THE FINITE WOMAN

MARK SALAMON

Book design by Suntrance Design.

Prologue

She struck him; a blur of motion followed by a ringing in his ears and the taste of metal in his mouth. He hadn't been hit by a woman since he was a child, when his mother slapped him for locking his cousin out in the snow. Men hit each other with fists. Now he realized how ineffective that was. You could hide behind pain, but humiliation was out in the open.

Women always had a way of improving on things.

~ ~ ~

The pounding rattled the doorframe. His son came halfway down the stairs. Tom put his hand up as he strode through the entryway. "I'll get it, hang tight." Dad's in charge. He swung the door open, ready for anything, and found a woman.

"Thomas," she said. She looked ready to lunge forward and bite him. He didn't respond. She stepped toward him and put the toe of her running shoe on the doorframe. "How old is your son?"

"Hello, Margaret. Would you like to come in?"

"Your son, Henry, how old is he?" She was framed in sunlight and smelled like roses and something sweet; a mix of sweat and adrenaline.

"How old? He's a—why?"

"Because, I came home to find your son having sex with my daughter. He had her bent over the back of the couch, her skirt hiked up and her shoes still on."

"Oh no, seriously?" Think before you speak, Thomas. The stupidest of all possible replies, and there it was, just running out in the street.

Her breathing was metrical, the kind learned in yoga class. Warm bursts pulsed his face. A vein throbbed on her neck. In this light, he noticed a hairline scar that ran off her bottom lip. Standing so close, she was all individual pieces: pulled-back hair, hard eyes, and light freckles spilling off her nose.

He remembered Henry and turned. His son was crouched on the stairs like an animal in the woods. There was a heavy bandage over his nose. That was new.

"My daughter is seventeen years old," Margaret said. Tom turned back to her. "If Henry is eighteen, I'm going to have him arrested for statutory rape."

Tom felt like he was being filled with ice water. "Oh, no, no, no," he drawled as his mind tried to close the curtains. "Wait—no. Now, that can't be. Please, something's not—" He squinted past her. It had stopped raining. Everything was rinsed. Her car, a black Mercedes SUV, was parked out front. One wheel had hopped the curb and was in the flowerbed.

"Please, come in Margaret. We'll discuss—"

"Is Henry eighteen?"

"Henry turns eighteen next month. December tenth. Did this just happen? He's home, if you'd like to speak with him."

Her anger shifted—a cloud passing—from red-hot to something darker. She took her foot off the doorframe and turned to go. That's when she whipped back and struck him, hard to the face, with the grace of a natural athlete. He watched her feet go blurry as his eyes watered. The wet sound, left hanging in the air, repeated in his head as the side of his face anesthetized.

"You're a terrible father," he heard as she turned and walked away.

~ ~ ~

Margaret drove home and played the image over and over in her head until a spot high on her forehead throbbed and the smell of him filled her. She made every effort to calm herself. She needed to find something like compassion—grab a corner and hold on—before talking to her daughter.

She tried the classical station as she drove down Sunset and crossed from Pacific Palisades into Santa Monica. She tried controlled breathing, like before she entered a courtroom.

Nothing. Just a crucible of fear and anger, chewing up her breath. She knew where it would lead if she couldn't control it, but she couldn't get the image out of her head; not of her daughter and seventeen-year-old Henry, though that would have its time. This was an older image, the kind that disturbed people carry around somewhere deep and hidden, always eager to rush in on a dark moment.

~ ~ ~

"Henry, eat your egg," Tom said. He put a glass of orange juice in front of him. "I boiled it exactly the way you like, nine minutes."

Henry poked his egg like he expected to learn something from it. Tom ran a finger around the rim of his coffee mug. He never ate breakfast right away, but had a habit of sitting at the table while Henry ate. Something about watching his son eat assured him he was still a parent in good standing.

"What her mother said, is it true?"

3

"Dad, come on." Henry had managed to avoid telling his dad exactly what happened the day before. He needed to talk to Justine first to make sure they had a strategy in place.

"Why weren't you in school?"

"You want to talk about this now? I have to go."

"Well, we're having this conversation. If not now, later."

Henry got up and hoisted his backpack with a flick of his hair. He looked down at his dad's swollen lip. "Damn, she really tagged you."

"Wasn't exactly expecting it." Tom touched his lip as Henry touched the bandage on his nose. "You should drive today. No motorcycle. Might rain again." His tone changed. "Or if you want, I could drive you."

Henry checked out the way teenagers do, staring at a secret in-between. "Nah," he said. Then he was gone.

Part 1

The Red Dress

Chapter 1

M A R G A R E T

"My God, you can't be that dumb. There are only fifty states, you flippin' retard."

Those were the words that changed my life. It happened on Tuesday, October 10, 1995. The screw-up that started it all. The day I created my own fork in the road.

I knew right away I'd messed up. Big. I didn't mean to say it. It was one of those things that just slip out.

Everyone around me laughed. I was finally popular, for about a second. Dwayne turned and looked at me—calm and deliberate. He had a different rhythm than everyone else.

That look has stayed with me like something burned into my soul. I think he was surprised it was me who said it, but he didn't show it. *I* was surprised. It was out of character for me, but character is a shifting thing in high school.

He stared, perfectly still, like it was something he'd practiced. Everyone stole glances at Mr. Janakowski as they waited for his reaction. I don't remember what question Mr. J had asked. I don't even remember Dwayne's exact answer, except it was something about fifty-two states. I think it was the *retard* part that got him. Dwayne was a tall, awkward guy, all limbs, with terrible acne. His pockmarked face and height made him look older. He actually looked more like one of the teachers than a student. He'd also been held back a grade, so he really was a little older. There was a rumor that when he was a kid, his father beat him so bad that he turned out a bit slow. He had an older sister who was huge—as tall as him and twice as wide. She used to go to our school and would beat him up when he was a freshman, I guess to look cool in front of her friends. I didn't really think he was dumb, just damaged. I always sensed there was a tragedy in him, waiting to birth.

"Margaret, you got something to add?" Mr. J asked, poised at the front. I could feel Song looking at me, but I didn't want to turn away from Dwayne. That would be admitting defeat, and I always have to finish what I start.

Mr. J dropped a book on his desk. Everyone jerked forward. "Hey! The learnin's up here, people." Mr. J was always trying to sound tough and casual at the same time, like he'd missed his calling as a superhero.

Dwayne was the last to turn back around.

While Mr. J gave us our homework assignments, I watched the back of Dwayne's neck turn a dark shade of red, like a heat rash. My mind began to empty—my thoughts too scared to stick around. Way to go, Margaret; piss off the creepiest guy in school.

When we were filing out of class, Song pulled my sweater and said, "Office." I figured she would.

~ ~ ~

Our "office" was the far north bathrooms that nobody used. They were near the old athletic field, which closed off. The school had been planning to redo the soccer field and replace the old bleachers since I was a freshman, but they'd stopped half way through so now the field was half dug up and scattered with weeds and trash. A tractor still sat out there, like they'd run out of money so fast they couldn't afford to store it. The only other thing on this side of the school was a big, boxy trailer meant for gifted students, which the school had been reluctant to add, loathe to discover there were two students at Saint Michael's High that actually qualified as gifted. I'm not sure what incentive you have to be deemed gifted if you're going to end up in a trailer. It didn't matter though because nobody used it. By the time the school finally got it, the two students were freshmen in college.

The women's bathroom used to be a men's room. The sign had *WO* added in front of *MEN* with a black marker. Inside was a storage locker where the urinals used to be. The lock on it was always open. Me and Song stole Mr. J's raincoat last year and put it in there as a joke. I figured the janitor would find it and put it in the lost and found where he'd get it back, but it was still in there. I keep thinking I should sneak it back and stash it under his desk before class or something, but I never do. I noticed he had a new one this year, but it wasn't as nice as the one we stole. He managed to dress pretty stylish, for a teacher, which I always kind of appreciated. At least he tried.

The far stall and the one next to it had a hole in the divider between them. It was just the kind of thing I always imagined would be in a men's room. When I got there, Song was already in the far stall. That was her office. Mine was the one next to it. It was great because hardly anyone ever used these bathrooms. They always smelled like an attic; dry and dusty, like something forgotten, as opposed to all the other bathrooms, which smelled like disinfectant with an undercurrent of fetid teenager. And this bathroom was the one place in the whole school that was warm in winter and cool in the hot months. Somehow they managed to get the temperature exactly right in the only place that nobody went.

"Mags," Song said, "you a crazy dumbass." Song's Korean accent made her insults sound funny. Sometimes, when I was down, she'd insult me non-stop until I'd crack up. One of our traditions was to talk really dirty while in our office. It seemed appropriate. Neither of us cursed much normally, but being in a bathroom stall with a hole between us inspired our seedier side. It had developed into a kind of contest to see who could be the foulest.

I wiped the seat, even though I was probably the last one to sit on it. There were paper protectors in a box propped on the plumbing at the back of the toilet. I put one down and sat quickly before it could slide away.

"Well, seriously, fifty-two states?" I said as I tinkled.

"He crazy motherfucker."

"He's not crazy, just dumb. Dumb as a fucking, shit... house."

"Didn't he torture cat or something?"

"I heard that, probably not true though."

"They a scar on side his face, from cat try to get away. Claw him."

"Really?"

"He no have it summer before, then he show up junior year with big scar and the Stokes—you know that fat girl, Rose, or Rosie?—they cat missing."

"It was her cat?"

"Yeah, he torture poor thing. It was calico, I think. Cute, orange little fucker. Real fuzzy. Poor thing."

"Yeah. That's... poor thing."

Song must have heard the fear in my voice. She changed the subject. "How you costume coming?"

"Good. I think I'm almost done. It's going to be awesome. Hey, did Nathan ask you yet?"

Nathan was the only guy in our shit school who was decent-looking, actually had a part-time job, and seemed fairly normal. Plus, he played guitar, so of course every girl was ready to lay down her life for him. Song claimed to be secretly in love with him. She had the obvious habit of falling madly in love with guys so far out of her league there was never any risk of actual interaction. She seemed to think that always being in a state of unrequited love made her more American. She got this from the movies, where in order to be an American woman you must be in love with somebody who actively hates you, wants to murder you, or is dead. Song pretended Nathan was going to ask her to the Halloween dance. Of course he wouldn't, seeing as how he didn't know she existed, but it would give her the opportunity to double down on her romantic misery and bring her one step closer to the feminine ideal. Really, I shouldn't talk. I had a mad crush on this guy, Simon, who graduated two years earlier and worked at a coffee house in Madison. I went there sometimes and ordered coffee and pretended I barely remembered him. Then I'd sit and read a book and try to look all mysterious and alluring. I guess I've seen a lot of dumb movies too.

"Not yet," she said. "He will though. I catch him looking at me other day."

"Gosh, really? Shit, really? No fucking shit?"

"Fuck yes. But he wear sunglasses, so it hard to know yes or no."

He was probably looking over her, I thought. Song was barely over five feet tall, and weighed about ninety pounds. "Do you have a costume? What are you going to go as if he—when he asks you?"

"I go as girl suckin' his dick."

"*Song! God!*" She always won. Damn, she could be nasty, and it wasn't even her first language. I heard her

11

giggle, victorious again. "You know, you can come with Vicky and me," I said. "If he doesn't ask you."

"I know this."

I shouldn't have said that. The truth was, we both knew Nathan wasn't going to ask her, and even if he did, she wouldn't be able to go, but it was the pretending that was fun. Sometimes I forgot that.

Song's family had moved here from South Korea two years ago. She had three younger siblings at home that she helped take care of. Her mother had some kind of horrible disease that kept her in bed all day and her dad was the traditional type who would never condescend to doing any kind of domestic chore, even though he'd lost the job that had brought them here and hadn't found another one. That kept them dirt poor, and left Song to pretty much run the house, raise her siblings, and take care of her mother. Sometimes I'd go over there and help her. She still managed to get perfect grades.

"I gotta go," I said and flushed. We came out and washed our hands. The sink had brown cigarette stains around the lip. I always wondered if the school bought the sinks secondhand from some flophouse, the kind you'd see in a crime movie.

"You have advance study after school?" Song asked. It should have been her in the advanced study program. She was crazy smart. I was pretty smart too, but mostly just with math. I was born with a brain wired for numbers and mathematics, which was going to be my ticket to college. Then I was going to go to law school. That was my planned path out of my shit hometown. At least I hoped. I hated it here. So did Song, which united us. She missed South Korea. The only things she liked here were the movies and the boys. I'd never been anywhere else, so I didn't have anywhere to miss. I just wanted out.

"Yeah, double class. They canceled Monday so we're doing both days today."

"Damn."

"Yeah, fuckin' shit. Fuckin' sucks ass," I said, warming up for next time.

~ ~ ~

I opened the refrigerator, hoping against hope there'd magically be something in it that wasn't there this morning. My dad wasn't home. He'd been spending more and more time at his girlfriend Teri's place. At first it was all very hush-hush, like I wasn't supposed to know, but it had gotten more and more obvious. He never bothered to sit me down and just tell me, like, *You're getting older now, Margaret, and I wanted you to know I'm going to be spending more time at Teri's.* Instead, he did it incrementally, and I was just supposed to figure it out.

My mom was in a mental hospital. Nobody told me that either. At first she was at a "retreat" to help with her "condition." "Condition" was code for her many suicide attempts. The first one I remember happened when I was nine and she made a half-hearted attempt to do herself in with pills. Every year or so was another attempt. I can remember the same paramedic, with the same armpit stains on his shirt, coming to the house for his annual visit. It became her identity—she was the type that was always trying to kill herself. The fact that she never succeeded added to her overall sense of incompetence.

Two years ago she took a gun and shot herself in the head. She was drunk and doped up, so the gun slipped off her temple and took off part of her skull behind her ear. There's still some blood stains on the wall in our dining room. She didn't die, but it put her in a state of shock, something the doctors called semi-permanent hypovolemic shock. She recovered, briefly, and came home for about a week, but her and my dad just had one long fight the entire time. I don't think they even slept. Then she went to the "retreat." I knew we couldn't afford a retreat any more than we could afford a Cadillac. I found out later when I tried to visit her that it was a state home for the mentally ill. At least then I knew who was paying for it.

As I looked through the fridge, I started feeling guilty about what I did in class. I kept running through justifications in my head. Dwayne was a colossal dick. He stole my entire chemistry assignment in sophomore year and turned it in as his own. The substitute teacher was apparently too dumb to distinguish a girl's writing from a boy's, so he got away with it. And someone once put a dead bird in Song's locker when she forgot to lock it and of course it was Dwayne. Still, I couldn't get past the way he looked at me. I kept trying to picture myself apologizing to him. I'd rather stick a fork in my eye.

Nothing much in the refrigerator. Basil, our mutt, came over to look with me, like we were in this together. Somehow my dad's military retirement provided us with enough money for an endless supply of Wild Turkey, but not much else. I made a peanut butter sandwich, sans jelly—same thing I'd had for lunch. The milk smelled iffy. I cut the crusts off and fed them to Basil. He was a rescue I brought home when I found him drinking some gross liquid dripping out of an alley dumpster. My dad never liked him. He didn't like any animal he couldn't shoot.

I was careful not to get any peanut butter on the crusts because I'd heard dogs can go crazy trying to lick peanut butter off their lips. We had enough crazy.

~ ~ ~

Because of my advanced studies class, I got to Vicky's later than usual. We'd probably only have about an hour to work on our costumes. I was going as Red Riding Hood and Vicky was going to be the wolf. When we were kids, we loved Halloween because it meant Vicky could sew the costumes. We still looked forward to it every year.

This year, I was sewing my own costume, which was Vicky's idea. She was always trying to get me to sew more, like at some point it would click and I'd become obsessed with it like her and we could be crazy sewing buddies for life. I could use a sewing machine, but I couldn't make a whole dress, and I certainly didn't think I could design one.

Vicky's bedroom was like something out of a downtown sweatshop. She had two sewing machines. There was an old industrial-sized one in the middle of the room and a small one against the wall. Bolts of fabric and pattern books were scattered everywhere, along with her design sketches. There were no girly posters on the walls, just color wheels, size charts, and fabric samples. She would lift and tilt her bed against the wall in the morning so she had more room to work. Vicky herself also took up quite a bit of room, as she was about two hundred and fifty pounds.

Vicky was a couple years older than me, but we grew up a block away from each other and had been friends since we were kids. Except for Song, she was the only friend I had at school, until she graduated. She was obsessed with sewing even back when we played pretend, and always used me as a model. She said when the money really rolled in she'd give me a commission for being her model all those years.

It might have started as something fun we did as kids, but over the years Vicky had gotten really good. She had some dresses in a shop in Madison that sold them on consignment. She'd even made enough money to buy an old van, and started paying me to pick up fabric for her. It was the only reason I got my driver's license. I used the money for food and other stuff parents usually buy.

I dropped my backpack on the floor and sat down at the small machine, which was the one I used. That was the way we were—I'd just come in and get right to work. Sometimes Vicky would be so absorbed in what she was doing, singing along to whatever song was playing, that she wouldn't even know I was there for a while.

She had *Duran Duran* playing. Her musical taste seemed to have locked in around 1985. It was a compromise. I didn't hate it, and it wasn't the awful country music she sometimes played.

Vicky's machine stopped. She came over and looked at my work, her arms draped in fabric. "You're almost there, kiddo," she said. "Use the machine for that part, then you're going to have to hand sew the rest, like you did the cuffs."

When I first started, I messed up half the fabric. I was clumsy, like a kid trying to play a new instrument, but Vicky kept encouraging me. She'd only instruct me, insisting I do it all myself, so in the end I could say I sewed the whole thing. She'd give me some pointers, then go to her machine and work. She could always tell by the sound of my machine if I was doing it right. "You're finishing too fast, slow down on that run," she'd say, while running her machine at a furious pace. She could sew a whole dress in the time it took me to go to the bathroom.

"How's your costume coming?" I asked her.

"Oh, shit, I didn't show you." She dropped the fabric in her arms and ran out of the room. She always moved in a blur of activity. She came back a second later carrying a heavy brown brocade cloth. "You'd never guess how cheap this fabric was," she said, throwing it around her shoulders. "I mean, after I treated it and dyed it, it looks like some serious quality shit. After the dance, I'm going to use it to make something else." She spread her arms out and opened her eyes wide. With her size, she really did look like something you wouldn't want to run into in the woods.

"Damn, that's awesome!"

"Oh yeah, this is so going to work. And I got the wolf's head at a costume shop, so now I've just got to figure out the feet and paws." She spun around in front of the mirror, hunched over and menacing.

Vicky's older sister, Alana, appeared in the doorway. "Hey," she said to me, ignoring Vicky's growls. Alana always seemed very exotic and full of older-girl wisdom, even though she was just a year older than Vicky; Irish twins, Vicky said, though they weren't actually Irish, and they didn't look like twins. They didn't even look like sisters, which always made me wonder.

"Hey," I said.

"What?" Vicky said to Alana.

"Nothing, freak," Alana said while looking at me.

"Well, go away, then. This isn't a locker room."

Alana smiled while still looking me over. "Don't get hostile." She leaned on the doorframe. She had on athletic shorts and a tank top, with a wrap around her right knee. "You still working on that thing for the Halloween dance?" she asked me.

"Yeah."

"What are you?"

"Red Riding Hood."

"Oh, that's right." She nodded. Alana had a way of looking at me like I was a meal. Vicky had her fabric spread on the floor and was down on her knees, pinning it. "You going as the big bad wolf?" Alana asked her.

"Uh, yeah," Vicky said, expert at talking with pins in her mouth.

"Well, you got the big part, easy."

"Bah-ha-ha, boy, that's funny. Wrong fairytale, jockstrap. Maybe it would help if you read a book, oh, ever. That's the three pigs. I'll just be a wolf."

"Aren't you guys a little old to be playing dress-up? Vic, you don't even go there anymore. That's the worst, seeing someone who's already graduated, trolling their high school. Pretty pathetic."

Vicky ignored her, but I felt compelled to reply. "I really wanted to go. I wanted her to go with me. They don't really check who's a student or not."

"Right," Alana said. "Because who'd want to go if they're not even a student there?"

"I guess."

Alana nodded and gave me another long look before sliding away. "What's she doing here?" I asked Vicky after she left. Alana was supposed to be in her second year at Madison on a volleyball scholarship.

"She tore up her knee. The team's on a road trip, so they gave her the option of coming back here for a while. She spends all day at the gym, working out with some other girl she's always with."

"Wow, that sucks."

"Yeah, I feel bad for her. She worked like crazy, and now if she doesn't heal fast enough, they won't renew her scholarship. Pretty fucked up. It's like if you slip in the bathtub, your future's ruined."

Vicky got up and hoisted the fabric onto her machine. She pushed what she'd been working on out of the way. She always worked in the midst of a mess, but somehow managed to keep track of it all.

We worked for a while without talking. I was being extra careful not to mess up because I didn't have any fabric left to spare. I liked it when we worked like this, with our backs to each other. Vicky usually had a way of dominating a conversation, but when she was sewing, she was a good listener, so I could go on and on about stuff. She'd grunt, or throw out some comment so I knew she heard me. Lately, I'd been telling her about my crush on

Simon, the guy at the coffee house. Vicky liked him because he once called someone a fucktard when they were making fun of her for being fat. It became her favorite expression for a while. Everyone was a fucktard.

"Yeah, we're going to look awesome," Vicky said, out of the blue. She did that sometimes. She'd just say something random, like a passing thought had slipped out. I hoped she was right. I tried not to let on, but I was really proud of my dress. I wanted it to be perfect. I felt like there was something special about it. If I did a good job, after the dance, I'd still have this awesome dress that I could keep; something beautiful that I'd made myself.

There was a Halloween party in Madison that a lot of older people were going to, and Vicky had wanted to go to that, not a stupid high school dance. She didn't want anything to do with high school anymore. But she agreed to go as part of a deal we'd made. Nobody was going to ask me anyway. It'd be like before, when we did everything together. Vicky liked to joke that when we were together, we looked like the number ten.

~ ~ ~

The reason I was sewing my own costume and the reason Vicky had agreed to go with me was because of something that had happened a few weeks earlier.

I was picking up fabric in Madison. Vicky needed Dupioni silk for a prom dress commission she was working on and sent me to a specialty store. I hadn't been there before and got lost in Madison's industrial area. I finally found the place, tucked behind a noisy machine shop. The owner was a hunched over lady that smelled like garlic. She reminded me of a brittle old bird. She was also hard of hearing, which was probably a good thing since there was a constant grinding sound that came from the machine shop.

There was no name outside the door, just an address. When I stepped inside, my eyes took some time to adjust. Everything seemed to vibrate from the machines next door. There were bolts of fabric everywhere, even on racks hanging from the ceiling. It was cramped, but organized, like an elaborate, color-coded geometric puzzle. I'd learned that textile shops were usually organized by fabric type, but this one was organized by color. The back of the shop looked like the dark end of a warehouse; after my eyes adjusted I realized it was a wall of black fabric. The colors on the next wall shifted from grays to browns, then to lighter hues. I turned a circle and took it all in.

I smelled garlic. When I turned back, the woman was there, surprising me. She was wearing a colorful wrap dress that blended into the fabrics around her, making her almost invisible. Her hands were bundled in front of her. She had a frozen smile and two missing teeth.

"I need, uh, some silk fabric," I said. "A certain kind, though. Let's see, it's—" She put her hand out. "Oh, right, I have it all here. Vicky wrote it down." I handed her the envelope Vicky had given me. She opened it with a gnarled hand. There was some cash, along with a note. She read the note and scurried off, probably glad for something to do other than smile at me. She disappeared into the surroundings like a woodsy animal.

I looked around. There was nobody else in the shop, but I guess it wasn't really the kind of place people just happened upon.

My math brain went on alert. That's what I called my predilection to break everything down into mathematical formulas—my math brain. It was an automatic response I seemed to have been born with. My mind just automatically wanted to pull things apart and rebuild them as mathematical constructs. It mostly depended on what was around me; it didn't happen with stuff I saw every day, but when I was somewhere new, like a fabric shop, it often did. I could reign it in with some effort, but sometimes it was fun to just let it go, especially if it found something really great to work with, like concentric rolls of fabric on racks, in complex geometric configurations, confined to a space that appeared too small to contain their mass and proportion. My math brain could do its thing while I thought of other stuff. It's like when you have a song stuck in your head and it's just there all the time.

The vibrations from the machine shop and the swirl of colors made the place feel like a trip room. In my freshman year of high school, I was friends with a guy, Danny Halverson. He was super smart. We studied together a lot. He was kind of an awkward, preppy type that got picked on because he had old style metal braces that usually had food stuck in them. He had an older brother he always talked about, who I guess fell in with the wrong crowd, because Danny started taking acid to be more like him. I went over to his house one day and he took me down to his basement where he'd built a trip room. It was actually a converted closet. He'd painted it all these bright colors and had a beanbag chair and a lava lamp and all this weird stuff, like a bag of day-glow marshmallows. I tried sitting in there with him but it kinda freaked me out. After a while he didn't want to study with me any more. He just wanted to drop acid, put on his headphones, and sit in his trip room. It was like he'd discovered nirvana. I stopped hanging out with him. I didn't realize people could change so quickly. Sophomore year, I saw him during the first week of school and he looked totally different, like he'd gone retro. His hair was long and he had on a weird denim jacket. He stood leaning over the third-floor railing, looking down at everyone. I had the queasy feeling he was going to go over and splatter on the concrete below. When you have a mom like I do, you see the potential everywhere. I never talked to him again, but I thought a lot about his mom, who was really nice. I wondered how she'd feel when she went down to the basement one day to store the winter coats or whatever and found his trip room.

I smelled garlic again. I turned and the smiling woman was back. She handed me a bag with the fabric in it.

"Great, thank you," I said.

She grabbed my hand and examined it. Her fingers felt like dry kindling. She looked up at me with her gap-tooth smile.

"Uh, I should go." I dislodged my hand. She stepped closer and reached up to touch my face. When I tried to back up, I ran into the table behind me. Her fingers touched my cheeks, which caused her smile to drop. I was starting to feel really weird, like I was being examined by an alien.

She stepped back, gestured for me to stay, and scampered toward the back again. I didn't want to offend her, but I really wanted to leave. I'd hoped to stop at the coffee house where Simon worked.

I turned toward the door and there she was again. I jumped when I saw her. It was like she had a twin and they were playing some freaky game with me. She was holding a bundle of red fabric. She ignored my startled yelp and spread the fabric across my front like I was a mannequin. The material was soft and silky, but I couldn't tell what kind it was. The woman considered me, her mouth a nest of puckered lines. Holding the fabric, she went around behind me and turned me toward a full-length mirror. I hadn't even noticed the mirror before. It blended in with everything else.

The fabric brought out the red in my hair. My hair was so dark that most people didn't realize there was any color in it. My pale eyes seemed to light up. Even my skin looked better. Vicky talked a lot about color—what colors worked together and what kinds of colors looked right on different people. She said everyone had a perfect color, but most people never found it. I always just pretended to understand, but looking at myself in the mirror, I actually got it.

"It's very nice, but I really just needed to get this today," I said and crumpled the paper bag for effect. She slid the fabric off me and began to fold it. "But, thank you," I added.

She handed the fabric to me.

"No, I can't buy this too. Vicky just wanted the silk." I tried to hand it back to her but she wouldn't take it.

She took my arm with a surprisingly strong grip. She led me to the door and kind of shooed me out like I was suddenly a pest. The door shut behind me. The bright sunlight and grinding sound from the machine shop made me feel like I'd just stepped out of one world and into another.

I told Vicky what happened. She listened as she examined the silk. I was anxious to get to the part where the woman gave me the red fabric because I wanted Vicky to look at it and tell me what it was—I thought it might be something exotic—but when I told her, she barely glanced at it. "It's just rayon challis," she said. "Nice color though. She's an expert with colors."

"Oh. I didn't pay for it, she just pushed it on me. She didn't say anything the whole time. Does she speak English? She was able to read your note."

"She doesn't have a tongue."

"She—what in the unholy fuck?"

"Ms. Barden told me about her. She only sells to people who have been referred to her. She was a Romanian gypsy who was raped, and the guy that raped her was afraid she'd say something so he cut her tongue out. He kept it in a jar."

"Her tongue?"

"Yeah."

"No way."

Vicky shrugged. "Then she had to leave the tribe or group or whatever it is gypsies run in. When the rest of them blew town, she had to stay here. Those gypsies are fucked up."

"Damn."

"But I guess she has some kind of old-world contacts because she can get fabrics that no one else has."

I ran my hand over the red fabric. When I held it closer to the window, I could see a light gray pattern threaded though it, like a vine. "Do you want it?" I asked Vicky.

"Nah, I don't really need it, and I'm kind of drowning in fabric I don't need. You should do something with it."

"Like what?"

"Like make a dress out of it." She took the fabric. "Hey, you know what?"

"What?"

"Red Riding Hood. This would be perfect for that."

"Really?"

"Yeah. That's what we could go as. I could be the wolf, and you could be Red Riding Hood. This would make a great dress, and you can do it all yourself. I'll help you design it. I'll be like your teacher."

"I don't think I can sew a whole dress."

"Fuck yeah you can. Hey, you wanted to go to your school dance instead of the Halloween party, so I'll make you a deal; you sew your own dress, and I'll go with you to your stupid dance."

"Deal."

Chapter 2

T H O M A S

The course of my life changed on Wednesday, February 21, 2012, at 8:50 pm, during a performance of Verdi's *Simon Boccanegra* at the Dorothy Chandler Pavilion in Los Angeles. I was anxious for the seventy-one-year-old Plácido Domingo, unsure how the great tenor would fare in this traditionally baritone role.

I drove home from work knowing I was cutting it close. I hated getting to a performance late. Whenever someone climbed over me in the dark to get to their seat, I wondered how they navigated the modern world without basic time management skills. It should be taught in schools. In Los Angeles, performances generally start ten minutes late to accommodate these inconsiderate types, who now of course consider ten minutes late to be the new start time, so they arrive some time after that, always whispering *traffic* as an excuse, which in Los Angeles is like saying you got caught in oxygen.

I was hitting every light yellow and running them all. I'd hoped to get home by six. Sex, shower, dinner. No, eat in the car. Leave by 6:20. A full hour to get downtown, with a ten-minute cushion.

I hit another yellow and gunned it while ducking. Why was I ducking? Like the traffic camera wasn't going to see my car if I duck?

The BMW 650i felt like a claw gripping the road as I came down Seventh, past San Vicente and through the weird turn on Entrada Drive that always felt like I was going back the way I came.

Shortly after I got the car, we took a weekend trip to Ojai. I told Francis I was going to the store for some wine. The dealer had told me to drive easy for the first hundred miles or so. The odometer read 104. I went out to the Maricopa Highway, opened it up, and hit 127 miles per hour. The car handled better the faster it went. When I got back, I told Francis I couldn't find the store. She noticed the red flush in my cheeks. "There's only one," she said. Driving this car in Los Angeles was like keeping a cheetah in a box. It was worth it though, for the few times I could let it loose. Two speeding tickets so far, in just over a year. One more and they'd suspend my license.

I had to break hard coming down my street. I pulled in the driveway and checked the dash clock: thirteen minutes and eleven seconds. Not bad. I always clocked my time from UCLA Medical Center to home. My fastest was 9:17. My longest was half a day, when a fire came down from Malibu and engulfed part of the Pacific Coast Highway, closing all the roads in the area. I ended up going back to the hospital and sleeping in the nurse's lounge. I went home the next morning, the LA skyline dark with ash and soot, as if the apocalypse had decided to come in from the ocean.

The engine clicked and whirred as I walked up our path. I perused our lawn and garden like I knew what I was looking at. Neighbors and visitors complimented us on how well we kept our yard. Our British neighbor, Joshua, was openly jealous; he seemed to think Americans didn't deserve such splendid floriculture.

I'd noticed a recent trend toward indigenous plants. Some of my neighbors have given in to this impulse for the native. Being first on a trend in LA brings silent bragging rights, especially when bundled with the rare chance to present as eco-conscious, and thus morally superior. Appearing to conserve water during a drought, forced or not, even as they headed off to the golf course and its acres of water-sucking greens, was enough ego boost to fill once-vibrant lawns with drab desert succulents, which, if it wasn't for symmetry, would look dangerously close to weeds. Los Angeles was semi-arid after all—not desert but close—despite the Malibu elite with their hillside vineyards. It'll be fun to watch all that careful topography wash away with the first hard El Niño rains.

"Would not have pegged you for the horticultural arts," Joshua once said to me in his nasal drawl. His accent seemed to get thicker the longer he lived here, instead of the other way around, as if his British allegiance could only be maintained via diction. "Being a man of science and medicine, I mean."

His problem was he insisted on doing it all himself, as if he'd be sent back to England if they found out he was using Hispanic gardeners. Except for the vegetable garden and the greenhouse out back, both of which Francis took care of, I had gardeners handle everything. Landscape engineers, or so said their invoice, a small team of them twice a week. I didn't know an azalea from a carnation, I just liked looking at it; and of course, everyone else looking at it.

Luca Brasi met me at the door, expecting me to pet him. I didn't want to have to wash my hands. "Hi, buddy!" I left him with a cocked head and took the stairs two at a time.

"How'd it go?" Francis asked when I came into the bedroom. She was pulling her pants off but still had her blue work shirt on.

"Oh, fine, an appendectomy and a spleen splice were the highlights." I sat on the edge of the bed, kicked off my shoes and unbuckled my pants.

"You're a saint." She came over and crouched between my legs.

"You still working on that piece?" I lifted my hips as she pulled my pants and underwear off.

"Just finished it, but started a new one." She straddled me. "Something a little different." I was going to ask her something else but the thought slipped my mind. Her hands moved over my face like a blind person searching. I slid my hands under her shirt. She ran a fingertip across my lips before kissing me. "My handsome saint."

The second Wednesday of every month I did volunteer surgery through a charity my friend Conroy and I had created: *Tykes Initiative*. It was for families in need. Babies, often infants, received surgery for free. Some were flown in from other countries and put up for recovery, all at no cost. It took us two years to set up. It required volunteer doctors, nurses and staff; then there was the insurance requirements, legalities, medical visas... on and on. Conroy and I ended up the principal donors, at least at first. Now we held charity auctions. We were both preposterously wealthy from something we invented when I was in medical school and he was working on a PhD in biomedical engineering. It was a small device that drew blood and tested it simultaneously, eliminating the need for a lab. The results were immediate, at least for the most common tests. Despite its obvious efficiency, when we shopped it around, nobody was interested. Labs have to make money, after all. Or rather, hospitals do, and labs are usually just another part of the hospital. Our device, clever as it was, cut into profits. This was all back when I had a different understanding of the role of hospitals and doctors. One comes to learn that hospitals are businesses, not unlike investment firms, only more consistently profitable. They invest in sickness and disease, and despite appearances, aren't always so eager to aid the body politic. We forgot about our little invention until a large medical equipment manufacturer bought the software and part of the patented design. The components eventually found their way into the architecture of artificial hearts. They are now used in nearly every fabricated heart device in the world. Conroy and I get a significant stipend for every one made. All this was possible because our lawyer had the foresight to patent the original designs, and of course to the prevalence of heart disease as it continues its relentless march around the world, owing to the influences of the west, and making us ever wealthier.

Something had to be done with all that guilt. Our charity was the result.

Francis started unbuttoning my shirt. "Wait, are you going to wear this?"

"Yeah, was planning to."

"Then I'll leave it."

"You ready now?"

"Yes, my love."

I spun her around, laying her on her back, and maneuvered over her.

Our sex was often like this. Minutes after one of us would come home, we'd be making love, as easy as asking about our day. After seventeen years of marriage, the sex was still frequent; sometimes quick and casual like this, and sometimes taking an entire Sunday afternoon while Henry was at band practice.

Ours was one of those odd relationships that began backwards. It started as a drunken hookup during my first year of medical school, when Francis was studying sculpture at Otis College of Art and Design.

I'd always had a nearly insatiable sex drive, but medical school left no time for such pursuits. After a couple weeks of avoiding it, my neglected desire would hit so strong it would frighten me. It was on one of these occasions that I met Francis. We had sex less than an hour after meeting at a bar. I was there for Conroy's birthday. She was there for drinks after a bachelorette party. I think we could smell the need on each other. We did it in her car, down and dirty.

That was that, I thought. I didn't remember giving her my number, but two days later she called me and we met a second time, this time in a parking garage, where we had sex in her car again. I found out later she got my number by calling my school and pretending to be my sister. She made up an elaborate story about our brother getting his hand caught in a machine at work and having to contact me right away. I don't have a brother. Or a sister.

A pattern of calling each other every week or two began. We'd arrange moments for hurried, greedy, often nearly public sex. It never happened at my place because I lived with three guys in a small place that at some point we concluded was too far gone for female company, unless the intent was to drive them away. I figured if her place was an option, she'd mention it, but she never did so I never asked.

This continued for months—one calling, the other only asking when and where. The bathroom of a Target, more times in her car (I always drove small cars), and once on the parquet floor of an empty condo her friend had just moved out of. I never knew a woman with a sexual appetite as ravenous as my own. She'd get her fill and push me out of the car, leaving me half dressed in the parking lot as she drove off, shaking her hair out.

We fell in love. I did, anyway. After months of blurry speed-sex, I was suddenly overcome with love, as if Cupid had nailed me dead center while I slept. I woke up choking on it. I didn't know if I could continue with our drive-by exchanges, but I also knew I couldn't stop.

She called one day. I asked when and where, weak with anticipation. A restaurant. I showed up, but didn't see her. I wondered if we were going to use her car, or maybe there was some spot behind the building she knew of.

She was standing right next to me. She was all done up in a black dress and heels. This perfect image of elegance and refined beauty had materialized out of the anonymous woman who'd been standing there a second ago. I'd never seen her wear makeup, much less heels. "Come on," she said, hooking my arm. "I'm taking you to dinner." Later, she told me. "I knew, Tom. I've been waiting for you to catch up. Is this how it's always going to be?"

We talked about art and medicine and opera until the restaurant closed around us. She listened like nothing else existed except me. I felt beheld.

We announced our engagement. "You're marrying your fuck buddy?" Conroy was concerned. He'd walked by our car that first night and seen us flouncing around inside.

Our sex life was something we'd learned not to discuss with others, except in very general terms. People either didn't believe we still had sex every day, sometimes twice a day, or they wanted to know the secret, like there was some mysterious elixir we both drank. So we kept it private. It was normal for us.

Francis was first. She arched back in the way I'm so familiar with. The tendons in her neck stretched. I followed a moment later.

I rolled off while still breathing hard. "Twenty minutes?" she asked.

"Yeah." I looked at my watch. "Twenty should be good."

She was already heading back to the closet. "I made some sandwiches earlier so we can eat on the way."

~ ~ ~

Oh, to have doubted Domingo. Who to know better the limits of their gift than the bearer? The rich texture of his voice was like a gift from another world, where beauty and perfection have many more reveals. I was transported, trite as that sounds. Having looked forward to this for a long time, I wanted to absorb every note and nuance.

I thought for a moment that Francis was crying. It wasn't like her. Between the two of us, I was the crier, at least when it came to opera, though she was kind enough not to notice.

She coughed. When I looked over at her, she had her hand over her mouth and her eyes were watering. Shortly after, she coughed again, filling a quiet moment. This time she leaned forward and gave me a sideways look.

She sat back, but soon her chest was bouncing again as she tried unsuccessfully to stifle another coughing fit. People around us shifted in their seats—the operagoers reprimand.

She got up. I stood. She touched my shoulder and gave me a look to say I didn't need to follow. I let her pass, reflexively breathing in her perfume, and sat back down. She coughed again as she exited to the lobby.

I turned my attention back to the stage. I figured she'd get some water and be back. We probably ate those sandwiches too fast. Ten minutes later, her seat was still empty.

The performance looked vapid now. It doesn't take much to turn opera silly, like a carefully built seduction ruined by the wrong word. I got up and whispered an apology to the person next to me as I climbed past with considerably less grace.

I found Francis sitting on a lobby bench. She stared vacantly with a tissue in her hand. She looked tired. She'd been working long hours in her studio to finish a piece she was donating to a charity auction to benefit the Tykes Initiative. I felt a pang of guilt as I sat next to her.

"You okay?" I asked.

"Yeah, I'm just"—she gestured—"I don't know, can't stop coughing." On cue, she bent forward.

I rubbed her back. "I think you're tired."

She sat back up. "No, I'm fine."

"Honey, let's just go."

"No." She put a hand on my knee. "Just give me a minute, I think it'll pass."

"It's opera, it goes on forever. Come on, let's go."

When we got home, she went into the bathroom. Her purse was sitting on the counter, half open. I glanced in on the way to the kitchen and saw a bloody tissue.

More coughing fits in the coming days were followed by fatigue and loss of appetite. She didn't want to see her doctor. She claimed she'd just forgotten to get a flu shot. It seemed late in the season for the flu, and it didn't explain the pseudohemoptysis, or sudden pallor.

On the fourth day, I pulled her out of bed and drove her to see her doctor, who diagnosed flu with a bronchial infection. He prescribed antibiotics. Shocked, I told him— with Francis glowering at me—that bronchitis is usually caused by a virus, not bacteria, so antibiotics would be worthless. "You're the reason antibiotics have become less effective," I lectured, "because incompetent doctors such as yourself overprescribe them, often without cause." He claimed the dark mucus was due to bacteria. I explained that early on it was blood, not mucus. We went back and forth, him arguing it was bacterial, me arguing it was viral, until we were shouting at each other. Francis left the room without either of us noticing.

I called Conroy. He wasn't a doctor, but because of our charity he actually knew more doctors than I did. I asked him if he knew a local internist who could come to the house and look at her. It was the kind of favor I didn't want to call in on my own.

"Yeah, of course. Let me get on the horn and I'll get back to you," he said.

"Thanks. I'm sure it's nothing."

"Of course it's nothing, but you'd rather make an ass of yourself than be wrong."

I stayed home the next day. A woman called early in the morning. She said she was driving in from the airport and needed our address. It was Doctor Simone Caruso, chief internist at San Francisco General. I'd seen her speak at a conference and had met her briefly. I couldn't believe Conroy had gotten her to fly in for what I figured would be a quick check to confirm it was just a bacterial infection after all; I'd had time to think about it and concluded her doctor may have been right. Now I wasn't eager to have someone so esteemed second-opinion my ignorance.

Dr. Caruso's briefcase contained an amazing number of diagnostic devices, most of which I was familiar with in their standard size. She had a graceful bedside manner, something I'd circuitously been told I lack. She asked Francis questions as she efficiently poked and probed. Telling Francis she'd be right back, she asked me to step out with her. Even in a private home, she maintained the procedural decorum you'd expect in a hospital. We went into the living room.

"You said this started four days ago?" she asked.

"Yes. Well, five now. She just started coughing. I know it's probably nothing. It sounds so strange for me to be saying that instead of hearing it." She didn't smile. "When I called Conroy, I didn't expect he'd have someone fly in. It's very considerate, and far beyond professional courtesy—"

"I'm also in town for a conference. And the coughing is still producing blood?"

"Off and on. That was my concern. She's on antibiotics. I was pretty sure it was viral, but—"

"I'd like to run a couple tests."

I'd said those words too many times. "Now?"

"Yes, I'll take a blood sample."

"Any idea what's causing it?"

"Not yet, but don't wait. That's my advice. I'd rather have her in a facility when I get the results back. Just to be safe."

"I understand." I felt unsteady, like my blood pressure was dropping.

"If I recall, you're at UCLA." she said.

"Yes."

She nodded and went back to the bedroom, leaving me standing in a space that felt very different than it did a moment ago.

Henry came home from school a short while later. "Dad, why are you home?" he asked as he slathering great gobs of peanut butter on a piece of bread. "And what's up with Mom?"

~ ~ ~

I checked Francis into Cedars-Sinai Medical Center.

After Dr. Caruso received the test results, she referred the case to an oncologist. She called me from the airport on her way back to San Francisco, but I missed it because I was meeting with Henry's guidance counselor. Henry, never before prone to violence, or any overt bad behavior for that matter, had hit a kid with the heavy bottom of a microscope in science class, splitting the skin above the boy's eye.

On the message, Dr. Caruso assured me the oncologist was the best, but she didn't give specifics about the test results. There is some information—the worst kind—a doctor is not permitted to leave on a message. I didn't know the oncologist, but after more tests, he met with me to discuss the diagnosis.

Stomach cancer. "This type of cancer is often late to reveal itself," he said. I sat across his desk in a mirror of what I'd experienced so many times.

It was eleven days since we'd gone to the opera. Because I dealt with children, I was used to rapid onset. When a child is struck with a terminal illness, they've not developed the defense mechanisms to put up the fight an adult body has. Mercifully, they often succumb with little suffering. I've too often seen the shocked and confused look on a parent's face: Our child was fine just last week, so what you're telling us isn't possible.

In a numb state of bewilderment, I went through all the scenarios I could think of, but still didn't see how it was possible that Francis could have advanced-stage cancer and had only begun showing symptoms now, when she was beyond the reach of most treatment options. There had to be a mistake.

Once revealed, Francis's demise progressed faster than I could formulate a next step. While we prepared for chemotherapy, I tried to get other treatment options from a second oncologist, a famous Canadian specialist who was teaching in Vancouver. I wanted immediate surgery, but her oncologist was adamant about starting with radiation treatments.

Desperate, I asked Dr. Caruso to come out again. She agreed, and Conroy arranged it. The next day, she evaluated Francis and met with her doctors. Afterward, she told me I should discuss with Francis whether she'd be more comfortable at home or in the hospital. I had a brief flash of hope before realizing what she meant. Francis told me, between morphine naps, that she wanted to go home.

Henry refused to go to school. He essentially lived next to the bed we'd set up for Francis in the downstairs library. She didn't think it was good for him to watch his mother die up-close, in progressive stages, so she made a deal with him. The late afternoon was when she usually felt best; if he went to school, they would work together in her studio for a couple of hours when he got home. She wanted to finish the piece she was still working on, and he could help her with it. It was that memory of her she wanted him to have, not the body in the bed consuming itself.

Henry was only sixteen, and though he was always a serious kid, he seemed younger. Minus the microscope incident, he was more momma's boy than rebellious teenager. He was so close to his mother that they'd often watch movies together on Saturday nights, curled up on the couch like a couple on a date. He knew what death was, but had not lived long enough to give it context. I'd watched the last breath of a child. Death was no mystery to me.

You never really know what you're capable of until you face an extreme situation. Hero or coward? For me, it turns out, coward.

Whether I chose to or not, I experienced my own pain through Henry. I found myself grieving not for my wife, but for my son. His trauma was anguishing to witness, but at least I could be there for it. I couldn't be there for what was happening to Francis. There was a barrier there, something I couldn't cross. It either wouldn't compute, or I didn't have the capacity for it. Yet there was my son, in a full season of pain, next to her bed. I marveled at his bravery, the way he could jump into the breach with all that suffering.

Some days we had grateful surprises. One afternoon, when Francis didn't have the strength to go to the studio, the three of us laughed. We were recalling when Henry was eight and had sat in the babysitter's car, refusing to get out. He wanted to go home with her and blubbered through tears that he'd love her forever. It was a moment of forgetting; Henry was animated and Francis's eyes were squinty with laughter.

Without my realizing it, the barrier dissolved a little each day, like I was creeping up on a silent enemy. What remained was a mysterious and profound intimacy.

We began talking late at night. Her medications turned her circadian rhythms inside out. I started sneaking into the library at around three in the morning. Henry was usually asleep in his sleeping bag next to her bed. If I heard his steady breathing, I'd check to see if Francis was awake. She'd let me know with a smile, even if her eyes were closed. I'd pull my chair close to the bed, lean in, and rest my head on the pillow next to hers.

We'd speak in whispers. She liked to listen to me talk and would guide me toward the things she wanted to hear. She especially liked to hear about our early relationship. Over and over, she wanted me to tell her about the time I woke up and realized I was in love with her. "Yes, but how did you *know*?" she'd say again, like we were playing a game. She'd shut her eyes and listen as I tried to find another way to describe it. I knew when she was listening because she had a slight smile. When it faded, I knew she'd fallen back to sleep.

Early one morning, just three months after her diagnosis, I was dozing in the chair next to her, lulled by the hum and stroke of the machinery. I woke to find Francis looking at me. She hadn't opened her eyes the day before, and was asleep when I'd made my middle of the night visit.

Her body was collapsed, leading the way out, but her eyes were lucid. We looked at each other for a long time.

The still, transposed moment grew to a long, silent communion until she motioned with her hand and I leaned in. "Henry," she whispered.

I went and nudged Henry. He woke immediately. "She wants you," I told him. He came around the bed and knelt over her. I stepped away to give them space. Left to witness.

She lifted her hand. They coupled fingers and formed a triangle. She pushed his hand flat to her chest. Her knobby knuckles were white with strain. Henry, surprised by her strength, flushed for a moment. She motioned for him to lean closer.

"Henry, my love," she said. "Don't spend your life trying to figure it out. It's love. That's all. Lead with love."

Chapter 3

MARGARET

I knew as soon as I felt him sit on the edge of my bed. I've always been one of those silent wakers—fully there before I move or open my eyes.

Because he had been spending most of his time at Teri's, and my mom was temporarily-permanently institutionalized, I guess my dad was feeling guilty. He decided we needed to do something together. For him, that meant hunting. I'm not sure if he ever considered that not many teenage girls want to go shoot something at six in the morning on a Saturday. For a guy who drinks like he does, I'm amazed he can get up at that hour.

It started a few months ago. "I'm going to teach you to hunt," he'd said, as if it was a skill I'd soon need. I wasn't sure how I was supposed to react, but he didn't pose it as a question, maybe because he knew what my answer would be. He'd taught me to fish a few years earlier, and seemed disappointed when I'd asked for the new Soundgarden CD instead of a fishing rod for Christmas. Didn't matter, I didn't get either.

"I want us to spend some time together," he said. It seemed to me there were other options for making that happen, but I went with him and we shot rabbits, a few birds, and I think a muskrat or meerkat or some kind of vermin-looking thing. I hated it. I hated everything about it. The blood and violence didn't bother me, though my dad kept giving me sideways looks to see if I was okay. It was the inanity of it. It was like stealing from a store and calling it shopping. I felt ridiculous in my orange hunting vest with dried blood on it and boots that were three sizes too big. And I hated that my dad thought of it as quality time together. It's not like we could talk or anything—he'd shush me for breathing too loud.

Deer hunting season was starting early this year, because of higher-than-expected birth yields or something. We'd been doing a casual form of hunting up until now, "Taking the gun out for a walk," as my dad said.

Deer season was different. Hunters respected the intricacies of deer hunting with a reverence that was nearly religious, and my dad was as devoted as they came. Of course, because it's a man's sport, there were all sorts of rules, exceptions, and procedures to learn. It was like football, with its tortuous complexity, which they claim is all part of the game but is really just dog whistle to keep the women away.

The night before, he washed our clothes with baking soda to get rid of any human smell. He packed the truck, except for the guns, which he leaned against the front door in their bags.

He sat in the living room and drank his whiskey. "Don't use deodorant or anything scented after you shower," he said as I was going upstairs to bed.

I'd hoped all this hunting and quality time together was going to last up until deer season—then he'd go off with his Vietnam buddies like he used to and I could have my Saturdays back. No and no.

So yeah, by the time he sat on the edge of my bed, I knew what I was in for. It was Saturday, it was 6 am, and we were going to go shoot some poor thing.

~ ~ ~

Fall was pushing toward winter. Every day was noticeably colder. It wouldn't start snowing for another month, but it had rained hard the night before.

It was still dark out when we left. My dad seemed to know where he was going, like he was following a beacon. He turned off the main road and took smaller roads into the woods, then cut across a swampy area and over a gully. The truck's headlights swept across bare trees, still dripping from the rain. I had visions of us getting stuck in the mud and being stranded, like the setup for a slasher movie.

I was relieved when we picked up the road again. We went about another mile, pulled off, and parked. The woods had turned a bluish gray as morning light crept in. The terrain looked exactly like every other spot in the area—mostly flat, with pale, twiggy trees everywhere.

We got out. It was quiet in the way the woods always are, where every unnatural sound, like a truck door closing, sounds twice as loud.

There was more equipment required for deer hunting then there was for killing smaller fare, most of which was a mystery to me, and it all had to be carried. Two guns now instead of one. We loaded up. My dad crammed things in my vest pockets. The cold made his breath steam. At least for once he didn't smell like cigarettes. He unzipped one of the gun bags and took the gun out. He handed me the other one. I started to unzip it but he stopped me. "Carry it in the bag," he said.

We started out. My dad walked faster than any time I could remember. With the gun, extra weight, and semi-darkness, it was tough going. I was wearing double socks and heavy boots that sucked the mud, so everything felt uphill. "Dad, I have to pee," I said, really just needing a break. "*Shhh,* later," he said, but finally slowed down.

He stopped, listened, and looked around. I was looking where he was looking, but all I saw was trees. The same tree over and over, like something designed to drive you crazy. The idea of doing this for pleasure seemed so absurd it took on an abstract form.

Then I saw it, far off, like a shard of light. A hint of movement. My dad moved behind me and started in a different direction. I followed, quiet as I could. He stopped again and waited. I caught another glimpse of movement, closer this time. We repeated this, getting closer, further away, closer. The terrain was starting to change. Not quite as flat. There was a light breeze, and a sound; something besides our footsteps and my breathing. It sounded like water.

We moved down an incline to a small clearing at the edge of the tree line. My dad slid off his pack and motioned me to the spot next to him. I crouched and looked past the trees to an open area that dipped down. It was just light enough to see a silvery stream running along the far end of the clearing, partly hidden by a group of rocks. There were two deer at the edge of the water, drinking.

They popped up, alert. They looked too far away for a shot. Squatting, my dad steadied his elbows on his knees and looked through his field glasses. He made a slight grunt and handed the glasses to me. I cranked the focus wheel to adjust for my dad's terrible eyesight as he set his gun.

I studied the deer. One's ears twitched, listening, as the other bent again to drink. I put the field glasses down and did some rough mental calculations. My math brain was happy to have something to work on.

Looking around, I tried to factor in all the elements. I have great eyesight. I didn't know how great until I hit a rabbit from a hundred yards and my dad looked at me like I'd just levitated. I concluded we were out of range, at least for my dad, who, like most men, had exaggerated ideas of his ability.

The breeze had picked up—a crosswind—and with this much distance, it would factor into trajectory. This was something my dad was bad at. Hunting with him showed me how bad a hunter he really was. Devotion and knowledge didn't equate to skill. Besides his bad eyesight, he didn't understand how wind affected a shot. He thought the bullet left the gun and hit or missed its target; what it did between those two points wasn't considered. The physics of it was lost on him. He also had whiskey hands, so he couldn't hold a gun steady.

My dad was set for a shot. I looked the other way as I waited for the crack of the gun. Nothing happened. I looked at him. He lowered his gun and motioned for me to open my gun bag. I unzipped it, quiet as I could, and slid the gun out.

It wasn't a gun I'd ever seen before. It was new; a black, shiny Remington. I hoisted it. It was center weighted, with a Nikon scope and a dark leather butt. I didn't know a lot about guns, but I could tell it was expensive. My dad leaned over and whispered in my ear. His scruffy beard stubble brushed my cheek. "Teri gave it to me. A gift. I want you to break it in. Show up your old man."

I checked the cartridge. Loaded. Safety was on. The mechanics of the gun were smooth and strong in my hands.

"Go ahead, take a sight, but don't fire," he said.

"We're too far."

"Take a sight."

I assumed a one-knee posture, took the cap off the scope, and adjusted the focus. The difference was remarkable. Everything moved forward. Now the second deer was drinking while the other one watched.

It was nearly light now, which helped, and the scope closed the range considerably, but it would still be easy to miss from this distance. I saw something move behind the deer, but when I tried to set the scope on it, I couldn't find it. I put the gun down and used the field glasses.

There it was—behind the two deer, tucked in the foliage and mostly concealed by rocks. A buck. It was his antlers that caught my eye. I passed the glasses to my dad. He adjusted them and nodded. "Yep, there he is," he said. "Thirteen-point whitetail. That's a trophy. I saw him at the end of last season and missed my shot. I didn't try again, hoping he'd come back."

It wasn't a clear shot, but looking at the topography and considering the wind, I thought it might be possible if the shot went right over the rock cropping and the wind pulled it just enough. While my dad watched the buck, I studied the wind as it banked off the trees.

"I tried from here last time," he said. "It's too far. My shot hit the rocks. We need to see if he moves closer."

I was beginning to think he was wrong, but didn't say it. I motioned for the field glasses and used them to study the area closer to the target.

There was a stand of trees off to the right, about thirty yards from the buck. The wind was rolling off them in a clear direction. I felt sure it would bring the shot down incrementally over the rock cropping. "I think there's a shot," I whispered to my dad. "The wind will bring it down after it clears the rocks, if you wait for a gust."

My dad shook his head. "No way," he said. "You'd end up shooting off an antler, if that. No, wait to see if he moves."

"He's not going to leave the water if he doesn't have to."

"He might, just sit tight."

We waited. The buck didn't move. The other deer finished drinking and disappeared back into the trees. The buck moved forward a few feet. He stopped, short of the water, and stood still.

My heart was pounding. My throat went dry. "Why doesn't he go to the water?" I whispered.

"*Shh*. Because... he doesn't know, but he understands." My dad had become Yoda.

The buck's antlers and part of his head were the only parts visible over the rocks. I kept studying the trees, and watching the pulses of wind. "What if I try to go around to the right?" I pointed. "And flank from that side."

"No, he'll hear, and once he does, this spot is ruined for the season. He's older, and smarter than you think. And you'd have less of a shot over there, it's lower."

He was right.

The buck still didn't come forward to drink. Why else was he there? He stayed in the same spot. Another five minutes passed. I was watching him through the field glasses when he turned and walked back into the woods.

"Should we track him?" I asked.

"No. We're done for today."

~ ~ ~

That night, all I could think about was the buck. I worked on the math. I wrote out diagrams and shot trajectories. One variable was the new gun. I'd used the other rifle and knew its range, but the new Remington was sure to be more accurate. My dad had bought higher caliber cartridges, which would affect velocity, which in turn would affect trajectory. The ballistic coefficient is also affected by cross variation—wind in this case. Hunting bullets are big, unlike pistol bullets. Wind will bend a rifle shot; not much, but some, depending on the length of the trajectory.

By midnight, I was convinced I could have made the shot.

I had the gun in my room. I ran my hands along its length. I lived in a house where everything was crappy, from the TV set to the chipped, mismatched dishes. The gun was crafted. It was designed. It had a duel aesthetic; symmetry and beauty balanced its fundamental purpose. I stayed up past one, studying it, leaning all its parts and practicing steady holds.

The next day was Sunday, which was church day for me. My mom used to take me to Catholic Mass when I was a kid, just the two of us. She seemed pretty normal then, at least for a time. I always liked the routine of it. Catholicism was a system, a complete framework that reminded me of a closed mathematical structure. I took comfort in it. I went to church alone now, but secretly I'd pretend I was with my mom. My normal mom. I'd have an imaginary conversation with her while I rode my bike there, and even during the service. It was weird, but it was the one dose of weird I allowed myself.

This Sunday, I completely forgot about church.

I was up and ready, sitting on the edge of my bed, when my dad stuck his head in my room. We loaded the truck and drove off without a word.

We drove to the same spot, but this time he kept going, driving off-road through most of the area we'd hiked the previous morning. We parked in a small clearing and walked the final distance, which meant trekking through more mud from the overnight rain. The fact that he'd driven in closer told me he was planning on hauling a deer to the truck. It occurred to me that he had planned yesterday as a trial. Even if he thought we had a shot, I don't think he was going to take it. Today was different.

We were at our spot a half hour earlier than the day before. It was still too dark to study the wind, but I could hear it and feel it. There was more moisture in the air. I was concerned I hadn't factored that in. What effect does air condensation have? I guessed it would change velocity, but not trajectory.

Trees appeared, like they were being etched before our eyes. The wind was stronger than yesterday, swirling and lashing up against the trees. I watched the pulses. It was coming in the same direction as the day before. I could picture it banking off the stand of trees and dropping down over the rock formation.

At the exact same time, movement appeared against the tree line as the two whitetail deer appeared for their morning drink. I unzipped my gun bag. My dad studied them through the field glasses. I positioned a knee on the ground, adjusted my set, and waited.

I saw part of the buck's antlers in the trees. It seemed impossible from this far away—it could easily have been tree branches—but I knew it was him. I didn't bother to tell my dad. I waited another minute, then tapped him and motioned for the field glasses.

I watched the buck move incrementally forward until I could see his whole head. "What do you see?" my dad asked.

"He's there." My dad made a noise that was probably the same that men made a million years ago when they spotted a wildebeest. The two deer turned back to the trees. The buck took a step toward the water and stopped. He was so still he appeared to be just another part of the landscape.

It was a waiting game. He eventually moved another tentative step, stopped, and waited. A few minutes passed. He repeated the process, until finally he was at the water's edge and fully exposed. I passed the glasses back to my dad.

I had to keep reminding myself to breathe. I checked the wind, noting the interval between gusts as it banked. Wind is not a dictative wave pattern, so it's not possible to calculate, but you can use the law of averages to come up with a rough predictive model.

The buck waited at the edge of the water, head up, alert, antlers reaching high. I had anticipated the last two gusts of wind and was accurate to within a second. He bent to drink. When he came back up—that would be the best shot. I was sure the next time he moved, it would be to leave.

I looked at my dad. He sensed it and took the field glasses from his eyes. He looked at me and shook his head, no. I didn't look away. I stared at him. My eyes started to water. "Dad, I can make this shot," I said. I tried to keep my voice steady and my eyes locked on him. He had shaved, as if preparing for something formal. His eyes were tired, the corners pulled down, like he was slowly melting. He wasn't that old, but his lower lip had the slight quiver that old people get.

He gave me a nod.

I felt myself go into a zone, as if enveloped in a calming blanket. I looked at the trees. My dad had the field glasses trained back on the buck. I waited until the bank of trees bent, as if pushed by an invisible hand, then watched them release. I started counting down as I positioned.

Looking through the scope, I could only see the tips of the buck's antlers and his tail over the rocks. I set the crosshairs just above the rocks and slightly to the right. My math brain burned as it triple-checked my calculations. The cool breeze tickled behind my ear. My finger cradled the trigger. I took a deep breath in.

The buck came up. His neck and back were visible. I began a slow exhale.

The wind would bank the trees in—*three... two... one.* The next gust hit the trees as the buck turned. I pulled.

It was loud. I expected the gun to be quieter, the way all newer things are, but the crack ripped through the woods. I looked over the rifle. There was a cloud of dirt where the buck was. My eyes struggled to adjust from the scope view.

I turned to my dad, who was still looking through the field glasses. "Did I miss?"

He turned and looked at me with wild eyes. "No, God damn it, I think you got him." He got up. "A buck doesn't always fall, he'll run out. Come on." He started moving. "Just bring the gun, hurry-hurry," he said over his shoulder.

When we crossed the clearing, I stood on the rock formation, where it was easier to assess the distance; I estimated about three hundred yards. When we made it to the stream, my dad went across. He was moving fast. I tried to keep up. Cold water filled my boots.

On the other side, we found scrambled hoof prints and blotches of shiny black blood, like holes in the dirt.

I followed my dad into the tree line and saw movement about fifty yards away. He was going in the wrong direction.

"Over here," I said.

He turned. "Where?" He followed me as I ran. "Gun up," he yelled, so I wouldn't go the way of my mother.

The movement stopped. I started to think it was something else, or a trick of the light. I turned to my dad, who had stopped. I followed his eye line.

There he was, lying in the shade of a tree.

When we came upon him, he was on his side, taking rapid breaths, which seemed to make his whole body expand and contract. We die in the most obvious places, I thought. The places we step over.

The shot hit him just to the left of his heart. Not perfect, but close. In the boiler room, as my dad had taught me.

He was huge, and somehow looked even bigger lying on the ground. His course fur was darker in the shade of the tree. Parts of his coat were gray and worn, with ragged patches. His shiny black eyes moved, opaque, searching for me. I stood over him with the gun over my shoulder. "Not too close," my dad said.

There was a sour smell in the air, raw and elemental. The buck's leg gave a violent kick.

"Stand back! Move back," my dad said, throwing an arm in front of me and pushing me back. The buck's eye followed me as his head slid across the ground. His antlers ground an arch in the dirt. It sounded like something being peeled apart.

"Margaret, you have to shoot him again. Damn, he's strong. Stand back and aim for the heart."

The hand holding my gun shook. Blood came out of the buck's mouth. His tongue spilled out and touched the dirt.

"Margaret!"

My whole body was shaking. The buck kicked again. His legs began peddling. He made a powerful snorting sound as his body jerked.

"Margaret, shoot him!"

I took a step back. I was shaking uncontrollably. My dad took the gun from me. I turned and fell to my knees. I heard the rifle go off as I vomited.

~ ~ ~

"That smell," I said. "God, I never knew it when you cut open a deer, that the smell would be like that. It was—I can't get rid of it."

Me and Song were back in our office. It was Wednesday. I'd missed two days of school, the first time that'd ever happened. I couldn't get out of bed or eat on Monday.

My dad had field dressed the buck. When he cut it open, the smell had made me vomit again. Since then, the stench was like something attached to me.

I helped drag the buck on a slide tarp back to the truck. We had to go down river to find a spot shallow enough to cross. I couldn't feel my feet by the time we made it back to the truck.

I continued to get sick on the drive home. I'd open the window to put my head out, only to smell the deer again in the back of the truck. At home, I took a long shower and crawled into bed. I felt like my whole body had been drained of fluids, as if it were me that had been split and gutted. It wasn't until Tuesday that I managed to eat a bowl of soup.

The smell of the eviscerated deer stayed with me like a virus. I kept thinking of that eye, searching for me. Maybe the smell was revenge, a way to reach through death and get back at me. Something to haunt me forever.

I accepted it. I deserved it.

"Wow, you hit one bullet?" Song asked.

"Yes."

"That good, right?"

"That's," I corrected.

"That's."

"Yeah, I thought so too, until I saw what I'd done. I mean, you're supposed to kill it with one bullet. That's the glory."

"But you dad proud."

"He was disappointed in me, for the way I was after." I was starting to cry.

"Oh, Maggy."

That was one of the things about our office. Usually we joked and played our game of who could be the nastiest, but sometimes we'd talk about serious stuff too. It was easier to say things that were private, or too personal to admit normally, because we were in our separate stalls and couldn't see each other unless we tried to look through the hole in the divider.

Song was a good listener. For all her joking around, she knew when to just be quiet. If you didn't say anything for a while, you knew she was still paying attention. I tried to do the same for her.

Once, she told me about something horrible one of her cousins did to her. She'd never told anyone about it before. It took a long time for her to tell me. She'd say one thing, than nothing for a long time. But I'd learned from her to be patient. We both missed our next class, but little by little she told me the whole story.

Our stalls were like confessionals, and when we got serious, it was like we were taking turns being the priest. Song was a better listener than the real priest I'd gone to for confession. I'd only gone twice, and once I had to make something up because I felt like the priest was anxious for me to finish, like he was on the clock. I guess everybody is, even God.

I got out of the stall. I didn't want to just sit there, crying. I hadn't peed. I hadn't peed all morning.

"You not look good," Song said as we washed our hands.

"I know, I haven't really been able to eat."

"I know you feel bad, but one shot, that still pretty good."

"Yeah."

We'd stayed longer than usual and had to hurry to get to our next class.

The sky was a dense gray with a steady drizzle. I always loved the summer, and every sunny day it brought, even the really hot ones. I dreaded the fall and its overture to winter.

On the way back, we took the narrow path along the fence that went behind the trailer. I noticed one of the windows was broken and someone had written *queer fuck* on the side with a felt pen, apparently going for the most value per letter.

Song was trying to make me laugh by insulting me. "You so tall skinny you no make shadow. Ha ha."

Dwayne stepped out from around the far end of the trailer. "What's up, dykes?" he said. Song and I stopped. It was rare to see anybody in this forgotten area of the school.

He had the same intense look he'd had in class, after I'd made the retard comment, as if he'd been holding on to it all this time. I'd forgotten about maybe apologizing to him. Weird how the more you don't want to do something, the easier it is to forget.

"I've been watching you freaks sneak off to the bathroom together. Your own little fuck-fest between classes?"

"Ha! You so funny," Song said. "And super smart, you not retard at all, no way." Most of the time people couldn't really tell if Song was insulting them or complimenting them with bad English. It gave her an advantage, which I think she used to humor herself. I could always tell though, so she never tried it with me.

"Yeah, that's us," I said. "Couple of dykes, like you say." What was one more rumor? This was my last year. I'd developed a pretty thick skin and figured I could handle anything by now.

"You should invite me some time, maybe I can turn you around," he said. He came up close and got in my face.

"Sure thing, and thank you so much, we will of course do that," I said, deciding on the no-fear approach, like you do with a dog that scares you. "We've got to get to class now." I tried to step around him.

He countered. "Sure thing, huh? Only the thing is, I really should bash your face in. I mean, you kind of have it coming. And then if I did, I wouldn't want to fuck you, with your face being bashed in and all. Who would?" He flinched like he was going to hit me. I jerked back and hit my head against the trailer.

"You can't no hit girl," Song said. "I mean, you too smart."

"I'd like to," he said. "Doesn't seem fair. But no, I wouldn't. I can't hit a girl." He was right in my face. "Not even a dyke-snob like you." His breath smelled like a wet ashtray.

"But I would," said a new voice next to me. I knew right away who it was: Dorie, Dwayne's sister. She'd graduated two years ago, and like her brother had been held back a year. I'm not sure if it was for the same reason. I didn't really know her, but I remembered in the locker room, when I was a freshman, the girls made fun of her because she had such a thick neck. It was like her head just went straight down to her shoulders. No one made fun of her to her face though. It was weird because Dwayne had a really long, skinny neck, so they were like opposite extremes. But she had the same bad acne as him, with pockmarks on her cheeks and red lumps spread across her wide nose.

"Hey, Dora, good to see you. Like those shoes. You still got that style, girl," Song said, unaware how obvious she was. Her voice was high and reedy, even for her.

"Fuck you, slanty, and it's Dorie, dumbass."

Song tried to step between Dorie and me. "Oh, see, I just meant—" Dorie didn't wait to hear the rest. I went to push Song out of the way just as Dorie grabbed her by the hair with one hand and hit her in the face with the other. The punch landed on Song's ear, but Dorie yanked her hair and swung again, this time connecting, making an awful cracking sound. The next punch hit Song in the side, just below her ribs. Dorie let go of her hair and Song fell to the ground in a writhing pile. Dwayne stepped over and put his foot on Song's hair. She started to get up but was yanked back like a dog hitting the end of its leash.

The pit of my stomach went cold, like when you know something really bad is about to happen. As Song was falling, I thought I could get one good shot at Dorie, but I knew it better be a solid one because she was much stronger than me. As she turned back to me, I took my swing. It was pretty pathetic, I guess because I hadn't eaten in a while. I went wide and barely grazed the side of her face.

I didn't even see her punch. She hit me in the same spot she'd hit Song—low on my side. My legs vanished and I collapsed at her feet. The pain was like a root canal on my whole body.

Dorie reached down and hauled me up by my armpits. She pinned me against the trailer and held me up by my neck. Her hand dug in just below my chin. She held her other hand to the side of my face, poised to backhand me, like something out of a bad mafia movie. Song was rocking on the ground in a fetal position.

"My big sis has been taking a class in self-defense," Dwayne said. His neck stretched high. He was the happiest I'd ever seen him. "In case a man were to try something she has not given her full consent to."

I felt dizzy and was afraid I was going to pee myself.

"This is for calling me a retard," Dwayne said. He was still standing on Song's hair with his arms folded over his chest. Dorie smacked me in the mouth with her backhand.

She must have learned some kind of technique because it was like getting hit with a brick.

"This is for sophomore year and trying to steal my chemistry assignment," Dwayne said. Dorie backhanded me again, in the same spot. I felt my lip split. My crazy math brain started calculating distance ratios and velocity. It concluded her technique must have something to do with her follow-through, like a hard tennis swing.

"And this is for calling my sister a thick-necked ogre," Dwayne said.

I shook my head. Dorie took her hand off my neck. "No," I said, sputtering blood. "I didn't say—"

Dorie rocked back and swung hard. She put her whole body into it. I think she was aiming for my mouth, but her punch landed on my left eye. I had started to slide down so she went a little high.

I was knocked back. The last thing I felt was my head hitting the trailer. Gray crept in from the sides until it filled my vision. I tipped into pure air. When I hit the ground, I heard the hard slap of wet cement. Then everything was peaceful.

~ ~ ~

I lay in bed and debated. The doorbell had already rung twice, and I was going through all the possibilities of who it could be. It was Friday, four o'clock, the worst hour of my worst day. I'm told most people looked forward to weekends. I equated them with hunger and my dad moping around until he could go to Teri's without legally being deemed criminally negligent. At least at school I could eat.

The doorbell rang again. Song? No, she was probably wiping her mom's ass about now. We'd talked a lot on the phone about what happened. She seemed to be bouncing back faster than me.

Vicky? No. Even though she lived close by, she never came to my house. She said it creeped her out. She's pretty honest that way. I'd called her, but didn't tell her what happened. I just wasn't ready to. Instead, I told her I couldn't come by for a while because I wasn't feeling well. She asked why I was lisping. I pretended I didn't understand her and said I had to go.

Truth was, I didn't want to face anyone. I'd missed another two days of school.

I finally decided to get the door. I figured that whoever it was would probably be gone by the time I got down there, but at least it would get me out of bed, which is where I'd spent most of the week.

I opened the door to a blast of cold air.

"Hey." It was Vicky's sister, Alana. She'd never come to my house. I didn't even think she knew where I lived.

"Hey," I said, but it came out sounding like I was drunk.

Her casual demeanor fell. "What the fuck happened to your face?"

I'd stopped looking in the mirror because my face seemed to look worse each time I did. My left eye was swollen nearly closed. A bruise had spread around it, extending to the bridge of my nose. The blue and black really stood out against my pale skin. My lip was so engorged it looked comical, like a costume prosthetic. The side of my head had a big lump, but you couldn't really see that.

"It's not as bad as it looks," I said with a lisp that made it all seem worse.

"What happened?"

"Nothing." I hadn't bothered to think up an excuse.

"Nothing? Because shit, if Halloween were tonight, you could go as a battered wife." For whatever reason, I started to cry. I wasn't expecting it—it just kind of hit me. "Aw, I'm sorry. I was just talkin' shit, trying to make you laugh."

"I know, it was funny."

"Shit. So, what the fuck happened?"

"Nothing." I didn't know what to say. The crying had thrown me off. Alana had a way of unsettling me. I was a little afraid of her but also wanted to tell her everything I was afraid to tell anyone else. It was confusing. "You want to come in?" I asked her.

"Nah, Vicky says your house is creepy."

"Yeah, it kinda is."

"She was wondering about you. She must not know what happened. She says you're never sick, so she's worried. I think she kind of likes being there for you."

"Yeah, she's good like that." I stared at my chipped toenail polish poking through a hole in my sock.

Alana stepped closer. She put her hand under my chin and lifted my face. She had a soft touch. She was tall, even taller than me, and very athletic, the kind of girl with ropey veins on her arms. Vicky told me she worked out at the gym sometimes twice in the same day. I was kind of surprised at how gentle her touch was.

"Hey, who did this?" she asked. She was looking at my face like a doctor would.

I hesitated. I noticed the wrap on Alana's leg was different. "Is your knee better? When are you going back to college?"

"Next week. Yeah, it's better. Who?"

"Dorie."

"Dorie? Wait a sec, I remember someone named Dorie when I went there. Ooh, Jabba the fucking Hutt? Her? She's not even in school anymore."

"No, but—"

"Oh, Dwayne, our village idiot—she's his sister. Was he there?"

"Yeah."

She still held my chin. "Did he touch you?"

"No. Well, not exactly, it was mostly just her."

"But he put her up to it." I shrugged. Her face tightened. "Yeah, I see."

She took her hand away from my chin but kept looking at my face until she settled on my eyes. Seeing the world through one eye makes it easier to look someone in the eye without looking away, which is what I usually did. She seemed like she wanted to say something else.

She turned and looked at her car parked at the curb. There was someone sitting in the passenger seat. I couldn't see them, just the cigarette they were smoking, and their long hair.

Alana faced me again. She leaned in close, like she was going to whisper in my ear, but she didn't say anything, just stayed like that for a moment. I wasn't sure if I was supposed to do something.

"You should come by, Vicky misses you," she said, and turned to leave.

I watched her walk to her car. She had the coolest car ever; a beat-up, primer-painted 1969 Camaro that sounded like death coming down the street.

Chapter 4

T H O M A S

I was always a doer. Whatever trouble came my way, I could solve it by taking focused, well-considered action. I attributed much of my success in life to this fortitude. When I had a problem, I'd imagine the problem as a black hole—always the same black hole, regardless the problem—and all the actions I took served to pull me away from the hole and closer to the shores of safety.

This stopped when Francis died. I let myself get sucked into whatever almighty singularity I'd always tried to escape.

With Francis, I was complete. I was a husband and a father. With her gone, I was neither. She was my cover, as I soon found out, allowing me to use those titles while I remained ignorant of the responsibilities. I was like the CEO that delegates everything until he realizes he doesn't know anything about the company he's assumed to run.

I missed my own father, a distant and intolerant man living in Santa Fe with his third wife. I hadn't talked to him in more than a year. Conroy called him and gave him the news, my dad being one of many Conroy called when it quickly became apparent that I was worthless.

In the weeks that followed, I became derelict in even the most basic ways. I'd already taken an indefinite leave from work. I called Henry's school to follow up with his guidance counselor, only to find out summer vacation had started the previous week. I thought Henry had been in school. Instead, he'd been in Francis's studio. She'd taught him the fundamentals of sculpting over the last few summers, like an apprenticeship. Instead of doing pretty much anything with dad—and I tried many things; ballgames, movies, even golf—he'd preferred Mom show him how to cast bronze and shape limestone.

Francis's studio was in our converted garage. Henry started spending more and more nights there. He took to playing the music Francis liked to work to. It drifted across the backyard at all hours. I'd tap on the door and stick my head in to find him hunched over a vat of something, safety goggles on (as she'd taught him), and put his dinner on the work table. He had the right to grieve his own way.

I had yet to find mine. Getting through each day was a push against gravity. I'd find myself stopping whatever I was doing and sliding into some other world; a flat landscape without horizon. The shower water would go cold and I'd snap out of it, or I'd be sitting on the edge of the bed, pants around my ankles and one shoe off, before realizing it was the middle of the night. I'd forget to eat. I'd read the same sentence in an article over and over without realizing it. My mind kept slipping back into a repetitive rut.

People began to look foreign, the way a word can seem like nonsense when you repeat it too many times. A trip to the grocery store would take the better part of an afternoon. I was easily confused, like an addled senior, trying to figure out if we still drank milk.

One morning, two months after Francis died, I turned on the kitchen light and nothing happened. I stood in the dark until Henry came downstairs and told me the electricity was off. "Did you pay the bill?" he asked me. I couldn't remember. I couldn't remember paying any bills.

Conroy came over that afternoon. He stood in the doorway, holding something wrapped in foil. I squinted at him.

"Gonna let me in?"

"Depends. What's under the foil?"

"Meatloaf."

"Alright, then." I let him pass.

"Patty made it. She's worried about you." He navigated the candlelight to get to the kitchen.

"She doesn't need to worry. Tell her I'm alright."

"No, I told her she's right to worry. You don't eat, or sleep, or, apparently, bathe. What else? Oh, pay bills. You know, you could just open the windows and skip the candles. The sun didn't go out, and it is July."

"Did Henry call you?"

"He did. I don't like meatloaf, but Patty said you loved it one time when you had it at our house. You're going to have to eat this because apparently you can't refrigerate it." He opened the refrigerator door. "Yikes." He slammed it shut and put the meatloaf on the counter.

Luca Brasi came skidding in. He looked to Conroy for salvation.

"Don't let him fool you," I said. "He gets fed."

Luca Brasi fell prostate at Conroy's feet, in full submission mode. Conroy fished a plate out of the sink and rinsed it off. He found a knife and cut some meatloaf. "Dogs grieve too. Here you go, buddy." He put the plate on the floor. Luca Brasi finished it before Conroy made it back to the dining room. He settled in across the table from me. "What were you doing?"

"What? When?"

"Just now, before I got here."

"Oh, nothing. Just… nothing."

"Just sitting there?"

"Yeah, I guess."

"In the dark?"

"I have these candles."

"They're nice."

"They were a gift. Christmas, I think."

"Potpourri."

"Po-what?"

"Pourri." He was confusing me. "The smell, that's potpourri."

"Is that what they call it? I think you're right, you always know that kind of thing, like a gay guy."

"I never thought of it like that." He ran his hand through his long hair, making him look feminine in the flickering light. "Where's the mail?"

"The mail?"

"Yeah."

"Oh, yeah, the mail. I've been putting it in the closet."

"I see."

"It's all together though. I haven't messed it up or anything."

"You mean by opening it?"

Things were bad, I realized, like the criminal who catches their reflection mid-crime, tire iron about to come down on grandma. The rationales stop holding up. I wasn't getting better. I hadn't finished getting worse. Francis's death was the neutron bomb. There was no other tragedy, no other bad, and no other sadness. Clocks stopped, and all the rest. That's where I had allowed myself to go, and was still going.

The only active part of myself left was the part that was trying to figure myself out. I'm cursed with an indestructible form of self-analysis. Medical school ruined me, I'm certain of it. My mentor, a doctor I attached myself to at Johns

Hopkins, had taught me that to be an exceptional doctor, it was necessary first to relearn how to learn. Our process of education is a failure, he'd said. You must take information and absorb it, digest it, allow it to become a living thing inside you, like planting a garden, then—and this was his main point—you must become your own teacher. And your first subject is yourself. It sounded a little creepy, like a cult's reeducation program, but I wanted to be exceptional. More than prestige or money or recognition, I wanted to be great. I burned to be great. So I relearned how to learn, and allowed him to mold me. But my mentor failed to mention that once absorbed, this self-analysis couldn't be turned off. Like a shadow self, it followed my every thought and experience, pen in hand. The worse I got, the more animated it became, always elbowing its way in. It sat across the table from me now, next to Conroy, observing, scribbling away like it was the first day of college.

"I'm thinking you may need some help, Thomas." Conroy stroked his chin. He was as wealthy as I was, but liked to play against it. He dressed in mismatched clothes; that and the long hair made him look like he might start a band any day now. He was the patient type. They've become so rare. If busy is admired, it's patience that's rewarded. He always appeared to react a beat late to whatever had just happened, but in the end he'd wind up ahead of everyone else.

"I'm thinking, maybe, we hire someone to look after things," he said. The moving shadows on his face now made him look menacing. The movie villain, come to square accounts.

"I can take care of Henry. And the dog."

"Good for you, that's not what I meant."

"Then, what?"

"Someone to clean things, open the mail, brighten the place up, maybe cook, that kind of thing. Just make it easier for a while. What do you say?"

"Alright. If you think it's necessary."

"Great. On the drive over, I figured it all out."

"Figured it all out? You live five minutes away, you could've walked."

"Yeah, well, the meatloaf. Anyway, I got it figured out. Henry can rest easy, and you can save your potpourri candles for the holidays."

~ ~ ~

I just assumed it would be a woman, but Conroy arrived a few days later, with Stephen.

It was a hot day. I opened the door and they came in. I'm sure they were hoping for air conditioning but weren't too surprised not to find it. Even the gardeners had stopped coming.

Conroy took a step back, braced himself, and entered.

"Tom, this is Stephen."

"Hello, Doctor Ackerman," Stephen said. He looked like an accountant with a killer weekend golf game.

"Hi." I shook his hand, confused. "Where is she?"

"Who?" Conroy asked. "And seriously, at least open a window in here."

"The, uh—the assistant person."

"I'm her," Stephen said.

"Oh." I didn't understand anything now.

Luca Brasi ran over and threw his paws on Stephen's thighs and buried his nose in his crotch like this new person was a long-lost lover. Stephen crouched and scratched him behind his ears. "You must be Luca Brasi."

I started to wonder how much this Stephen knew about my life. He stood back up and looked around, appearing to take mental notes.

"I know," Conroy said. "Don't be discouraged."

Maybe it takes having someone else in your house to see it with fresh eyes, but I saw the disaster all around me. I was embarrassed, though a part of me was glad for that. It was something. The shadow took note. I've always hated incompetence. Now Conroy had to hire someone to—to what? I couldn't remember exactly.

Henry came downstairs and went up to Stephen. They appeared to already know each other. I hadn't felt so excluded since grade school. "Hey, man," Henry said. I'd clearly missed a lot.

"I'll show Stephen around," Conroy said.

"Oh"—Stephen turned to me—"your electricity should be back on this afternoon. I took care of that right away."

~~~

Stephen proceeded to take over. There was nothing he couldn't do. He'd arrive at six in the morning and go home at nine, with Sundays off. Within a few weeks, the house was clean and organized. The gardeners were back. The kitchen was bursting with food. There was something cooking at all hours.

I began to think maybe Stephen wasn't human. An accomplished polyglot, he hired a Korean cleaning service and spoke to them in Korean; he spoke to the gardeners in Spanish, and I heard him on the phone once, speaking French. He could cook anything. He made the greatest coffee I ever tasted; he said he got it from somewhere in Venice that created a custom blend just for him. He had the uncanny ability to know what was going to happen before it happened. He'd start walking toward the front door before the doorbell rang. He was unfailingly polite, dressed impeccably, and could alter the way he spoke based on who he was speaking to—grunts, nods, and smirks for Henry—crisp, declarative sentences for me.

A month after he arrived, I came downstairs to find the bottom half of a stranger sticking out of the piano. "Having it tuned," Stephen said as he wiped his hands on a towel. "Henry wants to learn."

"Sure," I said. I'd tried about a hundred times to teach Henry how to play piano, thinking it might be something we could do together, but he was never interested, even though he'd developed a taste for classical music. Maybe that was why. He always felt obliged to pretend to like the music other kids his age liked. He played it at high volume as if to prove he was a normal teenager after all, even an angry one, while actually wearing headphones, listening to Brahms' *Requiem*. I eventually stopped playing myself. The piano had sat there like a museum piece for the last year.

Later, while in the library, I heard the piano. I came out to find Stephen playing Chopin's Sonata No. 3 in B minor. It was a piece I was very familiar with. The piano tuner was impressed, which I expect was saying something. Stephen paused and repeated a section with his head cocked over the strings. He stopped abruptly. "Sound's good," he said. The tuner looked relieved.

Stephen began teaching Henry to play, which seemed harmless enough, until Henry started playing scales at all hours.

Now I'd run out. Before Stephen's arrival, I had this vague idea of cleaning up my act. It was there before me, like something to aim for. Now Stephen had taken care of everything, and I was left with nothing but more grief ahead of me.

It wasn't just Francis's death; it was Henry as well.

Tragedy can pull a family together or push them apart. There was a widening gap between Henry and myself. It was my fault, but I couldn't figure out how. It was like we were no longer related. I missed my son, as if he'd died too. I'd daydream about the times he'd run and jump into my arms when I got home, smelling of boy. There was no hostility between us, just a drifting, like he was growing older, toward some horizon, and I was stuck in a never-ending limbo.

One day I was napping on the couch. When I woke, I couldn't remember his name. It was only for a few seconds, but a cold panic held me.

Maybe Francis was what kept us all from being strangers, and now, in her absence, we were regressing to our normal, isolated state.

~ ~ ~

I came to mistake grief for depression. This wasn't clear until the real depression hit, in stark relief, like an improved technology. One didn't fully substitute the other, but settled in like a good companion. What was gritty was now smooth and semi-opaque. It occurred to me that I was thinking like Francis, perhaps as a way to stay close to her. She would feel this new suffering in tactile terms.

I knew there was medication available for depression—I had a history—but not so with grief, which responds only to total submission or complete denial, and to neither well. But at least grief has context, unlike depression, which is holistic in its smothering.

Conroy again sat across from me, sipping chilled Chablis. The dining room table glowed like a precious metal and smelled of lemons. A wide bowl with fresh-cut flowers sat between us, some floating, like a faraway Japanese garden.

"Damn, where does he get this?" Conroy held his wine glass to the light and rolled the elixir.

"I know, it's everything." I waved a limp hand, my new go-to gesture.

"Nice."

"I guess."

"You should know, he's costing you a fortune. But I see you really get what you pay for."

"Usually that doesn't refer to people, at least not for a hundred years or so."

"We're all owned by someone, I'm afraid."

"Um."

I knew what was coming, just not when. I had actually called him, but hadn't told him why.

"How's Henry?" he asked.

"Good. He's become a pianist."

"Really?"

"About five weeks now. He can play some Chopin. Or at least that popular one that sounds like a nursery rhyme."

"Lucky you."

"Over and over."

"Haven't heard you play for a while."

"I haven't."

"Maybe he'll become a surgeon as well. Isn't piano supposed to be good for that, exercising the finger muscles or something?"

I didn't answer. That's the thing with depression—you don't really need an excuse for anything, and eventually forget you're supposed to try.

"So, what's up?" he asked. "You ready to come back to Tykes Initiative?" On to the heart of the matter.

"No."

"Soon, though, yeah? Could use you, and it might help. You, I mean."

"Or hurt. Not me, but if I'm not ready, I'd be putting people in danger."

"True, it's your call, you just let me know."

"I'm depressed."

"Really? You mean this isn't the new you?"

"I'd prefer to see someone I don't already know."

"I understand." He pushed his wine away and shifted into sincerity. He always saved it for when it mattered most. "Tommy, listen, I'm really sorry. You know how sorry I am about Francis."

"Of course."

"I want you to know I'm sorry for what you're going through. I didn't say anything before because I knew there were no words for it. I figured you'd rather I didn't try. We have that kind of relationship, I think."

"Nobody gets us."

"But now, I wanted you to know. I wanted to express it. I'm really, very sorry."

I reached across and took his wine. I swirled it under my nose. It smelled like a window box in Italy after a rain. Francis and I went to Tuscany when we were first married. Before Henry. I was ready for a lounging kind of vacation, but Francis was having none of that. She lectured me on the plane about what we'd be seeing. In that place of dust and cobwebs, I learned of her need for things expressed through touch. She thought sculptures should be felt, not put behind glass or placed up high. Good art changes your perceptions, she'd say, if you allow it. Down the boot to Rome and Naples, then back up the middle to Florence, she tutored me at every museum, church, and sculpture garden, grateful for my effort and always coaxing me forward. She carried the idea of tactile beauty the way a teenage boy carries lust. We touch what we love, her lecture continued, oblivious to the rain, standing at the foot of *The Rape of the Sabine Woman*. Our children. Her grandfather's old Plymouth, washed by hand every Sunday. The food we once ate with warm blood between our fingers. When she felt I'd graduated her school of sensory appreciation, we went back to our hotel and went to bed. She was so happy, right to have bet on this man after all. It was important, to be understood in this way. We spent the evening gliding fingertips, riding waves of tension; across the circle from our early, animal encounters.

"Do you know Doctor Gordy?" Conroy asked.

"Man or woman?"

"Man, at USC."

"It's like nobody graduates. No, I don't know him."

"I'll call him, unless you want to."

"I should."

Of course I didn't mean now. Conroy took out his phone and called his assistant, who called Doctor Aaron Gordy's office and transferred the call to Conroy's phone. He handed the phone to me.

I answered the questions from Doctor Gordy's assistant. I recognized some of them from the background chatter at work. The next available appointment was two weeks away. Conroy shook his head and motioned for the phone. He disappeared into the living room. I checked out until he came back a few minutes later.

"Tomorrow, at three-thirty," he said. "You want me to take you?"

"No, I'm allowed to drive."

"I'm not suggesting you can't, rather that you won't."

"I called you, remember?"

"That may have been all you had. I'll pick you up at two. You want to get there a little early to fill out all the forms." He got up to leave. "Tell Stephen I said thanks." He grabbed a foil-wrapped plate off the counter. Stephen had politely claimed to need to run to the store when Conroy arrived.

After he left, I stayed at the dining room table. I lost track of time again. At some point, I heard the piano; Chopin, same as before, rolling and dripping. I took a sip of wine. Warm.

~ ~ ~

I met with Doctor Gordy. He made me grateful I'd not gone his professional route. Psychiatry is a long slog, and none that I'd met could give me a clear answer as to why they'd gone into it. A fetish for self-analysis, using others as a mirror; a way to remain a patient forever, I concluded. They were all suspect.

It was a terrible system. With advancements in medication, clinical analysis was not only becoming obsolete, but a bit embarrassing, like using a Ouija board. Psychiatrists were now professional prescribers, more diagnostic technicians than medical practitioners, meeting annually to parse symptom into new diseases and naming them with the fun of hurricanes, digging new tunnels of revenue for the pill pushers. Of course there was always some analysis before the scratchpad came out, but largely as a formality, and nothing that couldn't be done over the phone. There were counselors and family therapists for those that still believed in a talking cure, but the best psychiatrist was no match for what came out of Pfizer's R&D department. Eventually, everything follows the money.

Doctor Gordy's office exuded the necessary calcified integrity, which required leather furniture and tall bookcases filled with reference volumes. A large window overlooked a hazy downtown Los Angeles. There was visible evidence this often-dismissed city center had found its legs; every few blocks sported shiny new buildings or dinosaur-like construction cranes.

We talked briefly of Francis, our marriage, and her death, like we were critiquing a tragedy. I was as honest as I could be. My answers were more direct than his questions. Being a doctor taught me the futility of lying to one, or even hedging the truth. Whether it's an embarrassing rash or something stuck up your butt, lying about it only makes for a worse truth later.

I did, however, allow one omission: my late-night conversations with Francis. They'd started as a sneaky indulgence, but had developed into something of a new relationship, and necessary for me to fall asleep.

He asked twice about my work. I reiterated my insistence that I was not ready to return. I didn't tell him I thought I'd never go back. I secretly believed I was retired; it was just too early to announce it. It would still seem reactionary. He talked about men—specifically men—getting their identity through their function in the world, usually their work, like it or not. It's what we bring home from the hunt, according to him.

"It was men that jumped out of windows during the Great Depression, never women, not because they'd lost their fortunes, but because they'd lost their identities." I sensed he'd used this line before. I nodded and wondered if he'd ever been sourced. I hated to think what he told women.

"If you go too long without work," he continued, "you begin to disappear. Not out there"—he pointed to the window—"but in here." He tapped his head. I'd been dutifully deferential so far in all the subtle ways, mostly out of professional courtesy, but this kind of tripe was making it difficult.

We plowed ahead, ticking off boxes: my history of depression, my relationship with Henry, and my trouble sleeping. In regards to my grief, he informed me there were support groups for those who had lost a spouse or other family member. Just my kind of thing.

"You need more people to talk to," he said. "You got that from your work before, and from your wife. So let's start close to home. I want you to have dinner with your son."

"Fine."

"That's your assignment this week. Pick a night. Even if you don't talk at first, sharing a meal is a bonding experience. It does more to keep families together than people realize." His look suggested he'd just tapped the source of the great unraveling.

I wanted to know the time but didn't want to look at my watch. I figured we were about done. I thought I was a nicely packaged patient and now I was ready for my drugs.

"Are you masturbating?" he asked, providing my first surprise.

"What, now?" I tried to joke. His eyes were as steady as his pen.

"You indicated you previously had a healthy sex life. Has that been an adjustment?"

"No, it hasn't, it hasn't even occurred to me." I felt a bit sick, like a kid who's secretly afraid he's a pervert.

"So, you're not masturbating?"

"No."

"Do you have any sexual interest?"

"No."

"None?"

"That's correct."

"Do you think that's unusual?"

"Everything is unusual. There no longer is any usual."

He opened the top drawer of his desk and pulled out the scratchpad. Finally.

"One last question."

"Sure."

"Do you want to get better?"

Chapter 5

MARGARET

"You tried to hit her? That's fuckin' awesome," Vicky said. We were in her van. It helped to tell her what happened. She made me feel pretty tough for not backing down. I hadn't thought of it like that. I just thought I'd gotten my ass kicked.

She was driving the way she usually did, like someone blind and drunk. She always seemed surprised there were other cars on the road, like it was really her road and she was just being kind in letting other people use it, but they really shouldn't take advantage by getting in her way.

I white-knuckled the armrest and pressed my feet on an imaginary brake. "Hey, didn't you say you were going to get seatbelts put in?" We careened around a corner and drifted half way onto the wrong side of the road.

"That was just to get you to drive with me. So you started it with her? Are you effin' nuts?"

"No. See, she'd already hit Song, so—it's complicated."

"You were protecting Song?"

"Not really. Well, I don't know."

"Whatever, Dorie's a Type A weirdo, her and her brother both. I'm not even totally sure she's a girl, I think she might have a dick." I laughed as she fiddled with the van's old tape deck. This was what I needed.

"She doesn't have a dick."

"I'm not so sure."

"*Fuck!*" I yelled and slammed both feet down. Vicky looked up and gunned it. We missed the light by about a hundred feet. A car stopped short in the intersection and honked as we zoomed past.

"We're not like—in a huge hurry—are we?" I asked.

"Kinda. Ms. Barden said to try to get there by eleven, before it gets busy."

"Shit, it's like after twelve." I tried to read my watch as we whipped around another corner.

"Really?"

"Yeah, so really no point in going so fast because we're already late and it's kinda freaking me out."

"Oh, relax, getting beat up has made you all uptight. We're almost there." She got the tape deck to work. Garth Brooks came on, mid-song. Vicky pounded the steering wheel in time and sang along. She even got the little catch in his voice just right.

We pulled up to Formally Informal, a clothing shop that catered to Madison's upscale clientele. Vicky parked the van between the last open spot and the handicap space, offending with equal opportunity. I realized I should have put something on besides jeans and a *Rage Against the Machine* t-shirt.

"Don't worry about it," Vicky said. "It's not what you wear, it's how you wear it. Actually, that's not true at all. Why don't you at least turn your shirt inside out."

"Here?"

"Yeah, who's going to see? It's not like you're peeing in the bushes."

It took me awhile because I could still only see out of one eye. I had to be extra careful pulling my shirt over my face. I could tell Vicky was trying not to laugh because the fat rolls on her belly were doing little bounces.

"Cool," she said when I was done. "With that fucked-up face, you look pretty badass."

"I don't have to go in."

I still looked pretty scary. The bruise around my eye had blotches of dark yellow. Most of the swelling had gone down on my lip, but I still had a bit of a lisp. I found out the hard way that I couldn't eat anything salty, which was my weakness. My side still hurt, especially when I walked, but my face had stopped hurting, so it was easy to forget about it until something reminded me, like when a kid stared at me and started to cry.

"Nah, I need you to help me carry some stuff," Vicky said. "You're not just here to look pretty." She swung out of the van and opened the back. She jumped up with an easy leap, like a world-class gymnast stuck in a big girl's body. "Here, grab these," she said. She pulled a bunch of dresses off a rod and handed them down to me. She hopped back down, twirling her keys.

"Hey, why shouldn't you tease a fat girl with a lisp?" she asked me as we walked to the door. Vicky liked to tell fat girl jokes. She said it was her way of disarming others. I guess a lisp joke, for my temporary benefit, was inevitable.

"Why?" I asked from under the pile of dresses.

"Because, they're thick and tired of it."

The door gave a pleasant jingle when we went in. The shop was cozy and warm, with a lavender-and-spice smell. It seemed like the kind of place where you'd drink tea. Everything was white or cream colored. Classical music played, like out of a romantic movie. It was one of those places where you knew right away if you belonged. I didn't. I felt like I might besmirch the air or something. Vicky breezed in like she owned the place and everyone in it.

Ms. Barden looked exactly like the type of woman who would own a place like this; around sixty, stylish, with flawless hair and perfect poise. Vicky told me she was actually pretty cool. When she saw us she broke into a wide smile and let out a big, "Vicky!" loud enough to make the shoppers all turn in unison. She excused herself from the customer she was helping to come over and give Vicky a hug.

Ms. Barden looked at me over Vicky's shoulder. My arms were still full of dresses. Her smile fell. "Good God, child—"

Vicky interrupted her before she could finish. "I brought more—I brought more just like you asked."

"Great. Yes," Ms. Barden said. She looked flustered. I felt bad that my nasty-looking face had dampened her joy at seeing Vicky. "Let's... let's just see what you have here, honey." She stole another look at me.

Vicky took the dresses from me one by one and laid them on the marble table.

"Oh, yes. My, these are wonderful. More sizes, though, honey. You need to do more multiples for size variations. Right now, you're designing a new dress each time, and that's just too much effort." She ran her hand along the seams and examined the fabrics.

"I know," Vicky said. "I just get all excited and can't help it. I don't want to make the same dress I just made, just to get one in a different size."

"Yes, but honey, that's what factories are for. You're too good a designer to spend all your time as a seamstress. Your work is exquisite. I'll take them all."

Vicky squealed. "Thank you, Ms. Barden."

"Not at all, I'm taking advantage of you, I hope you know. Should be illegal. Actually, it might be. Even with your commission, I'm making a killing." She picked up one of the dresses and ran her hand down the back. "I sure wish I still had the body to wear this. Vicky, you've got to get some business sense and learn to leverage your talent. You're going to do well, but if you're not careful, you'll get eaten alive. You don't want to end up with a shop like this, believe me. It's a glorified service job. Might as well work at the JC Penny. You're meant for better things, but fashion is a brutal industry."

"I know, I have that book you lent me. I'll read it."

"I already gave you this lecture?"

"Yes."

"Oh my, senior moments happening every day now. *Kimberly!*" she called in a sharp tone. A girl about my age came out of the back as if she'd been waiting to be called. "Take these dresses for tagging. Thank you, sweetie." The girl gathered up the dresses. I started to help her but she looked at me and stepped back. "I got it," she said.

"Oh, honey, there's a private commission for you," Ms. Barden said to Vicky. "I took her measurements and wrote everything down. It's based on the yellow drop-back you did. The paperwork is by the register, if you can find it. She'll pay whatever, so charge her a ton. And there's an envelope around there with your name on it. Your percentage."

"Oh my God! Oh my 'effin God," Vicky said. She ran behind the counter. Ms. Barden smiled as she watched Vicky rummage around the register. I was left standing there with nothing useful to do. Ms. Barden turned back and looked at me. I pretended not to notice. I thought of browsing through the dresses, but felt like I shouldn't touch anything, like I might soil it.

Ms. Barden wasn't shy about staring. Finally, I looked back at her. *What?*

"Someone do this to you?" she asked in a hushed voice.

"It was a... a fight. I lost."

"A fight with whom?" It was none of her business, but somehow she made me feel like she really cared, which seemed strange because we'd only met five minutes ago. My dad hardly cared. After the fight, he only wanted to know if I needed to go to the hospital. He decided I didn't, even though I was pretty sure my lip needed stitches. After the deer incident, everything was about the barest of parental responsibilities.

Ms. Barden kept staring as she waited for an answer. "A girl at school," I said.

"A girl did this to you?"

"Yeah. Well, there's some debate about her gender status, but yeah."

"My, how the world does change. We used to leave that kind of thing to the boys, try to set the better example."

"I would have done better in your era."

"Of course we were just as violent, but more subtle. Psychological instead of physical."

"That hasn't changed. This is in addition to, not instead of."

"Uh huh. About a boy?"

I looked at her with my good eye. "Not in the way you're thinking."

"I see. You're a smart girl."

"But not very tough."

"Oh, I don't know about that. I'd put my money on you, in the end."

Vicky walked up. "Ah shit, I didn't even introduce you guys."

"Vicky!" Ms. Barden said, smiling again.

"God, sorry, I got a bad mouth." She was bouncing on her toes as she clutched the dress order and her commission envelope.

"No bother, we made our own acquaintance," Ms. Barden said and gave me a knowing wink.

On the drive home, Vicky tossed me the envelope. "Open it," she said.

It was a check. "Oh my God, it's for four hundred and twenty dollars. Is that your commission? Is that all for you?"

"Hell yes. Actually, you get ten percent, so what, forty-two dollars, for being my model. Remember, I told you."

"Vic, you don't have to do that."

"You deserve it."

"No, I don't, you're trying to make me feel better. Thank you, but you've earned this money, you really have, and you already pay me for picking up fabric and stuff."

"I could use more help, actually. I need someone to do deliveries, so maybe you could do some on the weekends. I can't sew fast enough, and Ms. Barden says she knows a store in Milwaukee that will take my dresses. Of course, it'll be better when your face is healed and you're not terrifying to look at. This business is all about appearances, you know."

"Sure, I could do that, that'd be awesome. I can do deliveries, but please, can you put seatbelts in this thing?"

"We'll use your ten percent for that. I even had to open a bank account."

"Ms. Barden likes you. She treats you like a grown-up."

"Yeah, she's alright. She gave me a glass of wine once."

"Hey, Vic?"

"Hum?"

"Thank you."

She just smiled without looking at me and popped the tape back in. She was banging the steering wheel before the music even started.

~ ~ ~

I went back to school the following Monday. My face still looked pretty bad, so of course everybody asked me what happened. I kept changing my answer. I told one stupid girl that I'd had an allergic reaction after getting bit by a rabid dog that was still prowling the school.

I was amazed at how intimidated I was by all these people when I first started high school. Now, in my senior year, I didn't care what anyone thought. Not in a bad way—I didn't want to make enemies—it just didn't really matter one way or the other. The only friend I had there was Song.

I was focused on my grades, because a math scholarship was the only way I was going to go to college, and then to law school. I'd applied for a number of scholarships, and was hoping to hear back from Madison, but they all pretty much required I keep my grades in the top five percent. Not a problem, except I'd missed most of the previous week, so I was spending a lot of time begging my teachers to let me make up the work. After seeing my face, most of them took pity on me.

On Tuesday, I left my last class and was walking down the hall in a daze, having stayed up most of the previous night trying to finish a week's worth of homework. The hall was crammed with students, all talking and rushing for the exit. The last classes of the day were usually staggered so not everyone was trying to leave at the same time, but it seemed like the whole school was pouring out at once, as if it were the last day of school.

I followed the mass out. Though it was only late October, it was already in the thirties. Every day seemed to have a sky the color of dirty water.

I stopped on the steps. Everyone was moving to a certain spot on the schoolyard. It finally dawned on me that something out of the ordinary was happening. Probably a fight, I thought. The thought made my stomach twitch. I started down the steps and tried to get around the crowd, hoping to avoid whatever was going on. As I passed, I realized there was none of the typical goading and yelling you heard in a fight. It was strangely quiet. I drew closer. "Billy, what's up?" I asked a guy from my history class who liked to accidentally brush against my boobs about twice a week.

"I don't know, Mags, I'm too fuckin' short to see over all these fuckers." He started pushing through the crowd. I followed him. Everyone was converged around a spot. Something dead? That happened last year when they found a dead cougar in the middle of the basketball court; a prank from a rival school because our mascot was a cougar.

"Hey, Cassandra, what's going on?" I asked a girl coming the opposite direction.

"Oh, man," she said, shaking her head. "That's seriously fucked up." She looked at me. "And shit, so's your face. Damn, girl." I pushed my way in until I was finally close enough to see around the people at the front.

It was Dwayne. He was sitting at the base of the volleyball pole. His hands were tied behind him with heavy rope. He was naked except for a pair of bright pink panties, not big enough to cover his privates, which were spilling out. His lips were covered with red lipstick, smeared all over like a kid would do. His head was down. Red, irritated acne covered his shoulders and back. His knees were scraped and the knuckles of his right hand were bloody. His clothes were in a pile nearby.

Something was written in red lipstick on his chest and stomach. I had to maneuver to get a better look.

I HIT GIRLS

He sat like something abandoned, just staring at a spot on the ground between his knees. He didn't seem angry or humiliated, like you'd expect. He was probably beyond that. It was like he had separated from his body and was not really there anymore. Maybe he was hovering above, watching it all. I sometimes felt like that.

I looked at the people gathered around. I could tell some were pleased. Dwayne had made a lot of enemies, so it wasn't surprising.

"Oh, maaaan," Billy whispered next to me. "Good, fuckin' cocksucker."

Nobody stepped forward to help him. Nobody went to get his clothes. It was eerily quiet. A chain tinkled against the pole. He was perfectly still, like he was frozen. Despite the cold, he wasn't shivering.

Mr. Janakowski pushed though the crowd. He brushed past me and crouched to put a blanket around Dwayne, who still didn't move. Mr. J turned and shouted at us, "All of you, get out of here. *Now!* If there's anybody here in ten seconds, you'll be in detention for a week." He tried to cut the rope on Dwayne's hands using regular scissors. It seemed pretty obvious that wasn't going to work.

Dwayne looked up at me. It was like he knew exactly where I was standing. He stared at me with unblinking eyes.

"Hey, Billy," I rocked against his shoulder. "Can you walk with me for a second?"

Billy looked up at me and pushed his glasses up his nose. "Yeah. Fuck, yeah." We turned away and walked. I could feel Dwayne's eyes on me.

Billy kept taking sideways looks at my face as we walked. "Did you have, like, a farming accident or something?"

"Shut up."

"'Kay."

I looked toward the parking lot and stopped. Near the fence was Alana's Camaro, idling. She was in it, looking in my direction. The exhaust blew puffs of smoke in the cold air. Someone else was in the car. It was a girl, smoking a cigarette. She was holding something to her face. It looked like a bloody towel.

There was a distinctive growl as the car pulled away and drifted out of the parking lot like an old gray shark.

~ ~ ~

Dwayne wasn't in school the next day, or the next. On Friday, he still wasn't back. I sat in class and looked at his empty chair, only half-listening to Mr. J drone on and on.

I didn't feel any better after seeing Dwayne humiliated. I just felt sick and empty. Nobody thought I had anything to do with what happened. I hadn't told anyone at school that it was Dwayne and Dorie who beat up Song and I. Song hadn't told anyone either, and it wasn't like either of us had a big brother or a lot of friends who would do something like that for us. I had been looking forward to my last year of high school, but now that feeling seemed strange. It wasn't even November and I just wanted it all to be over.

After school, I went to Vicky's house to try on my dress. She wanted to do a formal fitting, which she said was part of the couture process. She wanted to make sure she practiced each step. Now that I could see out of both eyes, I could make whatever final adjustments were needed.

Vicky watched as I pulled the dress over my head. "Stop. First of all, how many times have I told you? You step into a dress like this. It's not a sweater. And I don't think you can wear a bra with it, or at least not that one."

I took off my bra, stepped into the dress and pulled it up.

"Awesome," she said and tugged the sleeves. She went behind me and tied the back. "Your eye holes match perfect." She came around the front. "Damn, Mags, it looks great. You did an awesome job."

"Thanks."

"Check you out." She turned me toward the mirror. I did look pretty awesome, except for my face of course.

"You're a good teacher," I said.

"Not really, I'm kind of a tyrant, but you bring out my soft side. The color is perfect on you. That gypsy hag knows her shit. You see what I mean now, right? After the dance, you're still going to have a great dress for special occasions or whatever. Now, I already made you a bonnet, and we'll add some other stuff to give the full effect, but shit, this dress is beautiful."

I looked in the mirror again. Even with my messed-up face, I felt like a more elegant version of myself.

"*Vicky, phone!*" a voice called from below. There was tromping on the stairs. Alana appeared. "It's that woman from the clothing store." She was wearing jeans and a t-shirt, instead of her usual gym shorts and tank top. She also didn't have her hair tied back like she usually did.

"Awesome," Vicky said. She leapt over a bolt of fabric. "And it's a fashion boutique, not a clothing store. And hello? Where's the fucking phone?"

"On the kitchen table."

"Oh, thanks for bringing it up, 'tard."

"No prob, skinny, figured you could use the exercise."

"She's the one from the Milwaukee shop that's going to take a bunch of my dresses," Vicky said to me over her shoulder before bounding down the stairs.

I stood there feeling foolish as Alana looked me over in her languid way, like she'd caught me playing dress-up. I guess she had. Her right hand had a bandage wrapped around it.

"Nice," she said.

"Vicky's been helping me with it," I said, like I needed an excuse.

"I know, I've seen the progression. How's your face?"

"Better, much better. I think it's healing, mostly." I was going to ask her about her hand, but I wasn't sure I wanted to know.

I could hear Vicky chirping on the phone downstairs. Alana stepped toward me. I felt like my feet were bolted to the floor. She came up close, very casual, and put the back of her bandaged hand against my cheek. Then her fingertips. I was surprised again by how soft her touch was. She nudged my face toward the light coming from the window. "Um, yeah, it's healing pretty fast," she said. "Your lip looks better, too. You might have a scar, though."

"At least I don't lisp any more."

"Um hum." She ran her thumb over the area of my lip that had split, just barely touching it. I was starting to sweat. She moved in closer. She had a bruise on her neck, just below her ear. She smelled musky, but in a good way, like the woods first thing in the morning. She had on dark red lipstick. I didn't think she wore lipstick. "I bet you think I'm a dyke," she said. Her breath was warm. "Like everybody else."

"No." My own voice sounded strange.

"No?"

"I mean, I don't know. I'm not..."

"You're not... what?" I could barely hear her.

"Sure."

"About what?"

"That."

"What?"

"That, what you said."

"What if I was?" She rolled her lips over and back.

"It wouldn't matter. I mean, I wouldn't care."

"You wouldn't? Don't you like that guy—hippy coffee house guy?"

"Yes, but he's not a hippy, he just has long hair."

"Don't worry, I won't beat him up. I know you think I did it for you, to be chivalrous or something." Her fingers slid off my face and grazed over the skin below my neck.

88

"Did you? Do it for me?" My voice came out shaky. I was starting to feel dizzy. She didn't answer. She just looked at me, all mysterious and dreamy. She pressed closer so her breasts touched mine. I leaned forward too, pushing into her. I felt like I was falling out of an airplane.

"I did it because I wanted to," she said. "Sometimes that's all you need." I was having trouble piecing together what she was referring to.

She closed her eyes and put both hands on my face. Her bandage was rough against my cheek. She rose up and kissed my forehead. My heart was pounding so hard I was sure she could feel it. She finally broke away and took a step back. I was left standing as I was before, except now it felt like my heart had dropped through the floor.

She went back to the doorway. "I go back tonight."

"Oh, yeah, I was going to ask you about that," I said from some other place.

"You're trying to get in there, right?"

"Madison, yeah, if I can get a scholarship."

"You will, you're like, a genius."

"No, I'm not."

"Yeah, right. When you get in, I could show you around."

"Okay."

We heard Vicky taking the steps two at a time. Alana stepped aside as she brushed past, but kept her eyes on me.

"Where's the bonnet?" Vicky asked. "I thought you were going to put the bonnet and sash on so I could see." She dug them out and handed them to me. "Here. Oh, you are so going to be making deliveries for me. She wants all the same dresses Ms. Barden has at her store. I think maybe they're kind of competitive." Alana and I kept looking at each other as Vicky busied herself tying the sash around me. "Plus, she wants a couple holiday dresses, which is kind of crazy seeing how it's almost November, but I'm going to try."

Alana slid away.

"It's going to be awesome," Vicky said and stepped back to look at me. "Damn, you look great. Really. Like some guy's wet dream."

~ ~ ~

Ever since the whole hunting thing with my dad, my weekend mornings were ruined. I couldn't sleep in. On Saturday, I was up at seven. I finished a homework assignment on differential equations, even though there was nobody to correct it because my math teacher didn't even know dynamical systems. He'd probably just write a general comment on it to imply he understood it, then give me an A-, like he knew enough to know it wasn't exactly right, but was just too busy to be more specific.

I wanted to get out. I decided to take the bus to Madison. The weather was warmer and I had enough money for both ways, plus some for coffee. Simon usually had the Saturday morning shift.

I found some makeup in the bottom drawer of my desk, left over from my makeup phase. I used it to touch up my face. When I'd finished, it was hard to tell if I'd made it better or worse.

It was ten o'clock when I got to Madison. I really had to pee, so I went to Peet's Coffee on the next block over and used their bathroom.

The place was crowded. When I was leaving, I saw Simon sitting on one of the big cushy couches. I was glad I hadn't seen him when I came in or I would have panicked. Now I just reacted without thinking about it. "Hey," I said.

He looked up from his book. "Oh—hey, Mags," he said with his lazy smile, giving me the good kind of shivers.

"Don't you work at the other coffee shop?" I asked, all casual.

"Yeah, but I don't start 'til eleven. The coffee there kinda blows so I usually come here first. I keep telling them they should just buy their coffee from here and brew it there and who's gonna know, right? At least it'd be decent. But management, you know? Hey, you getting something?"

"Yeah, I was going to."

"Cool, I'll save you a spot, if you want." He pulled his book bag off the floor and put it next to him on the couch.

"Yeah, cool. You want anything?" I said as I headed for the counter, which was dumb because I couldn't get him anything unless I wanted to walk home.

"Nah, I'm good."

When I came back with my coffee, he'd put his book away, which I took as a good sign. It meant he was planning to talk to me.

When I sat down, he looked at my eye and cocked his head. I could see he wanted to ask me about it but decided not to. I was so relieved I wanted to kiss him. Really, I kind of wanted to anyway.

We talked a bit about school. He was going to a community college and was planning to transfer to a university to study agricultural science. He seemed like the earthy type.

"That seems like it would be really interesting," I said. "You'd get to be outdoors a lot. Do you, uh, hunt?" I asked, hoping he'd say no.

"Nah," he said, almost embarrassed, like someone might hear. He pushed his long hair behind his ear. "I have, but I don't really care for it. I mean, maybe if I was going to eat it, but I don't eat meat, so... there's that."

The coffee kicked in and I became real chatty, talking about hunting with my dad and how I was good at it but decided I didn't like it. I left out the puking part. I talked about Song and Vicky, and making my dress, and doing deliveries for Vicky, and waiting to hear about my scholarship. He really looked at me when I talked, like what I was saying was important.

"That's right, I remember that about you, you're like a math freak," he said, smiling. "I mean, in a good way, like you're a math genius. I could probably take, like, a whole box of toothpicks and dump them all on the ground and you'd be able to tell me exactly how many there are, right? Freaky shit like that?"

"Oh, yeah, that'd be easy."

"Really? I was kidding, but you could really do that?"

"Sure, I'd just look at the box, it tells you how many are in it." He laughed. Really laughed. I don't think I'd ever had a guy really laugh at something I'd said. Vicky and Song, yes, they were easy to make laugh, but not a guy. It made me feel about ten feet tall.

"It's a little after eleven," I said.

It took him a moment to register. "Oh—right. I guess I should get going." He didn't seem in a hurry.

"Hey, um," I said as he was gathering his stuff. He stopped and looked at me. He had such soft brown eyes. I could never in a million years plan to do it, but somehow the moment was right and I suddenly felt very brave, so why the fuck not? "Next weekend, you want to catch a movie or something with me?" I asked him. My voice sounded pretty normal, but my heart had stopped beating, my lungs froze, and the world stopped spinning. My mind started doing math calculations on the earth's rotational speed and how long it would take to actually stop if it had twice the density. It was a ton of math, but my mind chewed through a lot of it in the second or so that passed.

"Yeah," he drawled out with that smile and slight overbite. "Yeah, that would be great. Let me get your number. Here, I'll give you mine too." He pulled a notebook from his backpack and tore off a piece. He handed it to me with a pen. I hesitated. My mind was blank. What was my phone number? He waited.

"What's yours?" I asked in desperation. He gave me his number and I wrote it down. Then—God showing mercy—I wrote mine down. I tore it off and handed it to him. My heart started beating again, crashing against my ribs.

"Alright," he said. "Well, thanks. I'll hit you up later in the week, we'll make plans."

"That sounds great," I said. We both headed for the door. Outside, he nodded down the street. "I'm headed this way."

"See you next weekend," I said. I started in the other direction. I desperately wanted to be alone so I could scream for joy. My mind immediately started on practical details; I'd have to ask Vicky for some of that commission money. I didn't want to assume he'd pay because after all, I had asked him, so I should offer to pay for us both. Maybe I wouldn't end up going to college pure as the driven snow after all if—

"Hey, Mags," Simon said, stopping me. I turned around. "I just wanted to be clear, are we just hangin' out, or is it a date?"

My throat constricted, like I'd had an allergic reaction. "Date," I squeaked out.

"Yeah, cool," he said, with that smile.

~ ~ ~

I couldn't wait to call Vicky. I knew she'd be proud of me because she was always saying I should just grow a pair and ask Simon out myself because he was never going to do it no matter how many cups of coffee I drank there, because men are just kind of thick that way, but it doesn't mean they're not interested. They just need a nudge.

"Especially with your looks. Unless they're partial to cock, no guy in the world would pass up a chance to tap that." She kinda talked like a guy sometimes.

I called her as soon as I got home.

"That's fuckin' awesome," she said. "I should call Alana and tell her. Hope she doesn't take her own life or anything. I think she was kind of hoping to break you in. Before she left, I caught her in my room. She was holding your dress. I think she was smelling it. Weird-fucking-o."

I didn't know she knew. I didn't say anything.

"It's alright," she said. "I pried it out of her freaky man-hands. Hey, when are you coming over to get ready? I'm sewing like a maniac. I worked through most of the night. You can come over early if you want, and help me out, payback for all the stellar advice I gave you on how to bag your hippy crush. I can give you some next-level advice, like how to make your first time last more than ten seconds."

That night was our school's first ever Halloween dance. It was made very clear that this dance was an official school event, and normal school rules would apply. If there was any trouble, it would forever ruin the possibility of future Halloween dances.

For as long as I could remember, everybody went to the Antista's for Halloween. Mr. Antista had an enormous house, twice as big as the next biggest house in Camden. He'd made a lot of money from all the bars he owned. He called our house once when my dad had passed out at one of his places. I had to go there and give him directions to our house from the back seat of his car while my dad sat crumpled over in the front.

Mr. Antista hosted a Halloween party every year so his kids wouldn't have to go anywhere and he could be sure they were safe. That's how it started out anyway, but after his kids got older, he kept having the party, and every year it got a little less kid-friendly, and a little weirder. He really went all out at the last one by turning his place into an elaborate haunted house. There were lots of drugs, mostly supplied by his kids, brother and sister twins who hated each other. He had a huge pool with underwater strobe lights that made everything distorted, especially with the drugs. One kid almost drowned when he kept swimming sideways in a panic, thinking he was swimming up.

Mr. Antista was having his party again this year, and it was going to be bigger than ever. He'd spent months recreating part of the set from the movie *Army of Darkness*. He'd developed some game where everybody was supposed to chase each other around with fake chainsaws, but someone started a rumor that he was going to sneak in a real one.

As word got around, parents took action. They insisted the school have a Halloween dance so they could be sure their kids didn't go to Mr. Antista's house, who they now thought might be insane. I think most of the students were relieved to have somewhere else to go, except the hardcore weirdoes and trench coat freaks.

Our school had a giant assembly hall, which was perfect for a Halloween dance. It wasn't good for much else because it was too big. When the school was built, the assembly hall was built first, as if they were planning for a much bigger school, or maybe they were just looking at the wrong set of plans. You could fit about five times our entire school's student body in our assembly hall, and all they used it for was school announcements and emergency drills. The place was so big the Red Cross used it one winter during a white-out when some power lines went down and they needed a place to bring people so they wouldn't freeze in their homes.

The student committee spent weeks decorating. They created a haunted maze and a hall of mirrors and a bunch of other stuff. I was really looking forward to it. I thought my costume looked great and Vicky was going to make a fantastic wolf, so I was really disappointed when Vicky's mom called me late Saturday afternoon and told me Vicky wasn't going to make it.

"I'm sorry, honey, she cut her hand open and had to get stitches."

"Is she okay?"

"Oh, yes, and it's her own fault. She stayed up all night sewing, and right through the day. I guess she's got some big project she's working on. You'd probably know better than me. She couldn't be bothered with sleep. I guess that's just for the rest of us. She was cutting fabric with those giant scissors she has and didn't even notice at first that she'd almost cut her finger off."

"Oh God, that's terrible."

"Blood everywhere. I was traumatized, but she'll be fine, they said. She finally fell asleep. She said you'd be coming by for your costume and to tell you that someone else might be able to wear the wolf costume. Tong, she said. I'm not sure what she meant, she's on a lot of painkillers, which work quite well, I must say."

"Tong?"

"I don't know honey, I'm just the messenger."

"Oh, *Song,* I think she meant Song."

"Song, okay, I don't know what's wrong with normal names."

I thought the chances were about zero that Song could make it, but I called her. I'd already decided I wasn't going to go by myself. Vicky made everything fun, so the thought of going alone was just depressing.

"So you could wear her costume and we'd have to pin it and stuff because it'd be way too big for you, but it's really cool with a full wolf's head and everything. I know you probably have to take care of your mom and stuff but I thought I'd check."

"I find out and call you back," Song said.

She called back a little while later to say she could go. By some miracle of coincidence, it was one of the few days every year that her mom felt well enough to get out of bed. Her younger brothers and sister were old enough to go trick-or-treating without her, and her dad played poker Saturday nights, though Song had found out he didn't know how to play poker so no one was really sure what he did on Saturday nights. Her mom told her to go out and have fun and meet a husband.

When I went to Vicky's to get the costumes, she was asleep in bed, snoring. Her left hand was in a makeshift hoist so it stayed elevated above her head. It was wrapped in a huge bandage, making it look three times its normal size. It kind of looked like she was flipping everyone off with her giant hand. I wished I had a camera because I bet she'd have loved to have a picture of herself like that.

I gathered the costumes and stood in her room for a moment. I wasn't sure why. Maybe I was hoping Alana would appear in the doorway. Then I remembered she'd already gone back to college.

~ ~ ~

We got to the dance late because I couldn't get the wolf costume to work on Song. I kept trying to pin it the way Vicky did, but nothing worked. No matter what I tried, Song still looked like one of those wrinkly dogs. I finally gave up and just tucked the extra fabric inside the zipper.

I looked pretty fantastic, I have to say. I even curled my hair into corkscrew pigtails, like I remembered from the story. Song took my picture so I could show Vicky the full effect. We looked kind of funny together because I was so much taller than Song, so she didn't seem very threatening, but she loved it.

"I look badass. Eat your head!" she snarled.

When we finally got there, it was already crowded. I'd never seen so many people in our assembly hall. It looked like a lot more people than actually went to our school.

The hall of mirrors was incredible. You could run through it and it looked like you were going to run into yourself, then you'd suddenly be really far away. The dance floor was lit with a big trippy disco ball. People were really creative with their costumes and sometimes you'd talk to someone not even knowing who they were in real life.

I danced a bunch with Song. It was great to see her having so much fun. I was about to stop to get something to drink when Nathan, the guy Song was crushed out on, came up to us. He was a zombie and was a little disappointed that we recognized him, but his costume wasn't that great, so it was pretty easy to tell.

"Mags, you wanna dance?"

"I am dancing."

"With me, brainiac."

"Just a sec."

A Sheryl Crow song started. I pulled Song aside and talked into her wolf ear. I wasn't really sure where her real ear was. "Nathan wants to dance with me."

The wolf head nodded. "You know he just use you to get to me," came her little voice from inside. She must have gotten that from a movie.

"Yeah, I'll pretend I don't know, play along."

"Good, I go to mirror hall, look for Cho." Cho was the only other Korean girl in school. "I tell her I go through scream house with her. She say she come as sunflower, I got to see, meet at office in half hour, okay? I want a full report card."

"Deal," I said.

"What?"

"I mean yes, that sounds good," I shouted in her ear.

Nathan and I danced for two songs. Between them he talked about himself and all the great things he was going to do. I told him I thought zombies didn't talk, just groaned or something. I don't think he got the hint. He seemed a bit drunk.

"I'm going to get something to drink," I told him after the second song.

"I'll go with you," he said.

We went to a table that had big bowls of lemonade with floating skulls. Nathan poured me one and pulled a little bottle out of his pocket, the kind you get on an airplane. He gave me a smirk, all bloody zombie gums, as he twisted the bottle open and poured it in my lemonade. He started talking about how he was going to move to New York after high school, blow this fucking place and hook up with his cousin who had a loft in Greenwich Village. "You know where that is?" he shouted, even though the music wasn't that loud. "It's this really cool place in the city—that's what they call Manhattan when you live there— the city. He's in a band and..." His voice began to blend into the background. I was thirsty but didn't want to drink the spiked lemonade.

I saw Billy walking by. He was dressed as the Joker from Batman. I knew it was him because he kind of waddled when he walked. "Hey, Billy." I lurched out at him in the hope that he'd save me. He spun around, confused, with his hands reaching out. I realized he wasn't wearing his glasses so he was probably half blind.

"Mags?" he said as he went past me.

Nathan was still talking. "So there'd be two guitar players, and I'd be the second one, but that's cool, I mean, that's what Pearl Jam does, you know?"

I decided on a firm approach. "I have to use the bathroom," I told him. "See ya." I stepped away before he could respond. When I looked back, he was still talking. The girl who had been standing next to me was also wearing a red dress. I wasn't sure what her costume was—Little Bo Peep, I think—so Nathan probably thought she was me and just kept talking.

I grabbed a cup of regular lemonade off the end of the table. I was desperate to tell Song about how I'd asked Simon out on a date. I'd been saving it for the office, but it hadn't been half an hour yet. Plus, I felt I needed to tell her she'd fallen for a guy that was kind of a dick. She needed a trigger to segue into her loved-and-lost phase, so maybe that would do it.

Billy came up to me. "Hey, Mags." He'd put his glasses back on.

"Hey, cool costume. Nice blend, like a nerdy Joker kind of thing."

"That's what I was going for." He looked me over. "What are you, like, a whore?"

"What? No! Fuck you, I'm Red Riding Hood."

"Oh. Yeah. See, I thought maybe you were a turn-of-the-century harlot kind of thing, like Jack the Ripper era."

"Jesus."

"Sorry, but shit—you can wear a dress." He'd only ever seen me in jeans.

"Whatever, come on, dance with me."

He was very well behaved on the dance floor, even when it got really crowded and we got pushed together.

"I gotta go pee and meet up with a friend," I told him after a couple songs. "Thanks for dancing with me."

"Well, fuck yeah."

I grabbed another lemonade and went to go meet Song.

I took the long way around, so I wouldn't have to walk past the trailer. It was cold out but the fresh air felt great. I realized I should be careful not to dance too much. There was a costume contest at the end of the night, and I wanted to look good for that.

The far end of the school was as quiet and deserted as always, but it seemed more so after the noise and crowds of the auditorium. The only people I saw were a small group by the defunct soccer field fence. They were passing a joint and looked at me as I went by. I imagined myself as someone from an old romantic novel, the heroine escaping in the red dress, running through the mist.

When I got to the bathrooms, Song was already in her stall. The bathrooms were nice and warm, which was good because I really did have to pee and didn't want to sit on a cold toilet seat.

"Is it hard to get your costume off?" I asked her. "Because mine kinda is. I can give you a hand if you need." I was trying to figure out how to get the sash off. It went on easy enough. "I know you're crushed out on Nathan, but I think you need to reconsider."

I could hear her moving. "Do you need help?" I asked. I smelled something. Cigarette smoke. I heard her door open. "Song?"

My door smashed in. I fell backwards and hit the wall behind the toilet. The wolf's head looked down at me. My body seemed to comprehend what was happening before my mind could make the shift. I tried to scramble under the stall divider.

He reached down, grabbed my hair, and yanked me up. I screamed as he turned me around. He wrapped an arm across my face, cutting off my scream and smothering me with the wolf fabric. I tried to bite him but couldn't get through the material. I kicked backwards. He reached down and lifted my leg. I flipped forward—my forehead hit the front of the toilet. He gripped my hair and forced my head down into the toilet. His elbow pressed into my back. He grunted and threw his weight down.

My face plunged into the cold water. A shock of adrenaline surged though me. My body bucked and I was able to throw him partially off—enough to get my head out of the toilet. I screamed. My own voice sounded foreign and maniacal. I twisted around and lashed out with everything I had. I tried to bite, kick, and scratch him all at once. It was impossible to get to him through the costume.

He hit me in the stomach. I lost my breath and buckled forward. He reached down, grabbed my neck with both hands, and vaulted me against the wall, pinning me there. I couldn't breathe. I kicked and missed. He let go of my neck and spun me around so he was draped over my back. I was coughing and gulping air. He grabbed my hair and snapped my head back.

"I will break your neck, I will." His voice was calm—much like the look he gave me in class—as if this didn't take much effort. Toilet water dripped down my front.

He never took off the wolf's head.

I'd always thought of rape as an event; a singular act, a particular, pointed thing—at least as much as I'd thought about it at all. I had never really considered the process, and the time involved.

It takes time. A lot of time. There's time to think about it while it's happening. There's time to die a thousand deaths while it's happening; to fight and lose, over and over. You have time to think about the pain as your mind runs circles like a wounded animal trying to get up and run.

And the physical force.

And what you can't see.

And you have so much time to be amazed by it, while it's happening.

Chapter 6

T H O M A S

I came in from the garage carrying a plastic bag of radishes and bok choy. Luca Brasi ran in, as if on cue, and pawed the plastic, every bag a possible prize. I outmaneuvered him with my human intelligence by setting the bag on the counter. Stephen was at the sink in his pressed floral apron, peeling something exotic. I had no previous knowledge of many of the foods I now ate.

"Are they red? Those look white," he said without looking. He was like the superhero that gets lazy about disguising himself—sloppy with his choice of phone booths. His extrasensory perception was now an accepted part of the household.

"They're mostly red," I said. "A little white. I didn't want to drive all over." He turned and poked the bag with a paring knife.

Stephen had taken to giving me small tasks that increased in complexity and importance a little at a time; a trip to the store for something he claimed to have forgotten (not possible), a post-it note to call Henry's dentist, small chores around the house. He, like Conroy, was trying to save me. Stephen's way was to make me feel needed, or at least useful.

"Where's the Aleppo pepper?"

"They didn't have it."

"Who didn't have it?"

"Whole Foods."

"Thomas, I said to try that little Middle Eastern shop."

"Oh, was that what you meant?"

"When I said to try that little Middle Eastern shop?"

The piano coming from the other room didn't sound like Henry's playing. It was a sonata I knew from my own playing days. "Who's that?" I asked as I tried to peak around the corner.

"A friend. Henry's friend. I've been replaced, it seems. Should have seen it coming. Likely his plan all along."

"Plan?"

"I thought you'd be gone longer. It's her first time here, so—"

"There's a plan?"

"—be civil."

"Her? A girl?"

"You miss everything, Thomas. Yes, a girl." Stephen gave me a look I didn't recognize. We'd grown accustomed to communicating with subtle gestures, like an old married couple where one has assumed dominance and can crush the other with a practiced look. Stephen usually kept his power restrained.

I wandered into the next room. Our house had a wide hallway that went from the dining room to the entryway. It had beautiful dark wood floors and high ceilings. I had taken to collecting art, since I didn't golf, and my favorite pieces hung in this area, mostly large mid-century abstracts, including a prized Rothko. The house felt too big now. Francis had filled it in ways I hadn't realized. Constantly walking into empty rooms sucks the life out of a home, like it's been lobotomized.

It was a girl all right, and very pretty. She wore a summer dress. The baby grand helped fill the wide hallway, and the way the girl was playing—Horowitz-like, with full bravado—filled the house. Henry sat next to her. He studied her hands as if to absorb the sequence by intense focus.

I was, once upon a time, a moderately accomplished pianist. I even thought I had a chance at being great. I'd started lessons before I could read a book, and stayed with it until I was seventeen, when I happened to read, *Of Human Bondage*, about a guy who wants to be a great artist, realizes he's destined to be a good artist but never a great one, and becomes a mediocre doctor instead. I felt an uneasy symbiosis and talked to my piano teacher. After a lot of hesitation, she told me I was good, but would never be great. That was unacceptable. I quit. It didn't matter if it was piano or something else, I had to be great. I had to be exceptional. When I gave it up, it was final, as any equivocating might diminish my pursuits elsewhere. Greatness was pure, requiring a single-minded clarity. I knew this even at that young age. After making my decision, I expected a battle from someone—parent or teacher—but my father was already gone by then, and when I told my mother, she looked at me like she was surprised I still did that. My teacher's only response was to chew his ever-present gum a little slower and pull out his calendar to mark off my last day. It seemed everyone else was aware of my tepid prospects. Luckily, it wasn't too late to try something else, and I, like in the book, settled on medicine, but had no intention of being mediocre.

My unequivocal reprieve from the piano didn't last long. In my first year of college, while drunk at a party, I discovered it could work a kind of sexual alchemy on women. Any prior life decisions were reconsidered in light of this. A week later, I had a small upright in my dorm room. Playing became an efficient way to help satisfy my prurient interests, and one I found didn't tarnish my drive for medical greatness.

Francis could also play some, mostly from years of sitting next to me, working through a bottle of wine and Elton John standards. She had the voice.

I stopped playing when she got sick. I hadn't realized it until months after her death, when I walked by the piano and noticed it as if it had just been delivered. By then, the ground had shifted. It was just another everyday object turned cold.

Henry knew I was standing there but was doing a good job of pretending he didn't. The girl played the piece at a different pace than how I had once played it. She found much more in the space between notes—the grout, my teacher had called it—than I ever did. She made it look easy; the surest sign of mastery, in art or medicine.

I knew the break coming up. "Hi," I said in a breezy tone when it arrived. The girl, hands still poised in an elaborate position, turned a large pair of glasses toward me. I was immediately envious of her self-discipline.

"Hello," she said.

"Dad, this is Justine," Henry said a little too casually, betraying a mental rehearsal.

She hesitated before giving up her hand position. I thought she was going to shake my hand, but instead she rested her hands in her lap. "Nice to meet you, Doctor Ackerman." She adjusted her glasses.

"She's showing me some stuff," Henry said. "On the piano."

"Hey, that's wonderful."

"Henry told me that you play too," the girl said. She appeared to look just past me.

"Oh…" I was caught off-guard, surprised that anyone would be talking about me.

"She taught me a new progression," Henry said, saving me. Or him. "Here Dad, check it out." Nothing happened.

After a moment, I realized he was inviting me to join them. "Oh, yes, I want to see," I said. They scooted over and I sat on the bench.

I'd been invited. Henry had taken the initiative to include me in something. This seemed huge. My bubble deflated some when I realized it was likely for the benefit of the girl. He wants her to think we're normal. My dad's a regular guy. He's cool. He'll even sit at the piano with us. We're not weird. Save all the messy stuff for later, when she already likes him and everything is diluted through that.

Henry took a focused breath and played a brief progression I didn't recognize. He didn't make it far before coming to a plodding halt. "Wait," he whispered to her, "how does it go?"

She took over and tore through the sequence like the piano was on fire.

"Shit, you don't have to show off," Henry said when she finished, flicking his fingers out.

"I wasn't, but I can, if you want me to." Teasing banter. I'd missed a lot.

"We should get going," Henry said. He got up. She placed a hand on his arm and stood. He seemed to wait for her before stepping away.

She's blind, I realized.

They headed for the front door. The girl turned back to me. "It was nice to meet you, Doctor Ackerman." I wondered why she bothered turning toward someone she couldn't see.

"Hey, you guys are headin' out?" I said.

Henry hesitated. "Uh, yeah. We're going to the library."

"To study?"

He grimaced and looked down, but I caught it. Maybe dad wasn't so normal after all. "Yes, Dad, to study. For school. Which we're both in."

"Of course, of course. Stephen driving you?" Henry was late to driving. He'd taken little interest in getting his license, which was a mystery to me. He had his learner's permit, but it required that an adult drive with him.

"Yeah, he was going to."

"I'll take you guys. That okay? You can drive." I was trying too hard, but I didn't care. I was desperate for redemption.

"Uh... sure, Dad."

When I handed him the BMW keys, he demurred. "That's cool, we'll sit in back," he said.

That's cool. It was like I was one of them now. "Yeah, sure."

Stephen always encouraged Henry to drive the Jeep when they went out together. It'd sprouted a few new scratches and a small dent. That was why Henry didn't want to drive, I realized. He didn't want to do anything in front of the girl that he wasn't good at. Humbled by the piano. He must really like her. I felt more pressure to come through.

I drove carefully, but also tried to be a little cavalier by rolling a stop sign. Not too uptight. Everything was under scrutiny. I probably wanted the girl to like me more than Henry did.

I caught a few looks at her in the rearview mirror. She had one of those faces that looked awkward when still, like the parts didn't all match, but when she moved, everything came together nicely. She had pale skin and the furrowed brow I often saw in medical school. She dropped from my mirror, like she'd forgotten her posture and had fallen into a slouch. Another sign she was comfortable around him. Damn, what I've missed.

They talked. I wasn't meant to hear. I thought maybe I should put on some music to acknowledge their privacy. I started to, but that would mean picking something. Picking music kids listen to would make me look desperate. Classical might be appropriate. Henry liked it, but I wasn't sure I was supposed to know that. I couldn't keep forgetting things.

I wanted to hear what they were saying. I caught fragments. It had an easy, familiar tone to it that made me hurt, like my son had passed me by. He was comfortable around a girl, without any help from me, but he was just a small, crushable child. Where had I been? Busy being selfish, the greatest of all time sucks.

If it weren't for them, I'd have pulled over and cried. Instead, I strained to hear while trying to appear cool. I tapped the steering wheel with my thumb. I was hoping to catch something tantalizing, maybe even a little alarming— sex, or drugs perhaps, something colorful and salacious. Scraps brought back from the living.

Their conversation got serious. Maybe something significant had already happened between them. I caught a few words and started stringing them together. Her high voice was easer to hear than his low mumble.

Classes. Teachers. They were talking about school, and the best study strategies. No time for trivial matters. It was so much easier to be an overachiever in my day.

~ ~ ~

When I got home, the house had a new level of silence—something I'd recently learned was possible— contrasted by the recent presence of a female voice.

I sat at the piano and tried the piece the girl had played. It rolled right out, but in aural contrast to her more accomplished rendering. I stopped at the same break and tried another. Not one of the songs I played with Francis at my side, as Justine had sat next to Henry, but one from my early childhood, when my mother would stand over me. Then another, from the middle period of my brief career, when I burned with ambition but had to play softly so dad wouldn't come hulking in from the next room, newspaper rolled up in hand like he was looking to swat the dog.

I was still at the piano hours later when Henry came home. He started up the stairs, but stopped and came back down and sat next to me. He smelled like ocean air mixed with something sweet. Feeling his shoulder against mine reminded me of the easy conversations we used to have, all the laughing and group hugs. Come gather around the patriarch of love and affection. Simple as rain.

Stephen appeared and asked if I'd eaten. He'd made a special pot roast and asked if I'd tried it. I lied and told him how good it was. The truth was my medication was wreaking havoc on my appetite and I'd had a beer and a cookie for dinner. I'd given some pot roast to Luca Brasi for cover. Stephen would probably know.

He knew everything.

~~~

"Promise you'll do one thing for me," Conroy said. He was sitting at the dining room table, plucking a piece of cheese off a wood board with a toothpick.

"Sure."

"No, not sure, you have to promise." He chewed. "Damn, that's good. I think I should move in. I'm only asking you to do this one little thing, but you're not going to want to do it, so before I ask, I need you to promise me you'll do it."

"You're not supposed to bully the depressed."

Doctor Gordy had asked if I wanted to get better. The hard truth, which I used to be all about, was no. I realized I should try to get better, but I didn't want to. I wanted to lie in bed and just go to wherever she was, even into nothing. And if it was just me, maybe that's what I would have done, but it wasn't just me, so there was no choice to be made. But still, getting better meant all sorts of things I didn't want anything to do with.

"It's a small thing," Conroy said. "A super small thing. You'll probably laugh when I tell you the little thing I want you to do." He had his fingers splayed at the base of his wine glass and was sliding it in a circle, something a sommelier—or Stephen—would do. The swirling golden liquid was the color of Italian sunlight.

"Fine, I promise." Didn't matter, the depressed are beholden to nothing.

"Good. I want you to start getting up at the same time every morning. That's it."

"What?" I was on a delay.

"You promised." He pointed at me.

"Why?"

"Just do it. I don't care what time you get up, but I want you to promise me you'll start getting up at the same time every morning."

"I already promised." I'd developed the habit of sleeping in pockets. A few hours here and there, then more time staring. I tried not to sleep. I hated that moment of waking up and realizing everything.

I did as he asked. This small change turned out to have exponential power. Conroy, the quiet genius.

I chose seven o'clock. Stephen would have my coffee and breakfast ready. For the first week, I went back to bed later in the morning, exhausted by ten from doing nothing.

The medication gave me a chemical reprieve. It created a strange gap in my mind, a blank spot that I'd normally cram with all kinds of information and analysis. It was like a place to hide, an alley between the buildings. My shadow self even went quiet.

Baby steps followed.

Restless one day, I went down to the basement and got on the treadmill and walked. I stopped after ten minutes. I stood on the sides with itchy legs, looking down at the belt go by. I felt a terrible guilt. I couldn't place it. Then it landed; it was because a part of me felt better, even just slightly. I went back to bed for the rest of the afternoon.

The next day I walked on the treadmill until my legs burned. I wept, and kept weeping as I walked at a brisk pace, sweat mixing with the tears dripping off my chin. A doctor terrified at the idea of his own healing.

~~~

There were other small victories. I set simple routines for myself; take Luca Brasi out for a walk at ten, read one medical article before lunch, run on the treadmill while watching the five o'clock news. I began practicing a little piano when no one was home.

I took comfort in these routines and fretted when I couldn't do whatever inane thing I had planned next. If it rained and I couldn't take Luca Brasi out, I'd wait anxiously until my next scheduled activity. I didn't get any enjoyment out of these things. I'd forget the article as soon as I finished reading it. I had no interest in the news, or anything else. It was the routine itself, the structure of hitting each point that allowed me to play at normality. That's where I found relief.

Hopeful green sprouts arrived unexpectedly. The adorable Justine had been by the house a few more times. Henry and her played piano and studied together. Nothing could be more normal than two teenagers stumbling over each other, and the fact that Henry felt comfortable bringing her to the house made me feel good. It meant I was providing him with a home. I thought I'd messed up again when I forgot they were in the library one day and went in there. I guess my own youth led me to assume they'd be fornicating on the table, but they were just studying. I tried to slip back out, but Justine said she was interested in medicine and wanted to know what it was like to be a pediatric surgeon. She said if she wasn't blind, that's what she would want to do. We ended up having a nice talk, and Henry didn't give me any warning looks.

As a reward for my diligence, I began to find an interest in things. I was watching the news when there was an ad for a show on the History Channel about the Napoleonic wars. It reminded me of a book I'd read in college, *Master and Commander*. It was part of a series. I had intended to read the other books at some point but had never gotten around to it.

I went to the bookstore. It had become a drugstore. I found another bookstore and bought the whole series, twenty-one books in all.

I read them all over the next month, sitting in my library, often forgetting to do my next assigned task. I went back to the bookstore and bought a bunch of mystery books and read all of them. I bought more. I preferred series books, the longer the better. Regency romances, thrillers, historical novels. I'd get to the end of a series and nearly panic if I didn't have something else lined up.

Stephen, tired of hauling boxes of books to the thrift store, suggested I get a library card. I wasn't sure why this hadn't occurred to me. I went to a local branch and told the woman at the information desk what kind of books I liked. She led me to Anne Perry and a number of other series authors. I'd found the mother lode.

Reading hardcover library books with the crackly plastic covers felt nostalgic, which was soothing in itself. It gave me the sense of being able to go back to a different time, when I could have done things differently. Craving more of this nostalgia, I spent more time at the library. I'd settle into one of the reading chairs and sometimes finish a book without even checking it out. I got to know the rhythms of the place. Tuesday at eleven was children's story hour, which was always packed. It was popular not because the kids enjoyed it, but because parents could drop their kids off for an hour, go do whatever, and feel good about it. Libraries seemed to carry some kind of moral weight.

One Tuesday, near Christmas, the reader didn't show up. The kids sat on the floor on pillows and blankets in front of a big empty chair with garland strung around it. The librarian, an anxious type to begin with, got jumpier as the kids got more restless.

The nanny of one of the kids attempted to fill in. She did her best, even wearing reindeer antlers, but her Hispanic accent was so thick that most of the kids couldn't understand her. One child started crying, which sounded twice as loud in a library. A couple of other kids rolled across the floor in an impromptu wrestling match. I left my book open on the chair and approached the librarian, who looked ready to bolt.

"I can read," I said. She looked at me like I might be dangerous. "I mean, to the kids. I could read to the kids, if you need someone. I noticed your reader hasn't shown up."

"Oh, *yes*, that would be great! Would you? That would be such a help." She came around and grabbed my hand. She pulled me toward the kids before I could change my mind. "I think she got her days mixed up," she said over her shoulder. "I'd do it myself, but I'm all alone at the front and our other volunteer is out today with whatever that thing is that's going around wreaking havoc. What's your name, dear?"

"Thomas. Tom."

"This is very considerate of you. I see you in here quite often. You're tall. You should meet my niece. She's coming to visit me later today and has such a wonderful disposition but has no patience for any man under six feet tall, though she herself is only five-five. I told her flat out, I think you've got a thing against short people. I don't understand it, frankly. And her tattoos, don't get me started. Boys and girls, special treat!" She clapped her hands. "We have Tim here to read to you today."

The kids eyed me. Children can be intimidating in packs, with their nappy hair and bruising honesty, but I was in my element, and these kids were healthy. No machines or nurses in sight. Piece of cake.

The librarian, speaking in her library voice, led me to the chair. "I believe she was planning to read, *Frog and Toad Are Friends.* It has a wonderful message, and that's the kind of thing we try to stick to. No Christmas stories, because of the Jews. We had complaints last year, and they're the biggest donors to the library. We're hardly allowed to decorate now. Don't get me started. Heavens, you're not Jewish, are you?"

"No."

"I have nothing against—well, never mind that. I have to get back to the front. You're a doll, thank you for doing this. Oh, this is the one." She handed me a book from the stack. I settled into the chair as she turned back to the kids. "You all be good for our guest now." She headed back to the front desk. I made a quick inventory of the other books in the stack.

The librarian came back. She leaned in close, smelling like dioxin and moisturizer. "Kelly is her name, and she only has tattoos in discreet places, not on her neck or anything, thank goodness. She's a very clean girl—woman, of course." While she was talking, I noticed some tables with art supplies; construction paper and crayons. Perfect. "Well, alright then." She hurried off.

The kids all looked at me. I knew this part. You have their attention for about three seconds; screw up, and you never get it back, so the first thing you have to do is throw them a curve.

I checked to make sure the librarian was far enough away. "This book is *dumb*!" I said, brandishing it from my throne. I threw it high in the air. It landed with a *thwack* on the tabletop.

"But this book is *aweeeesome*! It's got a dragon with huge teeth!" I swept my wide-eyed gaze over them as I held up *Harold and the Purple Crayon*.

The second thing you have to do with a group of kids is get them physically involved, so they take ownership. "Here's what we're going to do," I said to the group of O-mouths. "Everybody up—stand up—let's pull these tables together." The kids sprang into action. "That's it, help me slide them together. Good job. Now, grab a crayon and a piece of paper."

I got them all seated with paper and crayons. "After I read, you're going to create your own crayon adventure." Some confused looks and a couple hands shot up. "Nope, no questions. It'll all make sense."

"I know this book," an older girl said. "It's totally lame." She was probably five and already heavy, with wheezing breath and fat pushing out of the bottom of her t-shirt. I'd seen her mother drop her off earlier, a fully realized version of this poor girl's future. Her backpack had a name patch on it. "That's okay, Amy," I said. "You have special permission to draw whatever you want, since you already know the story. And you get to use as many colors as you want." She stared at me, transfixed.

I read the story and had the kids draw their own version. There was *Jackson and the Red Crayon, Yokum and the Yellow Crayon, Annabel and the Black Crayon*. Afterward, they took turns telling the group about the adventure they created and showed off their drawings; kids riding dragons, creating fairy factories, and building marshmallow cities. Even Amy got on board by drawing an adventure where she rode down a river on a magic carpet with a singing pumpkin made of glitter. Happy, healthy kids, laughing and shouting. No sickness or pain. I was having so much fun I didn't realize the hour was up until I saw a ring of parents standing on the periphery, watching with frozen smiles.

I drove home, pleased with myself for the first time in a year. It was the unmistakable feeling of improvement, like it or not.

~ ~ ~

My momentum didn't last. One step forward, two steps back. Henry was changing. But while my changes were incremental, his were leaps.

Henry's friend, Justine, was no longer coming around. Stephen informed me they'd had a falling out. All this before I'd had a chance to understand what their relationship actually was. Apparently, kids today eschew common labels of the past, both for individual identity and unions. I couldn't tell if Henry was sad about it or not. I was so used to him being touched by sadness that I could never be sure of its origin.

After finally getting his driver's license, Henry told me he wanted a motorcycle instead of a car. I made it my mission to prevent this, as any good parent would. We argued, which was unusual for us. I thought of it as my first parental challenge since I'd found my footing. I was out of practice. Or, more likely, was never in practice.

Christmas was coming, encroaching on the house like the fifth act of a tragedy. I began to sympathize with people who found the holidays difficult. They were made and packaged for complete families, not the fragmented. Stephen asked about decorating. Maybe feeling cocky about my improvement, I said I'd take care of it. I couldn't decorate a cupcake, but I felt a compulsion to lead—something. Francis used to do it all. She and Henry would pick out the tree together. She was also the one to go on the roof, wearing her old ballet shoes, which she said were great for traction, and hang an elaborate light display.

I couldn't find the decorations. I asked Henry and he showed me where they were in the garage. I asked if he wanted to help me pick out a tree. He declined, so I went by myself to a tree lot, where a cute teenage girl in a tank top hauled my pick to a workbench and took the bottom off with a chainsaw, like something out of a horror movie. I stood there like a dolt while she and another girl threw the tree on top of the Jeep and tied it down, all while talking about a guy they both knew who had recently drunk a bottle of perfume at a party, thinking it was alcohol. They still seemed to think he was cute, but agreed you couldn't fix stupid.

Turns out I can decorate a tree. It took me an entire day, and I had to refer to some online videos, of which there were many, but it came out pretty good. I even strung some garland and lights up the stairwell banister.

As Christmas got closer, Henry and I argued more about the motorcycle. In the end, I lost, but not before setting up an elaborate safety structure. I gave in because I couldn't stomach the idea of Christmas morning with just Henry and I. A distraction was needed. Something big and expensive with a bow on it. Something that could kill the user, even when used properly.

Henry surprised me with a gift; a leather bound copy of *The Sun Also Rises*. He also made me a card that he'd painted with watercolors. I cried in the bathroom.

The New Year brings either bold ambition or quiet guilt, or their succession, for both the healthy and the sick. I had no more stomach for guilt, so I decided I'd stop waiting to do things until I felt ready—I'd do them even if I didn't. I was going to take myself out of the equation. If I should do something, I'd do it. No more dithering. If I couldn't do whatever it was, well, I'd pretend. I'd fake it. It was a trick that worked, I knew from experience.

I'd brought that much back from the darkness.

Chapter 7

M A R G A R E T

A glaze covered my life. I no longer felt present. I was someone going through the motions of a girl named Margaret, and barely that. Part of me refused to believe it had happened. I wanted to take away the reality of it, not as a way to cope, but as a decision I could make. Advanced mathematics teaches us there is malleability to everything, even things that people think are fixed. There are few absolutes. Maybe I could twist the reality of my life like you could time and space.

I was standing over the toilet one day, flushing it over and over and staring at the water as it swirled down. While my math brain worked on a diffusion equation, I thought about the seven stages of loss.

Denial. It made sense, in a way. I did lose something. But it seemed so common. Underneath it all, I wanted to be an exception. Turns out, I'm common as dirt. I slid to the floor and cried, one of the things I hadn't yet done. Basil scratched at the door until I let him in. He crawled on my lap and licked my cheeks.

There was a reordering of my life; a change in perspective. Nothing was what it once was. Not school or friends or the circumstances that made up my day-to-day existence. I sat in a chair in my room most of the time. Not tired. Not anything. I just sat there, looking at nothing. I didn't go to school. I didn't think about what happened. I wasn't there. I wasn't anywhere. My dad checked on me a couple times. I had some schoolwork laid out that I could turn to when he came in.

"No school?" he said on Wednesday. It took him that long to realize I'd been home all week. He was hardly around any more.

"Fall break." Like there was such a thing.

"Oh, sure. You're not sick?"

"No."

"How'd you get that bruise on your forehead?"

"I told you about that, remember?" I'd learned this trick a long time ago. If I said I'd already told him something, and followed it with *remember?* he'd say yes, because he was an alcoholic, and alcoholics are afraid of being found out, because that would mean they'd have to stop drinking, so they learn to play along. Common as dirt, just like me. My new perspective came with a certain behind-the-scenes clarity.

"Oh, yeah, I remember," he said. "I bought some mac and cheese. And those frozen enchiladas, the good ones."

Two days later, on Friday, he came in again. I was exactly where I was before, probably wearing the same clothes.

"You alright?"

"Yeah," I said, watching the scene from somewhere else; the vagaries of a teenage girl and her awkward father.

"You got some mail. Thick envelope. Looks official. I left it on the kitchen table."

"Thanks."

"Listen, I wanted to talk to you."

"Okay." I tried to focus on him. I knew I should tell him, or tell somebody, but I couldn't remember why. The only person who knew was Song. She stayed with me that night and slept in my bed with me. She cried the whole night. The next day, we talked about it some. She said she remembered someone dressed as the guy from *Pulp Fiction* following her after she left the hall of mirrors. She didn't know it was Dwayne. With the music and commotion, nobody noticed when he pulled her into a utility closet. He took her costume, then jammed a chair under the door handle so she couldn't get out. He came back later, all sweaty, and gave her the wolf costume back. She had to put it back on and walk to the bathrooms, where she found me on the floor. She wrapped me in Mr. J's raincoat, which was still in the storage locker.

She understood, because of her cousin.

I couldn't go to the police. Afterward, when I was draped over the toilet, Dwayne said that Dorie would kill me and Song both if I told anyone. He wanted to know where he could find Alana and the other girl, but I had started vomiting uncontrollably, which freaked him out, so he left.

I didn't believe him about Dorie, but I'd been wrong about a lot of things. I couldn't tell Vicky, because she would tell Alana, and Alana would try to do something—something that would get her kicked out of Madison. She couldn't help me anyway. It seemed like the more people tried to help, the worse things got.

"What'd you want to talk about?" I asked my dad.

"You okay talkin' now? We can do it another time." He looked like he'd rather leave.

"Now's fine. Now's good."

He came around and sat on the edge of the bed to face me. He looked nervous. My change in perspective allowed me to be objective in a way I never could before. I realized what a weak man my dad was. He was small in the most important ways. He let out a sigh, put his elbows on his knees, and spoke to the floor.

"You know I spend a lot of time at Teri's place."

Wow, really? "Um."

"Well, I've decided—we've decided that I should move in there."

"You kind of already have."

"Yes, pretty close, but make it official."

"You're still married." I wanted to be cruel and didn't have many tools at my disposal.

"I'm aware of that, you don't need to tell me that." He ran his hand through his hair and wiped his mouth. He needed a drink, I could tell. He looked like a kid that had lost his mom at the mall. "I'm selling the house. I mean, it's for sale. I'm moving a lot of stuff out next week. The real estate agent wants to start showing it next weekend." I was used to being a couple of steps ahead of my dad, but my mind was so murky it had to swim to the surface, listen to the echo of what he'd just said, and try to make sense of it.

"You want me to live with you and Teri, at her place?"

"No. You're almost eighteen. It's a condition she—I'm going to give you the truck. It's yours now."

The full weight of what he was saying settled on me. "Dad, are you kidding? You want me to—what? I don't understand."

"You can stay with us for a few weeks, if you need to, but it's time to grow up now. I was out of the house when I was fifteen."

"Out of the trailer, you mean."

He glowered at me before going back to his script. "Your mother is not coming home, and I need to get on with things. It's all for the good. I think this—I think this will be good for you, in the long run." Teri's words; he'd never have said that. He got up and went to the door. "Oh, and some guy named Simon called a couple times." He put the truck keys on my dresser.

I left that night.

~ ~ ~

I told Vicky I had a fight with my dad and he kicked me out, and that he was moving in with Teri. I didn't lie, I just didn't tell her everything.

"What are you going to do?" she asked.

"I don't know."

"Stay here."

"Can I? Just for a couple nights?"

"Shit yeah, it'll be fun. Fuck him. That Teri has a string around his balls. Sorry."

"It's true."

"We'll make dresses and I'll boss you around. I need someone to cut fabric because I'm like one arm clapping here." She waved her bandaged hand. "So, are you going to tell me?"

"Tell you what?"

"Seriously?"

"What?"

"That big-ass bruise on your forehead. And there's a mark on your neck. Bang up job with the makeup, by the way."

"I told you, I had a fight with my dad."

"Uh huh. Look, your dad's no father of the year, but he doesn't knock you around, at least not that I know of. Does he?"

"No. No, he doesn't." I didn't say anything else. I just waited.

"Dwayne and the ogre were at the dance, weren't they? Did they come after you again? What happened?"

"No, it wasn't that."

"Come on, Mags, seriously, what the fuck?"

Tears were pushing behind my eyes. I was trying to hold them off, afraid if I started to cry, I'd lose it completely. I didn't trust myself any more. I used to be able to act a certain way, no matter what was happening on the inside. It was a kind of self-discipline I had. But I'd lost it. I didn't have the same control over myself that I once had.

Forever passed and started again while Vicky studied me. I kept looked at the ground. "You're really not going to tell me what happened? Really? You're freezing me out? Mags, you know I'm your friend, right?"

"Yes."

"And you know I'd slay a dragon for you."

I broke. Hot tears tracked down my face. "Yes."

"Enough said, you're staying here, but at some point, you're going to tell me what happened."

I watched my tears fall and disappear into the carpet.

~ ~ ~

I decided to kill him.

Maybe it was decided for me. I don't think I had much to do with it. I couldn't go back to school with him there. I just couldn't, and I didn't have a future if I didn't finish high school and go to college. I was stuck.

But it wasn't that. Those were just problems. It didn't even make sense. You don't kill someone because you have a problem—that's every history book—but that was the start of it.

There was something else. All that time I spent sitting in my room after it happened, all that time looking at nothing, thinking of nothing, living in a kind of void—something was happening. Something was developing inside me. An understanding. It took a while to work itself out, but it finally formed. It defined itself, independent of me.

Now it was clear to me. Like what addicts mean when they talk about a moment of clarity.

~ ~ ~

On Sunday, I went back to the house. I parked the truck up the block a ways. My dad was going in and out of the garage and loading boxes into Teri's SUV. I made sure he couldn't see me. I waited until he pulled away before going in.

He hadn't wasted any time. There were half-packed boxes everywhere.

I went to the gun cabinet. It was the oldest thing in the house, a real antique from before the turn of the century. It even smelled old when you opened it. The case had several heavy drawers with thick, ornate carvings. I opened the top drawer and found what I was looking for: the hunting knife my dad had used to split the buck.

I remembered watching him make the cut; a single slice from bottom to sternum, as if he was drawing a straight line with a pen. The body separated like a ripe fruit. He used a thinner knife for the rest of the field dressing, but it was that first-cut knife I was after.

I lifted it from the drawer. I unsnapped its case and pulled it from the fur-lined leather and steel sleeve. It was heavy in my hand and meticulously clean. Hard light reflected off it like it was lit from the inside. I re-sleeved it and tucked it in my backpack.

I went in the garage to look for some duct tape.

Monday morning, I got ready for school at Vicky's. I made sure she was still asleep, then used the bathroom to tape the knife to my stomach. I practiced putting my hand under my shirt, unsnapping the sleeve, and sliding the knife out without cutting my stomach open. I needed a baggy shirt to conceal it. The only loose shirt I had was the one I'd slept in. I put it on and put my jacket over it.

"Wow, is this a new look?" Vicky said from the bed when I came back in.

"You're up."

"Why'd you bring your backpack in the bathroom?"

"I've got half my life in there. Didn't want to use all your stuff."

She was sitting up and flexing her hand in front of her face. "I might take this fucker out for a test drive today." Her hand still had a heavy bandage on it.

"I thought you weren't supposed to use it for another week." I tried to subtly adjust my shirt.

"I just need it to push fabric through the machine. It's not like I'm gonna jerk off with it."

"You want me to help you tilt the bed?"

"Nah, I can manage." She looked at me. "You can borrow something of mine, if you want. Nothing that would fit you, but if you're already going for the baggy look, I have stuff that would look better than this little ensemble you've got going. Didn't you sleep in that shirt?"

We'd shared the bed. I hadn't slept well. I spent the night listening to her breathing, afraid if I fell asleep I'd roll over on her hand. "It's okay, I'm good."

"At least brush your hair, or is that part of this new grunge look you kids are doing? Because you've crossed over into something else."

"I gotta go."

"Okay, go get you some edgy-cation."

I stopped in the doorway. I realized I wouldn't see her again. They would take me away afterward. I thought maybe I should walk to school, so the truck wouldn't end up in the school parking lot. Maybe Vicky could use it. Then I thought of trying to walk all the way to school in the cold with a knife taped to my stomach. My dad would probably claim it later.

"Hey," Vicky said.

"What?"

"Your backpack. Don't you need it?"

"Oh, yeah. Duh." I grabbed it, even though it was empty except for a roll of duct tape. "Okay, see ya," I said.

"Yup."

It was awkward driving with the knife. The butt of the handle kept pressing into my hipbone. But I felt peaceful for the first time in a while, like I no longer had to figure out what to do. I already knew. I no longer had to be brave.

I walked to my first class, but when I got to the door, I kept going. I walked down the main hall while everyone else went the other way. I got to the end and went out the back doors, half expecting a teacher to stop me. I seemed to be guided by something. Part of me was hovering nearby, fascinated and eager to witness tragedy.

I walked toward the trailer. It had been raining off and on and looked like it might start again. I went to the area between the trailer and the fence.

I leaned on the fence and looked at the plastic siding on the trailer, where Dorie had pinned me. It reminded me of freshman year science class, when our teacher stuck insects to a corkboard for observation; when I looked with the magnifying glass, I could see one still moving, like he was the only one that didn't know to pretend.

Dwayne must have been watching Dorie and taken notes, because he'd done the same thing to me in the bathroom. I could feel both of their hands on my neck, and for a moment what they did became the same event, with just a brief pause for a change of location and fresh actors.

I ran my hand down the plastic siding, all the way to the bottom. I could see a pale pink splatter of my blood. I got down and looked closer. The outer rims on the blotches were dark red, where it must have dried first, but the rest was pale, washed away by the rain. Some of the rings were breached, spilling their centers. First to dry, last to die. Another one of those random, useless thoughts that seemed to crowd my head now, like they belonged to someone I hadn't been introduced to.

A steady rain began. I sat on the ground and leaned against the trailer. Raindrops plopped on the cement. The old tractor in the middle of the field listed to one side, as if the ground had shifted beneath it, ready to swallow it, knowing nobody would notice.

~ ~ ~

Second period. I sat at my desk as everyone came in, chatting and joking as they pulled out their books and binders. They seemed like characters in a story. I stared at the top of my desk.

Song sat down. I could see from the corner of my eye that she was looking at me and trying to get my attention. I hadn't called her since my dad had kicked me out. I guess I'd been avoiding her. She was still the only person who knew what happened. I turned to her and gave her a smile. Her expression made me turn back. What was it? My face was a wreck. I'd tried covering it with Vicky's makeup, but I think the rain had made it run. The bruise on my forehead was doing the yellow blotchy thing. As others sat around me, they got quiet and glanced at me, then each other.

No Dwayne yet. I couldn't have my hand under my shirt, so I rested it across my lower stomach. I could feel the snap on the sleeve, pressed against my inner arm. I had the hem of my shirt pulled up so all I'd have to do is slide my hand under, unsnap, and pull.

But still, no Dwayne.

I had blanked out some of what happened in the bathroom, but parts would come back to me in flashes when I wasn't expecting it, like scenes from a movie, full of horrible noises. When that happened, I'd think, oh no, that was no movie, that was me. A star at last.

I was able to piece together most of what happened from what I remembered and from the flashes, but not all of it. There was still a blank spot. Sometimes, when the flashes came, I'd throw up. I was hoping that wouldn't happen now. It'd be like with the deer—puking before the kill.

There was one part I remembered clearly, exactly the way it happened. I kept coming back to it. I could smell the bathroom and hear his raspy breathing coming from inside the wolf's head. It was when he grabbed my hair and pulled my head back. I didn't know I could bend back that far. All the horror seemed to stick there. When I thought about it, I could feel the twist in my spine.

Now I knew why. It was because I was going to do that to him.

I listened to my directions.

When he sits, give him some time to settle in. Then do it. Pull his head all the way back. His hair is short but there's enough to grab. Use the deep part of the knife, nearest the handle, and go just below the Adam's apple. It's best to do it all in one motion. Keep pulling the head back as you cut. Do it fast or you risk a reaction, which could interfere. All one motion.

My brain wanted to break it down mathematically, but I resisted.

The knife was heavy, I reminded myself, and very sharp. So sharp, there was the risk of cutting through to his spinal cord. He had a skinny neck. I'd have to be careful about that. Maintain steady control. I noticed the girl sitting in front of his desk—shit, I couldn't remember her name— was wearing a cream-colored blouse.

Still, no Dwayne. I stared at his empty chair.

I had one of those flashes: him getting frustrated and beating the back of my head. I could hear the strange sounds I made that I'd never heard before.

Thick, bitter saliva flooded my mouth. I swallowed it back. Mr. J was talking about essays. People were pulling pages out. Stapled sheets of paper. I willed my stomach down.

I realized I was still staring at Dwayne's empty chair. I went back to staring at my desktop and pressing the inside of my arm against the knife. The sounds in the room stretched and buckled, like the effects of a drug coming on.

I couldn't tell what Mr. J was saying. A student, Crystal, was answering a question, but all I could hear were the vowels.

There was a ringing in my ears. It sounded like it was coming from my neck. All the color in the room drained away and flattened into two dimensions.

No Dwayne.

Mr. J walked up and down the aisles. Students handed him their papers as he went by. He was saying something, but I couldn't tell what.

Another noise came from inside my head. It joined the ringing. It was my teeth. I was grinding them. Mr. J walked past my desk. He paused as if to acknowledge that I must be acknowledged, but nothing more.

Class stretched on. Little by little, I started to hear what Mr. J was saying. The Romans. Democracy. Advanced plumbing systems. I even laughed a little at something. A couple people looked my way. The bell rang. No Dwayne. I started to leave with everyone else.

"Margaret," Mr. J said as I went past his desk. I looked at him. "Your pack." I looked back and saw my backpack. I went grab it. "Are you alright?" he asked. "Are you sick? You've been holding your stomach."

"No. No, I'm not sick." My mouth felt heavy, like talking was unnatural.

"Margaret, if you need anything, you can come to me. Really, you can. You're the brightest of the bright, and I don't want you—"

"I'm sorry," I said. "We stole your raincoat. It was supposed to be funny."

~ ~ ~

After school, Vicky needed me to go to the fabric store. I asked if I could go to my house afterward to get some of my things while my dad wasn't there. I was pretty sure he would already be at Teri's. It was raining hard, so the van would be better than the truck.

I let myself in. Except for some furniture, the place was nearly empty. Basil came skidding around the corner and tackled me. I knew he was confused about what was going on. "I know, me too," I said as I scratched his neck. I went in the kitchen to see if there was something for him to eat.

I fed him salami and Cheerios as he followed me upstairs. I found a couple of empty boxes and packed up my schoolwork, some clothes, and some books. Basil finished the last piece of salami and immediately looked at me for more.

I opened my closet. The red dress sat crumpled on the floor. I remembered Song helping me take it off. I picked it up.

It smelled like him. My stomach lurched, but I kept it down. The side seam was split. Red threads stuck out. One of the sleeves was twisted out of shape. I thought of throwing it out or burning it in the backyard, but I couldn't. Vicky would ask me about it. She knew how hard I'd worked on it, and how proud of it I was. If it went missing, she'd want to know why. I threw it on the bed.

132

I went back to the closet and dug around for anything I wanted to keep. I found a scrapbook my mom helped me make when I was a kid. I sat on the floor and opened it.

The crackly cellophane pages had yellowed at the edges. There were lots of pictures of ballerinas I'd cut out, part of a phase that lasted about a year. I became so obsessed with becoming a ballerina that I'd mapped out my entire life, all the way until I was twenty-five. That seemed awfully old for a ballerina, so I stopped there.

There was a picture of Margot Fonteyn and Nureyev, in a triangular tableau. It captured a moment of perfect grace and beauty. I pealed the plastic back and tugged the picture until it lifted off the page, leaving a glue stain behind.

When I was young, I'd studied this black-and-white image for hours. I read all the world's splendor into those lines. I even tried to get my friends to start calling me Margot instead of Margaret. I wanted beauty like that so bad it consumed me. I'd sit in my closet with a flashlight, hiding this fragile treasure from the ugly world. I was its protector, until I could get there myself, and someone would take a picture of me in a moment of perfect beauty.

I closed the scrapbook, but kept the picture. I went back to the bed and finished boxing my stuff up, except the dress, which still lay on the bed.

I climbed on the bed and leaned against the wall. I was looking at the photograph when Basil popped his head up and eyed me. I pulled the dress over me like a blanket. Basil jumped on the bed and braced himself, legs splayed, like the bed was going to fly away.

"Oh, Basil," I said. He did an awkward lurch toward me. A box fell off the bed. He peered over at it, then back at me. The look he gave me told me I was about to cry.

The grief came. I'd felt panic, fear, numbness, and feelings I didn't know the words for. Now I was repeating them, starting at the beginning and going through them all again, like a merry-go-round that wouldn't let me off.

I was so tired. Not sleepy-tired, but tired like the requirements to keep going were just too much. I wanted a hole in the ground. A hole I could fall into and just keep falling. A forever falling.

I leaned over and hoisted my backpack off the floor. Basil eyed me. I took the knife out. My plan had been to return it to the gun cabinet before it was moved. I cradled it in my lap and picked remnants of tape off the sleeve. Basil watched, inquisitive, like it might turn into something to eat.

I slid the knife out of its sleeve. It was shiny and clean. Like drawing a line. I could see the buck separating. I still felt his smell. I never knew you could feel a smell, but I did, like a shadow-presence that would follow me forever. I began convulsing with sobs. I took some deep breaths and tried to calm myself but my heart was racing, like it knew something horrible was about to happen.

Breathe through it. Calm. Breathe. Calm.

Basil was alert, like when he hears a sound in the yard.

"Go on, Basil. Get." I tried to push him off the bed. "Get off," I yelled. I tried to sound mean but he didn't budge. I leaned over and shoved him. "Go!" He let out a surprised yelp and jumped to the floor. He moped to the door with his tail low, stopped, and looked at me over his shoulder. "Get!" I shouted. He flinched. I took another deep breath. He sat in the doorway, facing me. Defiant.

I tilted my head and held the knife to my throat. I adjusted my grip and positioned it as best I could.

One fast motion, with head pulled back. All the way back. All one motion.

I'd been practicing for the wrong killing. I gripped my hair with my other hand and pulled my head back. I felt the torque in my spine as I looked up at the stains on the ceiling. My pulse throbbed through the knife handle as I pressed the blade to my neck.

Do it fast. Fall in a hole. A forever fall.

I squeezed my eyes shut.

Basil growled. He never growled. He hardly ever even barked. I opened my eyes. He was baring his teeth. His growl grew louder. His eyes were slits. I started convulsing again.

I breathed through it. "Stop it, Basil. Please, I'm sorry."

I closed my eyes again. My palms were sweaty. I re-gripped the knife and placed it at my neck again. My body gave over and relaxed, resigned to its fate. I pulled the red dress all the way over me so Basil wouldn't see.

I grabbed a hand full of hair and pulled.

One breath, then in one quick move. All one motion.

I took a deep breath, and let it out—*three... two... one.*

Basil jumped on the bed and snapped the air with shrill barks. I pushed the dress away. He moved to my face and snarled through his teeth. "Basil, stop it!" He jerked his head back and forth, showering me with spittle.

I took the knife from my throat and let it fall to the floor. My body contracted into sobs again, betrayed for a final time. Basil went quiet and put a paw on my chest.

I fell asleep at some point. Basil was snuggled against me with his chin on my belly. I had one of my silent wakings. When I opened my eyes, Basil was watching me like a sentry. He closed his eyes as if he'd been sleeping too and exhaled dramatically.

The photograph lay next to me. I took a final look at it before tearing it into small pieces. I threw the pieces in the air like confetti. A piece stuck to Basil's wet nose. He looked at me, curious, unsure what to make of this new game.

I got up and gathered my things. I crammed the red dress in a pillowcase and shoved it in one of the boxes.

After carrying my things downstairs, I put the knife back in the gun cabinet drawer. The official-looking envelope my dad had told me about was still sitting on the dining room table. I grabbed it and put it with my other stuff.

After packing the van, I stood in the doorway for a final look at the house I'd lived in for seventeen years. The only good memories I had were the brief times when my mom was normal, or when I was too young to understand that she wasn't. Making Christmas tree decorations out of soda cans, or the time we planted an herb garden from seeds and she comforted me when I cried because I didn't understand why we had to wait for them to grow. All traces of those times had been sucked out of the house long ago. I didn't feel anything anymore, but I still wanted to take it in, like running a finger over an old scar.

Basil sat at the base of the stairs. He watched me. My dad would probably forget about him. Leave the next owners to find a dead dog in their backyard. I couldn't take him.

"Come on," I said. He ran for the open door so fast he skidded sideways like a cartoon before righting himself. He ran to the van and waited.

I guess I was learning that when you can't do something, you do it anyway.

~ ~ ~

It was a slow adjustment. I stayed at Vicky's about two days a week, which was all her mom would allow. I slept in her van the other nights, with an elaborate setup of blankets and fabric to keep warm. Alana had left her gym membership card, so I was able to use it and shower there on some morning. On days I had gym at school, I used those showers. I kept my clothes in the truck and in the back of Vicky's closet.

The real problem was food. I didn't have anywhere to put it and couldn't afford to eat out. I mostly just ate what they had at school, and skipped dinner.

Taking care of Basil proved more difficult than taking care of myself. When I was at school, I put him in the trailer by the soccer field. I had to knock out the broken window and crawl in to unlock the door. I taped cardboard over the window to keep it warm enough inside. I made a bed for him and put food and water in there. After school I would get him out and we'd walk to the library, where I would do my homework and he'd lay down on the grate outside the sliding doors. The building's heat came up through the grate so he'd stay warm and get lots of pets from people coming and going. I'd sit at a table where I could keep an eye on him. He became kind of a regular. I even saw the librarian go out there and sneak him some food once. He usually slept in the van with me, but Vicky let me put him in the basement on nights I slept in her room, as long as her mom didn't find out.

I was making some money helping Vicky. She was having me do more sewing, but mostly just easy stuff. I was also cutting fabric and stenciling patterns. It wasn't like before, when I was sewing my dress and we'd talk and laugh for hours. Now, I needed the money, so it was more serious, and Vicky didn't have time to goof around because she was getting more and more orders.

I started to feel a little better, but little was huge. It was a delicate balance. I was barely keeping it all together, but each day felt like progress, as long as I got to the end of it. I knew that one false step could throw me into a spiral, so I was very careful. Every day I just focused on the next step, without looking too far ahead.

I was concentrating on some cross-stitching one day when, between bursts of her machine, Vicky said, "I had your dress dry cleaned. You left it in a pillowcase and it totally smelled rank. I had to take some other stuff in, so no problem, you're welcome."

"Oh yeah, thanks, I totally forgot about that."

"Apparently I need to show you how to properly care for a dress too."

"Yeah." I tried to be casual, but I ended up having to go to the bathroom to vomit. I flushed the toilet and ran the water at the same time to cover up the sound, and used some of Vicky's hair spray to mask the smell.

My friendship with Song began to slip away. I thought we'd grow closer, because she was the only person who knew, but the opposite happened. Maybe she reminded me of it all, or I associated her with it. She seemed to sense it. She didn't push it, and was still friendly, even meeting me at the library a couple times and telling me about a new boy she liked. But it wasn't the same. I was different. It was my first experience disassociating from other people; the start of a long, slow process.

My math scholarship to Madison came though, contingent on a minimum SAT score. Vicky was super proud of me. She was the only one I had to tell. I'd bored her about a million times with my dreams of becoming a lawyer. We went to Madison on a Sunday and walked around the campus. She took me to a fancy dinner to celebrate and ordered me a glass of wine. She told me that in nice restaurants they don't really care how old you are if you acted like an adult.

I doubled down on my studies. I was worried I'd lose my scholarship if I didn't do well. The scholarship was my lifeline. Our school library had two books on quantum mechanics and one book that had a section on geometric topology. All the time at the library helped with my college prep class and my SAT study curriculum. The only subject I was naturally good at was math. Everything else I had to work at.

Dwayne never showed up. Word was he'd dropped out of school altogether.

Chapter 8

T H O M A S

"Good morning, Doctor Ackerman."

"Morning, Joyce."

I waited in the thick air. It was tough being on her end. Nearly a year since Francis died and there was no end to the people who had to face me for the first time. It was an awkward, graceless display for the both of us, like drunk ballet.

Joyce went for steady eye contact, determined ahead of time and bravely executed.

"Anything besides the consult today?" I asked with the kind of weary timing that says I'm not whole, but functional.

"Just that. Can I get you anything?" She started to stand, thought better of it, and sat again, smoothing her skirt. Unpracticed.

"No." I paused, knowing she needed it. Last chance. Then it came.

"I'm awfully sorry for your loss, Doctor Ackerman, we all are." Nice landing. Slight lip quiver. Her coffee cup had lipstick marks on it. I remembered her perfume; an older, singularly deceptive scent, not like the modern ones with their reckless complexity. A pastry bag was rolled up and tucked in her trash like contraband. I'd gotten used to having the time to notice everything.

"Thank you, I appreciate that." I did the tight-lipped half smile and went to my office.

I'd been doing consulting work via email and phone for the past two months, a slow seduction that didn't require getting dressed. I found it an easy distraction. I wondered why I once thought so much of myself as a doctor. It seemed easy to the point of trivial now. What did anyone need me for? Do what all doctors do—search Google. Of course, I hadn't picked up a scalpel in a year, and didn't plan to.

I didn't need to do any of this, as a practical matter, but being accidentally wealthy is paid for with a guilt that is impossible to express without expecting anything short of contempt in return. Being useful, it is assumed, is the sole province of the wage earner.

The first day, brief as it was, found many unwieldy moments. People laughing, then catching my eye and going solemn; caught being insensitive. I was like the grim reaper, there to extinguish the joy of living.

The consult went well, a simple hernia repair. They really were going easy on me.

"We were told there was no problem with us waiting," the wife said. "Until you were back. We were told you were the best."

"We wanted the best," the husband confirmed, puffing up a bit. Parents are often quick to inform me of this: *We wanted the best,* which is an end-around compliment, not for you but for them, as if other, less noble parents were out seeking mediocrity. Of course I heard my own voice, pleading with Dr. Caruso.

I had agreed to two days a week at first, only a couple of hours in the office. Then three. Just consulting. Eugene, head of the surgical department, smartly asked me to come in and give my opinion on a surgery.

"Now?" I looked up from my desk. He was in my doorway, in scrubs, which was rare. You don't walk this side of the building in scrubs.

"We're in part two of a lung repair, but there's complications with spina bifida. It's worse than it looked on the images. Just take a look."

"How old?" I found myself standing.

"Four months. Girl."

I scrubbed in and stood over his shoulder. He didn't need me; I saw his trick, easily enough, but even I thought it might work.

I came home that day to find Stephen sitting at the dining room table with his phone in his hand. Just sitting. This was unusual. Stephen never sat at the table. Doing so would cross an invisible but very real line of propriety he'd established for himself. I sat across from him, like Conroy did with me.

"Tom, I need to take the rest of the day off."

I was shocked. When Stephen started, I couldn't force him to take a day off. Except Sundays, he was there all day, every day. "You must have a life," I once said. "I've had an extraordinary one," he replied, which made me wonder all the more. He'd been with us eight months and had only taken one day off, to volunteer at the Veterans Administration on Christmas.

"Sure," I said. "Take whatever time you need, you run the show around here." He stood and put his apron on the table. He didn't fold it, which for him was the equivalent of slipping into hard drugs. "Everything okay?" I asked. It was easy to forget he might have problems of his own.

He looked at me like he didn't know me for a moment. "Hm? Oh, yes. Yes, I think so." He nodded like he was trying to convince himself. "I need to be there for someone."

I didn't pry.

A few weeks later, he asked to go part time, saying it would be temporary. He could return to full time later, if we wanted. For now, he'd work half days, leaving around noon, after setting things up for the rest of the day.

I called Conroy to let him know. He asked a few questions but I cut him off, letting him know I was just keeping him informed, not asking permission. I was pathetic, but at least I was aware of it. He didn't push back.

The consensus was that I was doing better, and was ready to handle more responsibility. This was more implied than stated. It's a quiet dance you don't know exists until you're called to participate. I was being given silent permission. It was okay with everyone now if I got better. Many people find it terribly insensitive if you try to follow your own pace of recovery.

~~~

You will eventually realize your suffering does not afford you any benefit.

This was something Doctor Gordy told me that actually stuck; perhaps the only thing. At the time, I was dismissive, out of habit by that point, but some part of my brain tucked those words away. Over time, they'd moved around in my head.

Nobody cares. That's what he meant.

It was painful at first, but liberating later. People are utilitarian animals, in the end, and the unfairness of it all turned out to apply to me the same as it did everybody else.

Nobody cares. Once absorbed, if still standing, it feels okay, given some distance. Like making it to the end of a tunnel. There's nothing specifically there, it's just a way out.

Nobody cares. Not even me, I tested, implying I'm somebody after all. My suffering, I found, when I could hold it up to the light and turn it, held little interest. I was finally bored with it.

The antidepressants, a new and improved version of what I'd taken years ago, came with new and improved side effects, which I never got over—primarily a dissociative feeling, like I was living a few seconds behind reality.

I began to ease off them. A bad, bad idea.

As a doctor, I would come down hard on any patient who did what I was doing, but secretly, I had stopped thinking of myself as a doctor. I got to be the irresponsible patient, sitting on the other side and acting reckless.

I was still consulting patients—rather, their parents—but feeling more and more like an impostor. Everyone was nudging me toward the operating room. I was good after all, on a fast track to great. I hadn't come up short there. I was also an asset—no trophy wife, I—a marquee name for the hospital, and I'd barely gotten started.

I held them off. I didn't want to crouch down and look into young, wide eyes, full of confusion. I didn't have the stomach for all the tragedy, and surgery required a kind of battlefield craving. Faith in the ends. I was soft now, all underbelly, and I wanted soft things around me.

I tapered off slowly, allowing at least that, cutting the pills with a razor blade. I got down to half a pill, every other day.

The first change surprised me. Lust returned, as if it had been doing pushups in the corner all this time.

It was a general longing at first, so unfamiliar I could hardly place it. Going up an escalator at the mall, I stared at the woman in front of me, as if under a spell. A woman coming up the opposite side gave me a hard look, causing the woman in front of me to turn and look down. She held my eye as my face burned, then she turned back around and took a few steps up where she waited, hip cocked.

I didn't want this new feeling. I was fearful of how far it would develop. As I remembered my bacchanal college years, the depths of my lust scared me. I had no place for that now.

I began to masturbate in the shower every morning, reduced to this banal act. The woman on the escalator at least provided a ready image. Before she turned. Attractive as she was, I wanted no identity.

Like a return to adolescence, I had an impulse I didn't know what to do with. As I looked around this new vista, I realized the world had changed in the twenty years since I'd met Francis. It was more than just the landscape. People prayed to devices now, trance-like, giving their full faith to new deities. A mass hypnosis was under way, and the masses were all in.

I chose to ignore it, as best I could. My previous solution had been to throw myself into my work. At the time, it was college and medical school. Then I had Francis. I had my insatiable sex drive to thank for my high station in life.

I had no easy solution now. I didn't want sex. The thought of it felt violent—an obvious trick of nature, who, I knew from experience, was always first with a violent solution.

It progressed in the ensuing weeks. I tossed and turned at night. I walked for hours on the treadmill. I did all I could to starve the beast. I upped my time at the hospital to four days a week. I wrote a few medical papers, the writing coming too easy to be useful. Joyce smiled with encouragement as she proofed my drafts.

One afternoon, after having left for the day, Stephen came back, saying he needed to talk to me. We sat in the library. I was expecting him to say he was coming back full time. Instead, he informed me he was leaving us altogether.

When I heard Henry come home, I called him in. I knew he and Stephen had a special bond. Before I could tell him, Stephen did, as if it was for him to do. Henry's face fell. Few things rend a parent's heart more than seeing their child try to hide emotional pain. I told Stephen he'd be welcome back any time, whatever the circumstances.

I was confident I could handle things; the practical aspects, anyway. I'd been on a pretty good roll lately. I didn't have to fake it as much. My mental state was improving. I began to think that maybe I had something to offer after all.

But I'd gotten ahead of myself. One step forward, two steps back.

~ ~ ~

I was at Cedars-Sinai, walking back from the labs and thinking about a consult I had coming up, when I smelled her. I hadn't seen anyone walk past, but I wouldn't because I'd developed the habit of looking at the ground as I walked, another regression into adolescence.

The scent was faint. I stopped and spun. A woman was walking toward the elevators. She had similar hair, but wasn't as tall. And judging by her walk, she was younger, but not much.

I followed her. My consult was in ten minutes.

She went left, to the elevator bank. I came around the same corner. She hit the down button. I pretended to look through the manila folders I was holding.

We waited. A young Hispanic couple joined us. The woman was pregnant. They both appeared battle-weary. They began a conversation in Spanish that progressed to an argument, restarting a paused fight they'd likely hoped to save for home or the car. I remembered those times with Francis. We didn't argue often, but when we did, it would last for days, picking up in the middle of the night or in line at the grocery store. The man stepped away, then came back. He'd forgotten her, like a piece of luggage. He took her arm and hauled her off toward the pharmacy.

It was now just her and I. She hadn't looked at me; just another drone in a white coat. She appeared distracted. I wondered if she'd just gotten a diagnosis. People go through a predictable process when it's bad news, starting with shocked silence at the indifference of their God. Deep down, we all believe something recognizes us as an exception.

The elevator dinged. Two nurses in blue scrubs got off, clutching white cups and phones, like it was required. They seemed impossibly young, as if they were continuing a game of pretend they'd started at home.

I got on the elevator with her. She hit the ground floor button. I pretended to immerse myself in my folders. The doors shut and the machinery whirred.

I breathed in, slow and deliberate. Yes, it was Francis's perfume. She'd bought it from a small shop in southern France; a specialty store that sold nothing but perfume. I remembered shelves of sun-soaked pastel bottles. No lounging, half-naked bodies in edgy ads. Years later, when I was in a nearby city for a medical conference, she made me go back for more. I got a harsh lecture from the alchemist about the evils of body wash as he sniffed the air between us.

The woman got off and I followed—her and her scent. She went into a coffee shop. I waited a moment, letting someone exit before going in. There were two lines, it being their busy hour. I stood in the other.

I had been there earlier and took away my own white cup. I always looked forward to it when I had business at this hospital. Nobody made better coffee than Stephen, but he'd essentially outlawed sugar from our kitchen, and I hadn't replaced it since he'd left. It was his only area of fanaticism that I could see. He was convinced sugar was a poison, and told me bluntly it contributed to my depression. He'd managed to bake without it, using all kinds of exotic substitutes and challenging Henry and I to tell the difference. He eventually rid the kitchen completely of the ruinous substrate, along with nuts because Henry's sometimes-friend Justine was allergic to them. When I wanted to binge, coffee was my choice. I'd buy a cup and add gobs of sugar.

I could still smell her, even through the artificial pumpkin spice seasonal assault. Maybe it was the memory that was so strong. Others didn't seem to notice, but my senses were on high alert.

The overhead florescent lights buzzed and vibrated through the watery, droll music. A gaunt girl behind the counter, bending over a machine, steamed milk with a loud, industrial whoosh. She had a worrisome mole on her neck. I once saw these things everywhere—the ominous mole, the concerning skin pallor, the telltale breath—and would try to be helpful. I took my oath seriously. But I was often rebuffed. People didn't want to know, and felt invaded. Just out to buy some shoes, they don't want some stranger pitching them doomey scenarios.

I tried to catch her reflection through the smudged, curved glass of the pastry case. The woman in front of me was bowed to her phone, headless, her child twisting at her hand.

Back outside, I threw my drink in the trash as I watched her cross the street. There was a mall across the way. The Beverly Center. She walked toward the escalators. The light turned yellow and I ran across, idiot in white.

I followed her into the mall. It felt official now. I could have convinced myself of something before, but not now.

It was early. The mall had few people in it, giving it the ambience of a movie set. She didn't meander, but went up another escalator. I drifted up just as she was stepping off. I caught sight of myself, reflected in a store window, moving in a diagonal line.

She turned a corner. I quickened my pace. My sweaty palms stained the manila folders. She disappeared into a store. I slowed and approached stealth-like.

It was a jewelry store. I backed off. I found a bench and sat, then stood and took my white coat off and folded it in my lap. I waited twenty minutes for her to come back out before I realized she must work there.

~ ~ ~

Back at the hospital, I made it through the consult, after an apology for being late.

"That's alright, it's normal, isn't it?" the mother asked, a little worried, as her child crashed toy cars. Early in my practice, I'd learned the odd logic that people unconsciously believe that if a doctor is on time, they can't possibly be that good.

The rest of the day was spent in the linear progression of an alcoholic, from morning remorse to five o'clock rationalizing.

I used the employee gym to shower and change. Since I no longer thought of myself as a real doctor, I'd stopped dressing as one. I'd abandoned ties and slacks in favor of jeans and knit shirts.

It was after six when I went back to the mall. Going up the escalator, I looked at my reflection again, this time sandwiched between others. My shaking head looked like an alien judging me.

The bench I'd sat on before was full. The mall was at full swarm, with lots of gummy teens with backward baseball caps. I leaned over the railing and looked at the floor below. I needed to think this through.

There was nothing there. I had no thoughts. I didn't know what I was doing, so there was no way to analyze it. The only thing I could determine was that I was acting irrationally.

As if compelled, I walked toward the store, weaving through the packs, and went in.

It was small, comprised mostly of a horseshoe glass display case. In contrast to the frenzy of the mall, it was quiet. No music played. The least popular store in the mall, like the lone kid against the fence far out in the field at recess. The only customers were a couple hunched over the glass counter, examining something displayed on a dark cloth.

She wasn't there. An older man was assisting the couple. But I could smell her, wispy in the air. The man looked up and gave me a pleasant smile.

With a push of scent, she came in from the back, polishing something. She set it on the cloth for the couple's inspection. They nodded and murmured.

I looked down into the display case in front of me. Necklaces. I could smell her approach, getting stronger, clear and potent at the same time. I saw her dark skirt through the glass case. It dropped past her knees and met the tops of her high boots, with just a crease of white skin in between.

"Is there anything I can help you with?" She had an accent. British. I looked up at her. She had a dressed-down beauty, with straight hair and bangs, like a kid whose mom cuts her hair in the kitchen. She wore layers, including a man's tweed vest.

"I, uh..." She looked at me and tilted her head. Something darted through her mind.

The couple passed behind me in a waft of rose water and tobacco. The sounds of the mall pulsed.

The older man behind the counter went to the woman. "You okay, then?" I heard him whisper. She turned and said something to him. He nodded, glanced at me, then went to the back.

Her attention turned back to me. "Are you looking for yourself?"

"For someone else."

"Someone else, I see." She looked down at my wedding ring.

"Yes, my—my wife."

"Oh, lovely, is it a special occasion?"

"It's her birthday." I didn't know where these words were coming from. It's amazing how the liar waits at the ready, like a more prepared self.

"Were you thinking of something specific, like a necklace?"

"No. Actually, I was thinking, maybe a ring."

She nodded and stayed on task. "We have rings over here." She pointed to the opposite display and walked around. I crossed over and caught a glimpse of the man in back.

When she approached again, her scent went though me like my own breath. "If you have something specific in mind, I can show you what we have that might match. If not, I can help you narrow down your choices. We can also do custom work, if your time frame allows." Graceful hand gestures. The waning told me she perfumed her wrists, probably as her mother had—the old pulse-points myth.

"I don't have anything specific in mind, I just thought a ring would be nice. I've done the necklace and earrings thing before."

"I see, but nothing specific. Sapphire is popular just now, in a silver setting. Personally, I think it only works well for someone with blue or green eyes. Are her eyes blue?"

"No, brown."

"Tell me about her and maybe I can be more helpful. Does she have a specific aesthetic? What does she like?"

She wore bookish glasses, which made her eyes look bigger. I overstepped and extended the look just beyond the acceptable. "She likes textures," I said. "Things you touch."

"Textures, did you say?"

"Sorry, that's no help at all. She's an artist. She sculpts. The ways things feel are important to her."

"Oh, now that is interesting." She spoke in a softer voice, as if we had skipped forward and had something to share.

"But I'm realizing that doesn't really help with picking out a ring."

"It might, everything's a clue," she said.

"It's not like you ask people to feel your ring."

"That's true." She smiled and lines at the corner of her eyes appeared. "But it's revealing nonetheless. What else does she like?"

"She likes bold statements, but with a subtle touch, if that makes sense. Probably not."

"Well—"

"She was much more social. Companionable, I mean, than I am. That's not a word, though, is it? And Europeans are so much more careful with their words. You're British?"

"I am."

"Sorry, I didn't mean to lump you in with the whole of Europe."

"Quite alright."

"England may be the last pillar holding up the English language. I think I read that somewhere. She could meet someone and a minute later they'd be telling her everything. She likes green. I'd turn my back, and she'd be hugging a stranger. And yellow. Those two colors. She likes gardening, so we always had yellow flowers everywhere. I never knew there were so many variations of yellow. You clearly have good taste. Maybe you could just pick something."

She waited, blinking. My stomach twisted. "Lemon quartz," she said.

"Is that a… is that a kind of jewelry stone?"

"It is, and it's companionable with many things. Do you know her size?"

"Her size? How big she is?" She laughed; teeth, lips, and tongue. "Of course you mean her ring size. I don't, I'm afraid." *I'm afraid.* It almost came out with an accent. I wanted to talk like her. I'm sure she didn't want to talk like me. I felt desire, lumbering about like a pacing boxer, waiting to be called out with a flourish.

"Well, sometimes we use this, at least for starters." She pulled out a mannequin hand, covered in dark cloth. She set it on the counter. She turned the fingers to face me. I didn't want to touch it. It looked like an elegant version of something dead.

"Her hands are about the same size as yours," I said.

We both looked at her hand. You'd think the scent would dissipate, but it didn't. It was in every breath I took, pushing and pulling through me.

She slid her hand forward. I reached and took it in mine, a courtier gesture, helping her alight. Her left hand. She wore a wedding ring.

I lifted it. It was warm and strong. Indoor hands. She had pale, elegant, feminine fingers. Not scarred from hard tools. I turned it. Faint, colored veins inside her wrist, like coded wires. The bashful drum beat, the throbbing, the push and the pull. I lifted it higher, leaning, and breathed.

~ ~ ~

There were no screams or threats. Just an awkward moment. An apology, sincerely meant and promptly accepted. The British have that on us. She was beautiful. Striking, even. She might be used to the erratic gestures of men. Probably had a go-to list of diffusing responses.

We both went back to our assigned roles and I ordered a ring.

~ ~ ~

That night, I spoke to Francis.

I often had conversations with her in my head, and not just at night. I don't suppose that's so odd, being the one left behind. Part of the grieving process, I'd told myself.

I'd be picking out something to wear and I'd hear her. *Really? There's green in that. You're going to wear it with the dark purple? Are you trying to look like a pimp?*

Her voice was real, with breath and realistic sounds throughout. She'd goad me to spend more time with Henry by trying to convince me that he really did want my company. *He's a teenager, of course it's not obvious. Everything is coded.*

But it was mostly at night. After rolling about in bed, I'd give up and turn on the light. I'd talk to her in whispers until I could sleep.

One night, she was working on coaxing me back to work. *For real. That means picking up instruments and cutting.* I fell asleep. I woke up seven hours later without having moved. I blinked at the lights. I wasn't sure if the numbers on the clock were AM or PM. It was the longest I'd slept in months.

I began to feel I couldn't sleep if I didn't talk to her first. Eventually, I didn't even bother trying.

Hands behind my head, I told her everything, starting with when I saw the woman and followed her on the elevator. I prattled on and on like a tween, trying to get it all out before she could cut me down.

Francis was quiet. Or gone. She was always a good listener, but seldom silent.

She remained quiet for the next few nights. I kept trying to talk to her, but she just wasn't there, so I didn't sleep.

I knew it wasn't her. I realized I was talking to the memory I had of her. I wasn't insane. Francis was dead, I was aware of that. But it still mattered that she didn't show up. This trick of my brain, whatever it was, must have served some evolutionary function, and had allowed me a degree of comfort. Now it was gone.

This was a practical problem as well. Without being able to talk to her, I couldn't sleep. I didn't worry until the sleepless nights stacked up. She seemed intent on depriving me. Except for a brief nap on the couch and once falling asleep in my car in a parking lot, I didn't sleep for nearly a week.

I received a message on my phone. A man's voice. The ring was ready for me to pick up. I could come by any time.

I didn't have business at Cedars that day, but I used the office they provided me to do some research. I followed the same routine as last time by changing at the gym.

I went back to the mall. Lack of sleep made me feel like I was walking though a performance without end. Nothing was real, so nothing much mattered.

Fatigue made me brave. I breezed in like I was ready for a laugh. She wasn't behind the counter. The man smiled. I had no choice but to pick up the ring and leave. I stood outside the store for a while like the kid who'd just lost all his money at the carnival.

The ring was beautiful. I'm not sure why I had such low expectations; none, really. Francis would have loved it. Mysterious yellow quartz threaded through bold lines of silver. It captured Francis perfectly. I secretly wanted to wear it.

That night, ready for bed, I put the ring on the nightstand and waited. I was willing to do anything she suggested. Lack of sleep proved a fascination at first, but no more. Now I'd entered a dark, twisty place. My shadow self made a rare appearance, showing astonishment at how adaptable we life forms are.

She didn't come. The ceiling began to move in waves. I closed my eyes and pleaded.

I went to the mall again the next day. Back on autopilot. This time it was late afternoon. Instead of going in, I looked through the glass. I figured I had one reasonable chance—to thank her, to tell her how much my wife liked the ring. It would be a coda. Then back to the identity I was supposed to have; respected doctor, widowed over a year now, rebuilding his life. *He's got a kid, you know.*

She wasn't there, or maybe she was in the back.

I went to the bench. A man was sitting on it. A woman came out of a store and gave him a lazy shrug. He got up and they went off together, a shopping ritual repeated everywhere. I took his spot, like a senior in need of respite.

I closed my eyes. The sounds of the mall mixed into an audio flotsam. I may have nodded off. I woke with my eyes still closed. Her smell. The memory of it, but so recent I could reach behind me and grab it. I opened my eyes and saw myself reflected in the window of the store in front of me, between the shifts of walking people. Sitting stoic, my face time-lapsed older.

Her smell. It grew stronger. I couldn't seem to move. I was stuck in a sleep paralysis.

Saturated. Her breath, her presence. I still couldn't move. A pack of them went by, jeans and jangling jewelry and rowdy hope. They passed and she was there, sitting next to me, in her dark skirt and boots. A long gap. I studied her, to make sure. She allowed it, looking with me, our shared image like a Hopper painting.

"Thomas." Breathing made me self-conscious, like it was something I'd just discovered. "I know you lost your wife." My throat constricted. More of them. Then us again, like a couple, talking it out, afraid to face each other; an exercise a therapist might assign.

"You followed me," she continued. "I know. From the elevator at the hospital. I didn't understand. I didn't know what to do. I'm sorry. I looked you up. Your name was on the receipt."

I wanted to turn to her but couldn't. I was still frozen, like in a dream where the hideous thing is about to engulf you.

"I can't help you," she said. "I don't know who can. But I can tell you, it's not me that you want. I am certain."

"How? How do you know?" I croaked.

"Because, I feel it too."

"You do?" I turned, released.

She sighed, long and weary, showing new wrinkles under the harsher light. "Yes. But I know it's not you." She looked at her hands. "I wear my ring, too. He left me. In

England. Not the same, of course. I came here. It was as far as I could go."

"You're—"

"No, Thomas."

"But—"

"No."

We took a break, as if we had a fully realized pattern.

"You remind me of him. Your eyes, mostly," she said. "They're exactly the same. What are the odds?"

"Your smell. Your perfume. And you. Something."

"I'm sorry."

"I know, me too. I feel foolish."

"Don't. I expect we're both projecting." She stood.

"Maybe there's something to it." My voice cracked. "Like you said, what are the odds?"

"There's not. It's just need. It finds a home."

"When do you leave? I mean, get off?"

She shook her head, resolute. "No."

"When do you get off work?"

"Just—no, I can't." She put a hand on my shoulder.

"I understand. But when?"

"Go home."

"When?"

"Thomas." She kept saying my name, like she was trying to convince herself I wasn't him.

"I'm sorry," I said and stood up. Her hand slid off my shoulder. I turned and started to go. I didn't want to miss my only brave moment.

"Six o'clock," she said to my back. I turned and watched her go into the store.

I went back to the bench and sat again. My reflection looked at me now. So old, like I'd passed my father. Anxious to get there, where she was. Waiting for the end of the movie so I could enter the bright light of day.

I walked the mall like a drunk man, fatigued and confused. I went down to the next level and walked the full circumference. I passed the mall's entrance and willed myself to leave.

Once more around. There was a blurring together of things.

The crowds thinned. Women in heels reached high and pulled down rattling metal barriers. I was across the way when she came out. She spotted me, like something in the woods. She turned abruptly and walked at a pace.

She took the escalators that zig-zagged the side of the building, down to the lower parking levels. I was far behind her. At first, she walked as she descended, head bowed and determined. She slowed, and finally stopped; drifting and waiting.

Windows everywhere reflected our shifts and slides. She saw me, one section up. Both of us still; machinists, caught in the machine.

She clicked across the cement parking lot with her keys out. Taillights blinked. I slowed to make sure she had plenty of time. She disappeared behind the pillar next to her car. I stopped and waited. I didn't hear a car door open.

I approached, quiet, and came around the pillar. Her keys were in one hand, her purse dangled from the other. She leaned forward, against her car. I moved behind her and connected.

"I know it's not me," I said to the back of her neck. I slid my arms around her. She grasped them. Her shoulders shook, slow at first. I parted the hair at her ear and breathed there, matching her breath and slipping in and out of gaps.

She turned in my arms and slid her glasses off.

Chapter 9

MARGARET

I began to see light at the end of the tunnel. I was busier than ever with school, studying for the SAT, helping Vicky, and taking care of Basil.

I'd made a few trips to Formally Informal and was getting to know Ms. Barden better. She tried to feed me every time I saw her. "Sweetheart, a strong wind could kidnap you," she'd always say, forgetting she'd said the same thing last time. I'd laugh anyway. Then she'd make me take a bag of food that she'd have all prepared. She did it like it was no big deal. "Just some leftovers." But I could tell she cooked everything just for me, wrapping it in foil and packing it all just so. It was always so good I could hardly wait to get to the van to eat it. I always tried to save some for later but never managed to.

If I just keep doing what I'm doing, I thought, I'll make it through the school year. Then I can work for Vicky through the summer, and be ready for college.

I'd lie awake at night in the van and think of the people I'd see on campus. The new faces. Young adults, not kids. Serious people, doing important things. All the smart conversations I'd have. I'd imagine my dorm room and wonder who my roommate would be. Sometimes I'd make her up and get carried away by creating every detail. She'd have curly red hair, and she'd love to cook. She'd be a year older and give me advice about boys and I'd help her with her math assignments and we'd be real friends. We'd borrow each other's clothes and go to movies together. I'd arrange every element of our dorm room, and she'd be amazed at how good I was at it. Some nights I'd debate if I should move my desk over to make more room for my bicycle, or where I should put the plant Vicky would buy me. I'd fall asleep thinking about the classes I'd have and already be worried about my pretend homework.

In December, my period was late. I hoped it was from not eating, or maybe stress. I also wasn't sleeping much. Now that winter was in full swing, I couldn't get warm in the van, no matter how deep I burrowed in the blankets and fabric. It was too cold for Basil so I'd been putting him in the basement.

A week later, still nothing. At night, I'd try to have my fantasies about college life, but I couldn't do it.

I bought a pregnancy test. I was sleeping in Vicky's room that night, but I didn't want to do it in her bathroom because I was afraid she'd walk in. She'd come in sometimes, lean against the sink and talk, like we were just hanging out. She didn't really get the whole privacy thing.

I brought the kit to school, thinking I could use the library bathroom that evening. But I couldn't wait. I wanted my dreams back. I wanted to be able to think about college all the time again. It was the warm secret that kept me going. After my third class, I went to the far bathrooms, where it all began. I knew I could be alone there. It seemed fitting. I hadn't been back there since it happened.

I opened the stall door. It was bent and made a grating noise as I pushed it open. There were tufts of fur from the wolf costume stuck to the damp area at the base of the toilet. I ran my fingers over the tile on the wall, where he'd pinned me. I looked at the toilet, where I'd hit my forehead, and where he forced my head in the water. It all just looked like normal bathroom stuff now.

I'd still get the flashes sometimes, but there was always that blank spot. A gap. A hidden part I couldn't remember. I wanted to know what was in there. That's why I came back here, I realized. I could have used any bathroom, but I wanted that missing part. I didn't want to be doing something years later and suddenly have a flashback and realize for the first time what happened in that gap. I didn't want anything to have the power to destroy my future. I wanted to cut off the diseased limb before the infection spread.

I closed my eyes. I could hear him, guttural and determined, the sound sharp off the hard surfaces. I could feel his grip on my arms, smell his sweat, feel the plastic nose of the wolf against my neck and the fur against my bare back.

All things I'd already remembered; but the blank spot, it was still there.

I took out the pregnancy test and read the instructions. I peed on the stick. It said results could take up to three minutes. It didn't take thirty seconds. Positive.

~ ~ ~

I went to 8 am mass. I didn't want to be one of those Catholics that crawl back to church only when they need God's help. But there I was.

I was early and felt awkward, dressed in my everyday clothes. I never liked the casual way some people dressed for church. My mom had taught me to always wear something nice, to show respect, but I hadn't packed any of my nice clothes. Now I was one of them, in my jeans and a blouse.

I looked up at the ceiling—something I usually avoided because all the ornate geometric lines and patterns would get my math brain going and I'd end up running calculations throughout the sermon. I let it go this time and it began a sequence loop, creating a background hum to my thoughts.

I didn't know why I was there. I hadn't been to mass in months. I'd been making deliveries for Vicky on Sundays, then I'd go to the library in Madison that was open late and had lots of advanced math books. No time for God.

Everything looked unfamiliar now. I was seeing it in a different context. I tried talking to my mom in my head, like I used to, but she wasn't there anymore. Even my fantasy version of her was gone.

I missed my life. This realization, from out of nowhere, gripped me as the choir sang an antiphon. My math brain stopped.

How could I miss a life I hated? Or thought I did. Maybe because I understood it, bad as it was, and from where I sat now, I didn't understand anything.

I closed my eyes and listened to the choir as I willed my mom back. I even missed my dad, I realized. I hadn't had a kind thought for him in so long I didn't think there was anything to miss. I wanted him to sit on the edge of my bed again. I wanted him to be proud of me again, even if it was for killing something. All their flaws didn't seem to matter so much, I just wanted them both back.

I was the one that found her. She was in the dining room. I'd heard the gunshot, from outside. I had gone to Vicky's house after school as usual, but left when she got in a fight with her mom, who was always on her about her weight. I was still two houses away. I thought it was my dad's truck backfiring, like it did sometimes, but his truck wasn't in the driveway. I opened the front door and stopped. The sound repeated in my head as if trying to get me to understand. Then I realized what it was.

"Mom?" No answer, but I heard a sound, like something sliding, or being moved. I went to the base of the stairs. I heard the sliding sound again and went toward the dining room.

It was dusk, but the curtains were open, so light was slanting through the room in bands. There was a faint red mist, like vapor, in the stripes of light. It was like something from a fairytale. The wall nearest the kitchen was dripping at the top, where it met the ceiling. My mom was moving around the dining room table, in a circle, in and out of the stripes of light. She was sliding one foot, as if that leg was dead. Her head was tilted up, the way blind people sometimes do. She was making a sound, like a baby: "boo boo boo."

I could see she had shot herself. Part of her head, near her ear, was misshapen. It was dark and wet. She held the gun pressed to her side as she continued around the table.

"Mom." She didn't seem to hear me, but she slowed, as if her leg was getting heaver.

Blood dripped off the end of the gun. It was a .38 long nose. My dad had taken me to the range with it.

A smudgy drinking glass sat on the table, with a bit of amber at the bottom and lipstick on the rim. Next to it was an open shoebox, full of old photographs. She'd drag it out sometimes and make me sit while she showed me pictures of when I was a baby and tell me about the people from her childhood. She'd point them out and clasp a hand over her mouth. Pictures scattered the table and floor.

She came around the table towards me. She was still looking up. Her eyes were wide. She didn't seem aware of me and continued making the "boo" sound. As she got closer, she walked into a band of light. Blood was pulsing down her neck and running down her arm.

I went past her into the kitchen and took the phone off the wall. I dialed 911.

"My mom shot herself, my mom shot herself." I remember saying this over and over and the person on the other end interrupting me, but I kept saying it, thinking they weren't hearing me, like we were on different frequencies. My mom appeared in the doorway of the kitchen and looked at me. She finally saw me.

She swung the gun toward me. An arc of hot blood stripped across my neck and cheek. "Boo boo."

Bobo. I remembered. It was the pet name she had for me when I was a baby.

My memory ends there. The rest is a blank. They found me outside, sitting on the ground against the side of the house. They took my mom to the hospital, but left me.

~ ~ ~

Father Brennan was well into the Liturgy. My brain was busy again reconfiguring the ceiling. I had planned to go to confession. I didn't know exactly what I was going to confess. Until now. Now it seemed clear. I was a bad daughter. *Bobo.*

I was the reason she did it.

~ ~ ~

I made it to early March, just a couple months short of graduation. I wasn't showing yet, but I knew I was close. I was sick most mornings. Bad sleep had become no sleep, except when I'd nod off in the library and wake with my head in my arms.

My mind was getting fuzzy. I couldn't concentrate in class. I would be doing homework and realize I'd been staring at the same page for ten minutes.

Worst of all, I had no plan. Before, I always had a plan. I could always figure out a way forward. I even used to practice planning variations of my future; how to become a geologist, or an astronaut, or how to move to another country and start a new life. It was like working through a puzzle. I'd analyze every aspect, refine it and fret over all the details.

But not now. Now I was pregnant, living day to day, with no plan.

I figured Vicky would be the first to notice. She thought I was getting sick from sleeping in the van, so she was making me sleep in her room more often. Her mom glowered at me but tolerated it. I tried to be helpful by cleaning dishes and emptying ash trays.

I was wrong. It was Ms. Barden.

It was a Saturday afternoon. I was delivering a custom dress that Vicky had just finished that morning. I had already driven to Milwaukee earlier to make a delivery. I hadn't eaten anything, figuring Ms. Barden would give me her usual bag of food.

She always gave me such a warm welcome when I came to her store. I looked forward to it. Not this time. I came in and waited for her to finish helping a mother and daughter that wanted a prom dress. There were a number of other customers, but I knew Ms. Barden saw me come in. She looked at me a couple times, but didn't give me any sign to go to the back or anything. I waited with the dress draped over my arm.

She finished with the mother and daughter but stayed there, across the store, looking at me. I smiled. She just kept staring.

She went to the back of the store. The girl who worked back there came out with Ms. Barden trailing her. "Double latte, with two of those raw sugars," Ms. Barden told the girl as she handed her money. "And get yourself something, if you want." The girl passed without looking at me. "Marsella, are you okay for a few minutes?" Ms. Barden asked her other employee. Marsella gave me a quizzical look. "Yes, I got it," she said.

I was still standing by the front door when Ms. Barden finally looked at me and nodded her head toward the back. I followed her.

She closed the door. "Sit," she said.

"Where do you want me to put—"

"*Sit.*" She took the dress from me and tossed it aside. She pointed to the desk chair, the cushy kind that swivels and automatically makes you feel important. I sat. She dragged a step stool over and sat so she was right in front of me.

"Young lady," she said, "I'm going to ask you something and so help me God, you're going to tell me the truth." I'd never seen this look on her face. "Are you pregnant?"

I wasn't expecting that. I thought maybe she thought I'd stolen something. I wasn't showing yet, or just barely. You couldn't tell with clothes on. I didn't think of Ms. Barden as being very aware, and she was always forgetting things she said. Her senior moments, as she called them.

"Are you?" she asked again. I nodded my head. Her expression fell. Seeing her disappointment made the tears start to fall. She reached out and put her arms around me. "Oh, my child," she said. Hearing her call me that made me wish she were my mother. She took more interest in me than any other adult. She treated me like I was special and always told me I was going to be a great mathematician. I never had the heart to tell her I didn't want to be a mathematician.

I cried as she rocked me. "There, there. It's going to be okay," she said as she stroked my hair.

After I stopped crying, she let me go and sat back. "Honey, you're such a bright girl, how could you let this happen?"

"I know, I just… It wasn't—it was a mistake."

"I assume as much." I stared at the floor. "Margaret, you don't owe me an explanation, but I know when a girl's in trouble. Does your family know?"

"No."

"Does the boy?"

"No."

"Does anybody?"

"Ms. Barden, I can't tell you that. I know you're trying to help, and I appreciate it, I do, but I can't tell you any more."

"Oh, Margaret." She was disappointed all over again.

She didn't give me any food.

~ ~ ~

I drove to Buy the Cup. I sat Basil by the front door. He was getting used to that.

The place was almost empty. Simon was behind the counter, rearranging the pastries.

"What can I get for you?" he asked, without looking up.

"A coffee, please. Small." He nodded and turned. He'd cut his hair, but left the length in the front so it fell in his face, like Johnny Depp. He was wearing a wide leather bracelet, like from the seventies, and a PJ Harvey t-shirt. A part of me, the part that didn't feel tired and nauseous and terrified of men, wanted to climb over the counter and kiss the shit out of him.

"Dollar twenty," he said. I gave him the money and he rang me up. I put the change in the tip jar.

"I'm sorry," I said.

"Hum?" He looked up at me. His expression changed as he recognized me. "Oh."

"Yeah, Margaret."

"Right. You look different."

"I wanted to tell you, I'm really sorry."

"Yeah, cool. Whatever."

"I really, really wanted to go out with you, but something personal came up."

"Yeah, well, I don't need details." He turned away and wiped down a counter.

"Okay. I just... I'm sorry. Take care," I said to his back. He didn't respond.

~ ~ ~

I drove back to Formally Informal and parked. I sipped my coffee as Basil rested his head on my lap. The cars left the lot one by one, except for an old Mercedes.

It was dark and the store had been closed almost an hour when Ms. Barden finally came out. She locked the front door. I got out of the van.

"Ms. Barden."

"*Oh, Jesus!*" She clutched her chest. Basil barked from the front seat. "Margaret, is that you?"

"Yes, I'm sorry I startled you."

"Good God, child, I may have wet myself. Are you alright?"

"Yes." I came closer. "I'm sorry about earlier."

"It's alright. I need a brighter light out here."

"Sorry."

She regained her poise. "Sweetheart, you need to stop saying that god damn word. You'll get old and realize you never had anything to be sorry for, and you'll only be sorry for all the wasted energy. It wasn't my place to interrogate you. I realized that later. I just think the world of you, that's all."

"Thank you."

"You drove back here just to tell me you're sorry?"

"No, Ms. Barden." I knew I needed to say it before I froze up or broke down. "Ms. Barden, I need your help. I really need your help."

"Okay." She put an arm around me. "No harm in that. But let's go get some dinner first, I'm starved."

～～～

I called Vicky and told her I was having trouble with the van and that I was going to stay the night at Ms. Barden's.

Her house was like something out of a romance novel. Everything was soft and elegant. There were lots of plants and antiques and beautiful old furniture. I guess she read a lot because there was a whole wall of books in her living room. The shelves went all the way to the ceiling. There was a rolling ladder you could climb to get to the ones on top.

I slept in the most comfortable bed I'd ever slept in. The next morning, I found Ms. Barden in the kitchen. She was feeding Basil eggs and toast.

I sat at the table and told her everything. The rape, the knife, my dad—all of it. When I was done, I realized how much I'd needed to tell someone. I felt like I could breathe again. She told me I was going to stay with her until I had the baby.

She insisted on knowing who raped me, and that I go to the police. I wouldn't tell her who it was, and told her I was not going to go to the police, no matter what she said. She threatened to talk to Vicky, or to go to my school and ask around if she had to, but she said she'd find out who it was, then she'd go to the police and report it herself.

I called her bluff and left. I got Basil in the van, though I could tell he was wavering. Ms. Barden ran out and stood in the way as I tried to back out.

We ended up back at the kitchen table, like two weary trial lawyers. She agreed not to try to find out who the boy was, but only if I went back to Camden and told the people I was leaving behind where I would be. That included my father. She reminded me that I was still a minor. She said we could hold off on going to the police for now.

I agreed to the part about going back and talking to everyone, but held firm on not telling the police. I wasn't going to do it, now or later. In exchange, she made me promise I'd finish high school in Madison, after I had the baby. She said we could set up a small nursery in the back of the shop and Marsella and her could watch the baby while I was in class. I would start in the fall and retake my senior year. I agreed, because I wanted to do that anyway.

Then she made me eggs and bacon. While I was eating that, she made me oatmeal. I couldn't believe how hungry I was, even though I'd eaten a big dinner the night before at an Italian restaurant where the cook knew Ms. Barden and kept smiling and nodding at how much I was eating.

"Go back and talk to them; Vicky, your father, and anyone else. You don't have to tell them everything, but you need to tell them you're going away for a while and you'll see them again sometime later. They'll figure it out. There aren't a lot of other scenarios for them to assume."

I'd have to drop out of school until the following year, which meant I'd lose my scholarship.

I went back to Camden, and started with Vicky.

Turns out, Vicky already knew I was pregnant.

"I figured if it was true, you would have told me. That's why I kept thinking it couldn't be. Then, the other day, I saw you in the shower. I wasn't spying or anything, but I had to go in there to get something and I could see part of you in the mirror, and I could tell."

"So, you knew?"

"Yeah."

I figured she'd ask me a million questions, but she didn't. She didn't ask me anything.

"I rented a place for work," she said. Her voice was flat. "It's just a small space in an industrial park, but I won't have to work out of my bedroom anymore. I'm a real business now. I have to move all my sewing stuff there by next weekend. It was going to be a surprise. I mean, I was going to surprise you because I talked to my mom and she said you could stay here, with me, if I paid her some, which I could do because I've been selling so much because you've been helping me. I was going to say you could move in here for a while, like for real. Because you're pregnant. I mean, once I realized, even though you didn't tell me. But I guess you don't need to now, because you've got Ms. Barden. Her name's Nancy, by the way. So I leased this place because my mom said it would be okay but only if I got all my sewing shit out of here. I guess I needed to anyway."

She went to her closet and came out with my red dress. It was wrapped in dry cleaner plastic. "Don't forget this." She tossed it on the bed.

"Don't you want to know anything about, like, who and stuff?" I asked.

"No. Not anymore I don't."

~ ~ ~

Song also knew. She was giving her sister a bath when I knocked on her door. She was surprised to see me and asked me to come back in an hour. When I came back, I went around the side of the house, like she asked. She was waiting for me on the back steps. It was cold and she had a blanket over her shoulders. She smiled when she saw me and held the blanket out, inviting me in. I settled in next to her.

"I know," she said.

"What?"

"That you pregnant."

"Fucking hell, everybody knows. How?"

"I went to bathroom at school and heard someone get sick. I could tell it you. I put together. I not know for sure, but you come here now, so I figure maybe that why."

"Everyone seems to know more than I thought."

"You keep it then?"

"Yes."

"What about college?"

"I don't know. I don't know much of anything, it seems. I guess it doesn't matter."

"I'm sorry you got raped."

"I hate that word."

"Yeah." She rocked forward and back a few times. "Can I say to you something?"

"Sure."

"I know we not really friends now."

"Sure we are."

"Okay. Just—I can't give no good advice much. But with this, yes. You have to call it rape. If you don't, you begin to think it something else. You lie to yourself, because it make it easier. But then you won't be able to—to, live with lie, even though it your own lie. It eat you. So you have to say it rape. Then you can get better."

"You can?"

"Not for long time. Not for long, long time. Not same. But better."

She started rocking again.

"How's your guy?" I asked her. "Are you still mad for him like you told me at the library?"

"Yeah, here him." She handed me a photograph she'd been holding like she was waiting for me to ask. I smiled when I saw it because he was short and kinda ugly. It was obvious she was gaga for him.

"He walk me home. He super smart."

"Of course he's smart, he likes you."

"He transfer here early this year."

"That's awesome, Song."

"He the only one for me."

~ ~ ~

I went to visit my dad. I brought Basil with me for support and drove to Teri's shit-colored stucco and terra cotta faux Mediterranean two-story home that I wanted to burn to the ground.

There was a new truck out front. He was in there, I knew. I really wanted to do everything Ms. Barden told me to do, but I couldn't seem to get out and walk up to the front door. Basil sat up and looked at the house with the same evil intent as me.

I was afraid. I didn't trust myself. I wasn't completely confident that I was fully in control anymore. I didn't want to hurt anyone. I had never thought of myself as someone that could hurt someone, but recent events had changed all that. I wasn't sure what I'd do if I saw my father in a sweater, smelling like hair gel. Or Teri, with her lazy eye that she always tried to turn away, like it was some horrible burden she had to endure. I was afraid I'd tear her face off.

Basil let out a low growl, as if he could smell familiar thoughts. "Okay, buddy," I said, scratching his neck. "We'll skip this one."

Chapter 10

T H O M A S

Tonight, I was going to sleep; I could feel it, like a divine promise held before me. I was sure of it.

But I didn't. Instead, it was the night I went mad.

"Dad, you said—remember?"

"Yes, I did, of course I remember. I just didn't realize I needed to dress up."

"It's a Halloween dance," Henry said. He was unusually shrill and looked stressed. "I don't think they even let you in without a costume."

"Great, I'm on it."

"So what are you going as?"

"I thought I was going as a parental volunteer, but I guess I'll need to come up with something else. What are you going as?"

"A circuit board. It sounds dumb but it's going to be really cool."

"That sounds very... expressive, and really cool."

I found all this confusing. I was deep into some experimental zone from lack of sleep. I had long lost count of the days. I remembered agreeing to volunteer for a school function. I believe it was part of my effort to coax Francis back. Or maybe I was trying to capitalize on my earlier momentum. I remembered the impulse, but little else.

Henry was disappointed in me, I could see that now, so either I'd either gained perceptive or he'd become more disappointed. Long gone were the days when my inattention was easily excused, or even justified.

I was doing so well there for a while. I'd been gaining his trust piecemeal. The illusive Justine had even been to the house recently, and I hadn't made any mistakes, at least that I was aware of. The three of us had a normal conversation. I took that as a sign we were all doing better. Her presence was like a barometer.

Maybe this was an exception. A brief, easily corrected relapse. I just needed sleep, I self-diagnosed—another thing doctors warn against.

"You're sure I'm supposed to dress up?" I asked. "It's not some joke, and I end up the only parent there in a costume?"

"It's required now, one adult for every twenty students. Because of last year, the thing with the goat. I volunteered you, because you said you wanted to, remember? For the hundredth frickin' time?"

"I know, I just—the costume thing is throwing me, but no sweat." I didn't understand why he'd want me there anyway. Who wants their parents at a school dance? Kids were supposed to be generationally more subversive, not less.

"And we're supposed to meet Justine there," he said. "Her mom's volunteering too."

"Justine's mom? Do I know her?"

"I need you to drive me because I can't drive in my costume. You said you wanted to do this."

"And I do, no problemo." I remembered now. Before he left, Stephen and Henry had been building something out of tubes and wires. I'd thought it was for the science fair.

I went to a costume shop and found the shelves empty, stripped of everything but princess outfits. The department store's costume aisle was decimated, like someone had gone through it with a leaf blower. Desperate, I called Stephen and asked if he was available for emergency assistance. He came over and turned me into an alien by creating an elaborate headpiece out of aluminum foil, and of course he was an expert with theatrical makeup.

Conroy stopped by, for the third time in a week. He was surprised when Stephen answered the door—immediately filled with false hope that he'd come back. I knew the feeling.

My sleepless nights had Conroy worried. During his last couple visits, he'd prodded me this way and that, trying to find the source. Of course, I couldn't tell him it was because imaginary Francis refused to talk to me anymore.

"How long since you've slept?" Conroy asked. He sat across the table and sipped wine as Stephen painted my eyes into big black orbs.

"Oh, I sleep."

"No, you don't. Stephen said he left you some herbs to take. They didn't help?"

"They would help if he took them," Stephen said.

"I'm not really the herbal type. Please, let's keep in mind I'm still a doctor. The real kind."

I heard clanging. Henry came in. He looked like a B-movie monster.

Conroy looked at him. "What in the world?"

"I'm a circuit board," Henry said from somewhere inside the contraption. A light snaked across his body. It was quite impressive. "But what if I have to pee?"

"Is that thing safe?" Conroy asked.

177

Henry had to bend to fit in the Jeep, and stay folded the entire drive. There'd been a debate about laying the seats flat and sliding him in like a coffin, but he proved too long. Now we were late.

As we drove, I kept looking at myself in the rearview mirror. I looked pretty good. Henry thought so too. Stephen's genius knew no bounds.

Henry's thin voice came out of a tube. "Shit, I'd have gone as an alien if I knew it would look that cool."

"No saying *shit*."

"Come on, dad."

"Just not around me. Let me pretend I'm good at this."

"Yeah, cool, pretend."

"What's Justine going as? You guys got something out of the studio for her costume, what was it?"

"I think she wants to surprise you, make you guess."

"How's it going with you guys?"

"You mean...?"

"Yeah, I mean are things getting serious again?"

"Again?"

I was going to run a light but thought better of it and stopped short, which threw Henry forward. Technically, I was driving without a license because of my numerous tickets. I used to get them for speeding, but I'd recently gotten one for reckless driving because I'd started to nod off and drifted across lanes on the freeway.

"*Fuuuck*, Dad! What're you doing?"

"Sorry. Don't you have your seatbelt on?"

"No. God, I'm practically pinned to the windshield here, how could I get a seatbelt on? That's why I said drive slow."

"I am, that's why I missed the light." The light turned and I crept up to speed. "So, things are good between you two?"

"Seriously?"

"What?"

"Dad, can I give you some parental advice?"

"Oh, please."

"Perhaps you could discern more opportune times to talk about these things. Like when you suddenly decided it was time to talk to me about sex while I was on the toilet."

"That was your mother's fault. I won a bet and she reneged, then—well, never mind, I see what you're saying."

"So maybe just not right now."

"Coolio, daddio."

I pulled into the parking lot and stopped as a witch and a cat-woman walked by. At first I thought there were four of them. Fatigue had caused my vision to blur, now it was doubling. They appeared to be wearing less than half a costume each. I'd forgotten how Halloween gave girls a one-day pass on propriety. I had to circle the lot twice to find a spot with enough room for Henry to unload himself.

It was already hot inside, and packed with youthful energy and unfamiliar music. A blob of pink puff approached us. From behind the blob appeared a tall version of Pippi Longstocking.

"Dad," Henry said. He referred to the pink blob. "Guess what Justine is."

"Don't tell me, let me guess. Okay—no, tell me."

"I'm bubblegum stuck to the bottom of a shoe," Justine said. I spotted her pink face poking out of the puffs like a detergent commercial. Then I saw the tennis shoe tied to the top of her head. Damn, kids are just awesome, even teenagers.

"Wow, Justine, that's very cleaver," I said, trying not to mess up. I turned to Pippi. "Now, you I can figure out."

"Doctor Ackerman, this is my mother, Margaret," Justine said.

"Hello," I said.

"Are you death?" Pippi asked me as she shook my hand.

"Am I what? Oh, no, I'm an alien."

Everyone wandered away from me. I seem to have missed something, or I'd slipped into one of my fatigue-induced time warps. Justine's mother went to the back of the auditorium. I figured that was where the other volunteer parents were. I followed her red pigtails. I thought this would be a good opportunity to find out more about Henry and Justine, if there was anything to find out. Henry was an enigma. Maybe girls talked to their moms more than sons talked to their dads about this kind of thing. I also needed something to keep me awake.

I found her leaning against the wall, watching the kids dance. I leaned next to her. "Looks like our kids have grown quite fond of each other," I said during a break in the music. "I think it's remarkable the way Justine—"

"I want your son to stay away from my daughter."

"Uh... what?"

"I want. Your son. To stay away from. My daughter."

"Is there something wrong with my son?"

"He picked her up on a motorcycle the other day."

"He—he what?"

My mind must have drifted. I think it was her voice. I recognized it, but couldn't place it. There was some association I had with it.

Time passed, I could tell, but I wasn't sure where it went. This had been happening more frequently. Both Justine and Henry were there again, as if teleported. Henry had only half his costume on and was sweaty, so I must have missed a lot. My life was like forever coming in late to a movie.

"You guys should dance," Justine said.

I didn't think I'd heard right. "Dad," Henry said, prompting me.

"Yeah? What?"

"You guys should *dance*," he said.

"Oh, well, sure." This didn't make any sense to me, but that was okay. If everyone was jumping off a cliff, I would too, as long as I knew that it was the consensus, and it was expected of me. I was at a place where the easiest way—really, the only way—was to follow the prompts of others. I just had to know what they were.

I looked at Pippi. I'd forgotten her name. "Lets do this," I said, trying for a playful tone and holding out my hand.

~ ~ ~

I stood in front of the bathroom mirror and looked at my big black eyes. I did look like death.

I still had my side, with my own sink. Hers had a dry water stain in the bowl. There were some boxes down at my feet where I'd put a few of her things. I'd pack something away, decide later to put it back, and obsess over where it was positioned. Boxing her things up was intended as a small step. Stephen had offered to help, but that would have reduced it to a chore. I couldn't just throw it all out, but it wasn't like I was going to store half a bottle of aspirin, a hairbrush, and some moisturizer, expecting to get some use out of them later. They needed to be thrown away, in with the dinner scraps and dead light bulbs. Things she pressed into her skin, pushed into a landfill. I thought maybe keeping things in boxes would be an easier first step. Nobody tells you how to do these things.

Her closet was something else. I made sure it was always closed. I couldn't smell her in there anymore, but I could trick myself into thinking I could. Her scent was like the evaporated water in the sink; it left a stain.

I was ready to sleep now. I had made it through the evening, and now everyone was home safe. It was a good day. Well done, and now I could sleep.

Henry was happy. When we got home, he was in a chatty mood. He took off his costume to the waist and gestured, half-naked as he moved about the kitchen, telling me about his friend who got kicked out because he dressed as Billy the Kid. Someone thought his guns were real and they don't take chances now and everyone had told him it was dumb to wear that costume because what did he think was going to happen?

My body twitched as I watched him. The twitches were the return of an earlier symptom, bigger now and harder to hide, like getting stuck with a cattle prod.

Henry ate all the time. He was at that age when they're never full. He pulled a plate from the refrigerator. Stephen had made him something before leaving, like he used to do, when he'd leave pre-portioned food in the refrigerator, toped with color-coded notes with heating instructions. Like his other uncanny abilities, Stephen always knew just what Henry would want. He'd come home from school or the library or wherever, open the refrigerator door and yell, *Awesome!* Stephen had found me less predictable, mostly because I tried to be, sometimes ignoring food I wanted just to maintain the appearance of complexity; always ready to feed my vanity first.

Henry plucked the note off and read it as he talked. He put the dish in the microwave and poked buttons with his back to me while he made his point with his other hand.

He was so beautiful; skinny and pale and vulnerable, with his bony arms, visible ribs, and knobs up his spine. It was hard to look at him without remembering when he was a boy. Francis was always there. I had few memories of him without her. She was the context for everything. I searched until I found one as I watched him in pantomime. He was three. I came home from work and got down on my knees. Henry did a jump-hug into my arms. I hugged him so hard he began to cry. It was the first time I'd left a dead child on the operating table.

Henry was still talking, now through mouthfuls of food, eating so fast he didn't bother to sit down. I listened, but his words slid around, too fast, then elongated. Sleep surrounded me in a creeping cloud. I looked forward to it, like a drug I'd sacrificed everything for.

~ ~ ~

Stephen had told me how to take the makeup off, but I couldn't remember. I was supposed to use a bottle of something. I started with soap and a washcloth and soon ruined two towels. I gave up and examined my face in the mirror. I looked like a melting goth rocker.

I went out to the hall and looked over the railing to make sure Henry had turned out the kitchen light. I wanted no loose ends. There was a stripe of light under his bedroom door. I could hear him talking on the phone with Justine, his voice bright as morning.

I went back to my bedroom.

I was so tired my breathing had gone shallow, like someone close to death. I pulled back the covers. When had I last slept? Really slept? I'd played this game before as the days added up, at first fascinated, then horrified. I ran a few mental tests, my analytical side the last to wink out. I couldn't add numbers. I wasn't sure of my age.

I turned off the lamp, stretched into the middle of the bed, and embraced the pillow.

Francis, I don't need you. Not now I don't. Not now.

I thought of the woman at the mall. I could do that. Her mouth, her breath, and her hand at the back of my head; the feeling of an eager, strong body, full of need and response. Delicate hands. To receive as a man. I'm a man. I'm a whole man.

I had forgotten sleep. How to do it.

You just let go. You just allow it, and there it is. It's not something you do, it's something you don't do.

I smelled Francis.

No.

It's a memory, my shadow self informed me; finally useful. He consulted his notes. Or you're confused because of what you were just thinking about. You can't even tell the difference now. Your brain is tricking you. I'm surprised there hasn't been more of this.

No, it was there. I smelled Francis. Whether I breathed or not, it was there, and I could feel it.

But you don't feel a smell.

I could hear my own labored breathing.

Please let me go, for the love of God.

Her perfume. That's it. That's all it is. It's in the bathroom. That's what happened—you just left the door open. You must have sprayed some. You've done it before.

I couldn't remember doing that.

Another gap, like sliding sideways. I couldn't tell if I slept, or was sleeping now. The smell was like something at the back of my throat.

I waited for the world to start again. I couldn't do any more.

I felt something corporal. My mind cleared, an ancient instinct that trumps fatigue. Light leaked under the bathroom door. My eyes had adjusted. I watched the bed slowly depress as she sat on it. There was nothing else to see. I felt the gentle tip of the bed from her weight. I waited, making sure, testing the corners of my mind.

I reached my hand toward the scoop.

Cold. Cold crept over me. Not an imaginary cold, but like a winter roof had come off. I felt pressure, like I was being pushed into myself and condensed into something. It continued until I couldn't breathe.

I clamped my eyes shut. I rolled to the opposite side of the bed, and rolled again until I hit the floor in a wad of bedding. I stood and disentangled, ready for a fight. Then I wept, and as I did, I remembered weeping, until I was back down among the bedding.

I crawled into the bathroom. Reaching up like a blind man, I took her perfume off the counter. Standing, avoiding my reflection, I went to her closet. Hanging there was her shirt, the one she always worked in, the real prize. I yanked it off the hanger and smothered myself in it. I sucked her in and consumed what was left. She lived there still, hidden in the fabric, sidestepping death, as if she'd been left in the waiting room.

I've been waiting for you to catch up with me. Is this how it's always going to be?

I felt it all. Even her death. I felt her tumor; wet, heavy and ignorant. I felt her sweat and heard her sounds and felt Henry's birth between my legs.

Mother of my child.

I made my way back to the bed and sat on the edge. I cradled her perfume, nestled in her shirt, and looked at myself in the full-length mirror on the wall. I sprayed, hazing the air with her. She would do this, then step into it, shaking her hair like she did after car sex. The light from the closet lit the mist in shimmering sparkles. I walked into it, closer to the mirror. My eyes were like smudgy black holes on a pale plate.

I found myself sitting again. I sprayed, stood, and stepped forward, even closer. My breath billowed off the mirror. Black orbs appeared in the clearing, with me at the center, ready to witness.

Are you death?

I did it again, coming through the sprayed mist and meeting the mirror.

I saw it.

So, it comes from the inside. While we keep a watchful eye, it sets up house in a cool place of smooth surfaces, let loose by the line, drawn by the scalpel.

Something hit me. Zooming. It was me, or something close, in the mirror.

I backed up, sprayed, ran. Again. Harder. Her shirt. My love. My love, wet in my arms.

Chapter 11

M A R G A R E T

On August 1, 1996, I gave birth to a baby girl I named Justine, and the whole landscape of my life shifted.

She was small, just five and a half pounds, but healthy. They put her on my chest, exhausted and messy, and I watched as she valiantly fought, with eyes closed, to scoot the few inches to my breast and suckle.

I was blindsided by love—just crushed by it—and from the moment I felt the weight of her little body on me, I felt the strength of a thousand suns.

Ms. Barden—Nancy—was there the whole time. A week before I was due, she told me to pack a bag, we were going for a drive; a long one. I put a change of clothes and a few other things in my backpack. She came in, hauling a suitcase. "You're going to need more than that."

She closed the shop for a week and had a neighbor take care of Basil.

We drove all day and through most of the night. We talked a lot on the way. I told her I didn't want to be a mathematician, and that my dream had been to go to college and then law school, preferably somewhere sunny and warm, and as far away from Wisconsin as possible.

We went south, to a place called The Farm, all the way in Tennessee. It was kind of a hippy commune with a natural birthing center. It didn't seem like the kind of place Nancy would go for, with her *no elbows on the table,* and *a lady does not raise her voice* ways.

"Hospitals were invented by men as a way to control women. That's why men hate hospitals. Being a patient in one, that is. They know. They only like it from the other side. That's why they always want to wait out in the hall. We're going to a place where giving birth is actually considered normal and doesn't require a team of men to muck it up."

Nancy didn't have children of her own. Her husband left her years ago. She was pregnant once, in her late thirties, but she miscarried. Her husband was gone shortly after. The girl in the dress shop was her niece. Nancy's sister had asked her to let the girl work there to try to instill a work ethic in her. "A lazy, vapid girl with no discernible life skills, which seems pretty common these days," was how Nancy described her. "Let's see if you can avoid that fate."

The strength I felt when I first had Justine dissipated over the first year, worn down by the reality of living a cliché: teenage mom high school dropout. Nobody cares how you got there.

I eventually managed to secure my independence and provide Justine with a healthy environment. A year and a half after she was born, I had graduated high school and was living in a studio apartment outside of Madison.

I was going to a community college and working as a math tutor for students taking summer classes at the university. That started when a girl, who was about six and a half feet tall, approached me at the university library, where I often went, using a student ID card that I'd found on the ground. I'd already gone through all the math books at the community college and the university library had books on math theory that I never even knew existed. The girl was on the basketball team and was about to lose her scholarship because she was failing math. She saw the books I was reading and said she'd pay me to help her. I ended up doing most of her assignments, which I would have had an ethical problem with, except I really needed the money.

She paid me a lot. She told some friends, and before long I had a number of athletes paying me to "tutor" them. Not just math, but other subjects as well. It was shocking how poor their academic skills were. Some lacked even the basics. A third-year football player tried to read something aloud and I made the mistake of thinking he was kidding.

I was making enough to have a sitter for Justine while I went to classes or tutored, but I wasn't getting anywhere. I had become one of those people I used to pity.

Vicky had taken a class in textile design at the Art Institute in Milwaukee. They ended up hiring her to teach. She also had three seamstresses working for her, and dresses in about a dozen shops. She bought an Audi for her frequent drives between Madison and Milwaukee.

I saw Nancy about once a month. She would sometimes take Justine for the day, but I maintained my independence, which she respected. I kept in touch with Song, but seldom saw her. She was all but physically attached to Vonni, the boy she'd fallen for. She finished high school, but said she didn't even want to go to college anymore. Vonni started a tech company with some friends, and all Song wanted was to be with him. I thought that giving up her future for a guy was a mistake, but it wasn't my place to say. My life hardly served as a shining example.

My world was very small. All I really cared about was Justine. I felt disconnected from everybody else, even other moms, who would strike up easy conversations with me at the park or grocery store, telling me about their husbands' shortcomings, I guess out of pity after a glance at my hand told them I wasn't married.

I had no interest in dating. Some of the male athletes I tutored would hit on me in a lazy way, but they had easier targets. College guys don't try that hard after seeing a toddler.

I had the vague but constant awareness of something I wasn't eager to face; I was twenty years old and I'd never been touched by a man in a truly intimate way. That part of my life was cut short before it started. The more time went by, the more my body seemed to want something I wasn't going to give it.

I bought a treadmill. The only place for it in our small apartment was the middle of the living room. I would run while Justine napped. It helped relieve some of my restless energy. I made rapid progress, sometimes going nonstop for more than an hour.

I could never lose the feeling I'd had since the rape. The rape, the rape, the rape. It was a feeling that the world was skewed in a way I didn't understand. I couldn't see where my place in it was anymore. There was no longer any border on things. It was like the whole world was diffused in some way.

I'd rediscovered math. I found comfort in its rules and structure. I'd always taken my math skills for granted and felt safe in the certainty that it would be my ticket to the future, but I'd never loved it. Now, without expectations, I began digging deeper, and found a new appreciation for it. It was like a faithful lover that had patiently waited for me to come back. After putting Justine down for the night, I'd spend hours working on contained structures. I'd create perfect patterns by combining fusion systems with algorithms and multi-variables, then work them to find and refine predictive behaviors.

I stopped taking classes at the community college and just focused on math. When I developed a perfect system, it felt like I'd created something beautiful. Like when I sewed the red dress. It felt complete.

A student I tutored called me one day to tell me he couldn't use me anymore.

"Why not?"

"My teacher found out I wasn't doing my own work."

"Oh, shit. How?"

"You left some pages of notes in with my stuff. I didn't know it and turned it all in. She gave it to someone. They want to see you."

When I did a student's assignment, I always insisted they transcribe it, so it would be in their own writing. While they were busy with that, I'd do my own work. Most of my work consisted of pages of formulas, sometimes with notes on theorems and proofs that I was working through.

"Do they know I'm not even a student there?"

"Yeah, she knows, I told her."

"Are you going to lose your scholarship?"

"I don't have no scholarship, I'm just a shitty student."

"Are you going to be suspended?"

"Shit no, my dad's a big-ass donor and I'm fuckin' first team, man. Suspended, that's funny."

I didn't see any point in going to see whoever it was that had my notes, so I forgot about it. A week later, the university called and told me I had an appointment, and that it would be in my interest if I went. I guess the student gave them my number. I wasn't sure what to make of it. I figured they probably just wanted to know who else I'd been helping.

I wondered if what I'd been doing was actually illegal. I worried I'd get a knock on the door some day. I decided to go. I couldn't get a sitter so I brought Justine with me.

It wasn't what I expected. I sat across the desk from a severe looking woman with a pinched face and frizzy hair. A man stood behind her. He looked straight ahead like he thought he was invisible. His glasses were so big it was like they were meant to be funny.

The woman had my pages of equations in front of her. She floated one across the desk to me.

"Did you really do this work?"

"Yes."

Justine lunged for the paper. She was at the age where she assumed everything was the start of a game. She grabbed the page in a balled fist and started swatting her knee with it. She giggled so hard she farted; one of those that are so loud it's hard to believe it came from such a small body. Glasses man was impervious. The woman gave a pained smile, like her shoes hurt.

"What do you say?" I prompted Justine.

"Scoosee."

"Our student tells me you graduated high school, but you do not go to college," the woman said.

"Right, I don't. I had a scholarship. To here, actually, but I lost it."

Pinch face looked at Justine. It was clear what she was thinking.

"We'd like to give you an aptitude test, if you're interested," glasses man said. He spoke to the air above my head, like there was someone behind me.

"What for?"

"To see if you qualify," he said.

"Qualify for what?" I was starting to think this was all some kind of mix-up. "Why am I here again?"

"The test is individualized, to determine your real level," the woman said. "From what we've seen"—she indicated the page of equations, which Justine was chewing on—"Madison may not be the best place for you. Doctor Jakobi chairs the Department of Physics at the California Institute of Technology in Pasadena, California. He thinks there might be a place for you there."

It still seemed like there was a misunderstanding. "You probably still have my application from before," I said. "It's got all my test scores and everything."

The woman held up a file folder with my name on it. "We know. We've been reviewing it."

"Oh."

"Would you consider relocating?" the man asked. He was finally looking at me. "If you qualify, we have an exclusive, privately funded scholarship that is available to a limited number of applicants."

~ ~ ~

Doctor Jakobi, the guy with the huge glasses, turned out to be pretty nice. He had a goofy laugh that sounded like a barking seal. He called me a couple weeks later to tell me I'd been approved for the scholarship.

I found out there are anonymous, private donors, usually alumni, who fund scholarships in specific fields. When they find the right candidate, things move fast. He told me they often don't find someone qualified and the scholarship goes unused. If I was ready, he said I could start the winter quarter at Caltech in January.

It felt surreal. I suddenly had what I'd always wanted, but my reaction was strangely muted. I was not as enamored with college life as I had once been. Much of the shine had come off. I'd seen enough from tutoring and community college classes to realize that not everybody in college was so smart and clever, or even grown up. Many of the students acted like they were still in high school.

I also didn't want to lie anymore. I didn't want to deceive anyone. I thought about it for a day, then called Doctor Jakobi and told him I wanted the scholarship, but my goal was to be a lawyer. I didn't want to accept the scholarship under false pretenses. He listened, then explained there was an advanced dual major in mathematics and applied science that focused on the application of math to other fields, such as medicine or law. It would satisfy the scholarship requirements and would be great preparation for law school.

I was so relieved after I hung up the phone that I let out a yell, which was so unexpected it caused Basil to bark, which frightened Justine and made her cry. I picked her up and squeezed her. I kissed the soft hair behind her ear and made goofy munching sounds until she giggled, saying, "More, more."

I'd forgotten what it was like to be happy.

I wanted to go out and do something fun. It was a hot, humid day, and the apartment's tiny air conditioning unit couldn't keep up. There was a nearby trail that threaded through a park where I liked to push Justine in the stroller and let Basil chase squirrels, but it was too hot for that. I decided on the mall.

~ ~ ~

Justine loved to look in the store windows. We stopped in front of a clothing store. The haughty mannequins in their akimbo poses made me think of Vicky. You don't realize how big a deal it is to always have someone to talk to, until you don't; especially when something good happens.

I didn't have any friends in Madison. I went to Buy the Cup once, during a weak moment, to look for Simon. I asked the woman behind the counter if he still worked there. She eyed Justine in the stroller with concern. "Simon? Oh, no. He left for college more than a year ago. New York, I think."

I pushed Justine through the food court. Six months after her first "momma," she was paring words into short sentences, usually in the form of a question. She twisted around in her stroller. "Puffa pezsel?"

"You want a puffy pretzel? Let's play first."

I parked the stroller in the kids' play section, where there was a padded romper area and an old style carousel. Justine pointed to the carousel and her favorite horse, a garish pink pony with its mouth in a frozen snarl. I always wondered why they made the carousel horses look so menacing.

I bought a token. When it was our turn, I strapped her on and stood next to her with my hand on her back. The ride started with a jerk. The horse slid up and down, forever coming up for air. After the first go-around, Justine pushed my hand away. "I do," she said.

After the carousel, I sat on a bench and watched her play. She found a smaller boy to play with and was showing off. He watched her climb the turtle and stake claim with a roar. I got distracted by the carousel and watched it spin. The horse's expressions of horror and glee shifted, depending on the angle. My math brain tugged at me. I began determining velocity and rotation ratio relative to circumference, then calculated the exact moment when the brown horse would come around and where on the ascent or decent it would be. An invisible rider pulled the horse's head back. Its front legs pawed the air like it was ready to fight.

I let my mind go. The horse came around again, eyes bulging and head twisted back. I felt a tug in my spine. On the next rotation, I was looking at the horse when there was a loud, piercing sound.

I looked at the play area. A girl was fighting with her sister; both wanted the same bouncy ball. The smaller one lost. She was letting out one impossibly long scream. She breathed in, finally, and let out another as the horse came around the circle again and drifted to a stop. The girl's mother lurched over and scooped the toddler up. The screaming stopped.

The horse looked above me. It seemed ready to take a few gallops and leap over my head. A foul taste flooded my mouth. I looked over my shoulder.

Behind me was a large window display for a seasonal store, the kind that changes based on whatever holiday is next. Halloween was coming up, so the display was filled with costumes.

Gazing down, as if for me alone, was the head of a wolf. It was from a movie that was currently popular. It had exaggerated yellow eyes and a red tongue hanging over its teeth.

The child screamed again as her mother hauled her off. My mouth coated with a bitter film.

As I stared at the wolf's head, a flash came. It had been a long time since I'd had one. Months. But I was right back there, trapped in the stall with him.

But this time was different. The gap—the part I couldn't remember before—came with clarity. Everything did.

The twisting, the bending and the breaking.

And his staccato voice. "You're crazy too, just like your mom. You going to blow your brains out too? Blow your fucking brains out?"

I don't know how long I was in a trance. I felt a small hand on me. I turned to find Justine standing in front of me. "Momma tersty." I gave her some juice and a snack.

She sat next to me and watched the other kids play as she munched goldfish crackers.

I turned and looked again. Next to the wolf was an alien with snakes growing out of its head. Next to that was a hockey mask and a large rubber knife.

"Come on," I said to Justine. "We have to go, sweetie. I have to stop in this store."

"Momma store?"

We went in and I bought the wolf's head.

~ ~ ~

I left Justine with Nancy for the night. It was ten o'clock in the evening when I pulled off the 94 onto Highway 73.

Teri's house was in the only planned development Camden had, back when they thought the city might actually have a future. My dad's truck was parked at the curb. Her SUV got the driveway. I drove past when I saw a flickering light on through the window. I parked a block up and walked to the house.

I knocked. No answer. I didn't hear any movement inside. I tried the door. Locked. I went around the side. I knew they didn't have a dog. Teri hated them. She was a cat person. The side gate was locked too, so I put a foot up and hoisted myself over.

I walked around to the back. The patio had cheap plastic furniture with faux textures, meant to simulate anything not plastic. Sad-looking Tiki lamps—fake versions of something fake to begin with—were propped along the back wall. A sliding glass door led to the dining room. I tried it. It slid along the tracks.

I had been on autopilot for the last week, ever since the mall, as if a spell had been put on me; guided by somnolent nudges. I slipped inside, stood still, and listened. I could hear a television on, down the hall, coming from the living room.

Even in the low light I could tell the kitchen was pristine and magazine perfect, painted in carefree yellow and pale blue, as if they expected a baby boy to be birthed there.

I went to the hall and slid along the wall toward the living room. There were pictures on the wall opposite. Family photos. A wedding. My dad in a tuxedo.

The living room opened off the hall. The TV was facing me. It was the only light in the room. There was an overstuffed easy chair in front of the TV. I could see my dad's feet propped on an ottoman. He still wore the same slippers. One of those cop shows was on, the kind where everyone wears an overcoat and there's always a dead prostitute.

I stepped into the living room.

"Dad," I said. He didn't move. I came all the way around. He was passed out, his head tilted back, mouth agape. I didn't recognize him for a moment. Cavernous and wasted away, he looked ten years older. I could smell the whisky. A highball glass sat on the small table next to the chair.

I backed up and sat on the couch. I studied him. I wanted to feel something, but he was just another stranger anesthetizing himself, as programmed as the TV show.

I looked around the room. There was a picture on the opposite wall. I couldn't tell what the image was, but I could see my reflection, sitting on the couch, in the shifts of TV light. Something was above my head. I looked up and saw the bottom of the buck's neck.

I started to weep, and progressed to great sobs. I tried to be quiet but I couldn't contain it. I was helped by the TV, where someone was being gunned down in typical TV fashion, with as many bullets as possible.

A voice called from another room, "Jordan?" The hall light went on. I put a hand over my mouth.

"Jor-*daaan.*"

A car insurance commercial came on. Teri appeared. She started toward the easy chair but stopped for a moment to watch the commercial.

"Jordan," she said. She went to the chair and pushed his shoulder.

"Ahhh." His head rolled like his neck was rubber. "Whada."

"Come on." She pointed the remote at the TV. Another commercial made her pause. My dad rolled back to his original spot. She turned off the TV and the room went dark except for the light that spilled in from the hallway. The tinny sound of the commercial continued down the hall.

She sighed. "Come on." She straddled the chair and threaded her arms through his armpits. He tipped into her.

"Lemme stay," he said. She braced her legs and hauled him up in a well-practiced move. He found his feet enough to stand and lean on her. They were like two tired dancers. She began a slow drag toward the hallway.

I often wondered what Teri saw in my dad, but now it made sense. She would get his military pension and life insurance when he died. He was a commodity, not a husband. From the look of him, she was doing a fine job with her investment.

They made it to the hallway. "Stop it now, you just— lemme alone," he slurred and disengaged himself. Using the wall for support, he slid toward the bedroom, his dignity reduced to this small assertion of self-sufficiency. I understood why they only had pictures on one side. "Well, hurry up, then," she snapped. "Show's about to start again."

I knew Teri had started seeing my dad before my mom shot herself. The week my mom came home from the hospital, she fought with him all day and night. I was too young to understand. Now I remembered, and the memory was like a wet hand creeping up my back. I'd heard Teri's name in the shouting. Maybe my mom shot herself when she found out about her. Her method of self-disposal was certainly different from her previous attempts. Perhaps that final indignity was just too much to bear. Maybe it didn't have anything to do with me.

The hall light went out. Their bedroom door closed.

My skin puckered as my tears dried. I stood and turned—looked at the buck. There was a reflection in his glossy eyes. They'd found a light source that wasn't there. He was having the final say. Again.

His eyes followed me out the front door.

~ ~ ~

I bought a used gun. The guy I bought it from wanted to take me out in the woods and show me how to use it. "In a safe environment." He assumed I didn't know which end of a gun was which. It was an older .270 Winchester. I would have liked something that took a higher caliber cartridge for more range, but I'd have to make do. I didn't want to wait. He gave me a few rounds.

"Be careful, darlin', always carry your ammo and gun separate." Thanks, sport.

I drove about a mile, went in the woods, and tested it. It was loud and kicked hard, but had a decent trajectory and the scope was clear.

I called Nancy and asked if she could keep Justine and take Basil for a few days. "Of course, love, I'd be delighted. Is everything alright?"

"Yes. I want to go see my mother. Maybe stay a couple days. She's not well." Lying could be like an old, comfortable pair of jeans.

"Oh, that's wonderful. I mean that you're going, of course. I hope she gets better. You so seldom mention her."

That night, I drove to Milwaukee. I tucked my hair into a baseball cap and went to Walmart, where I bought extra ammunition, tools, and some other supplies. I paid in cash. I got a cheap hotel, using a different name. I parked my truck where nobody at the hotel could see it.

Early the next morning, while it was still dark, I drove to Camden. I skirted the outside of the city. Some people in town knew my truck, or knew it when it was my dad's.

I'd found out where Dwayne lived by calling my old high school and saying I was a field officer with the Parole Board and needed to verify his last address for an arrest summons. The woman on the other end hesitated, asking: "Who are you again?" I had recorded some sounds off the hotel TV that were like the background of a noisy police station. I turned it up and told her my made-up name again, like she was really trying my patience. She gave me the address. I'd seen it done on *Law and Order*.

It was just starting to get light when I pulled off the road and drove into the woods. I parked where the truck couldn't be spotted. I took the field glasses and some supplies and hiked in about a mile. It was difficult to find a spot that fit my requirements; some degree of coverage and a clear sightline to his front door. I hiked the full circumference of his house. I went all the way around and back to where I'd started. The only clear area I could find was too far away. If I got closer, it was all open space.

The house was semi-secluded, like most in the area, but faced a neighbor across the way. I couldn't get a frontal location as it would put me behind the house directly across. Distance was one problem, but so was angle. I eventually settled on a spot farther away, with the deciding factor being that it was closer to the road for a faster escape if I needed it.

It would be long shot.

It was seven-thirty am. I set myself as comfortably as possible and trained the field glasses on the door. Every ten minutes I put the glasses down and looked at something else so my eyes wouldn't become fixed. I wore layers instead of a heavy coat, for better mobility, but I was starting to shiver, which made it harder to see.

After two hours, the front door opened. It looked like his father. I saw him once in a hardware store when Vicky pointed him out, saying; "Hey, there's freak show senior."

I watched him as he came down the porch steps and got into an old gray van. Smoke billowed out the exhaust. Because of my distance, there was a delay before I heard the faint sound of the engine.

It was nearly eleven when the door opened again and Dwayne stepped out. He turned and locked the door behind him. I mentally tracked his every move, my brain burning with calculations. He came down the porch steps in a lazy meander as he zipped his jacket. I studied him to make certain it was him and not a brother or someone else I wasn't aware of. He walked down the driveway to a dark blue pickup truck. He got in and started the engine, but left the door open. He propped a foot on the running board and lit a cigarette. About a minute later, he closed the truck door and drove off.

I checked my watch, put on gloves, and hiked down the incline toward the house. I did a rough distance estimate. I was out in the open, but my clothes blended into the surrounding environment. Anybody that saw me would never be able to identify me. It was late October. No snow on the ground, so I wasn't tracking.

When I got about eighty yards from the house, I stuck a small white flag in the ground. I estimated the overall distance at about two hundred and fifty yards. I went back up and flagged my set spot, then packed up and hiked back to the truck. I backed the truck out and used a rake to cover the tire tracks.

That night I bought a newspaper and sat in my hotel room. I studied the weather map. It had an illustration that diagramed the weather patterns with swirling arrows. It was essentially useless but it gave my brain something to work on. I didn't want to put pen to paper. I drew my calculations in the air, combining environmental factors with distance, trajectory, and velocity. I was in bed by eight o'clock.

I was up at four. I spent a long time getting ready. I smeared field dress paint over my face and put on heavy boots—not good for hiking, but I liked their stability and I wasn't sure what position I'd be taking. I put everything in the truck and went back to the room with a rag I'd brought from home and wiped down anything I'd touched. I didn't use the shower or anything else that wasn't necessary. I dropped the room key through a slot in the office door after wiping it down.

I drove to a park. I stayed in the truck and ate food I'd brought in a cooler and read a book on constitutional law. I read until eight-thirty, then used the park bathroom and drove out.

I parked in the same spot. I gathered the gun, tarp, field glasses, and backpack, and hiked to the spot. It was just after ten o'clock.

The angle between the house and myself was about a two-degree downslope. It leveled out for the last hundred yards or so. An erratic wind pulled the flag near the house in different directions. I'd already determined the wind would angle west off the downgrade. I moved the flag near me to an exposed area so I could assess the difference in wind direction.

I found firm ground for the tripod mount and got everything set. I checked and rechecked the gun chamber and safety. I studied the flags, counted the wind pulses, and tried to find an average duration and interval.

I was ready. I sat with the field glasses and waited.

At ten forty-five, I positioned myself at the gun and began a series of deep breaths. At five to eleven, I switched from the field glasses to the scope. I locked it on the front door. I could see the near flag, but the one closer to the house was too difficult to see through the scope. I chose instead to stay set on my target.

My senses pulled everything in. The damp vegetation had the pungent, compost smell common to the Wisconsin woods when summer gives way to fall. A cool breeze pushed the side of my face.

I expected nerves to kick in, or adrenaline. Nothing. From my distance, it was easy to believe that what I was doing couldn't penetrate the real world.

An owl hooted a warning in the distance, like out of one of the books I read to Justine.

At two minutes after eleven, the front door opened and Dwayne stepped out. He was wearing the same jacket as the day before. I flipped the safety off. My finger found the taught resistance of the trigger.

He turned to lock the door. The flag in my periphery snapped and pointed sideways. He turned back and came halfway down the porch steps and stopped. Some twigs cracked as a strong gust reached the trees. I had to wait. My center scope was over his head and left by a whole degree.

Trust your calculations.

He remained on the steps. His jacket zipper was stuck. He pulled at it.

The flag remained pointed, stiff in the wind. I stayed trained on him.

He tugged.

The flag dropped.

In through the nose.

I took in a deep breath.

He got the zipper up.

Out through the mouth.

I tracked him as he came off the steps.

Three. Two.

He came down the driveway.

One.

I pulled.

The crack made the birds take to the sky en masse, causing a shadow to move over me.

I lost him in the scope. I looked over the gun and saw the far-off smudge of his jacket.

I grabbed the field glasses and trained them on him. He was still standing, and seemed to be looking at me, like he knew exactly where I was—like on the playground at school that time. His figure was stiff, as if held up by a string. I could see the O shape of his open mouth.

He tipped backwards, like the wind had blown him over.

I stayed trained on him. His head was pointed away from me. All I could see was a small pile of color from the billow of his jacket as it fluttered with the breeze.

Minutes passed. Birds returned to their branches and picked up their conversations. Something moved. It looked like his leg. I scanned the area. Someone might have heard the shot, but that wasn't unusual in this area. It would be impossible to tell where it came from.

I grabbed my backpack and took off. I hiked around the perimeter, following the circular path I'd taken the day before, until I was positioned behind his house.

I came out of the woods and down the slope. I held the gun over my shoulder and moved as fast as I could toward the back of his house. When I got there, I rested against the sidewall of his garage. I looked around the corner and could see his blue truck, but not him.

I took off my cap and dug in my backpack. I took out the wolf's head and pulled it over my head. I had to make some adjustments so I could see out of the eyeholes.

I came out from behind the garage, walked around his truck, and approached his body. He lay on his back at the edge of the driveway, looking up at the sky.

His left leg was moving. He was dragging it in an arc on the pavement. When he heard me coming, he stopped. I walked around to his sightline.

His green jacket was dark with blood. The bullet had put a sizable hole in him, on the right side of his chest. In the boiler room. It was like a hand had reached down and scooped out part of his body, from front to back. As I got closer, his eyes got bigger. I leaned over him. My breath steam pulsed out of the wolf's mouth.

He kicked his leg and tried to push himself backward, but couldn't get any traction. I let the gun hang at my side. He opened his mouth and tried to speak, but coughed out a dark spurt of blood instead.

He moved his head side to side and let out a moan that went from low to high. Blood pumped into the hole in his chest. A dark, creeping pool formed on the driveway and spilled off into the dirt.

I positioned my right boot over his face and lowered it until it connected. He stopped trying to move his head as I pressed. He made a muffled cry and coughed more blood. I could feel the gush of it through my boot. I pressed down harder. He let out a high-pitched whine. Unable to breathe, his whine morphed into a mouthless scream that vibrated up my leg.

I bent my knee and pushed my weight up with my other foot. I stiffened my right leg and pushed my boot into his face with all my strength. I felt a hard pop as my boot heel dropped and his face collapsed.

Part 2

The Blind Girl

Chapter 12

Henry wasn't there because he liked school, though he did. Not that he'd tell anyone that. He was there because his mom died three months ago and he desperately needed a distraction.

The summer had crawled on and on, like the movie villain that wouldn't die. He just wanted it to be over. The start of school was a line, an event horizon that held the hope of something different—a place to go, something else to think about, a way to keep his thoughts from constantly turning in.

But the start of school was still a month away. In the meantime, there was this class he'd signed up for: *Junior Prep, designed for the motivated student to make the most of his or her upcoming scholastic challenges.*

They offered Junior Prep and Senior Prep—taught by actual college professors—held for three consecutive weekends at the end of summer. You didn't have to take the classes, so hardly anyone did. It was the bright idea of someone on the school board; part of a "solutions" package to improve student performance and test scores, thereby boosting college acceptance rates and the school's academic standing. It wasn't so much a plan for actual improvement as it was a plan to impress those in control of school budgets.

The program started with a big push and filled up the first year. School administrators flew down from Sacramento to witness kids so eager to learn they'd rather be in a classroom than at the beach. Neighboring school districts adopted the plan. There was talk of further expansion.

Instead of expanding, the program was scaled back the following year—once it was clarified that students could not include the class on college applications; it was considered a scholastic add-on, as worthless as community service. By the third year, the program was less than half its original size, and nobody on the board could remember whose idea it originally was. Now in its fourth year, it was more or less ignored altogether. The program's ten-year mandatory budget was the only thing preventing its quiet demise.

The students who showed up were mostly science and math misfits, anxious for the school year to start so they could get back to their clubs—French, anime, film—which often comprised their only offline social circle. The board acknowledged the program just enough to combine students from Santa Monica and Pacific Palisades into one class, likely to prevent the ultimate embarrassment of having the classes turn up empty before the ten years ran out.

This year, the classes were held at a nearby community college while Santa Monica High underwent construction to accommodate the ever expanding demands of earthquake retrofitting. Just walking onto a college campus and having somewhere to go made Henry feel important, even if it was just a community college. It seemed so adult. No blingy signs made of butcher paper announcing school events. He even saw people smoking, out in the open.

He was early so he sat outside on the cement edge of a planter. It was one of those hot days where everyone wore shorts and flip flops. Henry never wore shorts. He was convinced he had the world's ugliest legs, white and knobby like an old man's. He'd even stopped playing basketball because of it.

He watched a few students trickle in. All girls, so far. Great. It'd be like the pottery class he took the previous summer where he was the only guy and didn't even realize it until the teacher said, *hello ladies—and you, young man.*

A girl walked up and turned a slow circle.

"Lost?" he asked her.

She faced him. "What? No." She had on large glasses and a backpack. He wondered what she'd brought to the first day of a class that didn't require books.

"You're not here for Junior Prep?" he asked.

"No. I mean, yes, I am."

"It's in there."

"How do you know?"

"Because I can read a map."

"Oh, hey, that's funny, because I thought maybe you were the janitor or something, and that's how you knew where everything was." She turned away. He watched her walk past the classroom door and keep going.

A few minutes later he went in. He took a seat near the back; not the last row, but next to last. Henry had a theory that good students didn't actually sit at the front, as was commonly believed. The ones that sat up front had been told it's what good students were supposed to do, so they were the type that were eager to please, which meant they were anxious to begin with and only compounded the problem by feeling all those eyeballs on the back of their head.

So far, there were six other students in class, all looking around in hopes of seeing a familiar face. Henry was hoping for the opposite. He didn't want anything to interfere with his college daydream.

The students distributed themselves evenly, like elevator occupants. There was one other guy, who must have arrived early. He looked too old to be there and wore a cowboy hat. He didn't even look like a student, and probably wasn't, judging by the way he was eyeing the girls. You gotta be pretty desperate to poach this crowd, Henry thought.

He was disappointed to recognize the teacher when she walked in. Apparently, the school board had accepted total defeat and given up hiring actual college professors. He'd had this one for geography the previous year and remembered her as the frazzled type that wore barely appropriate clothes that looked borrowed from her teen daughter. Confused was her default state, which may have been cute when she was twenty and it was still optional. She started by mixing up where the front of the class was. She went to what she thought was the front and tried to push a desk out of the way. Puzzled, she looked up. "Why are you all facing the wrong direction?" she asked the air. "Are you havin' fun with me?" she added with a flirt, like a tick that came out when she was annoyed. Her eyes landed on cowboy-hat guy.

"Will you move this for me?" she asked him.

It was beginning to feel a whole lot less like college.

The girl Henry had seen outside came in. She stood in the doorway. Now Henry saw her white cane. Maybe she didn't have it out before. He replayed their conversation from outside. *Fuck.* She got around pretty good for a blind person; a lot of people probably didn't notice right away. She started toward a desk but stopped.

"Now, wait just a minute," the teacher said, like she'd been tricked. "I'm in the wrong spot, aren't I? In my normal class, see, the door is on the other side, so I just—oh, never mind." She moved to the front. "You put that desk back, now," she reprimanded cowboy-hat. "Yes, this is much better."

The blind girl seemed stuck. She backed into a desk, went around it, and sat. Henry leaned toward her. "I see you found it," he said from two desks over.

Her glasses turned to him. "What?"

"Nothing." Right, if she couldn't see him, she probably didn't know he was the one she talked to outside. Duh.

While unpacking a giant tote bag, the teacher began telling the class what they were going to be covering in this session and over the following two weeks. She paused to fumble through some papers. More notebooks and binders came out until there was a mess on the table.

The students began to stir as their fate sunk in. The teacher, apparently resorting to a plan B, looked up and announced they'd be working in pairs. She began the coupling, pointing and saying; "You two, and... you two." Being at the back, Henry and the girl got paired. At least he didn't get the cowboy. "Even number, perfect," the teacher said as she walked down the aisle. Her hand was still out from counting, like something she'd neglected to put away.

Henry had seen this trick before—the pairing-up thing. The way of the lazy teacher. He remembered when she did it in his geography class. Pair students up and give them something to do and they pretty much teach themselves while you go text your boyfriend or read some tie-me-up drivel on your laptop.

As the other students paired up, Henry moved to the desk next to the girl.

"You're the one I'm with?" she asked him.

"Yeah." He slid his desk closer. She did the same and clipped his hand between their desks.

"Ah—*fuck*."

"Shit, was that your hand?"

"Is there a problem?" the teacher asked.

"No," Henry said. He sat and squeezed his hand.

"Sorry," the girl whispered.

"It's alright. You got me back."

"How's that?"

"I was the guy outside."

"I know."

"Oh. I didn't realize you were—"

"I know."

Her eyes appeared normal, at least from the side. He thought blind people that wore glasses did so to cover their eyes because there was something freaky looking about them. He wondered if she could tell he was looking at her.

"*Okaaay*," the teacher said, as if the room had gotten out of hand. She turned and looked for something. "Oh, that's just great, there's no chalkboard in here. How am I supposed—"

"That's because we're at a college," cowboy said. "There's no crayons either." He laughed and looked around for support.

Henry watched the girl take a notebook and pen out of her backpack. The way she did things made it seem like she wasn't really blind. Why would she have a pen and paper if she couldn't see?

"But what am I supposed to write on?" the teacher asked the cowboy, like the only available man held the only possible answer.

The class wasn't the distraction Henry had hoped for, but the girl was. At the end of class, the teacher said they'd continue what they were working on the following week. Henry didn't hear her. He watched the girl push her hair over her ear and write something in her notebook. She tilted it toward him. A phone number.

"You can text me," she said. "If you want to get a jump on next week's assignment."

"How do you read a—never mind."

~ ~ ~

Henry soon forgot about the girl, which seemed strange. In class, he kept looking at her, unsure if he was attracted or just fascinated. She was like a mysterious jewel he'd discovered. He wanted to know everything about her, all at once, already wondering if he should text her right away.

What if she didn't come back the next week? He'd never see her again. It was a pretty stupid class, after all. Most of the students would probably be gone by the third weekend. It'd be just him and the cowboy, eyeing each other. What excuse would he have to contact her then?

Justine. Maybe he could find out more about her. A blind girl named Justine that went to Santa Monica High. He knew a guy from band who had moved to Santa Monica.

When the first class was over, Henry had gotten up to leave. "See ya," he said.

"Yeah," she said, already heading for the door.

"Need any help?" he asked her.

"With what?"

He didn't know what else to say so he watched her walk away, his brain stuck in the mud.

But by the time he was halfway to the bus stop, he'd stopped thinking about her. That was the weird thing about having a mom that died. Nothing was predictable. Everything becomes nebulous. You head down a path, and it just stops. It's like the blueprint for everything disappears, and you're left wandering.

Henry thought the girl might become his new obsession. He hoped she would. He needed an anchor, something to latch on to, like his infatuation with simulation theory a couple years ago. But by the time he got on the bus, he could hardly picture her face, despite all the time spent looking at her. And by the time he got home, he not only couldn't remember her face, he didn't care.

Stephen was in the kitchen, listening to opera while he cooked. The arrival of Stephen was a bright spot, a big splash of color against all the gray.

They needed the help. Following his mom's death, Henry's dad began closing windows, drawing curtains, and leaving lights out, as if pulling the house in on itself. Henry spent more and more time in his room, down the hall from his parents' room, feeling the house shutting down around him, like a succumbing animal kneeling in the white hot desert.

Father and son, left to fill a home. Stephen provided some padding.

When his mom was alive, the house always had music playing. Mostly classical, but sometimes old rock songs, like the Rolling Stones, which she said *her* mom used to listen to. His parents would act goofy and sing along, natural for his mother but a little awkward for his dad. After she died, all was quiet. For the first month, Henry didn't listen to music. He'd sit in silence. He could hear his dad down the hall, moaning and sobbing, often talking to himself, as if arguing with someone. It scared him—listening to his dad's muffled voice—especially at night, when his tone would rise and fall. Henry pictured a demon having replaced his mother, a bickering demon sitting on the edge of the bed, pick-pick-picking at his dad.

"Before you ask, it's truffled Taleggio pizza, and it's for dinner." Stephen said as Henry dumped his backpack on the kitchen table and started toward the kitchen. Stephen gave him a look. Henry moved his backpack to the chair.

"Can I—"

"And yes, you can have a taste." Stephen was already cutting off a piece. He slipped it on a plate and handed it to him with a napkin. "How was the class? Meet any pretty girls?"

"It was cool, I think it'll be helpful," Henry lied. The class had been Stephen's idea. Henry had never even heard of it when Stephen suggested it as a way to get him out of the house of gloom.

Stephen had only been with them a month but already seemed to know everything. Actually, he seemed to know everything about everything. "I just know a little about a lot," he told Henry one day. "Which used to be a good thing. Now people find it altogether unnecessary, if not a bit offensive."

It was Conroy that hired Stephen. It happened after their electricity got shut off because his dad didn't pay the bill. Conroy sat down with him one Sunday morning while his dad slept, and talked to him about having someone come to help around the house.

"He's a maid?" Henry asked.

"No, no—maids don't cost what this guy costs. He'll just be here to help. Look, Henry, I don't need to tell you, your mother held this house together. She also held your father together, and he's only now realizing it. It may be temporary, it may be long term, but you need someone to help take care of things and get you guys back on track."

"Will he live here?"

"No, it's a job for him. He comes, he goes. But I want you to meet him first. If you don't like him, we won't hire him, simple as that."

Conroy arranged to have Henry and Stephen meet at his place. Henry was used to walking over there to get food that Conroy's wife Patty made, since there was never any at home anymore. He found Conroy and Stephen standing in the yard, talking about the rose bushes.

He didn't know what he was expecting, but he was surprised to see that Stephen looked like a CEO, or maybe a business consultant. Someone other people worked for. Conroy introduced them. Stephen shook Henry's hand. Dry and secure. Okay so far.

"Do you guys want to talk inside?" Conroy asked.

"Henry, you ever play miniature golf?" Stephen asked him.

"No, I've only played real golf."

"Come on, we'll talk while we play. Conroy, I don't think we'll need you."

Miniature golf always seemed stupid to Henry, but it turned out to be fun because you couldn't really screw up. They talked a little while they played, but not about the stuff Henry was expecting. Stephen didn't ask about his mom dying, or how he was holding up, or give him any of those practiced *I'm really listening to you* looks that everyone had switched to, like they'd been collectively coached by a sensitivity committee.

They talked about science and physics, which Stephen seemed to know a lot about. When they were done, they got hotdogs and Cokes and sat at one of the sticky plastic tables with the chairs bolted to the cement. They watched a pack of girls taking turns at the batting cages and yelling, *you swing like a girl*, a joke that apparently never got old.

After miniature golf, instead of going back to Conroy's, Stephen drove them to Henry's house and parked in front.

"You know where I live?" Henry asked him.

"Yeah, Conroy showed me." Stephen was studying the yard, which used to be the envy of the neighborhood, with flower boxes bursting with color, exotic plants that looked like they belonged in a rain forest, and a wide expanse of emerald grass that was manicured every week. It had been like something out of an English country living magazine. But it was also one of those yards that had to be vigilantly maintained or it would all go to shit fast, like a high-maintenance woman precariously hiding her age; when it

218

goes, it goes hard. You could see what it was supposed to look like, but the summer sun had withering and twisted the delicate annuals into brown clumps. Stephen frowned, assessing it like a general overlooking a smoking battlefield. "But I can take you back to Conroy's if you want. Just thought I'd save you the walk."

"I don't need to talk to him?" Henry asked.

"About me?"

"Yeah."

"You can if you want. Or later. Whatever you want. Damn, it's like somebody put a hex on your yard."

"It used to be nice. The gardeners stopped coming."

"You can't push a lawn mower?"

"I don't think we have one."

"Um. Well, thanks for playing golf. I hadn't done that in a long time. And check out Laplace, he's kinda been forgotten."

"Yeah, I will." Henry waited with his hand on the door handle. For some reason, he didn't get out. Stephen was still looking at the yard and didn't seem to think it was strange that he was still sitting there.

"Oh, man, you have glory lilies," Stephen said. "Nice. Or they were."

"My mom used to love to garden. We have a whole big greenhouse in the back, the kind you walk into. She'd grow all kinds of crazy shit in that thing. I don't think anyone's even been in it since she died."

"Hope nothing comes crawling out."

They didn't say anything else for a while. Henry took his hand off the door handle. It seemed obvious now that he wasn't getting out right away. Some kids on bikes rode toward them on the wrong side and looked in as they passed, hoping to catch a bit of tragedy in progress. Something to pass on. They were the talk of the block; the young doctor who lost his beautiful wife—*she was an artist, you know*—and the poor teenage son, who hardly needed an excuse to wear black. *Perhaps we should do something. Maybe go mow their lawn. Do people still do that? Somebody should, for God's sake.*

Henry saw a curtain part next door. Their neighbor, Joshua, peered out like he was in a spy thriller.

"You guys have a dog?" Stephen asked.

"Yeah, he's just a mutt."

"Best kind. Cat?"

"No cat."

"Good."

"You don't like cats?"

"Don't tell anybody."

"Cool."

Henry cried. He was just thinking about their dog. Luca Brasi was named after a character in *The Godfather.* His mom used to do a great imitation. He was a big, clumsy dog they got from the pound when Henry was eight, after a year of begging, and only on the promise that he'd take good care of it. He had to prove his mature intentions with a succession of smaller responsibilities: a plant, a goldfish, a lizard, then finally the dog. He'd kept his word. It was different now, without his mom. She loved to cook and was always trying out different dishes. She often gave Luca Brasi the results of her experiments after sampling them. The dog had developed high expectations. Now, he'd not only lost Francis, but had to eat regular dog food. Henry was thinking about how his mom would sit at a certain spot on the end of the couch, close to the lamp. It was her favorite place to read. She'd prop an elbow to hold up her book. Luca Brasi would sit on the other end of the couch, watching her, waiting for it. When she lifted her hand, that was his signal. He'd lumber over, stepping awkwardly on the couch cushions, and put his head in her lap. She'd rest her hand on his neck, all without looking away from her book. Usually, when Henry came home, Luca Brasi would greet him at the door; if he didn't, Henry knew he was with his mom. He'd go in the living room, just to make sure, since Luca Brasi was his responsibility. His mom would stop reading and look at him, taking a moment to switch realities. "Hi, sweetie. How was band practice?" Luca Brasi would twitch an ear, anxious that someone was interfering. For days after Francis died, he didn't eat anything. Henry even tried to cook him a meal by following a recipe from his mom's cookbook, *100 Simple Italian Recipes*. Luca Brasi just sat on the couch with his nose in his paws.

Henry covered his face. The sound of his crying, wet and snotty, was embarrassingly loud in the car. Stephen didn't do anything. He didn't even look at him.

Stephen must have dealt with some kind of tragedy in his own life, Henry thought. Partly because he was old— probably over fifty—so even just statistically it was probable, but also he seemed to know what to do, which was nothing. Sometimes nothing is better than something, but doing nothing was hard for most people, or even impossible. Maybe Stephen's own mother had died.

Henry sat back, his face flush, and took a few breaths. He looked at Stephen, who turned to him. Henry was glad to see he hadn't put on the sympathy face. "I'm sorry this happened to you," Stephen said. "I bet she was glad you were there."

"People always leave when they're needed most," Henry said wisely. Stephen nodded. Henry wiped his face with his shirt.

"No cats, huh?" Henry shook his head. "Good. Fuckin' hate cats."

Margaret was recruited out of law school by the Los Angeles District Attorney's Office. After two years, she left to work for the California Coastal Commission. She won a case brought against the commission by a land developer that wanted to drain the marshland near Marina Del Rey, one of the last undeveloped coastal areas in Los Angeles, to build retro lofts. Seeing her argue the case, the developer was so impressed that he referred Margaret to his sister, who had a pending medical malpractice case.

The previous year, the woman's eleven-year-old daughter had jaw surgery to correct a birth defect. During the procedure, she contracted a virulent staph infection from an unsterile surgical instrument. The infection wasn't caught until after the girl was released. By then, scarring blisters had formed on her face and neck. The girl's mother was suing the hospital, who refused to acknowledge the infection came from them. The case was stalled, in part because of a change in partners at the representing firm. The developer thought his sister should fire the firm and hire Margaret.

Margaret had no experience in medical malpractice, and knew that taking a case without proper qualifications could get her sued for legal malpractice. She said no. The land developer kept at her, telling his sister he'd pay the settlement if Margaret failed to win it for her.

She finally agreed to look at the case. The first thing she did was call Orlando Apache at the DA's office, who originally recruited her out of law school. He had worked a number of malpractice cases before moving to the DA.

"It won't be a lot of money," he said after reviewing the case. "In California, punitive damages are limited to ten times the compensatory amount awarded. But it should be an easy settlement." He agreed to partner with her and oversee the work if she wanted to take it on. Margaret took a leave of absence from the Coastal Commission and took the case.

The previous firm had encouraged the mother to accept a private settlement, but the mother wouldn't agree to sign the no-fault clause the hospital was insisting on. The more Margaret dug into the case, the more she felt she was lifting a rock with one slithering thing after another under it.

The hospital's firm investigated Margaret. They couldn't believe their luck; they were now up against a single lawyer whose previous clients were spotted owls and eco-freaks. They threw a team of lawyers at her.

In interviewing the mother, Margaret learned the hospital's firm had been trying to intimidate her. If it couldn't be proven the infection came from the hospital, they told her, it would be assumed that she had caused it, perhaps intentionally, in the hopes of profiting. They threatened to contact Child Protective Services and told the mother she could be cited for child endangerment and have her daughter taken away. Margaret had never seen this kind of strategy. Beyond unethical, it was illegal, but the firm made sure there was no trail of their threats.

As she worked the case, Margaret found parallels to her own life. Shortly after moving to Los Angeles, just before Justine turned three, Margaret took her to the doctor for a skin inflammation. They ran an allergy test. A mistake at the lab led the pediatrician to rule out allergies. Later, while at daycare, Justine had a severe allergic reaction to a peanut butter sandwich. By the time the staff realized what was happening and found an adrenaline pen, Justine had suffered anaphylaxis, cutting off oxygen to her brain and causing a mini stroke. The result was cortical visual impairment, a condition that causes visual fluctuations from total to partial blindness. The lab took responsibility and the doctor's office admitted partial culpability. Their combined insurance paid a settlement and funded Justine's treatment. There was never a need to sue. And that's where the similarities ended.

Margaret hired two law students from UCLA to help her in the evenings. She turned her apartment into a war room. Orlando began feeding her precedent cases, which she studied obsessively. While the other side was waiting for her to come to them, Margaret became convinced the case should go before a jury.

The girl's mother wasn't so sure. Margaret got a call from her brother, the land developer. When he heard that Margaret had done nothing to pursue settlement negotiations, he screamed at her. He'd recommended her to settle the case, not drag it out. Margaret had researched him previously and knew his fortunes rose and fell dramatically, often in the span of a few months. She had one of the students look into his recent business transactions; he was not only in debt, but hemorrhaging money from multiple deals gone bad. Margaret realized he'd likely recommended her for the case in the hopes she'd get a quick settlement— he could then borrow from his sister and dig himself out of the hole he was in. Margaret ignored him and plowed ahead.

Everyone was on edge. Even the law students thought Margaret should be pushing for a settlement. The other side blinked first, unnerved by Margaret's silence. She got a tentative call, hinting they might be convinced to alter the settlement terms. She agreed to meet with them.

Orlando did some work behind the scenes. Most surgeons had their own malpractice insurance and work as contractors, so he was curious why the surgeon's private insurance wasn't taking this on. He dug around and found the surgeon was the nephew of the hospital board's president, and had a financial stake in the hospital. He encouraged Margaret hold to off on a settlement.

A trial date was set. Margaret went before the judge to argue against the other side deposing the girl. She lost.

During the deposition, the deposing attorney coaxed the girl along in a friendly manner—until the end, when she told her she'd have to testify, which meant showing her face in public. "So all your friends will see you. Everyone from school. They might even show it on TV, and on the internet, so it will be permanent. They'll all see your face, with those boils. Even the boys. And you're going to be a teenager soon."

Margaret began to have doubts. Even with Orlando's help and all the research she'd done, she feared she'd gotten in over her head. She was seeing a side to high-stakes law she'd never been exposed to. The other side had inexhaustible resources. It could be a long trial, and after seeing the tactics used, she didn't want to put the girl though it. The child was already looking at a long recovery, including multiple plastic surgeries to help with the scarring. There was also the real risk that she could lose the case in front of a jury.

A week before the trial, Margaret visited the girl and her mother at their home. She faced them as they sat side by side on the couch, wearing matching yellow sundresses. Most of the girl's sores were bandaged, but some were uncovered, requiring air circulation to heal.

The girl reminded Margaret of Justine. They were about the same age. She sat primly, feet and knees together. When she got distracted, she'd twist around like a boy, wanting to go out to play. Justine did the same thing when made to wear a dress. When the mother excused herself to go to the bathroom, Margaret leaned toward the girl, like they were coconspirators. "Tell me, Nicole. What do *you* want to do?"

Nicole had learned to move her face as little as possible when speaking, to prevent the boils from cracking. She looked toward the hallway, then back at Margaret. "I want you to make them pay."

Orlando was well known for his unorthodox legal strategies. His tactics, though effective, were not always welcome in the DA's placid environment. This case brought out his creative side. He got so involved he took to sleeping on Margaret's couch. Three days before the trial, he woke Margaret at two in the morning by sitting on the edge of her bed.

"Margaret, I've figured it out."

"Uh, what?"

"It's malice."

Margaret sat up and pulled a blanket around her. "What?"

"A hospital sells a product, like any other business, and it's not medicine. It's trust. That's their product. Trust. That's what they must protect, the public's faith in them, and that's what they fear losing. This case should be nothing to them, it's a write-off, even if a jury awards the maximum. Unless we can prove malice, beyond simple malpractice or negligence. That's what they're afraid of."

"Meaning they knew what they did and hid it?"

"That's right. I think that's what's behind this."

"We don't have evidence of that."

"I don't think we need it, they just have to think we do."

"So what do we do?"

"Nothing. That will terrify them."

The day before trial, everyone was crammed into Margaret's apartment. The two UCLA students took the day off from class. Justine stayed home. Orlando paced like a hungry lion. Late in the afternoon, opposing council called to meet.

Margaret went alone. Three of their lawyers showed up, only one of whom Margaret had met before. She was handed an envelope. "Is this an offer?" she asked.

"Yes."

"What are the terms?"

"There are no terms. Standard settlement offer."

"What's the offer?"

"I don't know."

"You don't know? We're meeting to talk about a settlement and you don't know what you're offering?"

"That's correct. We've been told not to open it. It comes directly from the board of directors and right now, they're the only ones who know. We're not to negotiate."

Margaret had never heard of such a thing, but this case had been a series of firsts. "I'll let you know," she said.

The offer was for a non-binding cash settlement far beyond any amount previously discussed. Margaret called Orlando from her car.

"When they go over like that, it's hush money," he said. "You're not legally obliged, of course, but it's their way of buying—well, asking really, in the parlance of counselors—for your silence. Or at least your discretion. It seems like a lot of money, but it's nothing to them. Congratulations, Margaret, it means they're officially afraid of you."

The hospital later fired their law firm.

After a second meeting to go through the formalities of accepting the offer, Margaret came home for a quick nap. Exhausted, she stripped naked and crawled into bed.

She couldn't sleep at first. She found herself hiding under the blankets, shaking. The full impact of what had happened hit her like a near-death experience. She eventually fell into a hard sleep. When she woke, Justine was standing there. Light reflected off her glasses like she was a visiting alien.

"Mom, I made you some soup."

"Thank you, sweetheart."

"Are you okay? You slept for three hours and twelve minutes."

"Yes."

"You're not sick?"

"No, I was just tired. Did you practice your piano?

"I didn't want to wake you."

"Oh, sweetie." Justine sat on the edge of the bed. Margaret touched the side of her face. "Are you alright?"

"Yes, Mom. So you won?"

"Yeah. It doesn't fix what was done to her, but it's all we can do."

"I'm glad. She's nice."

"Yes, she is."

"Good job, Mom."

"Thank you, sweetie. Hey." Margaret sat up. "Maybe I'll take some time off. We'll go do something fun."

"Can we visit Aunt Vicky?"

"Maybe. But you know what would be really fun?"

"What?"

"You know how we talked about someday moving out of this place and into a house?"

"Yeah."

"Well, I think we should start looking."

"Really?"

"We'll go together, so we can both decide."

"That'd be awesome. Can we get a place with a big kitchen? I can cook, ya know."

"Sure, a house with lots of room. But you know, if we get a bigger house, we'll need to get you a bigger piano. I don't think our old upright would work in a big house."

Justine hugged her. Margaret tipped back so they were lying down. Justine turned, facing away, with her back snuggled against Margaret's chest. Margaret squeezed her daughter and breathed in the sweet smell of her hair.

She didn't end up taking much time off. When news of the settlement got out, Margaret's phone rang non-stop. She considered offers from a number of firms before deciding, with a nudge from Orlando, to start her own firm. After giving them a bonus, Margaret promised the two UCLA students she'd hire them the moment they passed the bar. She stayed on at the Coastal Commission as an unpaid consultant.

As she built her firm, Margaret could afford to be picky. She focused on cases, big or small, that she felt had real merit, including a couple long shots. Her reputation grew with each win, and eventually prompted calls from east coat firms trying to pull her away. Her firm expanded over the next few years to include business and criminal law.

They moved a second time, this time to pricy Santa Monica. The house they found had a large backyard, a pool, and a big open kitchen.

And it was as far away from Camden, Wisconsin as it was possible to get.

Chapter 13

It was Justine who texted first. Henry and his dad were having dinner—their first attempt to eat together since it happened—and it was just as depressing as Henry feared it would be.

When Francis died, Henry's dad seemed to follow Luca Brasi's lead and stopped eating altogether. He became a vampire, pacing the house at night in a cloud of depression. He even stopped going to the grocery store, so after a few weeks, there wasn't much food. When Stephen arrived, his dad started eating again, and soon went to the opposite extreme; he'd wander into the kitchen to try whatever Stephen was cooking, only to be shooed out, usually with a plate of food. Then he went to a doctor for his depression and was put on medication, which made him not want to eat again.

Henry ate his chicken parmesan. His dad just frowned at his plate as Stephen hovered nearby.

Henry's phone pinged. He pulled it out of his jeans. Stephen snatched it before he could see who it was. "No screens at the table." He put the phone on the kitchen counter. "Something wrong with your dinner, Thomas?"

Tom looked at him through a medicated fog. "Hum? Oh, no. This is—it's—the..."

"Chicken."

"Chicken. It's very good."

"Do you want something else?"

"No. Maybe some wine."

"Not with your medication. I actually read the warnings, did you?"

"Oh, of course. I mean, no. But they put that on everything. Blanket defense. Lawyers rule the world, you know."

"I didn't."

"Okay, then. Nothing. I mean, I'm good. Stephen, why don't you sit with us?"

"No, Tom, I'm the help."

"Dad, nobody likes to eat with their boss," Henry said.

"You know, I never thought of that," Tom said.

"Eat your dinner, Tom."

It hadn't taken long for Stephen to take on this mothering role. Despite the initial explanations, Henry wasn't completely sure why Stephen had been hired, so after he'd been there a couple weeks, he asked him.

"So, what exactly were you hired to do here?" Henry was sitting on the kitchen counter as Stephen held up color swatches in their walk-in pantry. "And what are you doing to our pantry?"

Stephen circled the kitchen with a yellow swatch. "What do you think of this yellow, Henry?"

"It's nice. I mean, it's yellow."

Stephen nodded. "I think so, too. The trick with colors is to both complement and contrast, but in just the right amounts. See the pale green in the kitchen walls? The yellow complements it, but by using this warmer shade of yellow, it also contrasts the cool of the green. See? I'm painting the pantry, is what I'm doing. And as for why I'm here—well, you guys have had a rough time of it lately, and I'm here to assess what you need, and help provide it. When you don't need me any more, I'll leave. It's difficult to deal with practical things when you're going though something like this. Make sense?"

"Yeah. So how long, do you think?"

"You want to get rid of me?"

"God, no."

"We'll see how it goes. Every situation is different. These things take time, so I'll be here for a while. That alright?"

"Yeah, cool."

Stephen took care of all the practical things Francis used to handle. That was easy enough, but he soon realized that what Henry and Thomas really needed was a parent—a strict one—especially Tom, who seemed to take comfort in being told what to do without equivocation. By the time Henry's phone pinged at the dinner table, it was natural for Stephen to snatch it out of his hand, as any parent might.

After dinner, Henry took his phone and headed up to his room. His heart did a lurch when he saw the text was from Justine.

I use a text to speech ap, it said.

He texted back a question mark.

You were wondering how I could read a text. Right?

Yeah.

Question. You good at math?

He flopped on his bed and thought for a minute. *I kill at math. Why?*

What level?

Precal.

That was it.

The following Saturday, he went to class. It was down a few students, but Justine was sitting at the same desk as before. He took the one next to her.

The teacher had already created her prop display of notebooks and binders on the table. "Sit with your partners," she said. "Sit with the same partners you had last week, that worked out so well. If your partner isn't here, come see me. The rest of you can just carry on with the same assignment."

"Hey," Henry said.

Justine turned to him. "Hi, Henry."

After pairing up the stray students, the teacher disappeared behind her phone with a stupid smile on her face.

Henry and Justine spent most of the class comparing the differences between their schools. They talked about a couple people they both knew. Except for a few stifled laughs, nobody heard from the teacher again.

Justine did everything so normally it was easy to forget she was blind. Henry noticed she made a conscious effort to look him when they spoke, as if she could see him. He wondered if she'd always been blind, or if this was a habit left over from when she could see.

At the end of class, Henry went to turn in their assignment, which they'd knocked out in the last few minutes. When he went back to get his stuff, Justine was already gone.

He found her outside, sitting on the edge of the planter. He stopped. It was hard to tell if she knew he was there, so he made a little noise by hoisting his backpack and sniffling.

"Precal?" she asked.

"Yeah." He sat next to her. "I'd forgotten about that. Why?"

"Know any good Helen Keller jokes?"

"What? No."

"I kind of collect them. It can break the ice sometimes. Want to hear one?"

"That's okay. Aren't they, like, insensitive?"

"Of course, that's the point. Sure you don't want to hear one?"

He felt on uncertain ground. "Pretty sure, yeah."

"So, the math thing."

"Yeah, what's up with that?"

"See—" She hesitated before shifting to low voice, like they might get caught. "I need a tutor. Someone to help me."

"Oh."

"I'm okay at math, but not great. By okay, I mean okay by most people's standards. But my mom is kind of a math genius. She's one of those weird people that were somehow just born knowing. She doesn't even need to try. I mean, she watches physics videos and studies asymptotic theory for fun."

"Damn, that's awesome."

"Yeah, she's crazy smart."

"Is she a professor?"

"No, lawyer. But see, she kind of thinks I'm really good at math too. Like it's genetic. I mean, not as good as her, but good."

"Why does she think that—I mean, if you're not?"

She leaned closer. "I've kind of lied to her, without really meaning to. I cheated on some tests, and led her to believe I'm better than I am. I guess I kind of tricked her. The blind must be extra resourceful, you know. But lately, she's been trying to, like, talk math with me, like for fun. It's getting kind of hard to hide."

"Talk math?"

"Like she was saying someone had a new theory about the twin prime conjecture problem, and wasn't that interesting?"

"Oh, like is there an infinite number of twin primes?"

"See, I need you. I had no idea what she was talking about and had to totally bluff."

"So there's a new theory on that? I didn't hear about it. See, normally, primes don't—"

"Don't dork out on me."

"Why don't you just tell her the truth?"

"What are you, a teen counselor or something?"

"No, sorry. Why did you think I might be good at math?"

"Well, I mean, look at you." She paused. "See, that was a joke."

"Oh, blind humor, got it. You couldn't see, but I was laughing."

"That's the spirit. Anyway, I looked you up."

"Looked me up? How? What do you mean?"

She hesitated. "I can hack, and school records are the easiest."

"You don't even know my last name."

"Class lists are even easier. You're a pretty good student, Henry Ackerman."

"Yeah, I am, but what the fuck? So you just, like, hack into people's records? That's messed up."

"Don't get all weird, I only do it if I have a reason."

"You could just ask. That's what normal people do."

"I'm going to ignore that, and I did ask, if you'll recall, but I needed specifics."

"Plus, you're like, blind, aren't you? How do blind people hack?"

"I'm not completely blind. Or not always. My vision fluctuates. You know, Matthew Weigman went to prison for hacking. He's that good, and he's totally blind."

"That's your role model? A guy doing hard time?"

"I also use text-to-speech programs. You don't need to see to type."

"Wow, this is really fascinating. Blind hacker girl. Real niche. So like, did you find out all this stuff about me? Like personal stuff, like my family and stuff? My parents? I mean, who needs the fuckin' NSA, right?"

"Jesus, relax, Henry, I was just trying to see—never mind. I shouldn't have asked, mister sensitive. Didn't realize you were in witness protection." She got up to leave.

"That's not in my records?"

"Whatever." She pulled a fold-out cane from her pack and flicked it open.

"What was the Helen Keller joke?" he asked as she started to walk away.

She stopped and turned. "Okay: Helen Keller walks into a bar. Then a table. Then a chair." She paused. "That's it. Hardy fuckin' har, right? At least she didn't walk into a desk."

He watched her walk away.

~ ~ ~

She texted him that night. *I'll trade you something.*

What? HK jokes?

No. Sexual favors. When he didn't reply, she added: *Kidding.*

I know. She didn't respond. An hour later, he texted again. *What would you trade?*

You mean you don't want my body?

I'm gay.

Oh shit. Sorry.

Kidding.

Fucker.

Did I just crush your world?

Can you call me? Texting is a challenge.

"Hello, Henry," she said in a soft voice when he called.

"Hey."

"This is better. It's much easier to insult you this way. You know, texting is the exact invention blind people once had nightmares about."

"I thought you had some app you used."

"Yeah, it works, but it's not great. We're not a huge market."

"Why are you talking so quiet?"

"I'm in my bedroom. This is my bedroom voice."

"No, really."

"My mom. No boys. Not that you're a boy of course, mister manly man."

"Seriously? Just to talk to on the phone?"

"It's not that I can't, but I'd have to explain, which is worse."

"Damn. Raw deal."

"Tell me about it. Anyway, what should we trade?"

"What do you got?"

"No chance you'd do this just to be a cool guy? You could probably put it on your college application. Volunteering for the blind. They look for shit like that."

"Yeah, alright, just once, and we'll see how it goes."

"Really? I was kidding."

"I know, I gather you do that a lot. Is it a defense thing?"

"You mean defensive? I think defense is what they have in football and hockey and, like, baccarat."

"You can't stop, can you?"

"You really should be a teen counselor. You've got me all turned inside out here with your incisive analysis. I feel so exposed."

"I'm just wondering if I tutor you, if I'm going to be subjected to your nonstop standup routine."

"You think I've been kidding all this time? Maybe I'm just tragically unaware."

"Sure."

"You might get to like it." He was silent. "I can turn it off, don't worry, pumpkin."

"Are you in class next weekend?"

"Yeah, I guess. I think that teacher is retarded. Shit, sorry, didn't mean to insult retarded people. You don't have, like, a brother that's retarded or something, do you?"

"If I did, you'd know it."

"Ha! That's true."

"See you in class. I mean—"

"I know."

They hung up.

Justine lay in bed with her phone resting on her chest. Her heart was pounding. She detected the faint scent of her mother's moisturizer. There was a soft knock at the door. "Yeah, Mom."

The door opened. "Just checking on you, sweetie. You okay?"

"You mean you heard me talking on the phone."

"You're right. Sorry."

"It was a guy."

"That's fine. I mean, I'm glad. You should be talking to boys."

"Jeez, lady, what'd you do with my mom?"

"I trust you, honey."

"Por qué?"

She heard her mom sigh. "You've earned it. Just—just don't betray that trust. Our agreement, I mean. Please. It's the one thing."

"I know."

The door shut. Justine thought about Henry as she felt her pulse finally slow down. She thought about what she had to trade, even though he said he'd do it anyway. Not her body, apparently. Not that she would, of course. Besides, she didn't even know what she had in that regard.

Of all the things that sucked about being blind, or mostly blind—and there were a whole lot of things that sucked about it—one of the worst was also the most trivial. At least it probably seemed that way to everyone else.

Everyone thought things like writing would be hard, but Justine had learned to write around the same age as all the other kids, though she did have a private tutor. Her mom had insisted that if she was going to function in a world with sighted people instead of going to a special school, she'd have to work twice as hard. Most things weren't that difficult. Nobody understood what the *real* challenges were. Like not being able to see her body as it developed.

On those brief occasions when everything lined up in her brain circuitry and she could partially see, she'd try to get in front of a mirror as fast as possible, stripping if possible, and examine herself. But even when her vision was at its best, she could only get a vague idea of her shape. She had to rely on touch, the way she did for everything else.

She'd prowl the web using her text-to-speech program, searching for descriptions of whatever star was popular. It was a given that the reader knew what the person looked like, so descriptions were always along the lines of, *her amazing body*, but it wouldn't say exactly what was so amazing, except in general terms. Justine would stand with her earpiece in and run her hands over her body as she compared herself to the scraps of information she found.

She'd learned long ago that people love to do things to feed their egos, and nothing gave people more self-righteous satisfaction than collecting karma points for helping a blind person; they could go home, kick the dog, and still come out ahead. But she couldn't ask someone how she looked. How she *really* looked, not just the, *oh my gosh—you're so pretty*, she got from friends. She wanted to ask her mom, and almost did a few times, but couldn't bring herself to do it. Moms were never honest about that stuff anyway. She wanted to know what any girl wanted to know: what her boobs looked like, if her teeth were as big as she feared, what her eyes were like, if she looked good in dark or light lipstick.

She knew she was above average in height. She'd run her hands over her breasts and butt, hoping there'd suddenly be more, but always came to the same conclusion—that she had the body of a tall, skinny boy. That's about all she knew for certain, and that's what sucked the most about being blind and sixteen.

She got up and plugged her phone in to charge. She knew she should start getting ready for bed, but she could still hear Henry's voice in her head and didn't want to chase it away. He had a deeper voice than most of the guys she knew. It also had a beautiful texture to it that made her want to slip into the gaps between his words. He wasn't very talkative though. She would have loved to hear him talk for a long time about something just so she could absorb the sound. She knew other girls probably didn't think much about how a guy's voice sounded, but it was important to her. When you couldn't see someone, you had to get everything you could from what they said, and since most people, especially guys, would rather die than say what they actually mean, you had to find it in the nooks and crannies. Maybe next time she talked to him she could record it, so she could listen to it later. No, that seemed a little weird, and he was already pretty weirded out about the hacking thing. Sometimes it was impossible to know what would impress a guy versus what would freak him out.

Justine put her earpiece in and ran a search on her computer. When she found something, she stood and slid her hand under her shirt as she listened to the flat computer voice.

Sophia's got curves any woman would envy. Did she just win the genetic lottery? That may be part of it, but she maintains her amazing physique with a healthy diet and strict exercise program. What else does she do? This mother of one agreed to share her secrets with us.

~ ~ ~

Strong overnight winds had swept away the smog and urban detritus, cooling the air and leaving crisp, cobalt skies.

Henry sat on the edge of the planter before the start of the final Junior Prep class, listening to Bach's English Suites on his headphones. It always made him wonder why nobody wrote for harpsichord anymore.

For the previous three summers, Henry's mother had allowed him to join her in her sculpture studio as she worked. She had two conditions: he must follow every safety rule without exception, and she controlled the music, which usually meant classical or opera. Henry had a singular opinion of both. Boring. Music for hospitals and the kinds of movies he didn't like. She played it loud, which made it impossible to ignore. Sometimes a piece would cause her to stop working. "Henry, do you hear how she held that note, dropped two octaves, then went right into the next section without taking a breath? My God, what a voice. That one transition is years and years of training. Honey, appreciate that. Here, let's listen to that part again." She'd back up the CD—she was faithful to her CDs—and listen again; head tipped back, eyes closed and a hand dirty with sculpting clay suspended in the air. She talked to him as if he'd expressed some special love of opera. "Mom, I don't hear it. She just sounds like she's falling off a cliff or something." His mom would do her smile that was also a grimace and go back to her work.

One hot afternoon, Francis went back in the house after showing him how to create plaster molds. Henry stayed in the studio and practiced the technique. Mozart's *Requiem* in D minor was playing at full volume. He'd heard the piece many times before; background noise, like the rest. He would have turned it off if his hands weren't such a mess.

But then the strangest thing happened. In a single moment, he got it. It was like flipping a switch. He was resting on his knees, sweating, not even aware he was listening, when he felt the music in its totality. A connection seemed to open through time—lives that had heard and felt this music, loved to it and died to it; notes in the air pulsed through him, fresh and breathing, as tangible as the ground his knees touched.

The moment left him, as if an incubus had borrowed his spirit, found satisfaction, and moved on. He used the end of a paintbrush to back up the CD and listen to the section again. He closed his eyes, ready, but it was gone—a fickle lover that had changed her mind.

Maybe it was a fluke. Maybe it wasn't even the music, but something else, and the music just happened to be playing. Henry wasn't sure. For the next few weeks, he snuck his mom's CDs out of her studio and into his room. He skipped through them, listening randomly, and tried to find that connection again. He'd catch bits of it—or thought he did—but nothing like what he'd felt in the studio.

Later, after his mom died, Stephen was playing Mozart's *The Magic Flute* in the kitchen. Henry told him about his experience listening to Mozart. Stephen listened with a sly smile.

"But it was really just the one time. I tried to listen to the same piece again, but it wasn't there anymore. It was weird." Henry was sitting on the counter and dipped his finger in cookie batter. Stephen thwacked his hand with a wooden spoon, like his mother used to do. "I guess I don't really care for classical music."

"Nonsense."

"Nobody else I know does. People in band don't even like it. It's not for everyone."

"That finger goes in the batter again, you're losing it. I think you were able to slip into the music without realizing it was happening. It happened on its own, the way dreams do. Start with something easier. I want you to try listening to a Bach recording I have. Mozart can be like Scotch, it's not what you give a new drinker. And stay far away from Wagner, he's the heavy metal of classical, definitely an acquired taste—one I never acquired."

Henry listened to the Bach, but it wasn't happening.

"Keep listening," Stephen said.

He tried again. He sat on some pillows on the floor of his bedroom and dozed off with his headphones on. He was in that half-asleep state when he felt it; a warm presence. This time, it lasted longer. He kept listening.

"You're learning it's not just what you listen to, but how you listen to it," Stephen said when Henry reported back. "Which is pretty much true of anything."

A welcome breeze cooled Henry's cheeks as he drifted through the music. He felt a nudge. He opened his eyes and turned to see Justine. Her mouth was moving. He took his headphones off. "What?

"I figured it out," she said.

"How long have you been sitting there?"

"Awhile."

"How'd you know it was me here?"

"I asked someone walking by if there was a really ugly dude sitting here. You must be hideous because he didn't hesitate. What were you listening to?"

"Bach. What did you say before?"

"Thought so, you listen loud enough. Which?"

"English Suite one in A major."

"Damn. So you probably already play. I mean, if you know that."

"Play what? Like, am I a *playa?*"

"Hardy fuckin' har. Piano."

"Oh. No."

"Really? Because that's what I was going to say."

"Before?"

"Yeah, I was asking if you play because I do and I could teach you. That's what we could trade. You teach me some advanced math trickery, and I teach you the fundamentals of piano. That's what I just figured out, while sitting here listening to you dork out on your sissy music."

"I said I'd do it anyway."

"I know, but I'd feel better if we could exchange something, and since you don't want my body, I came up with this."

"I don't want to learn piano."

"Why not?"

"I just don't. Do I need a reason?"

"I'm thinking maybe you just don't want to learn it from me. I intimidate you."

"No. It's like, my dad used to always play and would try to get me to learn."

"Ah, you've been scarred."

"Shut up, it's not that, I just don't think I'm very musically inclined."

"Musically inclined? You're not being interviewed for the dweeb academy. And I thought I saw you were in band."

"Saw?"

"It's a universal expression, not to be taken literally."

"Fuck, how far did you hack?"

"It's right there, on your class schedule."

"From two years ago."

"Whatever."

"I played clarinet. In band, that's like playing third kazoo."

"So, it's something."

"I don't think I'd be any good."

"Hence, lessons. But I won't force you. Don't want to add to your distress. Though I could use a ruler and rap your knuckles when you do it wrong."

"That's an incentive?"

"Depends what you're into, guys are all weird. I could dress up as one of those parochial nuns, if that's your thing."

"Besides, you'd miss."

"What? Oh, with the ruler. Ha! Blind humor, I love it. Even late."

"That's all you really want, an opportunity to abuse me."

"Pretty much."

He watched her for a moment. "We should get to class," he said.

"Right. Wouldn't want to be late for a class that isn't graded and doesn't count for anything."

"I know, but I like to complete things."

"Okie dokie."

"Need some help?"

"With what?"

Henry called her that night and said he wanted to learn piano after all. She didn't ask what had changed his mind, which was a relief because he wasn't sure himself, except that it was another distraction and he needed as many of those as he could get.

They met the next day, on Sunday. He thought of saying he was busy that day, to at least make it seem like he had something going on in his life, but he couldn't think of anything fast enough.

He was afraid she would want to meet at his house. He'd already told her they had a piano. He pictured his overmedicated dad wandering around like a ghoul and Stephen cooking or painting the bathroom sage; even a blind person would think he had two gay dads. Then of course she'd ask about his mom, because she was the type who wouldn't be too worried that she was being nosy. She might already know anyway, depending on how far she hacked into his records.

"Let me just check with my mom to make sure it's okay if you come over," she told to him on the phone.

"Right, because she's all weird about guys. Is she going to, like, stand over us—make sure I don't take advantage of the blind girl?"

"Actually, she might."

"Really? Fuck me."

"It's not easy raising a blind kid, but she's cool."

"Just way overprotective."

"No shit about my mom."

"I thought it was guys that were supposed to be weird about their moms."

"If it wasn't for her, I wouldn't even be going to a regular school."

"You're aware that as a female teenager, you must hate your mother, right?"

"I know it's expected."

"Required."

Justine's house was on San Vicente Boulevard, on the seam between Pacific Palisades and Santa Monica. The living room was fronted by large windows overlooking the Riviera Country Club and a section of the shimmering Pacific Ocean. When they walked in, Henry almost said *nice view,* but caught himself. He'd done that a couple times already. In class, he'd said *see what I mean?*—twice.

"Aren't you going to comment on how awesome the view is?" Justine asked him.

"I was going to, yeah. It's great. I can see the ocean, even."

"Well, I wouldn't know, of course."

"Sorry."

"Kidding, Jesus, it's been described to me about a thousand times."

The house was light and airy—very different from the dark austerity of his house. The kitchen opened to the living room and faced the windows, creating one big room divided by an island. A concert-sized grand piano stood in front of the windows. A curved staircase led to a second floor. There was a wide hallway off the kitchen. Down the hall was another wall of windows, revealing a large backyard.

"Damn, I'm guessing your mom does pretty good as a lawyer."

"She's a fuckin' shark."

"Great, I feel like chum."

"Mom!" Justine called.

"Yeah, be right there," came a voice from another room. A door opened. "No, I was talking to Justine," a woman said into a headset as she came in. She looked at Henry and gave him a *this guy won't shut up,* look. "Yeah," she said and waited. "Yeah..." She rolled her hand in a circle. "Great, will do." She wasn't what Henry had pictured. She seemed too young and didn't really seem like the mom type; whatever that was. "Fine, got it, Orlando. Yup, bye." She hung up. "So sorry about that," she said as she pulled off her headset and walked toward him with her hand out. "Nice to meet you, Henry."

"Jeez, Mom, you could've waited for me to introduce you."

"That might be never, honey."

"Nice to meet you too, Ms. Shepard." She had a strong, man-like handshake and an unnerving intensity to the way she looked at him.

"Did you coach him, Justine? I'm Margaret, unless I'm suing you, but thank you. You guys are going to study together?" She maintained the hard eye contact.

"Yeah, I'm going to teach her—or, we're going to—" he stumbled.

"School doesn't start until next week, what are you guys studying?" She didn't seem to blink.

"I told you, Mom. We're doing prep work for the start of school. From our Junior Prep class. And I told Henry I'd show him some piano. He's interested in learning."

"That's wonderful." She didn't look like she meant it. Henry wondered if she'd gotten used to just using her voice with Justine and didn't bother to add the facial expressions everyone else used to sell a lie.

"It is?" Justine looked perplexed.

"But I thought you said that class was terrible."

"It was, so we're trying to make up for it." Justine seemed prepared for any question.

"Henry, make yourself at home. Are you hungry?"

"No, thank you."

"Thirsty?"

"Mom."

"Sorry. Listen—" She grabbed her purse off the kitchen counter. "I'm heading out for a bit to run some errands."

Justine turned. "What?"

"I'm going out."

"Now?"

"Yes."

"You're—you're leaving us alone?" Henry watched Justine's confusion.

"Yes, unless you need me to stay."

"No. No, we're good."

"Great. Now, there's lots to eat if you get hungry. I'll be back in about an hour." She squeezed her purse like she was trying to strangle it. "Maybe even longer."

"Okay, Mom."

"Great, good, I'm going to go, and I'll—I'll be back." She went to the door and pulled her keys out. "You call me if you need me." She paused with the door half open and gave Henry a forced smile. "Oh, do you need anything, honey, while I'm out?"

"Uh, no."

"Okay. It was nice to meet you, Henry. I mean—I'll see you when I get back, of course."

"Sure." He tried to give her a reassuring look. It must have come off wrong because she dropped her keys.

"Goodness. Graceful, Margaret." She bent and picked them up. "Ha! Okay, great then." She hesitated a beat longer before going out the door.

Justine remained still. They listened to her footsteps recede on the other side.

"I don't believe it," Justine whispered. "Seriously, I'm finding it very hard to believe she's actually leaving. I need to know she really left." They heard the sound of a car door closing. Henry went to the window. "Does she drive a big black Mercedes?" he asked.

"How would I know?"

"Sorry."

"*Jes-us*, Henry, I'm kidding, for fuck's sake. Yes, black Merc SUV."

"I think I'm just going to assume you're always kidding from now on, which means if you're ever serious, you'll have to let me know ahead of time. Yes, it just pulled out. She's actually leaving, though driving pretty slow, like she's still not sure."

"I'm stunned."

"It's that big a deal?"

"You don't understand, she's never—ever—left me alone with a guy. Even little things like taking that class was a big deal because she didn't know exactly who was going to be there. Last year, we were at the beach and this guy comes over and says hello, like on the boardwalk—because my mom's hot, right?—and she literally chased him off. I guess she thought he was talking to me. She took her shoes and earrings off, like she was planning to beat him up. I mean, I wasn't even allowed to go to summer camp as a kid. Even the one for blind kids."

"Why, what's wrong with summer camp?"

"Don't you know? It's like a nonstop fuck fest. It's where just about every girl I know lost her virginity. They turn it into a parlor game."

"Damn, I had band camp once. Nothing like that happened, at least not to me." There was an awkward moment where Henry tried to replay in his mind what he'd just said to see if he'd accidently confessed his virginity. "I've heard parents with one kid can be overprotective," he added in an effort to save himself.

"You have no idea."

He'd never asked if she knew what he looked like. Sometimes he was afraid to look at her because it seemed strange to look at her when she didn't know it, even if he was just looking at her like he would anyone else. He was pretty sure she was trying to look at him now though. She'd told him there were moments when she could see more than just vague shapes. The sunlight probably helped.

Maybe that's why their house had such big windows and was so open and bright.

He allowed himself to stare at her. She had the kind of hair that's different colors, like it'd never settled on one; dark brown, blond in parts, and now, in the sunlight, he could see streaks of red. It was long, almost to the middle of her back. She wore it down in a natural style, like girls did in pictures from the sixties. Her skin tone had a washed-out look; no feature really stood out, maybe because her glasses dominated her face. She didn't wear jewelry and the only makeup she wore was lipstick that made her mouth dark against her pale skin. He wondered how she managed to get it on so perfectly.

"Do you see colors?" he asked without thinking. When she didn't answer right away, he was afraid he'd said something wrong, but she kept looking at him, so he kept looking at her.

"Yes, sometimes, but I'm never really sure if it's the memory I have of colors, from before it happened, like maybe my brain is filling things in for me. I'm glad though, I'd hate to have someone try to explain color to me. But like, I know you're black."

"I'm not black."

"You're not?"

"I'm African American." She smiled. Then he wasn't sure. "I'm not, really."

"I know, I can kinda tell. And your school records say Caucasian. Here's something serious, ready?"

"Yeah, except I know it's probably a setup."

"You're never going to offend me, Henry. With the blind stuff. I know you're a sensitive guy. I actually like it when you forget and say things like, 'See?' It means you've forgotten I'm the blind girl, and I'm just a girl."

He couldn't think of anything to say to that. It became one of those thick moments where you become very aware of your own presence. He watched dust motes float in the streaks of sunlight.

"Want to see the rest of the house?" she asked.

"Yeah. Hey, I heard a Helen Keller joke, want to hear?"

"I'd rather see, but sure."

"How do you punish Helen Kell—"

"Put her in a round room and tell her to sit in the corner. Please, that one's older than history."

"Oh."

"Don't feel bad, new ones are like leap years. Come on, I'll show you the backyard. We have a pool and I haven't fallen into it once. What do you think of my mom?"

"She was... she's nice."

"I know, and she's hot, right?"

"Yeah, she is."

"Okay, chill, wild mustang."

Chapter 14

Breathe, Margaret, breathe.

She succeeded, briefly. Stopped at a light, she thought she was getting a handle on her anxiety until she realized she was gripping the wheel so tight the skin over her knuckles looked like it was about to split.

She let out a long, anguished cry and threw herself forward and back until she nearly tore the steering wheel off, then pounded on it as she shook her head like a wet dog. Music started blaring—a seventies-era disco song. The steering wheel was a small command center, with an elaborate array of buttons and controls. She found the right button, turned the music off, and tried to settle back in her seat. The windshield wipers slashed back and forth on hyper drive; she stabbed at buttons until she found the right one.

Deep breath.

She looked sideways to check if anyone had witnessed her display of lunacy. The light changed and she drove on.

Act normal. If you act normal, normal things happen.

Just, normal.

Why did she have to say, *maybe even longer?* An hour was torture enough. She turned the music back on. Ever since she got the Mercedes, with the satellite radio and options for every kind of music, Margaret found she had a secret love for disco. She hid it like a deviant sexual fetish. It had to be the old stuff though, like Chic or Sister Sledge. It was completely unexpected. She couldn't remember even hearing disco music before. It was like discovering she descended from pirates.

Now was one of those times she wished she drank. She could imagine herself holed up in a dark, wood-paneled bar, nursing a bourbon and doing a crossword as she comfortably waited out the hour. Maybe even longer.

Instead, she was going to shop for a trench coat. She had it all planned. Ever since she'd given Justine permission to have this new friend—or whatever he was, it was so hard to tell with kids now but it was clearly something to be concerned about—over to the house, she knew she needed a plan. Something she could do so she wouldn't have to think about it. Just get in the car and go. She didn't need a trench coat, but years ago, when she pictured herself as a lawyer, she was always in a trench coat, striding the halls of justice with briefcase swinging. Being a lawyer wasn't what she'd imagined. She'd imagined law as a system not unlike a mathematical construct, with rules and procedures that sculpted the unseen into an elegant, useful design, similar to how she once thought of Catholicism; ways to reduce God and morality to formula.

It wasn't anything like that, but she figured she could at least get the trench coat, even if she did live in Los Angeles, where nobody actually wore trench coats except poorly adjusted teenagers. Maybe something in a light color, like tan, or a smoky gray.

The anxiety had given her a case of ugly face. She didn't need to check, she'd seen it plenty of times before. It was mortifying. It made her look like a drug fiend about to scream or cry. Sometimes she could control it, sometimes she couldn't, and right now, she couldn't. She'd used up all her control at the house.

The trench coat suddenly seemed like a bad idea. It would entail talking to people. She drove to her office instead.

Solitude was needed. Something to calm her nerves. The long-delayed trench coat would have to wait. One of the yoga DVDs might do. They were forty minutes long. Perfect. She hadn't done one in a long time, so it should be okay.

She'd gone through a yoga phase a couple years earlier. She'd get to her office early and do a solo session before anyone else arrived. She had a series of DVDs that went from novice to advanced, color-coded from pale pink to royal purple. The last one had a hologram figure of a lotus flower that looked like a pentagram, giving it an occult look.

Her doctor had suggested, for the third or fourth time, that she find a way to control her anxiety. He'd prescribed medication, but she refused to take it. She didn't tell him she was terrified of any kind of drug after the fistfuls her mother used to eat. Back then, it seemed like the more pills her mother took, the worse she got, until Margaret forgot that medications were prescribed to alleviate symptoms, not create them. "You'll have to do something," her doctor told her. "Learn to meditate, perhaps." That seemed drastic, so she tried a yoga class, but found it wasn't for her. She liked the yoga well enough, but not all the self-conscious preening and catty pre-class talk. So she got the series of nine DVDs, donned baggy gray sweats, and did it in her office. After five months, with slow progression, she pulled out the final disc, with its hologram winking at her like an initiation key. By then she could nearly turn herself inside out.

The yoga helped with the anxiety, but came with an unwelcome side effect, which she discovered at the end of a session while clutching and releasing in the lotus position. She had an orgasm. It was completely foreign and unexpected. She panicked. Though she was alone, she managed to swat her office door shut as it was happening.

She assumed it was a fluke, but it happened again. Unnerved, she decided: no more yoga. Maybe it was too late because soon after she woke in the middle of the night from a vivid dream and realized she was again having an orgasm. Her hand was gripped between her legs. She lay there afterward, panting and clutching her pillow with eyes wide open.

Her anxiety returned full force. She began searching for another outlet.

He'd moved her law practice to the fifth floor of a building on the corner of Wilshire and Ocean Boulevard in Santa Monica. Her office window faced the Pacific. Directly across, near a path that wound through a grassy area, was a statue of Saint Monica, a reminder of the area's Catholic origins and the city's namesake. Most people mistook it for the Virgin Mary. It was the main reason Margaret picked this particular building for her law firm. The statue reminded her of her mother and the times they went to church together. From the ground, the statue appeared to watch passersby, overseeing their welfare, but from Margaret's office, it seemed to look right at her. It watched her watching others: runners, lovers, families, the homeless, tourists, and the herds of teenagers that moved in packs.

Margaret got to her office early one Monday to work on a brief she'd been pushing around her desk for a week. The sun was just coming up. She watched a runner use the base of the statue to stretch, leaning on it for leverage before she took off running. Her bright red shorts moved at a clip toward the pier. Margaret set to work on the brief. She looked up a short while later to see the runner come back and pass the statue. Every ten minutes or so, as the sun rose and more people came out, Margaret saw the red shorts zip by.

Early the next morning, she watched the girl go through her routine. She ran remarkably fast. Wednesday was the same. Margaret began coming to work early every morning. Seeing the girl became part of her routine.

One morning, the girl didn't show up. The next day, she was absent again. Margaret went outside and crossed the street. It was a chilly, early fall morning. The air had the tangy, metallic bite common to seaside mornings. Fog that would burn off by late morning hung above the sand. There weren't many people out at this hour, except a few surfers bobbing in the water, looking like monks in their black wetsuits. A dedicated pack of high-speed cyclists buzzed by like a swarm of neon insects—their chatter and laughter whooshed past in a rush of wind.

Margaret looked up at the sculpture. It didn't have the same power that it had at a distance. Up close, it was so many parts; a nose, a sad eye, folds of cloth that looked shallow and fake. Poorly constructed, like people. The base was cool and damp to the touch. She looked down and saw a shoe sticking out from the other side. She took a step back and saw the girl in the red shorts.

She pushed off the base of the statue and bounced on her toes. Margaret felt caught. Caught doing nothing; the American sin. She pretended to be interested in the statue. The girl looked over at her.

"Morning," Margaret said. She was young, Margaret realized. Just a teenager.

"She's weeping for her son," the girl said.

"What's that?"

"That's Saint Monica."

"The statue is?"

"Yeah. I like to use it to stretch but figured I should know what it is in case it's like, sacred. I don't want to go

to hell for putting my feet on something holy or whatever."
The girl looked up at it as she pulled a knee to her chest.
"She cries every night for her child, and because her
husband was a dick that cheated on her. Something like
that. Since you seem interested."

"That's—that's interesting, I didn't know any of that."

"You watch me."

Margaret turned to her. "Excuse me?"

"You watch me."

"I don't. I'm sorry, I don't know what you mean."

"From your office. You think the windows are tinted
and people can't see, but your window is the only one with
a light on early and I can see you watching me."

"I like—I get to work early. I'm not watching you, I just
look out the window."

"No, you don't, you watch me. It's okay."

"I just... I do, you're right."

"It's alright."

"I have a daughter about your age."

"My age? I'm not, like, ten."

"She has, uh—she's blind. Mostly blind, so she can't do
some of the things other kids her age do."

"Kids, yeah."

"So sometimes I see someone like you and I guess I—"

"You wish she could do stuff like run. That's cool, are
you a runner?"

"Oh, no."

"Who's your daughter?"

"Justine. Shepard. She goes to Santa Monica High—"

"No *shit?* Justine is your daughter? I so know her. Yeah,
the blind girl. I go to Santa Monica. I'm on the track team."

"You know Justine?"

"Totally know her. Damn, you don't seem like you
could be her *mom*. She's like, crazy smart. I mean, because
you look so young, not 'cause she's smart. She was in my

chem class and she'd ask questions where I'm like, whaaat?"

"Is that right? Well..."

"Yeah. You should run with me some time."

"But I don't. Well, I used to run on a treadmill, when I was younger."

"I could coach you. I'm a good teacher. I even coach some of my teammates 'cause our coach is new and she's pretty dumb, or just bad at coaching track. I guess she used to coach basketball or something, I don't know what they were thinking. See ya." The girl pushed a button on her watch and took off running.

The next morning, Margaret showed up at the statue, dressed in running clothes. The girl squealed. "Really? Oh, this is awesome. Fresh meat. I totally love this and I get to run with somebody. Justine's mom even. I can never get anyone on the team to run with me here because they're like, it's too *early* and we run in practice anyway, blah blah." She suddenly got very serious. "Now, we're going to start off slow, and I only ask one thing of you in the beginning: focus and commitment."

They started with fast walking and very little running. After a week, they'd progressed to less walking and more running. Soon after, they eliminated the walking. Margaret found running natural, like a skill she'd forgotten she had. Liz talked nonstop. Margaret enjoyed the chatter, especially when she realized Liz didn't really need her to respond, even when she asked a question. It was like listening to a teenage talk show.

Margaret asked Justine if she knew Liz. "Liz, yeah, I think she's a year older. And she doesn't shut up, like, ever. She's one of those people that doesn't really listen, just rolls you so she can talk more. So you're running now? What happened to yoga? You'd practically gone Indian."

After a couple months of running, Margaret asked Liz if she missed running faster. "It always bothers me that I'm holding you back."

"You're not," Liz said. "Two weeks ago you matched my speed. I've been pushing you faster and you didn't even know it. See, I told you I'm a good coach." When Liz went out of town with her family for Christmas, Margaret figured she'd take a break from running, but after a few days, her body got restless. She could feel her anxiety poking around, looking for an opening.

She went running alone. Instead of the short, fast runs she did with Liz, she went for a long run. When Liz got back and they resumed their weekday routine, Margaret added weekend runs, and increased her distance each week.

Running became an addiction. More than that, it was a cure-all. It relieved anxiety, cleared her mind, and kept all other physical needs at bay, especially that great beast that was always pushing at her from the inside out.

Margaret pulled her Mercedes into the underground lot. She saw the van from the cleaning crew and a few other cars, but none she recognized. It wasn't unusual for some of her associates to work weekends. She'd made Sunday trips to her office a number of times and found one or two working away in shorts and sandals.

She'd been lucky in her hiring—or smart in taking Orlando's advice: "Hire slow. It's easier to hire than to fire." One of her first hires was a sixty-four-year-old lawyer who had been out of work for three years. Gavin Tupps proved to be an exceptional attorney, and still driven to prove himself. He was sometimes in the office on Sunday afternoons; the only one in a suit. With two recent hires, Margaret's firm now comprised seven attorneys and herself, plus a number of paralegals, secretaries, interns and clerks—a total of twenty-three.

No more, she thought as she got off the elevator. The cleaning crew was just finishing. When they saw her, they turned off their radio and pushed their cart toward the elevators. They gave her a nod as she passed.

She looked around to make sure she was alone. It took some digging to find the yoga DVDs. A run would be better, she thought, looking out the window. Fifteen-mile runs were common for her now. Not today, though. Her body was so wound up she was afraid if she started running she wouldn't be able to stop. That had happened once before, when she was so racked with stress she was grinding her teeth like a coke addict. Beginning in the Marina, she'd run north all the way to the Palisades bluffs, then halfway back to Venice Beach, finishing in the carnival of pot shops and tattoo parlors. Twenty-three miles. Her legs had turned to jelly. She had to call a cab to take her back to her car. She ran again the next day.

Door shut and blinds down, Margaret opened the TV cabinet and loaded the DVD. She took her jeans off, figuring she'd do the session in her t-shirt and underwear. She pushed some things aside and sat on the edge of her desk as the intro played out. The varnish felt cool against the backs of her thighs. The familiar music and voice on the DVD brought back the memory of why she'd stopped yoga. She pressed her fingertips to her eyes and rocked forward and back.

She finally admitted to herself that the last thing in the world she wanted to do right now was yoga. Sometimes she felt like her anxiety would eat her alive. And then there were times, like now, when she was tired of fighting it, when she just felt like—*fuck it, eat me up. Make a meal of me.*

School started, finally, but it didn't bring the relief Henry had hoped for. He kept thinking about Justine. Not only that, but everyone seemed to treat him differently; that is, those who didn't avoid him altogether, like the asshole he'd hit with the microscope that had to get stitches.

It had been four months since his mom died. He hoped people would've forgotten by now. They didn't. Nobody wanted to talk about stuff like that, so they ignored him altogether. It wasn't a huge deal. It wasn't like he had a ton of friends to begin with.

He'd been to Justine's house twice now. Her mother was, without a doubt, a little strange. The first time he was there, she left, but when she came back, her eyes were all red and puffy.

The second time was different. She didn't try to be friendly like before, and she didn't leave them alone. She seemed to think Henry had some sinister motive, like he was waiting for her to leave so he could fondle the blind girl. She didn't stay in the same room, exactly, but she didn't leave the house either. It sucked because they were supposed to be working on Justine's math, but it was hard with her mother there, since she was the reason they were doing it. If that's what they were really doing; Henry wasn't even sure anymore.

He kept having these imaginary conversations with her where she'd say something really witty and funny. Later, he'd wonder where it came from, because *he* wasn't funny or witty. And her laugh. He thought a lot about her mouth when she laughed; the way her lips pulled just above her top teeth so you could see a little of her gums. In his mind, he'd say funny things so he could look at her mouth as she laughed, then he'd realize the bell had rung for the end of class and he was still sitting there.

They were going to meet at his house this time. Big risk. His dad seemed to be doing better, but he was unpredictable, and if he started acting weird, Henry might have to say why, and that would mean talking about his mom, which could turn into a big mess. Justine might make a joke, like she always did. There were all kinds of potential hazards.

Henry asked Stephen if he'd drive him to pick her up.

"You're meeting here?" Stephen asked.

"Yeah. She plays piano, so she wants to see our piano."

"Oh, I see, the piano, what a coincidence."

"So, can we pick her up?"

"Sure, what time? I'll send your dad out on some worthless errands to get him out of your hair."

"That'd be awesome."

On Sunday morning, Henry texted Justine to say they'd pick her up. She texted back saying she'd take the bus. He was going to ask why, but realized it was probably because she'd told her mom something short of the truth about where she was going.

Henry kept checking the time on his phone. She'd said eleven o'clock. At twenty to eleven, he heard Stephen's voice. He came out of his room and leaned over the railing that overlooked the entryway. Stephen was talking to his dad in the dining room. The sound of keys, his dad's docile voice—still hard to get used to—and the sound of the kitchen door that led to the garage.

Great, that's done. Thank you, Stephen.

He thought of taking another shower. He'd gotten up early, so it'd been a few hours. No, that was dumb. He tried to read, listen to music, play some of the games he'd put on his phone and hadn't tried yet—but his focus kept wandering. He tried looking over the math outline he'd agonized over. He'd realized from their last session that a very different approach was required to teach a blind person advanced math concepts. He stared at the pages like a blank-minded idiot.

He settled for lying on his bed with his arms folded over his face, trying to calm his heart, which was pounding like it did before he had to get up in front of a group of people and talk. There was only one class he ever had to do that in—French—and that teacher had scarred him forever. She would make students come to the blackboard and write a phrase in French, then turn to the class and articulate it, like they were eight years old and in some French Colonial school. Henry seemed to sense exactly when the teacher was going to call on him. His heart would start to pound out of his chest, like his body knew before he did, then the teacher would turn to him with those weird thyroid eyes. "Henry, we haven't heard from you for a while. Staring at your desk won't help. How about, *J'ai pris mon vélo au magasin.*"

He heard voices downstairs. Stephen, and Justine's friendly sing-song. He swung his feet over and sat on the edge of the bed, suddenly weary. Thinking about Justine all the time could be exhausting; now here she was and he felt used up. He went out to the railing and looked down.

He'd told Stephen about her. Not much, but some. "Oh, and by the way, she's blind." He tried to make light of it by saying, "At least she won't have to look at my ugly face," or something like that. Stephen, without looking at him, said, "Henry, I can assure you, you don't have anything to worry about in that department." That made him feel good because Stephen had good taste in just about everything.

She was standing a couple of feet inside the entryway with the door still open. She formed a tall triangle framed in white light. It took him a moment to realize she was wearing a dress. He'd only seen her wear skirts that went past her knees and plain, loose-fitting blouses. She had her cane out. As she talked to Stephen, she used her cane to find the bottom of the door and close it behind her. Henry was glad to see that Stephen knew enough not to try to do it for her. Should have known; Stephen always knew the right thing to do.

~ ~ ~

"I'll be in the kitchen," Stephen said, leaving them alone at the piano. "Where I'll stay. Unless you need me. In which case, Justine, just hit a high C a few times and I'll come running." He already had her laughing.

"Damn, he's funny," she said when he left.

"Yeah."

"He's the guy your dad hired to help you guys?"

"Uh huh." Fuck, here it comes, a question about his mom.

"You know he's totally gay, right?"

"Picked up on that, yeah."

"Cool, hope that wasn't offensive."

"No."

"You can tell me if I'm being offensive. I love gay people."

"Great."

"I mean, I'm not. Myself, I mean."

"Right, I know."

"You do? How?"

"Oh, man."

"Are you?"

"What? No!"

"Chill, I knew that, just giving you shit. I mean, you drool all over my mom."

"I do not."

"It's alright, men find her irresistible."

"I don't."

"Really? Because last time I thought you were going to have to go in the bathroom and pull one out."

"What the fuck?"

"Forget it, lets play some piano, stallion." She situated herself and felt around. Her leg touched his as she played a few bars. "Fuckin' A, this piano is gorgeous. Perfect tune. Tight strings, though, doesn't anybody play it?"

"My dad plays, or he used to, but he stopped."

"This place is a tomb. Is there a way to get some more light? It helps sometimes if I can see a little."

"Really? I wondered about that."

"You can always ask. Actually, I've been praying for a miracle and I figure if God answers my prayers and I'm suddenly sighted, I don't want to be in a dark room because I might not notice."

"I can ask Stephen for a lamp. Which is the high C?"

"That's way beyond your level. Forget the light. Quit stalling, let's get started—*fuuuck! Is that a dog?*" She grabbed his arm.

"Oh, yeah, that's just Luca Brasi. He's friendly."

"O-kaay, rule number one is always-always-always let the blind girl know when there's a dog because you know we can't *see*."

"Shit, sorry."

"He's friendly you said?" She was squeezing his arm so hard his hand had begun to tingle.

"Yeah, totally friendly."

"Damn, Henry."

"Sorry about that."

"You owe me for that one. Like, big. Like if I ask you to help me bury a body, you say okay, no questions asked." She loosened the grip but still held his arm.

"Sure."

"Like even ten years from now."

"Alright, sorry. You don't like dogs?" It was a soft touch now, but still there.

"No, I love dogs. I love dogs as much as I love queers, I just need to know they're there, before I feel their cold nose on my thigh. Hello, Luigi." She let go of his arm to pet Luca Brasi with both hands.

"It's Luca Brasi."

"What kind of name is that?"

"Haven't you ever seen *The Godfather?*"

"Jesus, Henry."

"Fuck, sorry."

"I wanted a dog for the longest time. We had one when I was little, when I could still see regular, and for a time after. It's one of the few things I really remember seeing."

"How old were you when it happened?"

"Two, almost three."

"Shit, you remember back then?"

"A little. I think it's different for me. I remember our dog, I think because it was a before-and-after kind of thing, and I could touch and feel him. When I found out later that some blind people got their own special dog, I begged my mom, but she said no. She wanted me to be able to do everything like regular people."

"That's harsh."

"I hated her for it at the time, because how could she know what it's like?"

"Right."

"And she was making these decisions for me. But later I realized it was probably a lot harder for her that way, so she really was doing it for me. It would have been easier if she just threw me in with the other blind people."

Henry noticed Luca Brasi lay down on her feet. "Wow, we just had, like, a serious conversation," he said.

"I have my moments, and seeing as how we're in your house and you have no sense of humor, I figured I should try to accommodate."

"Thanks for that."

When they got started, she commented on how fast he was picking things up. He had to confess that Stephen had already shown him a few things.

"Could have told me that and we would have just started with scales. Now, forget the black keys." She reached over and took his wrist. "They're mostly there to make you feel inferior so don't let them, just say, *suck it, little black keys.*" She slid her hand up his arm. "Are your elbows straight out? Keep them level. Maintain your posture. Start good habits early. I don't want to have to bust out the ruler."

She kept her hand resting on his arm as he played the simple scales she showed him. "Wait," she said.

"Did I do it wrong?"

"No."

"Then what?"

"Nothing, sorry." She put her hands in her lap. "Proceed."

He was conscious of her hair touching his arm, and her smell. Vanilla. He noticed it more when she moved, like when she'd held his wrist. She was nodding her head to the sound of the scales. Her shoulder grazed his upper arm. He looked over at her. Her eyes were closed.

"Stop," she said. "What are you doing?"

"Sorry."

"You're way off."

"I know, I got distracted."

"By what?"

"I was—by you. I got distracted by you because I was looking at you."

"Okay."

"Sorry."

"That's alright."

"Can I just say?—it's weird, but sometimes I look at you, or want to look at you, and I don't know if you know

I'm looking at you so I don't know if I should be, or if that's weird."

"I think I understand."

"I don't want to be the weird guy."

"That's thoughtful."

"And you had your eyes closed, not that it matters, of course. I mean, I don't know."

"If it helps, I usually know."

"You know if I'm looking at you?"

"Sometimes. It's strange, I know, but I can tell. Like at my house last time."

"Really?"

"It's like a developed sense. Would it help if I gave you permission?"

"To look at you?"

"Yeah."

"No, that's weird. I mean, isn't it? Let's just keep going."

"I want you to. I mean, I'd like you to."

"Like, right now?"

"Yes." She turned to face him. "You have my full permission to look at me. As much as you want. This offer is good for the next two minutes."

"This is way fucked up."

"It is, but you started it. Do you want me to stand up or anything?"

"No."

"You're sure? I know I offered you my body before and you turned me down, and frankly that still stings a little, but you can still look, if you want. Last chance."

"No, I just wanted—just your face."

"Okay, go."

"Can you see me at all?"

"You're a pale-skinned blur, so no, not really."

He leaned closer. He could feel her breath. She took her glasses off and opened her eyes wide. They were dark brown with flecks of gold, with a dark ring around the iris. She had a long, elegant neck, and a soft fuzz of fine, translucent hair around her earlobes. Subtle expressions moved across her face, like ghosts glimpsed in a mirror.

"Good?" she asked. Her voice sounded different. He saw her swallow.

"Yeah, good."

She put her glasses on and turned back to the piano. She playfully nudged him with her shoulder.

"Are my two minutes up?" he asked.

"I think they better be." She began playing a sonata.

His dad was home. Henry knew right away because Luca Brasi got up and ran into the kitchen. Justine, absorbed in the music, was playing like he wasn't even there.

His dad came in. Henry knew he was standing in the archway but pretended not to notice. He hoped he'd just wander away on his own. No such luck; he continued to watch as Justine played. When she paused, he said, "Hi."

Justine stopped but kept her hands at the keys. "Hello," she said to the new voice.

"Dad, this is Justine."

~ ~ ~

The library was crowded. Everyone starts the school year with the best intentions.

When two people got up from a table, Henry guided Justine over to grab the spot. She was comfortable enough to touch the top of his arm as they walked. He was getting used to making sure there was space to his right when he walked, to keep her from getting clocked by a doorframe or bookcase. He liked it. It gave him a sense of purpose, like she trusted him to protect her.

Justine stood back up as soon as they sat.

"Shit," she said, and started digging in her backpack.

"What?"

"Nuts."

"Where, here?"

"Someone here was eating nuts." She took a wet wipe out of her backpack and wiped down her chair.

"Let me help. Can I go in your pack?"

"Sure."

"Wow, you carry a lot of stuff in here." He took a couple wipes out and used them on their area of the table. Others looked over at them.

"Yeah, it was a condition my mom had so I could go to a regular school. She checks my backpack every morning to make sure I have everything. This package don't travel light." When they finished, she put her pack on the floor and sat down.

"So, you're like, super allergic."

"Yeah, I can tell right away." He sat across from her. "Even traces trigger it. Believe it or not, I have trouble flying. I sit there with my EpiPen ready, like a terrorist about to trip a bomb. Those stewardesses can be careless with the peanut packs."

"Shush," someone at the far end said.

"Jeez," Justine whispered. "Why not just piss a circle around the table?" Someone on the other end made a big show of putting ear plugs in. Henry realized that Justine wasn't bothered by other people's reactions because she couldn't see them, so the mean looks and rude gestures—from the blatant to those calculated for subtlety—were lost on her. She'd already told him that there were actually some advantages to being blind. This seemed to be one of them.

They didn't work on math. They sat with their chins on their hands and whispered to each other for over an hour. The lesson outline Henry had worked on sat untouched.

"So, no dad?" Henry asked.

"No dad. He left when I was still in my mom's belly."

"Damn, and you don't know anything about him?"

"No, my mom just says he left. I gave up asking a long time ago. She says there's nothing more to tell. I've always thought it was weird how easy it is for men to leave."

"Maybe he didn't know about you."

"Maybe."

"So we're both down one."

"But I have my Aunt Vicky, she's awesome."

"You seem to think all the adults in your life are awesome."

"I know, I'm screwed up, right?"

"It's pretty bad."

"She's not really my aunt and she doesn't live here but she visits a lot. She's a famous fashion designer but you probably haven't heard of her because you're a dude."

"That's all true."

"She's the one most responsible for my pithy sense of humor. She's also my best source for Helen Keller jokes. She says it's better to make fun of yourself before anyone else can. Believe it or not, I used to be shy."

"No shit?"

Another *shush*. They slid their faces closer until Henry was almost lying on the table.

"Yeah. She tells me stuff my mom doesn't and always has great advice, like—*ruin lipstick, not mascara.*"

"What's that mean?"

"It's basically everything a girl needs to know about guys. According to her. So, what the fuck? Stomach cancer and she just dies, just fast like that?"

"Yeah."

"Jesus fuck, that's harsh. I'm really sorry."

"Yeah."

"I can tell you'd rather not talk about it. I just—I guess I have all these questions. I can be nosey. I mean really I'm just interested and I care, but I've been told I can be nosey or insensitive or whatever. At least my mom says so, but she's a bit uptight, as you know. Or a lot uptight. She says it's my Aunt Vicky's bad influence. I won't keep asking you about it. I'm just really fuckin' sorry."

"Yeah, thanks."

"Your dad seems really cool."

"He is, I guess."

"He's a doctor?"

"A surgeon, but he's kind of on leave, because—"

"Sure."

"—yeah. He's been majorly depressed. He's been a little better lately though, I think because of something a shrink prescribed him."

"Drugs to the rescue."

"Pretty much. We're not really getting anything done."

"I know."

He hesitated. "Can I tell you something?"

"Let's see. Yes."

"I have a feeling you don't really need help with math."

"Really? Why?"

"Well, you're a hacker, for one, which generally requires math skills."

"It helps, but isn't absolutely necessary. And I've kind of given that up, or I'm trying to. They put people in jail for that shit now."

"You mean for invasion of privacy, fraud, identity theft, that kind of thing?"

"I know, weird."

"So, why did you ask me to tutor you in math?"

She pursed her lips and went quiet. He waited. He'd learned this in debate class. If someone is uncomfortable and doesn't give you an answer right away, don't do anything, just let the silence hang there. Most people can't stand an awkward silence, so they fill it by answering your question, even if they didn't want to. He'd never had the occasion to use it in real life. She sat up and pushed her hair behind her ear. He stayed with his chin on his hands. She finally came back down, closer this time.

"Do you ever feel like you've outgrown your friends?" she asked. "Where it's like, nobody's interesting anymore?"

"I don't know, I don't have any friends."

"I've noticed this about you. Why is that?"

"Because I'm not funny."

"That's true."

"Funny people always have a lot of friends. You're funny, so you probably have a lot of friends."

"Well, you're half right."

Now he sat up and leaned back in his chair and she waited. "I gotta go to the bathroom," he said.

"Actually, I do too. I'll come with. We'll be like girls. You think our stuff's good here?"

"Yeah, I don't think anyone's going to boost your wet wipes."

When he got out of the bathroom, she was standing by the windows that overlooked the football field. She must not have gone to the bathroom, unless she was a lot faster than most girls. He stood next to her. She gave him a slight nod. She always did something subtle like that to let him know she was aware he was there.

"Henry, is there anyone near us?"

"Right now?" He looked around. "A few people, yeah."

"Can you—? Fuck. Can you take me where nobody can see us?"

"Now?"

"Yes." She put her hand on his arm.

"Sure." Since they were at her school's library, he didn't know his way around as well. He led her along the windows to the science section. There were glass box displays of award-winning science projects. Even though they were encased, somehow they were still covered with dust. He guided her down the aisle that had the chemistry periodicals that nobody read.

"Here," he said. "There's nobody here. But it's not as bright as by the windows."

"I know, this is good. Thanks for not asking why."

"Sure."

They stood facing each other, like they were waiting for the music to start. He could hear his own breathing. *Journal of Materials Chemistry*. Red and blue circular orbs on the cover. Sometimes the world seemed full of fascinating things he couldn't quite understand.

She stepped closer. He didn't move, but his heart started to pound, like it did when he knew he was about to be called on in French class. He willed it to stop, afraid if he looked down it would be like one of those cartoons of a heart popping through a chest. Maybe she could hear it, because she put her hand flat on his chest.

"Good," she said after a moment. "I thought it was just me. It's like there's an angry animal in there." With her other hand, she touched his face. He tried to hold still. She traced her fingertips over his eyes and nose, like his face was made of something fragile, then along the contours of his temples and forehead, and over his ears and chin. Her fingers rested on his lips for a moment before she trailed them over his cheeks and down his neck.

Her mouth was slightly open—her face still with concentration. Her fingers went over and around and back up. He could see where her lipstick tracked along her lip line. There were little flakes, the color of dark roses, in the ridges of her bottom lip. She kept her other hand pressed to his chest. A smile crept over her lips before she finally took her hand from his face.

"Thank you, Henry."

It was after five o'clock, but only starting to feel like dusk. They walked down Ocean Avenue through Palisades Park. The walk to her house was longer than he'd thought, but she didn't seem to mind, and the weather was warm. October was always a tricky month; summer was long over but then there'd be a string of hot days that made it seem like it was back. After the library's florescent lights and air conditioning, the breeze and ocean air felt nice.

The only time she touched his arm was when they crossed the street. "I used to walk around here a lot," she told him. "When my mom moved her offices near here. I got to know the area pretty good."

"What's the worst thing about being blind?"

"Stepping in dog shit."

He felt comfortable asking her anything now. If he wanted to know something, he didn't run it around his head a hundred times first, he just asked. She always seemed happy to answer whatever dumb question he had.

"I never thought of that."

"I know. It sucks. People that don't pick up after their dogs are the worst kind of people, followed by assholes on bikes that zoom by as close as they can and are all like— *watch it, idiot.* Fuckers. I had someone spit on me once. But the dog shit is the worst. I used to wear only really cheap shoes—I'd buy like five pairs—and carry an extra pair in my pack so if it happened I'd just throw away the pair I was wearing. The only thing worse than stepping in it is trying to clean it off so I just decided, fuck it. My mom would be all like, *where's all your allowance going?* Like maybe I was spending it on drugs instead of at Payless."

She wanted to tell him that the worst thing about being blind was not being able to see what she really looked like. She almost did. Somehow she felt like he'd understand.

Still, it didn't seem quite right. It was a strangely personal thing to tell someone—maybe her most personal thing, and he wouldn't understand, being a guy. How could he? So she told him the dog shit thing, which was true, but far from the worst thing.

She put her hand on his arm when they crossed Montana Avenue. When they got to the other side, she let go. He took her hand in his. It just kind of happened. But then he was conscious they were holding hands and got a little panicky. She squeezed his hand ever so slightly and rubbed her thumb once over the padded part at the base of his thumb. He stole a look at her. She smiled, to let him know she knew. It was a mystery to him how she did that.

"How was the library?" Stephen asked, pulling a u-turn in the Jeep.

"Good."

"Sorry your dad came home early. Thought I sent him on a task that would take longer."

"That's cool, he wasn't too weird."

"But a little."

"He insisted on driving us to the library, but it was fine. Thanks for picking me up."

Stephen nodded as he looked at the houses. "Nice neighborhood."

"Her mom's like this super successful lawyer."

"Yeah, I know." Of course he did. He knew everything.

They rode in silence after that. Henry wished Stephen would ask him about Justine, like—*Anything going on with you two?* or—*You guys seem to be getting along pretty good.* The kind of things parents say, all casual, while they're doing something else, like driving, or helping you fix your bike, or showing you how to pour a plaster mold.

"Can we stop and get ice cream?" Henry asked as they waited at a light. He felt like a kid. He didn't really want ice cream, but he couldn't think of anything else, and he really didn't want to go home yet.

"You haven't had dinner," Stephen said.

"Yeah, you're right."

Stephen looked over at him. "Actually, screw that. The pot roast came out terrible. Let's get some ice cream."

They went to the Ben and Jerry's on Main Street in Venice. Stephen got all worked up when a Porsche tried to take the spot he was backing into. He threw the Jeep in park and popped out, like getting in a fight was something he'd been meaning to do all day. Henry twisted in his seat and watched. "Seriously?" Stephen said in a big voice with his arms stretched out. The driver hesitated a moment before putting a hand up and backing out.

"Fuckwit," Stephen said when he got back in. He seemed like a chameleon sometimes, able to morph into whatever was needed at the moment. It occurred to Henry that maybe he should have gotten out too. There were parts of the male code he found elusive.

They sat on the cement steps, eating their ice cream and watching the parade of sidewalk traffic. The first push of warm Santa Ana winds arrived in a cluster. The sun had just gone down so the light was the kind that painters always trying to emulate. Girls walked by, happy for more warm weather and another chance to wear summer clothes. Hot wind snapped their clothes against their bodies and threw back their hair.

Henry, halfway done with his ice cream, was thinking that if he wanted to talk about Justine, he'd probably need to initiate it. He was trying to formulate a question. He was almost settled on—*do you think Justine is smarter than me?* Not much to show for all the effort.

They watched a distressed girl in a man's white dress shirt and jean shorts. She twisted and gestured on the sidewalk as she talked on the phone, crying and choking out words—well past the point of caring. Or perhaps she was making a public show of her drama on purpose. Henry thought she looked like the kind of person who needed tragedy to color her life, with her two-toned nail polish and wild eyes. He knew plenty of them, always finding conflict, afraid they'd forget they were alive if they didn't throw themselves against a wall a few times a day and have everyone witness it. He wondered what that would be like, to open your wounds for everyone to see.

The girl wiped away glistening tears and snot with a cuffed sleeve before her hand disappeared back inside. She wasn't much older than him. He wondered if he knew her. What in her life could cause such anguish? A guy, probably. A guy or her mom. Probably a guy. The shirt probably belonged to him and had his smell.

Maybe they weren't so different. He'd gone into his mom's closet a few times since she died, to bury his face in the flannel shirt she always wore in the studio. He'd even brought it to bed with him once. He had to sneak back and replace it the next day while his dad was downstairs talking to Conroy.

What if the shirt belonged to the girl's father? Maybe her father died, and that's why she was past the point of caring. Henry saw her differently now, like they were allies. What if his dad died? He'd never thought of that, but he'd never thought of his mom dying either. Then it happened.

"Henry," Stephen said. "Finish your ice cream. You don't want to face that pot roast."

Henry looked down; ice cream was dripping down his hand. He didn't want it now but wasn't sure what to do with it. He'd asked for it, after all.

When they got home, Stephen disappeared into the kitchen. Henry heard the piano and stepped into the hallway. It was his dad. Except for earlier that day, it had been over a year since he'd seen his dad at the piano. It seemed like another good sign.

He started up the stairs, but stopped halfway. Stephen appeared in the archway. They exchanged a look. Henry came back down and sat next to his dad.

He watched his dad's hands. He was playing something he'd never heard before; a simple melody, the kind they teach kids to build their confidence.

Tom finished. Not the end of the piece, but a drifting off. He put his hands in his lap. "I've been practicing a bit," he said. "You've inspired me."

"What was that one you tried to show me a long time ago?" Henry asked.

"I don't remember. Before?"

"Yeah."

"Did you eat?" Stephen asked Tom.

"Stephen, that pot roast—you should really ditch us and open a restaurant." Stephen smiled and went back to the kitchen. "Oh—I know," Tom said. He played the opening cords to *Hey Jude*.

"Yeah, that was it, The Beatles, right?"

Tom nodded. "Oh, this is super easy. Here, let me show you."

"Is that a C?"

"Yes. It's just C, F, A. Simple. Try with just your right hand to start." Henry tried the opening measure. "Good. It just repeats. She's very pretty."

"I think she's smarter than me."

"Um, you'll find that's the case sometimes."

"I need to get my driver's license."

"Sure, I can take you, we'll go together."

"Cool, thanks Dad."

"Now the left hand."

Chapter 15

When Justine got home from school, she knew her Aunt Vicky was there because of the music booming through the house. It sounded like one of those eighties bands they played during retro hour on the radio. That also meant her mom wasn't home.

She could never count on Aunt Vicky coming until she arrived. Sometimes she'd plan to come and not show up, other times she arrived unannounced. Justine figured wild, glamorous people like Aunt Vicky were probably all equally unpredictable, which was part of what made them so awesome.

"Auntie V?" Justine yelled from the living room, then the kitchen, then the office. She tried the bedroom. She turned down the music and called again. "Aunt Vicky?"

"Oh—*shit!*" a voice called from the backyard. "Yes, hon, I'm back here!"

"Where?"

"In the pool, on one of these floaty things. Careful, hon, the door's open." Justine went out back. "Sorry, babe, I had my headphones on and forgot I still had the music on in there." Vicky drifted in the center of the pool on a raft shaped like a chaise lounge, pushing the limits of its floating capacity. A cocktail rested on her swollen belly.

Vicky loved pools, and there was no pool she loved more than this pool. She'd always hated swimming, and barely tolerated water. Stretching a bathing suit over her ever-expanding girth was, in her words, positively medieval. It wasn't until she had back problems and a chiropractor—who eventually became her second husband and was currently trying to bleed her dry, despite Margaret's valiant legal efforts—made her use a pool that she found what she'd been missing. It was like discovering true love.

Weightlessness. She still avoided swimming, and could even do without water in general, except for bathing or as part of a view, like as a backdrop to her Chardonnay, but floating, being held up, getting a break from the plague of gravity was like being cradled in God's hand.

Her condo in New York had a pool. It was gorgeous. It was so beautiful, the doormen had to make sure tourists didn't come in and clutter the elevators just for a peak at it. Encased in glass and half the length of a city block, the sight of it teased Vicky with every elevator descent from the fifty-third floor. It was a marquee feature of the condo tower—a result of the Darwinian extremes of New York developers—and displayed itself like Cleopatra on the middle floor, suspended in weightlessness with steam drifting across its glassy surface and over slipstream edges. Every surrounding surface was clear. Even the decks were textured glass. Like a human aquarium, it was visible on all sides. It was an engineering marvel, in large part because it had to meet so many extra safety regulations and building codes, making it one of the most expensive pools in the world. Whooshing past in the glass elevator, Vicky watched the silent swimmers pushing frog-like through the water and divers leaving white trails like jet exhaust. She had only recently discovered her love of floating when she bought the condo, and had dreamy expectations of weightless evenings.

But she hadn't used it once in almost three years. The first time she tried, she looked up and saw the elevators drifting past. Faces turned in her direction. She couldn't display herself like that for every rise and fall of the glass box. This came as shocking news to her. Until then, her bravado had known no bounds. She had a hard time acknowledging this small weakness rooted in, of all things, vanity. She had to finally admit that she'd become guilty of buying her own image.

Vicky was the Red Queen. When she moved to New York, she was confident that she had better skills than all but the very best, most seasoned designers. She started at the bottom, because that's what you do, splitting seams and sewing cuffs and collars, all the while continuing to create her own designs. After two years, she thought long and hard about the direction she wanted to go in and how to get there. She studied every aspect of the fashion market and made a decision; instead of working her way up, she was going to burn down the door.

She used her savings to hire a top publicist. Together, they created an image for her—the Red Queen—which would also be the name of her brand, making the personality and the product synonymous. They mapped out every aspect of her public persona and began a careful strategy to spread it through interviews and social media.

She borrowed money from her sister and took out high-interest loans. She knew she had one roll of the dice. By the time she debuted her line at New York Fashion Week, everyone was talking about the Red Queen. Critics, initially prepared to pounce, were won over. All fell prostrate and hailed the Red Queen when she strolled out at the end in her now signature blood-red outfit.

Retail orders flooded in. Vicky had to rent three warehouse spaces and hire seamstresses as fast as they walked in the door. The whole enterprise nearly collapsed under a debt burden in the first year, but she soon found her feet and thrived, even as the faltering economy left most businesses like hers in ruins.

She'd discovered a trick. There was an enormous amount of money in the fashion industry, and the rewards matched the extremes. More important than having money and success was looking like you had money and success. If you mastered that, even in lean times, the money would eventually flow back.

The Red Queen was a marketing gimmick. Vicky knew this because she helped create it, and she knew where she left off and the Red Queen began. Usually. But there were times, after multiple fifteen-hour days, when she would begin to confuse the two. Over the years, she'd gotten more used to thinking as the Red Queen than as Vicky. It was just easier to be the larger than life crazy genius that yelled at people and slammed her fist so hard her assistants would scurry for cover. It was being Vicky that was difficult.

The Red Queen bought the condo with the floating pool, but it was Vicky who wanted to use it, and it was Vicky who couldn't bring herself to put on a bathing suit for all to see. The luxury hotels she stayed at during her frequent travels always had marvelous pools, but they were also visible from dozens of windows. Her bathtub wasn't big enough. That left Margaret's pool as the best option. A private pool where nobody but her oldest friend could see her; not even Justine.

"How's my little hacker?"

"I'm good. Where's Mom?"

"Still working honey, but she'll be here soon. We spent most of the afternoon at her offices. She needs some real help there."

"What do you mean?" Justine pulled her shoes and socks off and was about to sit on the edge of the pool and dip her feet in.

"Wait, honey, before you do that, can you pour me some more of this? It's in the blender. Try some. No, wait, you're not old enough. I've got my glass here."

"Sure, I'll get it. You don't sound close. Should I use a different glass?"

"Shit, I'm not. No, wait." Vicky tried to air paddle to Justine's side of the pool by kicking her foot. "I looked for some of those plastic cups I used last time. Damn—I'm cramping. Do you have one of those poles they use to get the leaves out?"

"I think so."

"No, never mind, I don't want you to fall in. Ah, fuck this. Sorry, honey, you know I got a bad mouth. Takes me a day or so to adjust."

"I don't mind," Justine said, grinning.

"Know what? I'm good, I've had two of these already, maybe three, so never mind. So, you're mom's offices. I know she has very little aesthetic sense, I mean she dresses nice and all—now—but that's mostly my influence, and even that was the result of me forcing her to email me a picture of what she was wearing every day for a month. You know she used to wear t-shirts and jeans every day? I mean every-single-day. Well, the offices she moved into—and by the way, when did her firm get so big? A few years ago she had three people on staff, today, she couldn't remember the name of one of her own employees."

"I know, she's been very successful."

"I thought I was doing alright."

"You are. I keep reading online about you, and now everybody wants you to do their dresses for award shows, it's like the first thing they say—*Oh, my dress was made by my good friend, the Red Queen.*"

"You freak me out a little when you say you read something, honey."

"It's a text-to-speech thing I have."

"I know, but still. Anyway, your mom's offices are the equivalent of her t-shirt and jeans. Plain and boring. If they were white instead of tan—*tan,* a color that shouldn't exist—it could be a biology lab."

Justine laughed and kicked the water. Visits from Aunt Vicky were just about the best thing ever. "How long are you staying?"

"Oh, longer this time. A week or so, I think, if your mom can stand it. Long enough to redo those offices." Vicky had drifted toward the far end of the pool. "Come down here, honey, I don't want to talk to you over my shoulder." Justine went to the other end and sat. "Here, hold your hand out, I think I can grab it. There, that's better. Now, put your foot on the edge of this thing and that'll keep me from drifting off. Perfect. My God, look at you, sweetie. When did you get so beautiful? I was here six months ago and told your mom, that Justine's becoming hot-hot-hot. She didn't like that, but I was right. You're prettier, much prettier, than the girls I design for. Even the Europeans. And you've got boobs. Do you realize how hard it is to design a dress for someone with no figure? I sure wish the tide would turn on that one. I should design something for you."

"I *wish* I had boobs."

"There's such a thing as too much, believe me. Yours are perfect. I bet you have to carry a stick around to keep the boys away."

"Hardly."

"Your mom told me you've got a friend."

"Yeah."

"Yeah? It's got her worried sick."

"I know."

"She's even started biting her nails again, like when she was a teenager."

"I didn't know that."

"Well, you can't see, honey."

"I know."

"So, tell me about him, is he pushing you toward the finish line, or have you already crossed it?"

"No, God!"

"I know, I'm a horrible woman, but I wasn't born yesterday. You still have this agreement with your mom?"

"Yes, I think it's carved on my arm somewhere, followed by, *It's all I ask.*"

"It's important to her."

"Clearly."

"But listen, honey—before your mom gets here—if you need anything, like help with anything, or have a problem you can't talk to your mom about, you call me. I know you have this agreement with her, and you're the best kid ever and she's got nothing to worry about, but sometimes things like that just don't stick. For whatever reason. If something happens or you need anything, you can come to Auntie V, understand?"

"Yes, thank you."

"Not that you'd need to of course, because you're too smart, but if you did. I wouldn't want to find out later something happened or you needed help and I didn't know about it. I've had that happen before."

"Alright."

Vicky looked toward the door. "And for God's sake, be safe, alright? I know your mom's got her rule number one, but this one is mine. Be safe. Promise me that."

"I am."

"Am?"

"I meant will—I *will* be safe."

"And you know all about that stuff, right?"

"Of course, everything's out there now. I mean, you can read about whatever."

"Freaking me out again with that."

"Although now girls watch stuff together and talk about it, like to learn how to do stuff."

"Are we talking sexual stuff?"

"Yeah, and they talk about how they're going to try that, or if they have. But of course I can't see that stuff and if I try to just listen all I hear is a bunch of—"

"That's enough, I get it. How I hate this age we live in. I don't envy you. Listen, don't you worry about any of that. Believe me, honey—and I've been around the block a few times—usually stumbling, but still, I speak from experience, I mean not that kind of experience necessarily, but experience—and you're better off. You're at an advantage over those girls. Honestly. You know, I may need another drink after all."

"Want me to get you one?"

"Actually, no. How's our project going? Is your mom seeing anyone?"

"No."

"Still no?"

"Still no."

"Not any anything?"

"Nope."

"Never, ever?"

"I think I'd know."

"Goodness, that woman, she's not human, that's all I can figure. Any leads? I'm having a hard time doing anything from New York."

"Maybe. One. I think so anyway."

Vicky perked up. "Really? When did this happen? You didn't let me know. See, this is what I'm talking about, I hate finding out after the fact."

"Nothing's happened, she doesn't even know."

"Well, shit, honey, tell me—" They both heard the sound of the sliding door. Vicky twisted toward it.

"Hey, ladies!" Margaret called. She held up a hand to shield her face from the late afternoon sun. "I stopped at the store and got steaks."

"Oh, for fuck's sake," Vicky mumbled, then shouted; "Hi, Mags!" She turned back to Justine. "Later, I want to hear."

~ ~ ~

Things weren't right. Henry's heart felt like a car racing down a dead-end alley. He didn't want to eat, sleep, or study. At home, in school, riding his bike—he thought about Justine all the time. But it didn't feel good, because of the guilt. He'd been thinking about his mother all these months, but now thoughts of Justine clawed away that and everything else.

It just felt good to think about her, which also made him feel bad. It all swirled inside him: guilt and desire and joy and dread. And a lot of fear. He didn't understand how it was possible to feel all that at once, and at the same time feel a kind of numbness, like the moment after getting hit in the head.

They'd seen each other three more times since the library; on consecutive Sundays at his house to play piano and study. Because they went to different schools, there wasn't an easy way to meet up during the week. The time between Sundays was a blissful kind of torture.

Despite his progressive desire, nothing had happened between them, which seemed normal to him; normal in the sense that he didn't think of them as normal to begin with, so not-normal was normal. They just acted like friends that were getting more and more comfortable around each other. They talked about her mom and his dad, but avoided talking about his mom, like they both knew not to. He'd say little things about her here and there, testing the water, like: "My dad's an opera nut. My mom kinda was too."

Stephen had taken an immediate liking to her. He loved bringing them snacks when they studied or practiced piano. He always assured her there were no nuts in anything. The kitchen had been purged of any nut-containing product. His dad liked her too. He came into the library once when they were studying and ended up sitting down with them and talking. She asked what it was like being a doctor. She said that if she weren't blind, she would definitely go into medicine.

"You know, it's not just you; I think she's smarter than me, too," his dad told him later.

Now he wasn't sure what to do. She'd invited him over to her house the following Sunday. She wanted him to meet her Aunt Vicky—the one she was always talking about. They could practice some piano and use her mom's office to study. She made it seem so easy-breezy.

But nothing was that simple. He'd recently been struggling with an overwhelming need to tell her how he was feeling, but the thought terrified him. Everything in his head now had this dual aspect. Maybe that was why adults looked so miserable. All he had to do was imagine saying something like, "I think about you all the time," and the ache in his stomach would contract and his head would feel like it was about to explode from the pressure. He knew he couldn't do it, but he had to do something. All this head traffic made him both look forward and dread seeing her.

On Saturday, he went to her school's library to study, even though his own school had a very nice library. He told himself he really needed to get his head into his schoolwork before it was too late, and using her library would be better because he wouldn't run into anyone he knew. Dumb excuse, he realized later, because he didn't really know that many people; and he didn't get any studying done. Instead, he ended up in the aisle with the chemistry periodicals, which he pretended to look at while reliving every moment of the time she'd touched his face.

~ ~ ~

Margaret's offices were a mess. When Vicky insisted she be allowed to redecorate, Margaret had said fine, imagining something like a few new pieces of furniture and some artwork on the barren walls. She didn't even bother to tell the staff—it would be no more than a minor inconvenience.

They were now at day five, and nowhere near done. The place looked like it had been turned upside down and shaken. It reminded Margaret of years ago, when Vicky would throw herself into sewing projects with an obsessive energy that devoured sleep and every other human rhythm.

Vicky had gutted all the offices and common spaces, pulled carpet, laid hardwood flooring, repainted twice after changing her mind on the color, installed natural wood baseboards and crown molding, and revamped the entire lighting system. This last part required a small army of electricians and a visit from the building's owner, followed by an inspector from the city of Santa Monica. The owner argued that Margaret was now in violation of her lease. She was sure he was right. Fortunately, he did an about-face when he discovered who Vicky was, and transformed into a star-struck groupie, giddy to be asked his opinion on fabric swatches for the furniture by the Red Queen herself.

"You didn't know?" Vicky told Margaret later. "I'm huge in the gay community. I'm the new fuckin' Cher. I actually have followers, like a cult leader."

On the third day of the project, a ladder fell on the desk of a terrified paralegal, who went running for the elevators. Even Margaret's obsessively committed assistant, Heidi, was complaining. Margaret decided to let them all work from home, and asked that they return to the office on Monday.

Now it was Friday, and things didn't look any better than they had on Wednesday. With the workers gone for the day, Vicky and Margaret took refuge in her office, away from the wood varnish fumes and loud noise of the industrial fans being used to speed-dry the floors. Even Margaret's office was a mess. Everything had been taken out except her desk and chair. She sat, tipped back, her tennis shoes propped on the window ledge as Vicky sat on the floor, surrounded by a mess of fabric samples, pottery brochures, paint swatches, phones, two open laptops, and a tablet on video connect with an interior design consultant who was half asleep in a hotel bed in Brussels.

Margaret gazed out the window with the detachment that comes from complete surrender. She wondered about Liz. They'd run together through the fall, but had to stop when Liz started training with her school's team again. Margaret missed her gabby camaraderie. She'd stuck to her long weekend runs, often covering the equivalent of a marathon in two days, but had missed the previous weekend because Vicky had arrived, and she'd miss this weekend because her offices were decimated. Her body was getting that itchy feeling, a warning that she needed to get some miles in.

Margaret chewed her fingernails as she watched a pack of teenage girls waiting to cross the street: slouchy, half dressed, and constantly distracted. The new cool seemed to revolve around ignoring everything except their phones. What did they fear? Same as every teenager, probably—not finding their place in the world before it left them behind. No catching it on the next rotation. For a moment, Margaret pitied their mothers, before realizing she was one of them.

"*Amaryllis red*, that's what she was saying," Vicky said.

Margaret heard her, but a beat late. "I'm sorry, what? Are you still talking to that woman?"

"No, she fell asleep. I kept thinking she was saying, *I'm ready for bed,* and you heard me, I'm like, *I see you're ready for bed, because you're in your bed, but I need to know what the trim color should be.* Well, shit, she was saying *amaryllis red,* not *I'm ready for bed.* I mean—I get it now, but not until I told her fine, go to fucking sleep, and signed off. I'll have to call her tomorrow because you know what? That color is perfect. I was thinking maybe a warm tone, but nothing as hot as that even occurred to me. I should be nicer to her, she's really very good."

"Vic, I need my offices back. Bad. I'll go broke if this keeps going. I've got contracts, things I've signed."

Vicky held two paint swatches side by side. "I know what a contract is, counselor. It'll all be done by Monday. Ish." She heaved herself off the floor—a three-part process. "It looks worse than it is. That's always the case with these things, then you walk in and it's like *holy shit, it's done!* I'm doing all this pro bono, you know."

"Yes, and I'm grateful," Margaret said, fatigue settling into her voice. "But that doesn't make it free."

"You couldn't afford me."

"I'm sure you're right."

"What do you do for sex?"

"—wait, what?"

"I'm inquiring what you do for sex." Vicky hoisted herself onto the desk with a glimmer of her youthful athleticism and propped her stockinged feet on Margaret's chair.

"What do you mean?" Margaret asked. "I don't do anything for sex. I suffer, like all normal people." She looked out at the statue of Saint Monica—watching her watching others.

Vicky made one of her stretching yawns that ended like a cat getting strangled, then slid her toes under Margaret's legs. "I get it, you don't have the same basic needs as the rest of us mortals."

"It's not that, there's just no *there* there."

"I've never been clear on that expression."

"It helps to live here. A writer used it to describe Los Angeles. Perfectly."

"No help," Vicky said without considering it.

"Think about it."

"I hire people to do that."

"You're looking for something that doesn't exist but seems like it should."

"Are we talking about God? I was just talking about sex. Or even companionship. I don't think you even have someone to talk to."

"Really?"

"Am I wrong?"

"No," Margaret sighed and looked at the ceiling. "No, you're not wrong. What about you?" Her head tipped sideways to look at Vicky. "Divorce was over a year ago."

"I do fine."

"Do you now—who? I want to hear." Holding up her end of conversations like this felt like heavy lifting.

"There's no *who*, at least not specifically."

"Not specifically, or not singular?"

"Not either."

"Vicky, what do you do for sex? You've asked me, I answered, now I'm asking you, because I know you're not seeing anyone, and you're not one to go without, and I'm not good at this kind of girl talk."

"That's true, but you could at least pretend."

"Believe me, I do." Margaret took her feet down. "I'm tired, let's go home. You float, I'll cook. Having you here is improving my barbecuing skills."

"Wait, before you get up."

Margaret was half out of her chair. "What?"

"I may need to talk to you about something."

"Something else?"

"Yes."

"Now?"

"Yes, and it's something that's hard for me to talk about."

"Then don't—let's go."

"This one's bad."

Margaret sat back down. "I'm worried now so don't fuck with me, Vicky. What is it?"

"You were asking me about sex, right?"

"*You* were asking *me*."

"Yes, but just so you'd ask me."

"Which I did—or I tried to. What the fuck, Vic, just tell me."

"You know, you've become quite the potty mouth since you lost your Catholicism."

"It comes out when I'm tired. Lawyers are worse than cops, but I'll make an effort. *Speak*."

"I'm saying it would be easier for me if you were to keep asking me about sex, like you're forcing me to tell you."

"Oh, Jesus." Margaret rubbed her eyes. "Like a deposition?"

"Yes, exactly."

"Fine." She turned to face Vicky. "Who are you having sexual relations with, on what occasions, and under what specific circumstances?"

"Men."

"More than one?"

"Yes."

"At the same time?"

"Yes."

Margaret blanched. "That was supposed to be a joke. You're having sex with multiple partners at the same time? In the same bed?"

"You should never try to be funny, Mags. Not always in bed, but yes, I have."

Margaret shook her head and stood. "Vicky, what are you doing? What's going on?"

Vicky slid off the desk and took the chair. It made a new sound under her weight. She looked at her lap. "Alright, here it is. Please, no judgment." She took a deep breath. The chair wheezed. "There are professionals, as there are in any industry, including the one we are speaking of."

"Industry?"

"Or, that I'm trying to speak of. Women, of course, but there are also men, who—"

"What?"

"—men whose job it is to administer pleasure to—"

"*Jeeesus* on a bicycle, are you talking about prostitutes?"

"Don't interrupt me or I won't get through this."

"It's just that before you wanted me to ask you questions."

"Just, shut up now."

"Fine, no prob—"

"A couple times I've paid for... it. It's very formal and, and organized. I know it sounds horrible, but I'm a fat woman in her sexual prime who is now moderately famous and, well, you'd be surprised at how much that limits my options. And they're good. My God, Mags, you get what you pay for, and I have considerable resources now and holy moly these men know what they're doing. Then they leave, and for a few days, I've got a bit of a buzz. You know, I think more women would do it if they knew—" She looked at Margaret. "Okay. Well, I was talking to one after we'd—you know—and he says I should really treat myself to him and a couple of his friends."

"At the same time?"

"Well, yes."

"Oh—like a package deal."

"Exactly."

"Thrifty."

"I thought so. Of course I laughed at first, but he mentioned it again the next time and showed me some pictures, and, well, without all the details, it happened."

"Oh, my dear God."

"Stop it!"

"I'm sorry. Go on. Or not. Is that all? I'm fine if it is."

"Well, these guys do it for the money, obviously, so it's no surprise they do other things for money. And while I was... distracted, one of them filmed me, and they sold it to a news website, which contacted me for comment—as a courtesy, they said—and they're building a story around it and plan to release it in a few days."

"Oh, my God." Margaret sat on the desk and slumped forward.

"I've got two verbal agreements to design for the Academy Awards. That will disappear, along with every other contract I have, and probably the Red Queen retail expansion that's just getting started."

"I need a second to get my head around this. So, it's a news site that bought it, not a, a... pornographic site?"

"Yes, that's right."

"Did you give some kind of consent?"

"For what?"

"To be filmed."

"No, of course not. Jesus, Mags."

"And you didn't know they were doing this? The filming? I mean, while it was happening?"

"No, I didn't. Does it matter? I was distracted. I remember one was standing while the other two were—"

"Stop. Don't ever say what you were going to say."

"But is there anything you can do? Legally?"

"No, I don't think so. They're not doing anything illegal, especially if they've notified you. The person who filmed it without consent, maybe, I don't even know, laws are different state to state—privacy versus creative expression type of thing—and I have no experience with that kind of law, just like I have no experience with divorce litigation like I told you a million times, and see how that worked out."

"What does any of that mean?"

"It means there is no legal solution to this because the law is completely inconsistent in this regard. For instance, prostitution is illegal, but—"

"I'm aware of that. I don't need a lecture about—"

"Oh, you're getting a lecture. I'm saying—listen—exchanging money for sex is illegal. That's prostitution, which is illegal, except in parts of Nevada. But exchanging money for sex and filming it is not illegal. That's pornography, which is a protected form of creative expression. Those actors don't work for free, after all. So money for sex is fine as long as there's a camera present. Then it magically becomes something else. Legally."

"Why do I care about any of that?"

"Because, it means maybe you weren't breaking the law. You were, by paying men to have sex with you, but once someone started filming, it became art. Or not exactly art, but legally protected."

"Again—"

"You essentially went from law-breaking criminal to legally protected employee. You became the talent. Because of a camera. Which you didn't even know existed.

You see how fickle the law is? Although you were paying them, not the other way around, so now I'm not sure."

"Everybody hates you."

"Do you know which one took the video?"

"I don't even know their names, much less—"

"Did you get a receipt? Okay, sorry. Let me think. Now, this may be a dumb question, but is it possible this would help you instead of hurt you? It seems to happen an awful lot, the whole sex tape thing, like it's planned or something, for publicity purposes."

"I thought of that, believe me. And, no. I don't mean to be crude, but if you've noticed, all those other people are attractive. You *want* to see them doing whatever it is. Who doesn't want to see that?"

"Me. Me times a hundred."

"But I'm fat and nobody wants—well I understand there are some who have a fetish for my type—"

"Please don't use that word. I'm really trying here, Vic."

"The point is nobody wants to see me doing that. Believe me, I've seen it. The news site sent me a copy. Or at least the vast majority of people don't. It wouldn't help. I'm pretty sure it would kill me."

"There may not be any immediate legal recourse to stop them, but if a crime was committed, you should report it. You could go to the police."

"Right. Comedy hour at the station. Should I report myself first for engaging prostitutes?"

"No, of course that wouldn't work."

"You're a real help."

"I'm sorry. I really think you should consider embracing it. If it's going to happen anyway, what else can you do?"

"Mags, you don't know how hard I've worked and what I've gone through."

"Is that why you did all this?" Margaret waved her hand toward the outer offices.

"No. Maybe. I needed a distraction. A big one."

"At least you told someone, that's got to be a relief."

"I guess."

"You know I don't judge you, Vic. I don't always understand everything you do, but that doesn't matter."

"Aren't you even a little curious?"

"About what?"

"What they do? What they do that's so great?"

"No."

"There's really no going back once you've experienced it. It kind of ruins you."

"Well, that certainly seems to be the case."

Chapter 16

Most people thought the Red Queen was the scatterbrained-genius type. That was part of Vicky's well-crafted image, and one she usually enjoyed projecting, but the truth was, she was as sharp and organized as a military commander.

She'd tried to take care of this the right way. It didn't work. Now it was time to get creative. Her specialty. She had an alternate plan, and it involved Justine.

While Margaret barbecued out back, Justine and Vicky worked in the kitchen. Justine was making a peach pie. Vicky had been assigned to cut vegetables.

"I need your help with something," Vicky said when she was sure Margaret would be in the backyard awhile.

"Jeez, Auntie V, you can't even cut vegetables?"

"Not that. How hard is it to hack a news website?"

"Like CNN or something?"

"No, one of those tabloid types that are always intent on ruining people's lives."

"Like CNN."

"Okay then, like CNN."

"Depends."

"On what?"

"Well—"

Vicky heard Margaret's tennis shoes squeaking down the hall. "And *then* I'm going to add some big pottery bowls to each of the floor stands, so it brings the whole thing together."

"Wha—? Oh, yeah," Justine said. "I see. How big are they?"

"Huge, like ancient urns."

Margaret dug in the refrigerator. "Barbecue sauce," she mumbled.

"What if they fall?" Justine said. "We have earthquakes here, you know."

"They weigh a ton," Vicky said. "Any natural disaster, they'd be the last thing standing, like the chimney that's always in a picture after a fire."

"Oh, right."

"I really should have marinated first," Margaret said as she squeaked back toward the backyard.

"So," Justine said when the coast was clear, "this would appear to be something you don't want my mom to know about."

"It would be better if it was just between us girls." Then, without specifics, Vicky explained the situation.

"You realize I'll need a copy of the video," Justine said.

"No way."

"I have to get any coded imprints off it. It's essential. It's not like I can actually see it. What is it, anyway?"

"Just something I'd rather people not see. It's something a jealous competitor made to try to damage my reputation and—"

"Oh, my God!" Justine dropped the bag of sugar. "It's a sex tape."

"No, it is not a sex tape."

"It is *so* a sex tape. Auntie V, I didn't think you could get any cooler. You have a sex tape?"

"You stop that right now, it is not—" Squeaks approached.

"Honey, you alright?" Margaret asked.

"Um hum." Justine said. "Just... dropped the flour."

"Sugar," Vicky said. "I'll clean it."

"Vic, you've cut one tomato—what've you been doing in here?"

"Sorry, I'm on it." Vicky bent over the cutting board and started hacking at a bundle of carrots.

Throughout the night, in bits and pieces, Vicky told Justine everything and answered all her questions: How long ago? How many copies are there? Was it shot on a cell phone? Is it all one piece? Is there sound? (oh, there was sound). All information Justine claimed she needed to determine if hacking was a possible solution.

"Everything okay?" Margaret asked Justine later in the evening. "You're so quiet."

"I'm fine, just tired. I think I'll go to bed early. Auntie V, will you tuck me in?"

"Of course, sweetie, I'll be up in a few minutes," Vicky said. She turned to Margaret. "*Tuck me in.* That kid is just the sweetest thing ever."

"Um." Margaret said. "I count my blessings."

Later, when Vicky sat on the edge of her bed, Justine got right to the point. "I think it can be done, but it depends on a lot of factors I won't know until I get in there. And I'll need help. Some of it's beyond my skill set— most of it actually—and it has to be done fast. But I know some people. They cost money, though."

"You *know* some people? Heavens, you sound like the Mafia. 'Gotta see a guy about a thing'—kind of thing. Well, whatever it costs." Vicky's breath was heavy with wine. "You're not going to do anything dangerous, are you?"

"No, but illegal. You need to be aware of that. We'll be breaking the law."

"Jesus fuck."

"I'm alright with it. This is about the most exciting thing ever."

"Fine, let's do it. I'm terrible. I'm just a terrible, horrible person. Thank you, sweetie, you're really saving me if this works."

"You're welcome."

Vicky started the process of getting up. She bounced up and down a couple times for momentum. "But I want something in return," Justine said as she was about to get flung against the wall.

"Oh." Vicky stopped. "Sure, hon, anything."

"Something very specific. Actually, two things."

"What are they?"

"One, I want you to tell me what I look like."

"Oh, honey—"

"No, don't say it. Honestly. Very honestly. Otherwise, forget it. I'm going to get naked and you're going to tell me exactly what every part of my body looks like, in detail, and if I think you're lying, I'll send your video to the New York Times."

"Jesus fuck. Now?"

"No, later. We'll figure out when. And two, I want you to tell me about boys. Men. Things other girls know because they can see stuff. Every tip, trick, and technique you've learned. I want it all, in detail."

"Holy mother of God."

"That's the deal."

"Your mother would absolutely fillet me."

"Deal?"

"You're a horrible child."

"Deal?"

"You're satanic."

"*Deal?*"

"Yes, deal."

Justine squealed. "Oh, *thank you thank you thank you.* You're so awesome, I love you, Auntie V."

~ ~ ~

By the time Vicky woke up the next morning, Justine had made significant progress. She was coordinating three people on the East Coast, including a guy who called himself Charlie Horse, who specialized in source-tracking video and imaging codes and charged more per hour than a brain surgeon.

Justine sat through an antsy breakfast with a bleary-eyed Vicky. Margaret was fidgety and gnawed her nails, anxious to face the disaster at her office. Justine was itching to get back to her computer.

Vicky and Justine managed a whispered exchange. Vicky wanted to make sure she remembered their conversation correctly. She held out hope that Justine had changed her mind about her conditions, but Justine confirmed their deal and gave her a quick update on her progress. "I think it'll work," she said.

~ ~ ~

The following Tuesday, Justine skipped school.

Vicky told Margaret she needed half the day to meet with contractors. Margaret, who had segued from surrender back to panic, just grunted, afraid if she made eye contact she might throw Vicky out the hole that was once her office window; the math required to do so flashed through her mind: weight, leverage, distance.

Margaret had shown up on Monday with a new attitude—how bad could it be?—and found herself shocked by her lack of imagination. She had to send out a staff email saying the offices were not ready to be safely occupied and to stand by for day-by-day updates. Taking a moment to force deep breaths while willing her bleeding fingers away from her mouth, she calmly rationalized that when Vicky showed up they would immediately come up with a strategy. Perhaps she'd not been clear enough in emphasizing the urgency of the situation.

Not only had her office desk been removed, but her window was missing. It was to be replaced, eventually, with a new polarizing version. In the meantime, the sound of traffic filled her office, along with a bracing ocean breeze.

Margaret was using a door laid over two sawhorses as a desk. Power saws buzzed outside her office. She was focused on transcribing a deposition, which the paralegal would normally have done, but she'd quit. That was when Vicky came in to explain she'd be gone for half the day. Margaret grunted because she couldn't speak—her stomach was clenched so tight she didn't have the air. It was a good thing she didn't know where Vicky was really headed.

The Beverly Wilshire. Once she gave over to the idea, Vicky decided to go all out with Justine's unusual request.

The hack proved easier than Justine had expected. Thank God for cloud storage. The news site that bought the video had just switched not only to cloud backup, but cloud-based applications. That made for an easy snag. Filtering emails and text messages led them to who had copies, which were harder to herd up, but not impossible. The hardest part was getting the original, which, thankfully, they tracked to a cell phone. In trying to get the phone, Charlie Horse followed the owner around the Upper West Side all day Saturday, then in and out of a Knicks game at Madison Square Garden the following day. Impatient, he finally followed the man into a restaurant bathroom. He washed his hands over and over until another patron left; he then put on a big pair of sunglasses and kicked in the stall where the man sat, texting. The man dropped his phone as he tried to stand. The phone skidded across the tiles. Charlie Horse stopped it with his foot, grabbed it, and was gone.

The final step was putting a trace-bot on the video's data code, in case any other copies popped up. If they did, they'd be pulled before they could be presented for public consumption.

In return, Justine got what she wanted. Vicky took the task seriously. As Justine lay on the Beverly Wilshire's cream-colored sheets, Vicky answered honestly the many detailed questions Justine had about every part of her body. Justine had Vicky look at pictures of other girls and describe them so she could compare and contrast. Vicky made some suggestions about how she could improve her looks by accentuating her best features.

The second part was harder to deliver. When Justine began to sense that Vicky was dragging things out a bit too long, she suggested they move on to part two.

"I don't know if I can do that," Vicky said as Justine put her skirt back on. "This has been hard enough."

"You have to. It's not just sex I want to know about, it's everything, but we'll start with sex."

"What's the point, really? You've promised your mom."

"I know, but—"

"Your mother's very smart, by the way. She's a brilliant woman, so this is not wise."

"You said you'd do this."

"And I'll tell you something else, she is the only woman in the world I'm actually afraid of."

"Auntie V."

"She has a potential in her."

"You agreed."

"You're not going to need any of that stuff for a while yet. When it's time, we'll talk. Promise. I'll fly you to New York, just for our talk."

"I think it's probably the words that make you feel uncomfortable, but remember, I've heard all the words, so none of that's new. I mean, I heard a lot of them on your video."

"Oh, God."

"Especially the guy with the Italian accent, that dude was like captain nasty."

"No, no, no."

"What was he doing to you?"

"Just—stop."

"They're just words. But I know you're weird about it, so I'll say some, just to get them out in the open so you don't feel so bad using sex words with a sixteen-year-old."

"I can't do it."

"Fuck, cunt, pussy, tits, blowjob, anal, cock."

"Jesus."

"Dick, snatch, balls, lick, suck, lesbian."

"Stop."

"Anal."

"Said that."

"Cunt, um, sucker... fuck, clit, threesome, spank, asslick—er."

"*La la la* I'm ordering room service lunch and a tray of Bloody Marys."

"Auntie V."

"How about a turkey-melt?"

"Remember what I said."

"I know—go ahead, send it to the New York Times, I can't do it."

"Auntie V."

"I'm saying I cannot do it. I know I said I could, but I was intoxicated."

"No, you weren't."

"Then I was coerced."

"No."

"You're like your mother, you make people say things."

"Auntie V." Justine sat on the edge of the bed. She could feel her tears welling up and tried to hold them off.

"Just, forget it," Vicky said as she picked up the phone.

"Aunt Vicky!"

"*What?*"

"I've never been kissed by a boy. Or been touched. Ever. I'm asking for your help. Please." It felt like forever before she felt her aunt sit down beside her.

~ ~ ~

Henry's lungs burned as he peddled up the long hill. He kept thinking that he really, really needed to get his driver's license.

His plan had been to ride his bike partway to Justine's house, then take the bus the rest of the way. That didn't work out because the bike rack on the bus was full. Now he was standing on his peddles and leaning over his handlebars as he made incremental progress on a hill that went on so long the local triathlon club used it for training.

By the time he made it to her house, his pants were shellacked to his legs with sweat. He lifted his bike up her porch steps and took a moment to catch his breath before knocking. The door swung open immediately.

"You must be Henry—holy *shit* you are good-looking." A large woman dressed in red filled the doorway. Synthesizer music blared from behind her.

"Auntie V, you were supposed to let me open the door. You're always taking advantage." Justine appeared behind her, smiling, her face flushed like she'd been laughing.

"Well, I'm fat, so I figured we were evenly matched. Come in, Henry."

"Thank you." The red mass stepped aside. She smelled like lavender perfume.

"Did you swim the English Channel? My God, hon, you look like you're melting. You don't believe in shorts? Justine, get the man a cool refreshing something to drink."

"I'm fine, but that is a very long hill."

"Wow, you are sweaty," Justine said when she took his arm. "I can feel the heat coming off you. Let's get something to drink, I'm thirsty too. My aunt has been making me sing along to horrible old music with her."

Vicky turned down the music. "This music was a cultural high point."

"So, Auntie V, this is Henry. Henry, this is my aunt that's not really my aunt, Vicky."

"Oh, he doesn't care about any of that crap. Listen, kids, I'm going to go float—you guys need anything?"

"No, but I thought you were going to go help my mom."

"I am, I just want to experience some of the day first. Your mother, God love her, is not easy to take at full strength first thing in the morning."

"It's past eleven, but okay."

"I'm on East Coast time."

"Then it's after two."

"And that's why I got to bed so late, see? Nice to meet you, Henry."

"Yeah, you too," Henry said.

Vicky started down the hall. "Listen, Henry." She stopped. "You've seen the pool out back, yes?"

"Yes. I have. I've seen the pool. I have. Seen it."

"I wasn't going to press charges, hon, I was just going to say you don't need to see it again, right?"

"Uh, no? I don't think so."

"I'd advise you not to, because there's going to be a great big fat woman floating in it, and nobody really needs to see that."

"Oh. Who?"

"Ha! Me, dingbat, but you sure are sweet, acting like you don't know. Cute, sweet, and knows just when to lie."

Justine handed Henry a glass of iced tea. "Come on, we can use my mom's office. She usually keeps it so perfect she'd know if a paperclip was moved, but it's got a bunch of junk in it now because they're redecorating her work offices. There's enough room and it's quiet."

"Where's your mom?"

"Work. She's practically living there now, trying to get it all put back together."

"You look different," Henry said as they sat down at her mother's desk. Justine had cleared it off so they'd have room to work. She let Henry have the normal side with the big cushy chair while she sat on the other side, straddling a swivel chair backwards. Her hair was in a loose braid down her back, which opened up her face. Her skin wasn't as pale, and she was wearing an aqua blue polo shirt that was tighter on her than the bland, loose blouses she usually wore. She had a necklace on with turquoise stones and wore snug, faded jeans instead of a skirt. "I mean, good. You look different in a good way."

So far, so good, Henry thought. He'd been having so many thoughts and fantasies about her that he wasn't sure if he could act normal around her, like maybe his ability to function in the real world was slipping away. He was afraid he'd say something stupid or make a gigantic fool of himself.

Then, he did.

"Yeah? Check this out," she said. "I didn't want to throw too much at you at once." She took off her large glasses and put on a smaller, thinner pair, like a sighted person would wear. Her dark brown eyes were so clear it was like she was really looking at him.

Henry's body went slack. "Wow. Shit, you're so fucking beautiful," he blurted out. *Fuck.* "I mean—"

"Thank you."

"It looks like you can see," he stumbled.

"That's what my mom said. I hadn't replaced my glasses in three years. I guess they've made some advancements so they don't need to be as big and thick. But I can't really see any better."

"I just meant that... you look good."

"Yeah, thanks, my Auntie V has been helping me. I did her a favor and she took me shopping. How's your dad?"

"My dad? Good, I think. He's developed a reading obsession. Like he's reading a book a day."

"That does sound obsessive."

"It's kind of his personality."

"Sounds familiar. Your dad and my mom could share a therapist."

"And he's working a little, part time, so that's good."

"He was really cool to talk to me that time about what it's like to be a doctor and all. He's pretty awesome."

"I guess."

"What do you want to study?" she pulled open her backpack.

Nothing, he wanted to say, but didn't. He just wanted to look at her forever. "I've got a lot of geography. And chem. Your aunt's a trip."

"Yeah, she's got this thing for our pool. Even though she has this ginormous pool at her place in New York, she..."

Justine kept talking, but it all began to blend together. Henry's fantasies started up, eager for their chance. He watched her mouth move and looked into her eyes and watched the animated hand gestures she made when she was making a point or emphasizing something.

Henry's fantasies usually revolved around saving her from great peril. She'd get turned around on a hiking trail and end up stuck on a ledge, afraid to move, desperate for

313

his help. He'd rappel down on a rope, which he'd tie under her, then climb freestyle back up the shear cliff face and hoist her up. He wouldn't accept her thanks—this is just what a man does. Or they'd be at the beach and despite his warnings she'd insist on going in the water, and she'd get pulled out by a freak riptide and the lifeguard would be busy talking to a blond girl, and only Henry would be smart enough to know she couldn't be reached through the current, and only Henry would be strong and brave enough to sprint to the end of the pier, dive in, and grab her while he held a piling and the rip tried to pull her past. Sometimes a man had to take on nature to protect his woman. Always cool under pressure. Just what a man does.

All his fantasies involved some sort of athletic prowess that he completely lacked in real life. There was the near-death horseback riding accident, and pulling her from a burning car in a burning parking garage under a burning building. He'd looked into African safaris because there were lots of possibilities there, with all the ferocious animals she couldn't see and deserts that went on forever. He liked a touch of realism, which sometimes required research. He pretended her wild, adventurous spirit came out only because of him, because she knew her man would always be there to rescue her and keep her safe. Her friends would shake their heads and tell her how lucky she was to have this guy, and they'd pull him aside and whisper, *she never really started living until she met you.* He had just the right laconic expression ready for such an occasion. Just what a man does.

Justine was on a roll. She was talking about someone named Charlie Horse, and how part of some agreement meant this guy was going to be able to use her aunt's awesome pool for a year. Henry just had to nod and ask a question here and there, and for that he got to look as much as he wanted; at her eyes and mouth, precious glimpses of her tongue, the tendons in her neck that stretched when she got excited. Her arms were more muscular than he'd realized. God, that bit of her upper gums when she smiled big or laughed—it made his insides churn and his mind whirl. She leaned forward and he could feel her breath, warm and tangy.

He became conscious of his staring. Sometimes Henry had to rescue Justine from himself. A bigger, better version of Henry chastised him in an effort to protect her privacy. *Stop staring, creep,* better Henry told regular Henry. He smiled to himself and looked past her.

She was still talking. He took pride in his quiet chivalry. He was looking absently at the boxes, stacks of paper, and piles of file folders on the table behind her. A droopy potted plant poked out of the mess. He looked without seeing as he listened, dreaming and sliding into a free-fall. He gazed at the same spot until it became an abstraction. Justine kept talking. Now she was imitating someone's voice. She leaned across the desk again and whispered, then dropped back with a big laugh.

It changed. Henry had been looking at the same spot when it shifted into something else. A magic trick. *Tada!* Like spotting the animal in the trees, perfectly still, part of the landscape but really watching you all this time.

That was how Henry saw his mother's statue.

It was sitting next to the droopy plant, on one of those sturdy cardboard boxes that bankers and lawyers use. He remembered it. It was one of her last pieces. She'd labored over it for a long time. Some of her sculptures would take a few days, some would take months. A couple took years. The size was irrelevant. "The piece already exists," she'd told him. "My job is just to excavate it. Some are buried deeper than others."

Henry went cold. He'd been still, but now it was more than that. He was frozen. His mind wound down; it chugged to a halt like an old truck refusing to go on.

His mother's statue, there, as if it had come up from deep water. It was incongruous, like a character from TV walking into the wrong show.

Something was fundamentally wrong.

There was a buzzing in his ears. He tried to think, but it was more like his mind was talking to him. Better Henry talked to regular Henry.

Math. She wasn't bad at math, she was good at math. Her mother bragged about it once when Justine was in the bathroom. No way she could trick her mom like she'd said. Her mom didn't miss anything.

Class. That class they took, where they'd met, she didn't need it, but she knew he'd be there because she'd hacked his records.

"Henry?"

"What, yeah." His own voice was so quiet he wasn't sure if he'd spoken out loud.

His dad. She was always asking about his dad, saying how cool he was. She'd asked his dad what it was like being a pediatric surgeon—he'd thought it was strange because he hadn't told her that's what he was, only that he was a surgeon.

Her mom. She was always talking about how great her mom was. Scattered hints; your dad and my mom could share a therapist.

"I've been talking to you," Justine said. "I've been asking you something."

"Oh. You have?"

Piano. They both had one. His house. Her house. The lessons. That was all her idea.

"Yes, I have," Justine said. "And you haven't been answering."

"Um."

"Henry?"

"Yeah."

"What's wrong?"

"Nothing. Nothing's wrong."

"Yes, there is, you sound different. Something's different. What just happened while I was talking to you?"

"Nothing."

"Not nothing—something. I feel it."

"That statue. The sculpture. The one behind you."

"What? What statue? There's no statue behind me."

"There is. It's a sculpture of a single figure. A woman."

Justine's chest moved in rapid breaths. "That's here?"

"Yes, on the table, behind you."

"That belongs at my mom's office."

"We're in her office."

"No, her work office, where she works."

They were quiet as each waited on the other. Justine began grinding her teeth. He'd never seen her do that. He could hear the slide of her molars as her lower jaw moved side to side.

She finally spoke. "That—yeah, that's—is that your mom's you said?"

He stared at her. "You already know it is."

"I don't. I mean, I didn't. I didn't know that."

"You're lying. Why do you have it?"

"Henry."

"Why is it here? Why do you have it? Why do you have my mom's sculpture here?"

"It's—I don't know. I can't see it. I can't see, I'm blind, so, I'm not sure what you mean."

"Yes. Yes, you do. Answer me. Why? Why is it here?"

"Henry, you're scaring me a little."

"Why do you have it?"

"Henry, stop."

"Answer me!"

"Henry."

"Now, or I swear I'll—"

The words came out as fast as she could speak them. "My mother bought it at a charity auction—something to benefit kids—about a year ago and I was there and your mom was there but I didn't realize it was her until later because I didn't talk to her and—"

"My mom?"

"But I didn't *know* it was her. I looked her up and found out she died and I didn't understand, I mean it was just a short while later so I couldn't believe it, she was so alive and what she created was so beautiful and I remembered your dad." She was crying now and trying to talk through it. "Because he spoke that night and was so smart and funny and my mom laughed like she never does and I thought about my mom because—"

"You met my mom?"

"Because... because, my mom is beautiful too—my mom is beautiful too—fuck, Henry, my mom is beautiful too—"

"You're trying to replace my mom?" He stood up.

"No."

"You want your mom to replace my mom?"

"You're really scaring me now."

"What is wrong with you?"

"No, I don't."

"Why?"

"Henry, really, I didn't think—I didn't think you would be you, I mean, I thought—"

"You did all this to, to..."

"No, Henry, please." She stood and reached out. "Oh, please, Henry."

Vicky opened the door. "Justine? Kids—Henry! What is going on?"

Henry hissed the words at Justine. "You go fuck yourself."

"*Henry!*" Vicky's voice boomed. Henry turned to her. She held a towel to her neck. He went around the desk. Vicky, dripping on the floor, filled the doorway. "*Move!*" he shouted in her face—so loud she rocked back into the hall.

He ran outside to his bike.

~ ~ ~

Henry flew down the hill, going faster than the cars. Runners coming up twisted around with wide eyes as he flew past. He went through the intersection at 7th Street. His speed increased as he hit the bottom half of the hill; across 4th Street as horns blasted. He went through the crosswalk at Ocean Avenue like he'd been launched from a slingshot.

Someone on the sidewalk shouted—"*Hey-hey-HEY!*"—as a car skidded and slid sideways in a wide arch.

Onto the cement area, Henry made a wide turn and flew past others on bikes, their conversations halted as they banked and wobbled to avoid him. Losing control, he swerved away from a woman pushing a jogger, went up on the grassy area, and slammed into the side of a bench—launching him over his bike and through the air.

He landed on the grass with a disappointing thud.

People gathered, some to help, some yelling at him and calling him a fucking asshole. *You could have killed someone.* When the distorted face turned to them they backed away. He ignored their words and went to his bike. The front tire was crumpled and the frame was twisted and bent.

He couldn't push it so he picked up the front and wheeled it. A pain shot through his side from where the handlebars had caught him on his way over. He walked crooked down the path, pulling the bike and favoring his side as observers dropped away.

He didn't want the bike. He'd never want to ride a bike ever again. He wanted to leave it next to one of the trashcans dispersed along the shoreline, but he continued to haul it, dragging his way to Golgotha. Penance for being such a fucking retard.

He'd been played.

A group of homeless men, encamped on their small patch of million-dollar real estate, heckled him with slurry, sing-song insults. *Think yer tiire's flaaat. Ha ha ha.*

I deserve it, he thought. All of it. His face burned.

The pain in his side caused him to finally set the bike next to a bench and sit. He faced the water. The breeze slowly chilled his tears.

The sun streaked through gaps in the clouds. Thin lines like angel hair lit the ocean surface in shimmery patches. He watched sailboats in their incremental march and airplanes pulling advertising banners as they buzzed slowly along the shoreline. The thousands on the beach below looked like colorful trinkets tossed across a sand garden.

He was seized by an overwhelming loneliness. A giant, invisible hand squeezed and torqued all the life out of him. He buckled over with his head between his knees and gave over to the anguished sobs that are sole province of the teenager. The pain didn't stop, but coursed though him with continuous, mechanized efficiency. He heard jogging footsteps go past and walking footsteps hesitate before moving on.

He was all alone and he wanted his mom. He wanted her so bad he was ready to die to see her again, to smell her and hear her laugh and feel her touch. Her hugs that cocooned him in warmth and comfort. Her kisses with both hands on his face and nips on his nose. *My baby.* Sitting on the floor with him, making a house from popsicle sticks, laughing and messy with glue and letting him play the music he wanted. To be understood in that invisible way that only she had. Her sympathy, swaddling him in a blanket and rocking him with a soothing voice and strokes on his neck and whispered encouragement. His mom. He was ready to die for her in that easy way the young have, anxious to cash in their lives for the here and now.

He sat up and wiped his face with his shirt. The world went on, uninterested.

He got up, careful, like an old man. He left the bike behind and walked the path along with all the others; just another part of the machine. His mind cleared. No thoughts rushed in to fill the gap like they usually did. He was left with a singular clarity. It was pleasant, in its way. Peaceful. The peace that comes from no longer having anything real to care about. The suicide, before the suicide.

He got on a bus without knowing if it was the right one. It seemed headed in the right direction. He dug change out of his pocket and came up short. People behind him waited to board. The bus driver waved him on with a frustrated gesture.

After he sat, he noticed a guy about his own age trying to get his bike on the overcrowded rack. He eventually gave up. The driver shook his head and pulled the bus out into the traffic.

She texted a number of times. He read the first one: *I'm sorry. Very very. I was trying to make people happy.*

He deleted the following ones without reading them and blocked her number.

The next morning, Henry found a cardboard box outside the front door. He opened it to find his backpack. When he pulled it from the box, he got a whiff of lavender perfume. A note fluttered out:

H,

I hope that's not the last we see of you because I like you and I know she does too, but if you ever talk to her like that again, I will drown you in the pool.
No shit.
Auntie V

~~~

Margaret's staff trickled back, stepping on tarps and sharing a single bathroom. Margaret had taken a two-day business trip—grateful for the distraction. When she got back to the office on Friday morning, everything was done. The moment she came in, an excited Heidi took her hand and pulled her around, gleefully pointing out one thing after another.

Orlando stopped by in the afternoon to take a look. He stood in the common area and turned a slow circle. "My gawd, Margaret Shepard, I believe this makes you legitimate."

The carpet had been replaced with blond hardwood flooring. The pale yellow walls and dark red trim were offset by heavy, royal blue furniture arranged over antique area rugs. The desks and tables were made of matching sets of mahogany and ash. The common area was now open and took up most of the floor. Rather than paintings on the walls, Vicky had built-ins made that held antique pottery pieces, each floating in a glow of museum light. Bursts of color came from large, wide vases on low, white marble tables that overflowed with plants and flowers. The few private offices were opened up, including Margaret's—now enclosed only with a waist-high half wall. Natural light from the polarized windows filtered through. Opening the space and using outside light gave the environment a sense of time; morning looked and felt like morning.

Two of the old offices were combined to create a quiet room, which could be used for anything from research to meditation. Margaret was sure Orlando would get a laugh out of that, having spent so many years in the DA's office, where having a quiet room would be like having a place to finger paint. He poked his head in and looked around as Margaret told him what it was for. "Brilliant," he said, nodding his head.

"Not the reaction I expected."

"There's a whole new science about adapting work environments to our natural rhythms," he said. "Hell, if it were me, I'd throw a few futons in there for naps. It's proven to increase productivity. You're ahead of the curve." He ran his hand over a desk. "If I wasn't such a dedicated public servant, I'd come work for you."

"Anytime. You can run the place." He didn't look at her but she could see she'd made him smile. "I mean it," she added. "Anyway, it all cost a fortune, but Vicky did her part for free."

"That must be the Red Queen. I figured she had to have a real name."

"I don't even have a total yet. I may never. I told Heidi to hide it from me."

"Not surprised. My wife bought a Red Queen dress. I thought that last zero was a typo."

Her employees were happy. Margaret was afraid she'd lose more than the paralegal in the carnage, but the staff buzzed about, exploring each other's work areas and taking turns behind the barista bar in the new kitchen.

Margaret christened the conference room with a meeting to review all the pending cases. She was surprised by the amount of work her staff had managed to get done from home. Afterward, they took a group picture to send to Vicky, who had gone back to New York while Margaret was out of town.

That evening, Margaret drove home with the windows rolled up and the disco music blaring. She went down her mental checklist. Nothing came back demanding an immediate stress response, and tomorrow she could go for a nice long run. She tapped her thigh and allowed herself the luxury of feeling good.

~ ~ ~

Justine was usually in the kitchen when Margaret got home.

"Honey?" Margaret called. No response. She looked in her office and checked down the hall. "Sweetie?" she called louder. "Justine?"

"Yeah, I'm out here."

Margaret slid open the glass door to the backyard. She peered into the darkness. "Where?"

"Here." Justine's figure was illuminated by warbling shifts of light from the pool water. She sat at the edge with her pants rolled up and her feet in the water.

Margaret turned on the light and stepped out. "Honey, you okay?"

"I'm fine."

"What are you doing out here?"

"Just—nothing."

"We'll have dinner in a bit, okay?"

"Sure."

"Unless you think we should order out." Justine didn't answer. Margaret went inside and started toward the kitchen, but stopped in the hall. She took her heels off and went back outside. "I'm going to sit with you a bit. That alright?"

"Sure."

Margaret pulled her skirt up and sat. She dropped her feet in next to Justine's and watched their ghostly white legs shape-shift in the water.

Justine was slouched forward with her face down. Margaret looked at her. Justine usually made a small movement with her head to let her mom know she was aware. It was part of the silent, hidden communication the two had developed, a complex network of nuances built over the years. People sometimes asked Margaret if it was frustrating trying to communicate with a blind daughter. She always gave the same answer; *oh, it has its challenges.* But she actually felt their communication was better than most mother-daughter relationships, but required a different kind of attention—a practiced focus that had become second nature.

"What's up, sweetie?"

Justine kicked the water. "Nothing, Mom. Nothing's up."

"Are you missing Auntie V?"

"Maybe. I guess."

"What else?"

"Nothing."

"Honey, is it Henry?"

Justine shrugged, but her face began to contort. Her lips pulled wide like a tragic clown. She cupped her forehead with both hands and shook.

"Oh, baby," Margaret said. She put her arm across her shoulders and pulled her close. "Sweetheart, what? What happened?" Justine cried like a child; long and hard. Margaret started, as if something had bit her. "Wait, honey, did Henry—"

"No, Mom, it wasn't anything like that. Really, I promise."

"Okay, so—what? Did you fight? Because these things happen."

"It was more than that."

"What? Please tell me."

"I can't."

"What do you mean, you can't? That frightens me."

325

"There's just—Mom, I do everything you ask me to do, right?"

"Yes, you do."

"I don't act like a lot of the other girls, right?"

"That's true, and I'm so grateful."

"It's not always easy, it's really not, but I really try hard."

"I know you do."

"But—but, I mean, there needs to be something I get for that."

"I don't understand."

"You ask things of me, now I want to ask something of you, because I'm an adult now."

"Well—"

"Mom."

"Alright, you're mostly an adult."

"So, I'm asking you for this. That you not keep asking me what happened, or what's wrong, or try to find out. I've earned your trust, so respect that. Just be my mom. You don't have to know everything." She'd started to cry again.

"You're right. I don't have to know everything. I just—I love you more than the world and everything in it, that's all."

"That's all I need right now."

"Okay."

"Mom, can you leave me alone now?"

"Sure. Sure, I can. You just—yes." Margaret forced herself to get up. She fought the impulse to pick Justine up in her arms and smother her.

Margaret tracked wet footprints back to the house. From the other side of the glass door, she watched her daughter. The light reflecting off the water painted Justine's face and cast a glow around her. With her long hair draped over her shoulder, she looked like a Rembrandt painting; the girl of a thousand sorrows in tragic repose.

Justine stood up. Margaret took a step back, thinking she was coming inside. Instead, Justine took her glasses off and set them on the ground. She pulled her shirt over her head and took the rest of her clothes off. Naked, she sat back down. After a brief pause, she slipped into the water, feet first. Margaret watched as she pushed off the wall. Her legs kicked out in a triangle that thrust her through the water, causing her billow of hair to flow over her lithe body. When she surfaced and rolled on her back, her arms stroked the water like a ballet dancer stroking the air.

What does she fear? Margaret thought as she watched Justine stare up into a different kind of darkness. *Me. That's what she fears. Me.* She didn't know where the thought came from. Like so many things in her life, it seemed to have no origin.

Chapter 17

Henry never did ride a bicycle again. He got his driver's license, but he didn't get a car. For Christmas, he got a motorcycle.

His dad had said; "Absolutely not, no chance that is ever going to happen." It was the most animated Henry had seen him in a long time. "Do you know what doctors call people who ride motorcycles?"

"No, Dad, enlighten me."

"Organ donors."

"That's a good one."

"Except it's not a joke."

For the whole of December, Henry pressed his dad. "Any car you want," was Tom's response. His dad even took him car shopping, figuring once Henry got inside the new Mini Cooper or a two-door Audi, he'd forget the motorcycle. When that didn't work, Tom solicited Stephen for help.

"He listens to you," Tom said.

"Nope," Stephen said. "This one's all you."

Henry and Tom went back and forth. At one point, Henry even said, "Mom would have let me." Tom was so surprised by that sucker-punch he couldn't respond.

Out of options, Tom asked a doctor friend who had a brother on the police force to send him crash photos of motorcycle accident victims. "I'm asking a friend to break the law so I can show you this," he told Henry as he spread the pictures over the library table. They bent over them together.

"See? See that helmet on the side of the road? That has a head in it. Paramedics will tell you—they find body parts fifty yards down the road."

Henry began to wonder why he was putting up such a fight. He didn't really want a motorcycle that bad. He hadn't expected such a strong reaction from his dad, but faced with so much resistance, he'd dug in. It awoke something in his dad, and the more they argued about it, the better Henry felt.

The final deal was complex and hotly debated. Henry would take a motorcycle safety class. He would wear a full set of leathers at all times, and would not be allowed to ride on a freeway for the first year. No riding at night, or in the rain. A single citation would mean no riding for six months. Finally, he could only have a standard road bike, not one of the crotch-rocket style speed bikes that created young corpses with factory efficiency. They settled on the sedate—but still more powerful than Tom would have liked—Triumph Bonneville. When it finally sat in the garage, Tom couldn't help but admire it, and even snuck out there a few times to sit on it.

Maybe riding a motorcycle gave him confidence, because a couple months later, Henry kissed a girl.

It was his second time. The first was when he was thirteen. A new family had moved into the house behind them. They had a fifteen-year-old daughter who talked in a fake French accent. Francis had suggested that Henry invite the new girl to the community pool with his friends. The girl pretended she was doing them all a big favor by going. She didn't even go in the water, she just sat there reading a magazine and chewing her gum. When he walked her back to her house and said goodbye, she said, "You have to kiss me."

"Why?"

"Because, it's what you're supposed to do."

So he kissed her. He caught a little tongue without meaning to.

"That was terrible," she said, and pushed her sunglasses up. "American boys don't know how to kiss right."

"My dad says you guys are from Baltimore."

"I told you I'm adopted but you don't listen. Here, I'll show you." She grabbed him and kissed him with her mouth open. She rolled her tongue in his mouth like she was showing him a trick. He didn't like her and she wasn't very attractive, but he still liked the kiss, which seemed like its own thing, somehow separate from the girl. She kept kissing him. She had a sweet, fruity smell from her gum. He started to get queasy from the smell and all that tongue. He stopped and pulled away.

"So you do it like that," she said, chewing her gum again. "You can practice with me sometime, if you want." The girl's little bother, half hidden behind the curtain, watched through the window.

"Great," Henry said, but he already knew he wouldn't.

In March, about four months after his fight with Justine, Henry kissed a girl for the second time.

The girl drove him home from the school science fair. It had been raining that morning so he couldn't ride his motorcycle. His chemistry teacher offered extra credit for anyone going to the fair, and chemistry was the one subject Henry wasn't very good at. The girl had been his lab partner once. In class, she was quiet, but on the drive home she was chatty, talking about the fair and college and her theory that cellular signals probably give you brain cancer because she knew someone who had that but then when they stopped using their phone it went away. She stopped in front of his house and said; "Damn, you live here? Nice." He turned and kissed her without warning. Surprised, she backed off. Then a different look came over her and they kissed again, starting slower and building up as she made breathy sounds. He touched her breasts over her zip-up sweatshirt. She pulled away. "Wait, no," she said. "I mean, only because I have a boyfriend."

"Oh, sure. Sorry." He was relieved. He wasn't sure why he'd kissed her to begin with, or if he even liked her, though she was really good-looking in that athletic, bouncy way that he always thought he didn't like but then found exceptions for.

Henry had the sense he was falling behind. He felt that at his age, he really should be further along. The whole mom-dying thing had thrown him off track. If he didn't catch up soon, he'd be left behind for good, and he'd end up one of those weirdo virgins that lives at home and goes to science fairs because they actually like it. Or maybe it wasn't that at all. Maybe it was because of this new thing he'd been trying out. It involved doing something first, then thinking about it later, instead of the other way around. It turned everything into an experiment by flipping the hypothesis to the end.

The athletic girl looked like she regretted what she'd said. She leaned toward him and bit her lip in a practiced way. "I mean—"

"So, thanks for the ride home," Henry said and got out.

In class, the girl went back to being quiet. She kept making eye contract with him over the next week, like she expected him to say something profound. Then her looks got cold, until finally she just ignored him altogether.

The truth was, he didn't want her, or any other girl in school. Despite himself, he still thought about Justine. During the day, it wasn't so bad; he always had something to distract himself. But at night, it was impossible. He fought it every time. When thoughts of her crept in, he'd try to switch to sexual fantasies, grabbing the first one that came to him: the entire girls' volleyball team, one of his teachers who gave off that vibe and always leaned over him a little too close, those sisters who both had braces and always talked over each other. Anything to avoid thinking about Justine.

But she was like a magnet. Without realizing it, his thoughts would drift back to her, leaving the teacher waiting, spread-eagled on her desk.

Fantasy mixed with bits of conversations and moments they'd had. He'd catch himself, and have to remind himself that he hated her, that the Justine in his head didn't exist. The real Justine was a manipulative liar.

It didn't always work. He tried other tricks, like playing games on his phone until he fell asleep. But his phone would end up lying on his chest as he stared at nothing and remembered when she touched his face, and how she smelled like vanilla, and how her face changed expressions, and the glimpses of her gums when she laughed, and how she held her hand over his heart that time and said it was like an angry animal. He wouldn't fall asleep until it was almost morning, then he'd be too tired the next day to fight off thoughts of her and he'd end up in class in a daze and remember something funny she'd said—he'd laugh, but wouldn't realize it until people turned and looked at him.

The worst thing about all this was thinking about the very last time he saw her. That look on her face, like it had collapsed. After all his fantasies of saving her, of being her hero and her protector, he couldn't get that one image out of his mind. The one time he destroyed her.

"Hey."

"Hey."

"Didn't know if you'd answer," he said.

"Didn't think you'd call," she said.

"Yeah."

"So, what?" She didn't sound like she used to.

"I wanted to talk to you about something."

"What?"

"You were trying to get our parents together, right? I mean, before, that was like, your plan?"

"Are you going to freak the fuck out?"

"No. Shit, that was like a really long time ago."

"Henry, what do you want, because I gotta go."

"I just thought—I think maybe you were right."

"About *what?* God, you still talk around things like everything's so delicate."

"My dad's doing good, or better, and I think maybe him and your mom might—that maybe they could meet, and we could, you know—I don't know. If you think your mom might want to."

"No, it was a dumb idea. She didn't know anything about it. She'd kill me. I don't think she'd be interested in meeting your dad, or any guy actually."

"Oh."

"Just not part of her scenario. But I'm glad your dad's doing okay. I really did think he was pretty cool."

"Yeah. I mean, I know."

"That all?"

"Yeah. No. I mean, except I wanted to—I'm sorry. For how I reacted, back then. I mean, I was mad." It seemed like forever before she responded.

"I know."

"And I just, I don't know. It was a long time ago, but—"

"Yeah, you're kinda late here."

"I know, but really, I'm sorry. And how I was with your aunt, or whatever she is."

"You can't ever do that again."

"I know."

"If we were ever to see each other again, like if that ever happened, you could never do that again."

"I won't, I swear."

"I was really scared, Henry. I thought you might attack me."

"I'd never do that. Shit, Justine—"

"Because I can't see, I imagine the worst."

"No, see—"

"I just won't allow myself to be treated like that, to be yelled at."

"Justine, I—"

"I hope you can understand that. I mean, you have to understand that."

"I can, I can. I'm sorry. God, I'd never hurt you. Or anyone."

"I know, but people say that."

"Fuck. I mean, fuck."

"I just—I don't make a thing of it, but you know, because I—I just, I have to be able to trust people I'm with. Like really trust them, no matter what."

"Sure, of course."

"Alright," she said, and it was like before, when they could be quiet for a while and it was okay. "And Henry, I'm sorry, too. What I did was... was really dumb, and—"

"You were trying to help people."

"No—yeah—but I just did it all wrong. So wrong. I tried. It's just weird how that happens, like the opposite of what you're trying to do."

"It's alright."

"I'm really sorry."

"It's alright, really."

They talked again the next night, mostly about school and things that had happened since they'd last seen each other. Henry told her about his motorcycle.

On the third night, they talked strategy. Justine had a plan. "So, I'll get my mom to volunteer and you get your dad to volunteer. Think you can?"

"Yeah, I think. He's easy. But your mom—what are you going to tell her?"

"That for safety reasons the school has asked for one adult volunteer for every twenty students expected to attend. And I'll tell her this is the easiest volunteer thing she can do, and every parent is expected to do at least one thing a year, and if she doesn't do this, she'll be assigned to the decorating committee, which meets every Monday night for a month, because that's the only other volunteer spot left."

He laughed. "Jeez, I forgot how resourceful you are. You realize this means we have to go too, right?"

"Yeah, but I don't want them to think something's up, so we can't go together. We'll just meet there and act all awkward because we haven't seen each other in a while, then our parents will have something to talk about."

"About how awkward their kids are?"

"Oh, yeah. Parents love to pretend their kids are all super sensitive."

"Except it'll be true."

"I'm not sensitive, you fuck."

"No, that we won't have seen each other for a while."

"Oh. Yeah."

"Unless we do."

"Right. The plan is flexible."

"Okay, so then what? We go off, and they—I mean, what happens then?"

"That's why this is brilliant. They won't have anything to do because these things are totally boring for them, so they'll naturally talk to whatever adult is there, and that will be them. They'll shake their heads and talk about music today, or whatever."

"Then what?"

"I don't know, I'm not writing a script here. Maybe nothing. Fate takes over."

"Okay. So, costumes. What are you going to go as?"

"I don't know, I have to think about it. We got—what—a few weeks?"

The following night was devoted to costume talk. Justine had an idea for one, but it required a lot of puffy material she would need to dye the right color. Henry didn't ask how she knew she needed to do that, much less how she'd actually do it, but he thought the material his mom had used for shipping sculptures might work. There was a big box of it in the studio. "Want to come by on Sunday? Or if you want, I'll pick you up on my motorcycle."

"Ha, that's funny."

"Yeah, I didn't think so. Thought I'd offer though."

"You know what my mom says when someone zooms by on a motorcycle?"

"What?"

"Oh look, someone playing the idiot lottery."

"Our parents really were destined for each other."

"If she saw you come near me with a motorcycle, she'd pick it up and throw it at you."

"I get the picture. No motorcycle. I'll see if I can borrow the—"

"Now, wait, I said she couldn't see it, not that I wouldn't ride with you."

"Really?"

"I'm practicing being a rebellious teenager, making up for lost time, and we live pretty close, so it wouldn't be that far."

"I don't want to cause trouble."

"I'm trying to do things outside my comfort zone, and this is so far outside it's like on another planet, so I'll be good for, like, a year. So—yes, before I chicken out. But you can't come to the house. You'll have to text me and pick me up at the bus stop."

On Sunday, Henry stuck to the plan. He stopped a couple blocks away and was about to text her when she called.

"You can pick me up. She just left for the store."

When he got there, he had a safety speech all prepared. He wanted to have something to focus on because he wasn't sure what it would be like to see her after all this time. He didn't get the chance to use it.

"I know, hold on tight, keep my knees in, and lean when you lean," she said. "I've been researching it."

"Here, you need to wear my jacket. Just put your arms out." He slid it on.

"Ooh, it's all warm and Henry-like."

"And here's your helmet."

"Had an extra lying around?"

"Something like that." After talking to her earlier in the week, he'd bought a used helmet off eBay and had it rush delivered. "Here, let me adjust the chinstrap."

"I feel like a real badass. Let's go get tats. I'll be your biker bitch."

"Easy, Hell Flower."

"What? I can't hear for shit with this helmet on. Now I'm blind and deaf."

She slid on behind him and pressed against his back. Her hands went around his waist and across his chest. "Hope you know what you're doing," she said in his ear as he started up. He caught her smell, as familiar as his thoughts of her.

He was a safe rider—despite his blasé reaction, those images his dad had shown him stuck—but he was extra careful now. He didn't take the most direct route. Instead, he took Ocean Avenue to the California Incline, then went up Pacific Coast Highway to Temescal Canyon. Lighter traffic made Sundays a great day to ride.

He could tell she trusted him. She held tight, her body entwined with his, but she wasn't tense. She leaned easily on his cue, even when he powered hard through the long curves.

When they got to his house, the first thing she said when she slid off was, "Your hair is longer."

"What?" He pulled his helmet off.

"Your hair is longer. I could feel it against my neck, that's all."

"Oh, yeah."

"That was so crazy fun. I'm all tingly, like when your leg falls asleep, except it's my butt and everything."

"You get used to it."

"I'm not sure I'd want to."

When they went through the house, the door to the library was open. His dad was sitting by the window, reading a book. Henry had told him that Justine might be coming by, which prompted Tom to nearly say something, think better of it, and play it cool instead.

Henry hesitated. "Hey, Dad, Justine's here."

Tom looked up. "Oh, hey guys." Maybe it was because he was with Justine and had already slipped back into seeing for her, but his dad suddenly looked different to him; exhausted, maybe even sick.

"Hi, Doctor Ackerman," Justine said.

"Hi-ya Justine, so nice to see you again. And call me Tom, like you used to. You know, it's been so long, I thought you two were—"

Henry cut him off. "We're going in the studio. I think mom had some stuff we might use for a Halloween costume."

"Mom's studio?" Tom asked.

Justine felt the shift.

"Yeah," Henry said slowly. "That alright?"

"Of course it is. This is for the school dance?"

"Yeah."

"Henry told me you're going to be a volunteer," Justine said. "That's awesome."

"I am, yes. I hope I don't embarrass you guys."

"Oh, well, we're not really going together," Justine said.

"We'll probably just meet there," Henry threw in.

"Yeah. Meet there."

"Well, great," Tom said, and went back to his book.

~ ~ ~

"Where's Stephen?" Justine asked as they walked though the backyard.

"He's not here as much now, just part-time. He has to take care of someone."

"Wow, how do you manage?"

"I know, right? We're going to step through the doorway now." She took his arm.

In all the hours Henry had spent in the studio after his mom died, practicing what she'd taught him, he was always careful to keep his work confined to specific areas. Everything else was much the same as it was, like she might walk in any second, wiping her hands on her shirt and cocking her head the way she did when a piece of music grabbed her, even if it was the hundredth time she'd heard it.

There were half a dozen partially finished sculptures on the workbench. A few were barely formed at all. Francis's process had been to develop five or six pieces, using different materials, and work on them in turn. As they progressed, she'd focus on two or three, until eventually her attention shifted to just one—the one she'd develop to the end. Early drafts were used to test finishes before being melted down or discarded.

Henry had helped his mother with her last sculpture. She'd spent the previous two summers teaching him the primary patina and distressing techniques. She'd asked him to do the finishing on her final piece, but he still hadn't done it. Her final sculpture sat at the end of the table. He had mixed a dozen trial finishes and tested them over and over on the unfinished versions.

Henry went to the big box of padded fabric as Justine stayed in the doorway. He brought some of the material over for her to feel.

"This is what I was thinking might work," he said. "And it's white, so I think it would be easy to dye. I could help you if you want. I think the drug store has those dye kits."

Justine felt the material but seem distracted. "That's good, I think. I'll leave the color stuff up to you. Henry, can you tell me what's in here? Describe it to me?"

"Oh, sure. It was a garage. Our house is one of those old ones that had a separate garage. But now it's my mom's sculpture studio. Where she worked."

"I mean, what's in here, specifically."

"There's a long table by the windows. My dad built the windows along the wall there because she wanted the natural light. And the table—"

"Over here?"

"Yeah. Careful, there's some cords on the ground. That's where her sculptures are, the ones she was working on. Then on the other side are more worktables. She'd roll her chair between the two. On the far end are some finishing tanks. On the other wall are a bunch of tools, and some storage cabinets. She kept a lot of material stored in a shed behind the studio."

Justine moved closer to the windows. "This is the table, here?"

"Yeah. Just a little farther."

"Can I touch?"

"Yes."

"There's nothing wet or toxic or whatever?"

"No. Some are covered, but I'll uncover them."

"Sculptures? There's some here on the table, now?"

"Yes."

Her hand met the first one. "Oh, yes." Something about her changed, as if she had just materialized and become present for the first time. The statue was unfinished copper, but the light from the window cast her and the statue in the same golden color. She put both hands on it.

Henry's world went still.

She moved her hands over the piece. It was an early incarnation, little more than a blob with motion. *Every sculpture has action, Henry, energy pointing it in a certain direction, either out or in—or, if you're a genius like Rodin, both.*

"Henry, can you tell me more about your mom?" He was silent. "It's okay if you don't want to, or would rather not. Really. But if you want, I'd like to know more about her. I really would." She'd moved on to the next piece.

She was touching the fourth statue before he said anything. "She said the secret to sculpting was to realize it's not a visual medium. It was better to think of it as something people should feel compelled to touch, not just look at."

Justine paused and turned to him. "That's what I did when my mom bought her sculpture. I couldn't stop touching it. Your dad brought it over and put it on our table and talked to my mom. Then your mom came by and they talked, but I wasn't paying attention."

"Did you talk to her? My mom?"

"No. I wanted to. She was talking to my mom for quite a while, but I kept feeling the statue. I finally tried to say hello because I really wanted to meet her, but she was already gone."

"Oh. I thought maybe you'd... never mind."

She turned back to the sculptures. "Tell me something bad about her."

"Like what? What bad thing? Why?"

"I've found it's easier to know somebody if you know something bad about them. But you don't have to say, if you'd rather not."

"I don't think I know what you mean."

She put her hands on the edge of the table and picked her words carefully. "It's like everyone is good in the same kinds of ways. People are good and they do good things. But people are bad in very different ways. Nobody's all good. And I think whatever is bad about someone tells you more about what they're really like."

She went back to touching the sculptures, each in turn.

"She could ignore you," he said. "I know that doesn't sound bad, but it is. You could be right there, and sometimes she wouldn't even know it. She'd kind of zone out on whatever she was doing and it was like you didn't even exist. She did it a lot. You're at the end of the table. That's her last piece in front of you."

"The one you're going to finish?"

"Yeah."

She put her hands out and touched it. "They're dancers."

"How'd you know?"

"Because they're exactly what I've always imagined dancers to be. Except there's three of them." Her face was in shadow but the edges of her hair were lit. She turned to him. "Maybe she felt like *she* didn't exist. It sounds weird coming from me, but maybe that's the only way we know we really exist, because people see us. We're witnessed."

"Yeah, maybe."

"Henry, can you come closer to me?"

"Sure."

"Maybe even a little closer. I want to tell you something that I wasn't really honest about before."

"Okay."

She spoke in a low voice, like she was afraid of being overheard. Like in the library. "Since we're being honest and I wanted to make sure there wasn't anything else, and I realized there was this one other thing."

Henry heard the scrape of leaves in the doorway as they scuttled on the cement floor. "What?"

"When I touched you in the library."

"Yeah—I mean, I remember, I think, that time—sure."

"It wasn't so I could tell what you looked like. That's something people believe about blind people but isn't really true. I guess I can tell a little about how you look by touching your face, but only the same stuff anyone else could if they closed their eyes, like if you have a big nose or oily skin or whatever. So it wasn't that."

"Oh. So—"

"I wanted to touch you because I liked you."

"You did?"

"Yes. That was the only reason. I just really wanted to touch you."

"To... you really wanted to touch me?"

"Yes. I think I even needed to." She reached out. "Your hair is longer."

"Yeah, it is."

Then, he kissed her.

~ ~ ~

After the kiss, the first thing they did was stay away from each other.

Justine floated through school the next day. She was in trouble—real trouble—and she knew it. She could feel it all over. It might be necessary to talk to her mom, she decided. Except for a few things she only talked to Aunt Vicky about, she felt she could talk to her mom about anything, and this new thing really needed to be talked about.

She tried that night, but couldn't seem to do it. She decided to keep it to herself, at least for a little while. If she shared it, some of the magic would go away. It was a beautiful, delicate secret she got to carry in her pocket. It was like the time she knew a butterfly had landed on her hand; it was a day where the shapes were there and she could see the little blob of color, like a far-off planet, and could feel it, whispering to her without sound, for just a moment. Then it was gone. But for that moment, all beauty was just for her, and she knew if she tried to tell someone, it would ruin it.

Instead of talking to her mom, she sat in her room and relived every detail of the kiss—every incremental nuance. Then she backtracked to the motorcycle ride. Then back earlier still, to the phone call, going over every part and working her way forward to the kiss: the sound of his voice, the silky warmth of his leather jacket, his hair whipping her chin while her body buzzed, his dad in the library sounding wobbly and far away; and the studio, touching the statues, hearing about his mom, the most beautiful Francis, and learning about her in a new, private way, a way few people could know, because there are some things about being blind that are impossible to explain. Or that nobody would believe.

And, finally, the kiss. She didn't realize she had her mouth open as she thought about the kiss until drool hit her hand. She didn't care. She wanted to stay in this magical place for as long as possible.

Henry was scared. The kiss was about the scariest thing he'd ever experienced. It was like he'd done something that was so good that it had to be bad. There must be some consequence for a thing like this. The natural structure of things demanded it, like in physics; for every action there is an equal and opposite reaction. What would be the opposite of the kiss? What was he in for? What's on the other side of the most incredible thing ever?

When his dad asked him to come into the library and he saw Stephen sitting there, he thought maybe he had his answer. Something had happened; Stephen was normally gone by noon.

Stephen told him he was leaving. For good. Henry wanted to ask why but his throat felt thick. He was afraid if he spoke, his voice would crack and he might cry.

"Stephen needs to—" Tom looked at Stephen. "Well, he's got a life outside of us, of course, and his attention is needed elsewhere. But hey, this means we're doing well enough to captain our own ship, so that's good, right buddy?"

Henry went to his room. He wanted to ignore what Stephen just told him—at least for now—and go back to thinking about Justine, which a moment ago was so fresh and new.

There was a tap on his door. Bad things came in pairs. This must be part two.

"Come in."

The door opened. "Hey," Stephen said, his hand on the doorknob. He looked around. "I don't think I've ever been in your room. You keep it so clean, I never needed to. Your dad told me you even wash your bedding every other week." There was no response from Henry. "Can I talk to you a minute?"

"Sure," Henry said from the bed.

"Alright if I come in?"

"Yeah."

Stephen sat on the floor with his back to the bed. He stretched his legs and kicked the door shut.

"So, why are you leaving?" Henry asked. It was easier to ask when nobody was looking at him.

"Someone needs my help, and I'm afraid it can't wait."

"So? Leave. Why are you still here?" Despite his efforts, he started to cry. He tried to hide it at first, but then figured Stephen would know anyway. He knew everything.

Stephen waited before saying anything. "Your room—seriously, I think it's the cleanest room in the house."

"Are you going to make some kind of Martha Stewart joke? Because I've heard 'em."

"She's actually kind of my hero."

"Fine, whatever."

"Tom told me Justine came by the other day."

"Yup."

"Sorry I missed her."

"Um hum."

"How is she?"

Henry didn't answer. Stephen let the silence build until Henry slid off the bed and sat next to him.

"I kissed her," Henry said. He was reminded of when they sat on the steps with ice cream and watched the world go by. He'd wanted to talk about Justine then but didn't know how to bring it up. The girl in the white shirt; how had it worked out for her? "But now I don't know what to do."

Stephen tipped his head back and looked at the ceiling. "The kiss, was it nice?"

Henry's eyes followed the horizontal and vertical number patterns on the periodic table he had taped to his wall to help him with chemistry. "It was like... I finally understood what all those stupid songs are about."

Stephen sat forward and nodded. "You want my advice?"

"Yeah."

"Don't fuck it up."

"Okay, thanks for that. I'll really miss your stellar advice. So why are you leaving again? Really this time."

Stephen pulled his knees up and hugged them. "You remember when we first met, and we talked in the car?"

"Yeah, sure."

"You said people always leave when they're needed most."

"Oh. Yeah."

"You were right."

"And we don't need you most?"

Stephen nodded. "Not right now you don't."

Chapter 18

She remembered him from the charity auction, but he didn't seem to remember her. At least he didn't appear to when Justine introduced them. After the kids went away, Margaret found a spot along the wall. Tom followed her like a lost child.

It was hard to believe this was the same man. It wasn't that he looked different; it was impossible to tell what he looked like, dressed as whatever it was he was supposed to be—an alien, she thought he'd said—but the confident, graceful man who'd held a room enraptured was now tentative, slow, and spoke in a slurry monotone, as if drunk.

The music wasn't the heavy kind Margaret remembered from high school, but a puzzling hybrid of electronica and hip-hop, mixed with folk. She rather liked it, which made her wonder why teenagers would.

~ ~ ~

Justine was trying to remember the DJ's name. He'd been in one of her classes the previous year.

"Henry—the DJ—is he a big Italian guy?"

"Yes, big Italian guy. Doubt I could take him. Why?"

"I wanted to see if he had a set list, or if he's just improvising."

"Why again?"

"To see if there's a slow song coming up so one of us—probably me—could casually mention to our parents that maybe they should dance together. Then, when they say okay to appease us, would ya look at that? It's a slow song! I think they've been talking long enough, it's time to move things along."

"Why you?"

"Because I'm better at deception than you. You're far too innocent, even with the motorcycle."

They'd been there over an hour. Their parents had been standing near the back wall, talking, but it was hard to tell if they were getting along. Their body language was erratic. It looked to Henry like they were arguing.

The auditorium's AC was on a timed system that went off after school, but nobody had programmed it to go back on for the dance. With a few hundred teenagers in close proximity, it was sweltering. Henry was shedding costume little by little by making periodic trips to the trashcan and stuffing it with silver painted cardboard piping. The heat was making Justine sweat too, which was making her costume itch like crazy. Another reason not to waste any more time.

"*Vincent*—that's his name," Justine said. "The DJ."

"Sounds right. He looks like a Vincent, or a Paulie, maybe a Tony."

"Here, take my drink and offer it to him. Say, *You're doing a great job, Vincent. Keep up the good work.* Then see if you can check out his set list."

Henry took her drink. "What is it?"

"Apple juice."

"I doubt that'll fly."

"You got any ideas?"

"I got twenty bucks. I'll just give it to him and ask him to play something slow and boring."

"That motorcycle has killed your innocence. Okay, try it, but hurry up because I'm turning into a puddle here."

"Here, hold my head, I'm going in." He handed her his cardboard head and made his way to the DJ platform.

~ ~ ~

"Hey, guys!" Justine exclaimed as she arrived in a pink puff. Henry came up beside her.

"You guys having fun?" Margaret asked.

"Yeah," Justine said.

"Can't be having too much fun if you're here talking to us."

"You guys should dance," Justine said. She appeared to be talking to Tom, who, in his semi-catatonic state, really did look like an alien.

Margaret glanced at Tom. "No, honey, we're not even—"

"But you're supposed to," Justine persisted. "It's like a thing, all the volunteer parents are expected to dance at least one dance. It's like a tradition." As she spoke, Justine had the sense she'd pushed too far. An awkward moment passed as the music thumped.

"Dad," Henry prompted.

"Yeah? What."

"You guys should *dance*."

"Oh... well, sure." Tom turned to Margaret, who was chewing her fingernails, and held his hand out. "Let's do this."

Justine grinned. The look on Margaret's face made Henry wince. His dad pretended not to notice.

"Sure," Margaret said. "Love to."

As the two of them made their way into the swarm of sweaty teen flesh, Henry sent a text to the DJ.

"Was that as awkward as it felt?" Justine asked.

"Worse," Henry said. "Robots kissing level awkward. I don't think this is working."

The DJ pointed to Henry. The music shifted to a slow song and the dance floor cleared.

~ ~ ~

Justine sat in bed with her phone resting on her chest. "He couldn't even tell what she looked like, because of her costume. I think he'd like her more if he saw her better because that's so important to guys." She was trying to keep her voice down so her mom wouldn't hear. She'd already gotten ready for bed so talking to Henry would be the last thing she did before sleep.

"I'm familiar. I don't think that was the problem, but what was with the Raggedy Ann thing? She should've worn something that at least made her look good."

"She was Pippi Longstocking, perv."

"She looked like the bride of Chucky."

"I'm disappointed, aren't you?"

"I guess. Seemed like a long shot. Wait, let me take the rest of this off. Hold on a sec." Henry set the phone down. He had to do a funny dance and hop on one foot to get out of the bottom half of his costume. "I'm back." He climbed on his bed and sat with his legs pulled up.

Justine rubbed lotion down her legs. "Did your dad say anything? Like on the way home?"

"Nah, but guys don't really talk."

"You're not some separate species, I'm sure somewhere a guy has met a girl he liked and told his friend about it on the way home."

Henry was picturing her sitting in bed, same as him. "I'm his kid, not a friend. Very, very different dynamic." A loud thump shook the walls. "What the fuck was that?"

"What? Henry, I heard something too, what was it?"

"It was like a car hit the side of our house or something." He slid out of bed and stood in his socks.

"Is there someone in your house?"

"Why are you whispering?"

"I don't know, but—"

"I don't think so. My dad already went to bed and—" There was another loud crash. "*Fuuuck*, there it is again. Seriously, the wall just shook."

"Is it an earthquake?"

"No, Luca Brasi always barks when it's an earthquake."

"Henry, seriously, maybe you should just get out of there."

"No."

Another smash. Henry was sure it was coming from down the hall. "I gotta go," he said.

"Henry, please be careful, don't—"

He dropped the phone on the bed and opened his bedroom door. He looked out and scanned the hallway, then slipped out in a stealthily move, like he was in an action movie.

Another smashing sound came from his parents' room. He crept down the hall until he was just outside the door. "Dad? You okay?" He opened the door a crack and peeked inside. There was just enough light coming from the open closet to see.

He saw his dad lunge from the bed toward the wall and smash into the mirror, as if he was trying to go through it. Shards of mirror shone wet. His father staggered back. He still had his makeup on—white face and smudgy black eyes. He had something in his arms.

His dad turned and looked at him; inquisitive, then puzzled, like the demon Henry used to think his father talked to at night.

"Dad. Dad, what are you doing?" Henry crept into the room. "Is there someone else in here?"

His dad staggered, as if holding out for the bell. "Are you death?" he asked Henry, his face bloodied and dripping red. A mirror shard dropped from his head and stuck in the carpet at an angle. It winked at Henry as it tipped.

Henry moved closer. "Dad, it's alright."

"It's alright?"

"Yes, yes it is."

Tom turned back toward the mirror. He straightened and squared his shoulders as his head lolled. He lunged forward.

Henry was there before his dad's foot landed. He remembered from his brief experience with football; hit center and follow through. Wrap and hold with both arms. Drive all the way to the ground.

Even before they hit the floor, Henry had time to feel what his dad was holding: his mother's shirt. He felt the soft fabric against his forearm. He felt her presence. Then he felt pain.

~ ~ ~

Tom was brought to Cedars-Sinai hospital and diagnosed with a severe concussion. After a CT scan, the doctor determined it was safe for him to sleep and gave him a high dose of Klonopin. A nurse picked glass out of his forehead and stitched him up as he slept. When he'd slept a full twenty-four hours, they put him on an IV. He woke briefly, then slept another nine hours.

Conroy handled everything. An hour after Henry called him, he'd supervised Tom's transfer from the ER to a private room, just down the hall from where Francis had been. After consulting with Doctor Gordy, Conroy used his contacts to keep Tom's situation private, knowing few things could end a surgeon's career faster than questions of mental stability.

"He stopped taking his meds," Doctor Gordy told Henry in the hallway outside Tom's room. "It's as simple as that. I'm not sure why, but this is the result."

"How do you know he stopped taking his medication?" Henry asked.

Doctor Gordy had his hand on Henry's shoulder. They huddled together like two conspiring politicians. Henry liked the way Doctor Gordy talked to him like an adult, instead of just pretending to. "I've already seen his blood tests. He was doing better, and he'll continue to get better, but he wasn't ready to stop his medication. There's a process for that, and he didn't follow it."

Stephen came back to help out for a couple days. He drifted through the house much as Tom had in the early days; like a ghost. He made food for Henry and froze it in batches with notes taped to the top. He cleaned up the mess in the bedroom. He took extra care with the shirt—picking the glass out of it and lifting out the bloodstains with ammonia and a special soap, eliminating any remaining traces of Francis in the process.

Henry was at the hospital when his dad woke on the second day. "You had a breakdown," Henry told him. He wanted his dad to see him first when he woke up. "You're okay now. You're going to be fine, Dad."

Tom looked old. His face was gray and stubbled. He looked at the IV line with confusion. "Just nourishment," Henry said. "You slept so long they thought you needed fluids and vitamins and stuff." Tom rolled his tongue in his mouth.

"Water?" Henry asked. Tom nodded. "You're at Cedars. Conroy arranged it."

As he sipped, Tom looked at Henry. "You never hit that hard when you played," he rasped.

"You remember that?"

"About all I remember. Tattooed me." He touched his head.

"You've got some stitches there."

"I let you down."

"No, Dad. You didn't let me down, I'm fine."

"I really messed up."

"Dad, listen, it's just something that happened." Tom shook his head. "Dad, I'm probably the only one that knows how hard you're trying."

"Why am I so tired?" Tom asked. He closed his eyes. After a moment, Henry realized this was his dad's way of asking to be left alone.

~ ~ ~

Henry stayed away the next day. He filled Luca Brasi's bowls with extra food and water, then rode his motorcycle north all the way to Big Sur before turning around. At night, he went inland from Santa Barbara, winding through the roads in Rattlesnake Park. He sat on Rincon Beach in the morning and watched the surfers way out on the peak, bobbing on the water like flints of graphite.

He came home that night to an empty house. He'd had his phone off all day. When he checked, he found updates from Conroy, letting him know his dad was being transferred to a rehab facility for a few days. Stephen was gone again, but left a note letting him know there was extra food in the freezer.

He made a sandwich and sat at the piano. He ate while practicing scales. Later, when he went upstairs, Luca Brasi followed him up.

He went in his parents' room, turned on the light, and sat on the edge of the bed. He looked at the wall where the mirror had hung. Stephen had taken it down. There were two holes from the hooks. There were still a few dark spots on the carpet, there to map the family's tragedy, here as everywhere. Luca Brasi lay down in the doorway and pretended to be uninterested.

The closet door was open. Henry could see the shoulder of his mother's shirt. It moved, turning away, bashful.

He went in. The shirt hung square on the hanger with the top button done. Its previously dull colors buzzed with a fuzzy, vivid vibrancy. Henry unbuttoned it and slid it off the hanger. He took it back to his room, where he crawled into bed and slept with it.

~~~

On Sunday, Henry worked in the studio. He'd been avoiding the house, only going in to use the bathroom or to get something to eat. The empty house had its own ominous presence that grew in power the longer it was vacant. He'd slept the previous night on the cement floor of the studio—the only place left that still felt full of his mother.

He worked on successive batches of glazing solution for the final sculpture, and found something wrong with each one. He used the unfinished pieces to test, like she'd taught him. Mix and retest, over and over. He finally came up with a batch he couldn't find fault with. After applying it, he walked around the test piece and checked every angle. It glowed in luminous copper and mercury tones.

From nowhere, Justine appeared in the doorway, like the leaves that skidded in for short visits.

"Luca Brasi's not much of a watchdog," she said.

"He knows you."

The light always seemed to cast her in a perfect glow that only she couldn't see. Her hair was down, the way she used to wear it. She also wore the dark red lipstick he remembered from the first time they met.

"Is your dad alright?" she asked him.

"Yeah, I think so."

"Kind of a bummer how that happened."

"Yeah."

"I don't want our parents to get together."

"Me either. They'd fuck each other up exponentially."

"True that. What about you?"

"What?"

She was still framed in the doorway, bathed in holy light. "You, Henry, are you okay?"

"Sometimes. When I'm in here."

"I smell something strong."

"It's the finishing solution I'm working on."

"Is it okay to come in?"

"Yeah. Did you take the bus here?"

She took a tentative step. "Uh huh."

"I could have come and got you." He came closer.

"I texted you. And called."

"Oh, fuck. Sorry. I don't know where my phone is. I kind of forgot about it."

"Probably better. I wouldn't have wanted you to come by. My mom's been weird, asking me all these questions, getting all lawyerly."

"Parents." He stood in front of her.

"Yeah, full of surprises."

They had one of their quiet moments where everything stopped.

"Henry, would you rather be left alone? I would completely understand. I really wouldn't mind at all."

"No."

"What are you working on?"

"I want to finish my mom's last sculpture. She wanted me to. I guess I'd been avoiding it."

"How's it coming?"

"Good, mostly. I just need to turn some stuff off and we can go in and get some iced tea if you want."

"That sounds nice." He began shutting down the studio. "Or I don't mind being in here while you work."

"Nah, I'm thirsty."

When they walked across the backyard to the house, she didn't touch his arm but relied on her mental map to find her way.

He poured their iced teas and they stood in the kitchen and drank. The house was so quiet it seemed to be watching them. The only sound was the buzz of the refrigerator.

"Do you want to sit?" he asked.

"No." She felt for the counter and put her half-finished glass on it. She heard him put his glass down as well. She smelled him closer. It was one of those days where she could see a little, mostly just small variations of light. When he stood in front of her, he filled the space with a richer black.

"I'm taking your glasses off," he said.

"Okay," she whispered. As he touched her glasses, she put her hand forward, flat against his chest, finding the distance. He moved closer until she felt his breath, then his mouth and his lips, open and wet and turning, and finally his arms sliding around her.

He took her wrist and led her upstairs. He didn't wait for her to touch his arm. Luca Brasi followed them halfway, then stopped and plopped down on one of the stairs.

He kissed her again as they stood in his bedroom. Her hands moved over his face and neck and around his shoulders. His hands went down her back and up her front, grabbing with increased intensity. He hesitated. "Yes, Henry," she said in his ear, as if she was inside him. "Yes, it's okay." She pressed against him and felt the whole length of his body against her as she gripped his shoulders.

"I should take a shower," he said.

"Oh. Sure."

"I mean, if that's okay."

"Yeah." He led her to the edge of the bed. She sat as he pulled his shirt off. He started to take his pants off, but stopped. "It's okay," she said. "It's not like I can see you."

"I know, I just didn't know if it was weird."

"It's not." She heard his belt and the slide of his jeans. Then nothing. "Are you naked?"

"Yeah. I'll just be a couple minutes."

She nodded, serious. "Wait. Henry, can you—"

"What?"

"No, nothing."

"What?"

"I mean, can—oh, nothing."

"No, what? Please."

"I just—I mean, can you, would you please come closer to me? Yes, like that, but closer. Yes. Closer." Her hand shook as she reached out. She felt, then grasped and put her mouth on him.

Justine sat, still fully clothed, the taste of him everywhere as she listened to the sound of the shower. Her body felt shiny and new, as if she'd been sprinkled with magic pixie dust. She reached behind her and touched his bedding.

She leaned down and breathed him in. Her hand landed on something. She sat up and pulled it on her lap. She felt buttons and realized it was a soft shirt.

The scent of soap wafted from the shower. She knew where the window was—that side of the room was warmer. His desk would be there. She could hear the hum of his computer. She felt for his desk chair and draped the shirt over it.

She took her shoes and socks off and stepped out of her skirt. The water stopped. She took her blouse off, unhooked her bra, and let it drop. She took the shirt off the chair and slipped her arms through it. It smelled like him.

Henry came in from the bathroom with a towel around his waist. "I—" he stopped short. She turned, facing him, in her panties and open shirt. "What—what are you doing?" he asked.

"Is this your favorite shirt?"

"No."

"It's not?" She felt his voice more than she heard it.

"No, it's not my favorite shirt. It's not even my shirt."

"It's not? It was on your bed."

"It's my mom's shirt."

"Oh, God."

"Why are you wearing it?"

"Oh, God. It was supposed to be hot. Henry—"

"Why are you wearing it?"

"Henry, don't be mad."

"I'm not. I'm not mad, honest, I'm not."

He began to cry. It was sudden, like being run over. One moment he was standing, dripping, and the next he'd fallen to his knees like he'd been sucker-punched. He covered his face and leaned forward until his forehead touched the carpet.

He cried so hard he couldn't breathe. Justine didn't move or speak. He finally rocked back and caught his breath.

"I miss her," he said in a monotone. "I miss her so much." His face curled up again. "I just don't want to miss her so much, all the time, and my dad, I don't want to lose him too." His sobbing finally stopped, allowing him to breathe in gulps.

He looked up at her. She was shaking.

"Henry, I love you," she said. "I just—I love you. I do, I love you, Henry. I love you. I love you, Henry." She was shaking uncontrollably. He stood and grabbed her. He gripped her so hard her feet came off the ground. She was bony and bare and naked against his warm damp skin, jerking in his arms. He held her until she stopped shaking.

He pushed the shirt off her shoulders and let it fall to the floor. "I'm taking my towel off now," he said.

"I want to be naked, too."

He got down and slid her panties down. He pressed his face to her and wrapped his arms around her hips. She leaned forward and slid her hands through his wet hair and over his shoulders.

He went to the bed and yanked the covers off, leaving only a sheet.

"I know it's light in here," she said. "Don't make it dark. I want to know you can see me."

"I can see you," he said, and led her to the bed.

He lay on top of her. She felt herself open up, welcoming and fearless, like she was being born and rushing out of the darkness.

~ ~ ~

They came downstairs that evening and ate at the dining room table, naked, quite, and ravenous. They held hands with one hand and ate with the other.

Justine had to go home. After she left, Henry went back out to the studio and finished his mother's sculpture.

~ ~ ~

There was only one thing about sex that confused Justine, and it had to do with satisfaction. If sex was so great—and she now thought it was possibly the greatest thing ever—and if it was so satisfying, which it was—so, so insanely satisfying—then why did you always want more of it? To be satisfied meant to be content, but with sex, the more they did it, the more she wanted it. It didn't make sense, though it did explain a lot about the world.

361

And how was it that she'd never even thought about sex before? Well, except as something to avoid until she was eighteen, so her mother wouldn't come completely undone, and of course she always wanted to know the best ways to do things because she was at such a disadvantage. Thankfully, Aunt Vicky had helped with that, even if her advice about wearing his favorite shirt didn't really work out.

Now she thought about it all the time. Sex. Specifically, sex with Henry. She'd gone from never thinking about it, to thinking about it like it was something she fundamentally needed, like food and sleep. If they went more than a couple days apart, she felt like she was going to scratch her skin off.

There were logistical challenges. Justine's mom posed some problems. Margaret was always quick to suspect, and now that they were actually guilty, they had to be extra careful. Henry's dad wasn't home as much because he was working again, but it was usually around the same time they were in school.

Henry started driving the Jeep more often instead of his motorcycle. The Jeep had tinted windows. He'd lay the seats in the back flat, which worked okay, but was awkward. They had to be careful where they parked, and couldn't get too wild because the car would bounce.

Henry had started buying condoms in bulk. They'd decided it was his responsibility to make sure they had fast access to them at all times because she couldn't have any with her in case her mom found them. He had them stashed everywhere. They could complete the act remarkably fast when the occasion called for it. If an opportunity presented itself, they were quick to take advantage. They did it multiple times at Justine's school—against the wall behind the administrative offices where the only person Henry ever saw was a janitor who used the area to smoke. Justine loved going to class right after. Sitting at her desk, she could still feel him inside her, like an imprint.

They explored a lot of positions and discovered their unique preferences. Justine wanted Henry to describe everything he was seeing as they did it. It took a lot of coaxing at first. She had to assure him she wouldn't be offended by all the descriptive words. Like with her Aunt, she used them first so he'd know it was okay.

"Pussy, cock, ass, sperm, dick—"

"I get it, Jesus."

Justine found an appreciation for movie theaters after all. Comedies worked best. Henry would use his fingers until she'd claw his arm. He was good at timing it to the funny parts so she'd be covered by the laughter.

They got a hotel room once. Henry sold all his old video games to get the money. They didn't stop until they were sore and stinging raw. Another time, on a weekend, Henry's dad actually went somewhere for the day and they spread blankets in the backyard. It was a bright fall day with a cool breeze. They did it once while Justine wore her dress, which Henry liked, then a second time naked. He described the goosebumps on her skin and the pucker of her nipples as she arched back and twisted.

They got caught once, in a dressing room at the mall, which was especially awkward because Henry had the bright idea to tell the clerk he was Justine's brother, and that he had to go in with her because she was blind.

They had a secret, and they protected it. The secret wasn't sex. The secret was their discovery of each other. They were the only two people in the world fortunate enough to have found each other. A part of Henry wanted to brag, to tell every sort-of friend he had about his girl, a girl you'd probably just walk past and maybe even avoid because she was blind, so she might ask for help or do something embarrassing. But he liked their secret more than he liked bragging, so he didn't tell anyone.

Justine enjoyed their secret in part because she knew it wouldn't last; she'd have to talk to her mom soon. This was the first really big thing she'd ever kept from her mother. She'd broken her promise, over and over again, and she'd have to face it. Getting her mom to understand would be a delicate dance through a minefield. It would require strategy. Henry was for not telling her at all, but Justine assured him it would be okay. Probably. But she found it easy to put off, telling herself she wanted to enjoy their secret just a little longer.

They never did it at Justine's house. Henry didn't even like going there, especially if her mom was home. He felt like she'd know, just by looking at him, like she could read his thoughts.

The exception was a Thursday in November when they hadn't seen each other since the previous weekend and were desperate for some time together. They'd planned to meet after school and go to the park. Justine called him in the morning, just as he was leaving.

"Are you driving?" she asked him.

"I just got in the Jeep."

"There's construction on my street."

"You mean now?"

"Yeah, my mom already left for work. She's been going in early. It's also raining and I hate to walk when—"

"I'll be right over, I'll give you a ride."

"It's really just the construction. Walking through it freaks me out a little. They apparently have to tear up our street because of some emergency water thing, and they weren't required to notify us or some such shit, at least according to the vegetable on the phone."

"Who'd you call?"

"The city's Municipal Planning department. Not the first time. They kinda know me. There are many civic issues only a blind person would be aware of. They always appreciate my input."

Henry had a hard time getting to her house. There was already a long line of cars backed up. They'd blocked off the middle of the street, leaving only a single lane on each side for traffic.

He arrived twenty minutes late. They'd been texting while he was stuck, so he expected her to be ready when he got there. Instead, she opened the door and pulled him inside.

"Sorry it took me so long," he said as he stumbled in. "Wait, I don't want to get your floor all wet."

She kissed him. She kissed him like he was a solider back from a great war. Her backpack fell to the floor.

"You know," she said, now kissing his neck. "I was thinking, while I was here waiting for you, that I'll miss my first class anyway, and it's raining, so we won't be able to go to the park after school, and it's been days and days, and if I have to sit in class all day and think about it, it's going to really be detrimental to my education, and I'm trying to get into college, you know"—she lowered her voice to a whisper and stood on her tiptoes so she could talk in his ear—"and I know it's kind of pervy of me but I like it when"—her voice turned to hot breath; she bit his earlobe, wet from the rain, and pulled a fistful of his hair—"when you fuck me really hard and then I go to class and I can still feel it."

He kissed her—rough—as his hands slid under her sweater. She found his ear again. "And I'm ready now. Like, right now."

"Where?" he asked.

"Here, right here, fuck me here."

A second later his belt buckle hit the hardwood floor; Justine turned and pulled her skirt up as she leaned over the couch. He maneuvered behind her. She let out a low moan as he pushed in. He could tell this one wasn't going to last long.

Justine screamed. Henry felt her body go rigid. He stopped, confused.

Margaret's perfume—Justine had smelled it.

Henry looked up and saw Margaret's reflection in the window, then a blur of motion and another sound— Margaret's cry blending with Justine's scream.

Margaret grabbed Henry by the hair and pulled him backwards. He twisted and tripped over his pants. Her contorted face hovered above him as she pulled him across the floor. He tried to cover his face when her foot came down. It landed on his neck. Justine screamed again when she heard the sound.

Margaret stomped a second time. Her foot slipped past his arm and hit his face. She fell on him, her knee to his neck, and grabbed his hair.

Justine leapt off the couch toward her mother's voice. She knocked Margaret off enough for Henry to scramble away by kicking his heels on the floor and sliding on his back.

Justine held her mother's leg. "Go, Henry!" He stood and pulled his pants up. "Go!"

"No." He stood facing Margaret.

He got hit from behind. A construction worker, hearing female screams, had run to the open door. He saw the only man and tackled him, knocking him face down. The man landed on Henry's back. Henry felt the scruff of the man's face on his shoulder and the lip of his hardhat on the back of his neck before his face hit the polished hardwood floor.

~ ~ ~

366

Margaret had been running north, enjoying the rain. She'd had the idea of doing a triathlon for a while. As much as she loved to run, there were times when it got monotonous. The bike part was easily enough, but the swimming would be a challenge. She could swim in a pool, but triathletes swam in the ocean.

She'd seen the local triathlon club use her street to train. Instead of her normal route near the beach, she decided to try running up the San Vicente hill. She'd planned to go as far as 14th street, then cut across and come back down to Ocean Avenue. She could still make it back to the office before anyone else arrived, except Gavin Tupps, who was always in early. She thought about the times she'd driven down San Vicente and seen the runners coming up; she always thought they were a bit nuts, especially on a cold, rainy morning. Now she was one of them.

She waited for the light to change. The construction trucks caught her eye. They were farther up the street than when she'd left the house. She thought of Justine as she jogged in place. As independent as she was, the one thing Justine hated was a construction site.

Better call her, Margaret thought—see if she made it to the bus okay. She took her phone out and looked up the street as the call connected. She thought she could see Henry's Jeep parked in front of her house. She crossed between cars to get a better look. Yes, that was his Jeep.

She ran toward her house.

~ ~ ~

Henry was up before the construction worker who'd tackled him was able to stand. The man groaned; he'd wrenched his back and stayed on his knees as he tried to piece together what happened. He could see that the guy he'd tackled was actually a kid, who now had blood gushing from his nose and down his front. A girl was crying and saying, *Who is that smell?*

Three other hardhats crowded the doorway, including the foreman, who was telling the man on his knees that if he was hurt, he couldn't file a claim because he was in a private residence, and was no longer covered by the company's insurance policy, as he'd voluntarily left the worksite.

Henry felt woozy. He looked at Margaret. She looked in shock—all the color was gone from her face. He went to Justine. "Are you okay?" he asked her.

"Go," she whispered to him.

Another worker arrived in the doorway. "You crazy fuck," he said to the guy still on his knees. Henry held his shirt to his nose as he pushed past, down the steps, and to the safety of his car.

At home, he took a shower and bandaged his nose. He checked his phone impulsively, expecting a text from Justine. One finally arrived while he was lying on his bed with his head tipped back to keep his nose from bleeding again.

Are you hurt?

I'm okay but what the fuck was that?

I don't know. She's on her way over there.

Henry looked blankly at the screen, like the message might change. He was leaning on an elbow. Blood started to fall in dime-sized splats on his wrist.

What the fuuuck?!!!, he texted back, then added, *Should I call you?*

No just wanted to warn. Is your dad home?

Yes.

She wants to talk to him.

Margaret sprinted back to her office. When she got there, she ran through the reception area. Her wet shoes squelched across the floor.

It was a quarter to nine. The receptionist only had time to look up as Margaret went past, leaving a wake of wet tracks. Heidi was sharing a joke over the phone with her youngest son's second grade teacher. Her smile fell when she saw Margaret.

"Margaret, you—"

"Not now," Margaret said over her shoulder.

Heidi followed her into her office. "What happened?"

"Keys!" Margaret yelled. Heads popped up and turned in their direction.

"*There-there-there!*" Heidi said and pointed to her desk. Margaret grabbed her keys and ran out.

~ ~ ~

She knew she was driving too fast. She willed herself to slow down as she sped down Lincoln and weaved through traffic. *Recalibrating,* the car's GPS intoned. She decided to go left on Montana and try 7th Street, which cut across to the Palisades.

Slow down.

She squealed a hard left through an intersection and raced to the light at 7th. She stopped to turn right—*come on come on come on*—she inched forward, looking for a gap.

It had stopped raining. The sun was out, shiny and bright. A group sat outside the Starbucks. A small blond girl, maybe six, stood on the corner, holding her younger brother's hand. She was looking across the street in the other direction, squinting in the sun. Even in her current state, Margaret thought, *Where is your mother?* At least the girl knew to wait. Margaret looked left again. A gap opened. Turning back, she took her foot off the brake and was about to stomp on the gas when she saw the smallest wisp of blond hair bob over the hood of her car. She slammed her brake. The car lurched.

Paralyzed, Margaret watched the girl and boy pass in front of her and continue across the street. The girl's hair was tied on top with a scrunchie, which caused it to stick up a few inches. Was it the mother that Margaret had just secretly reprimanded who had done that? A whimsical touch, made on impulse, that just saved two lives?

Margaret's heart was trying to escape from her chest, throwing itself around, pounding in whooshing thuds in her ear. Everything joined in, the car and the street and all the people—*whomp whomp whomp*—all trying to turn her head inside out. Like a landed fish, she gulped for air.

Another sound. Light taps of the horn. Not rude, just a suggestion. Margaret crept around the corner, staying close to the curb. She parked in the red and slumped forward.

Anxiety took over; a merciless machine that stripped, shook, and squeezed her like squealing factory stock—dropped her down to where the air was thin and grainy. Images ran through her mind: her foot about to stomp on the accelerator, on Henry's head, on Dwayne's head. The lurch of the car. Handsome, beautiful Henry, his face red and his fists balled up like an infant, vulnerable and naked and excited. Justine, with a look Margaret had never seen. Fear. Real fear. Of her.

The one person she was most devoted to protecting.

Where is your mother?

She gripped the wheel. Someone walking by slowed to a stop and peered in.

Margaret squeezed her eyes shut and it was all right there—the bathroom stall, Song's voice, his grip and the smell of his breath, Basil snapping at her, and her mother with her pulpy head.

You going to kill yourself too?

She got out of the car and found her way to the sidewalk. A heavyset man looked at her. "I don't think you can park there." He tilted his head. "You alright?" He reached out.

"Yes." She recoiled and turned back to her car.

She drove.

Pretend to be fine. Pretend to be okay. Take the physical actions. Take the normal, physical actions and everything will be okay. Breathe. Take deep breaths.

She was driving fast again and nearly passed the house. When she tried to park, her wheel hopped the curb and landed in a planter of flowers.

Henry had spent the previous half hour debating if he should talk to his dad. Was it better to warn him of what was coming? How could he explain it all? He was still weighing the pros and cons when there was a pounding on the door. He came out of his room and started down the stairs, realizing that—yes—judging by the sound of the pounding, he should have warned his dad.

He was halfway down when his dad strode into the entryway and thrust a hand toward him. "I'll get it, hang tight."

When his dad opened the door, Henry couldn't see her at first, but he heard her voice, loud and clear.

"How old is your son?" she asked.

"I'm sorry, would you like to come in?"

"Your son, Henry, how old is he?"

She put her toe on the doorframe. Henry crouched on the stairs. Now he could see her. She was coiled tight like a cobra. Her chest was rising and falling. He was having trouble hearing what they were saying. His dad turned and looked at him, puzzled, then turned back to her. A moment later there was the sound of a hard smack and his dad's head snapped back.

"You're a terrible father," he heard her say.

Chapter 19

The scariest feeling in the world is realizing you didn't really know someone after all. You think you know everything about them, the entire minutia that make them who they are, then this other part comes out. A hidden part. The real part.

Where was it all this time?

~ ~ ~

When Margaret got back from confronting Henry's father, she went to her study and called her office. She told Heidi she wouldn't be in and hung up as Heidi tried to ask her what happened.

She sat rigid, looking at her shaking hands. Her stomach burned.

Her eyes locked on the sculpture. It sat on the table that ran along the wall by the closet. When they redecorated, the statue ended up staying in her home office. It was the first thing her eyes fell on when she sat at her desk. It was so much like the statue that was outside her office that she'd come to think of it as the same presence, watching her watching others, like the moon that followed her as a child.

Her medication. She seldom took it. It took the edge off her thinking and made her groggy the next day. Today was an exception. Anxiety would lead her math brain to search for something to grab hold of. If she didn't head it off now, her mind would soon be filled with repetitive patterns and equations, cycling over and over.

She dug through the drawers for her pills. There was half a cup of cold coffee on her desk; she used it to wash three down. The sustained anxiety had made her neck so stiff it felt like her vertebrae had been fused. Her hips and legs ached from the long sprint back to her office.

To be taken with food, the label said. It was almost noon and she hadn't eaten anything, and wasn't about to now. She rolled the bottle around in her hand. Expired nearly a year ago. Still safe to take. Didn't she read that somewhere?

She looked at the statue again. Some time must have passed because she felt the pills take effect. Invisible arms comforted her.

She pulled her running shoes off. They were dry but her socks were still damp. She peeled them off her pale feet as the medication released layers of calm. She rested her head on her arms and listened to her breathing and heart rate slow down, like water finding its level.

Her phone vibrated in her pocket. It was an odd feeling. It took her a moment to realize what it was. She took it out and looked at it. She didn't recognize the number, but it was her area code.

"Hello?"

"Is this Margaret?" a man's voice said.

"Yes."

"This is Tom. I got your number from Henry. Did you hit my son?"

"What?"

"Did you hit Henry?"

"No."

"I've had some time to piece this together. Henry won't tell me what happened, but he comes home with his face smashed in, you come here making assertions and threats, then assault me. I'll ask you again—did you hit my kid?"

"No, no I—"

"And how old is *your* kid?"

"What?"

"This happen at your house, am I right?"

"Wait—"

"Your house."

"Yes, but—"

"Listen to me. If I find out—and I will find out—if I find out you touched my kid—consider this a threat if you like—I know you're a lawyer but guess what? I can afford lawyers too. You come here—*I'm* a bad father? You come here—you're a menace—you stay the hell away from my kid."

The call ended. Margaret dropped the phone on her desk and covered her eyes. The calmness of the medication evaporated. She cried in her hands until she forced herself out of the chair and trudged up the stairs.

She used the soft knock that precedes an apology. "Can I come in?" No answer. Margaret cracked the door. Justine was curled on the bed. She had her glasses off. Her eyes were open but she looked blank, like all the light had gone out of her.

"Honey? I wanted to talk to you."

"I don't want to talk to you right now."

"But can I come in?" Justine gave a barely perceptible shrug. Margaret lay on the bed and slid behind her. She tried different angles in her head, but the words wouldn't come out. Her thoughts were like something screened off. She closed her eyes and breathed in the smell of Justine's hair.

She came out of a sleepy, gauzy place to the sound of Justine's voice.

"You spy on me," Justine said in a flat voice. "I've been thinking about that, and what a lie it was. But I also realized I was lying to you, because I knew and didn't tell you. It was only recently that I had to get rid of stuff I didn't want you to see. You used to say that other people would put limits on me because I'm blind, but I should never put limits on myself. But now I see that it was you. You were the one that put limits on me. No matter what I did or how good I was, it was always you. I couldn't decide about sex for myself. I would have talked to you about it if I actually thought I had some say. I never betrayed your trust, but you read my email and texts and I could even tell when you would go through my stuff. You thought I wouldn't know because I'm blind, like other people would think. I could smell your hand lotion in my drawers. Why?"

Margaret didn't answer. She opened her mouth, but nothing came out.

"It's funny," Justine continued, "because for the last few weeks, I've been trying to figure out how to talk to you about Henry. How to tell you we've been having sex. How I feel about him. About how... full I feel. I broke my promise to you. I knew it was a big deal, and I wanted to tell you in a way that would make you understand. And really I just wanted to share it all with you. The last month has been the best month of my whole life, and I wanted to tell you all about it, every detail, until you were sick of hearing about it and teasing me to shut up already. That's what I imagined, because you're my best friend. But I'm laying here thinking that I only had the best month of my life because I finally betrayed you."

Justine could feel her mother against her back, shivering, like she'd long been left out in the cold.

He didn't answer. Somehow she wasn't expecting that. She hung up when she got his voicemail. After thinking about a message to leave, she called again. "Yeah," he answered on the first ring, throwing her off again.

"It's Margaret." There was no reply. "I'm sorry. I was mistaken in the assumptions I made. I understand that now. And I'm sorry." She waited. "Is—is Henry okay?"

"I remember you," Tom said. "We spoke briefly, and you talked to my wife. At the charity auction. When you and I saw each other at that godawful dance—our kid's thing—you thought I didn't remember you. But I do."

A cold feeling crept over her. "Yes," she said. "I remember that too. I recall talking to you. And your wife. You're right, I didn't think you remembered." She listened to the faint sound of his breathing and waited. "I can tell you what happened, if you like. With Justine and Henry. And how Henry got hurt."

"No, I can talk to my kid."

"Is he alright? And you?"

"Full of good intentions, I see. We're fine."

"I'm sorry I hit you."

"I won't sue."

"Well, that's all I wanted to say. Take care, Tom."

"What did you talk about?"

"What?"

"You and my wife. I'd like to know what you and my wife talked about."

"I don't—I don't remember."

"There's nothing left of her, so when I find something new, like a conversation or something, it's nice to know. Even the trivial stuff matters. It's impossible to express how much. But you don't remember. That's okay. Thanks for calling."

"She said she'd have preferred to be a lawyer. Instead of an artist." She waited. "If I remember right," she added. "Yes, she did say that."

"Did she say why?"

"I asked her. I remember now—I asked her why anyone who could create things as beautiful as she could would ever want to do something else."

"What did she say?"

"She said it wasn't what people thought. Being an artist. Artists haven't mattered for a long time, she said. It's a— what did she call it? You're limited, or restricted I think she said. She used a word. I told her I'd wanted to be a dancer, when I was very young. I bought one of her pieces."

"I remember that, yes."

"I'm looking at it now. She said—the sculpture, the one I have—it was as close to a self portrait as she'd ever tried to create."

~ ~ ~

"So, no sex?" Henry paced his room. "We're agreed?"

"I think that's a little extreme," Justine said, sitting up in bed. Talking to Henry had become a necessity before sleep.

"I think it's important. For my safety, if nothing else."

"Don't you think it's a little ironic that we've been having sex and keeping it from our parents, or at least from my mom—"

"Keeping it from my dad would really just entail not doing it directly in front of him."

"—and now that they know, we're going to stop?"

Henry flopped on his bed. "Ironic, yes. I think. I've heard people often misuse that word."

"Not I. You know, I think you're just afraid of my mom."

"That's entirely true."

"Fine, we'll stop, I can do that."

378

"Really? I was kind of counting on you to turn me around."

"No, you're right, at least for a while. See how long we last. Though I hate to think our last time ended with you getting assaulted. How's your nose?"

"Better. My dad said it's not broken, so there's a rainbow."

"It's not like we'll never do it again."

"I know."

"Just until things calm down and we can approach our parents as two mature young adults, capable of independent thought."

"Let the healing begin."

"I'll tell you, Mister Henry, I've gotten very used to you, in that way. Maybe now, since we're not having sex, it's a good time to tell you what an amazing lover you are."

"See—now, already you're making this very difficult."

"What?"

"And you express yourself better than I can so there's a problem, because I'd never in a million years be able to tell you what an awesome lover you are."

"Okay, that didn't hurt. How long do you think we'll last?"

"I don't know. What time is it?"

~ ~ ~

"What day is it?" Justine asked. It had become their opening routine.

"Nine," Henry said.

"I think I'm getting hives or something."

"Relax, people go without sex for, like, years."

"Not with you as their lover. The way you touch me."

"Stop."

"And the way you describe everything as it's happening. God, I love that."

"Me too."

"Mmm, so miss that."

"Go easy or I'll have to get some tissues."

"Have you been thinking about it a lot?"

"I'm a guy, so that never really changes."

"Like, how do you think of me? Wait, it is me you think about, right?"

"Of course."

"Now I know you're lying. It's fine. Hey, have you heard your dad on the phone recently, like at night?"

"No. What do you mean?"

"I keep hearing my mom late at night and I thought I heard her say *Tom*."

"You mean like she's talking to my dad?"

"Yes, Tom is your dad."

"I'm not slow, but we were talking about sex and it takes a while for the blood to make its way back up to my brain."

"The burdens men suffer. I'll wait. Are you back yet?"

"Not really. Almost."

"Maybe stand on your head."

"No, I'm good. So, when was this?"

"The last few nights."

"What day is it?" she asked.

"Thirteen."

"So, you heard him?"

"Yeah. I felt weird, so I didn't really listen to what exactly they were talking about, but it's the third night in a row, and it's definitely your mom he's talking to."

"Henry, this makes me nervous."

"I know, me too."

"I don't want them liking each other."

"Me either."

"It's like, we were here first."

"I know."

"Because, what would that mean for us? I thought this was temporary."

"Yeah. Wait, you mean our abstinence?"

"Well, yeah. It's almost two weeks now. I thought it'd get easier. Then we could talk to them together, like starting new."

"Then fuck like rabbits."

"Exactly. It's just—if they start something, it gets complicated."

"In a whole lot of ways."

"It's our fault."

"No it's not. We failed at that, remember?"

"What day is it?" she asked.

"Fourteen."

"I listened as much as I could. Did you?"

"Some. They're talking about some weird stuff."

"I know. She was talking about being a kid. Things I'd never heard."

"Some dark shit."

"Right? But I think they're enjoying it."

"I was going to say the same thing."

"This is a serious problem."

"What day is it?" she asked.

"Fifteen."

"I'm going to break."

"Hang in there."

"I was thinking."

"Yeah?"

"What is sex?"

"You're not sure?"

"Not entirely."

He let out a long breath. "I've failed. Let's talk about something else."

"No, I mean, what exactly constitutes sex? Is it the point of insertion?"

"Tab A into Slot B kind of thing?"

"Yeah, it seems a blurry line at best."

"How so?"

"If I suck you, is that sex?"

"I won't be able to speak clearly if you continue."

"When you finger me at the movies, is that sex?"

"Daaahhbleeergflasm."

"Or like if you were to imagine me, right now, like while we're talking on the phone..."

"Okay, stop."

"And I was on my knees, between your legs."

"Uh."

"And you looked down at my face, turned up at you. Henry? Are you there?"

"Uh. Huh."

"Do you need to get some tissues?"

"I'm going to need a towel."

"And you put your hand in my hair, maybe grabbing it a little rough because you've gotten inpatient."

"Fa-fa-fuck."

"I've made you wait all this time and now you're done being the considerate guy."

"Done with that."

"So you're impatient and rough and grab my hair and I put my mouth on your dick."

"Oh—fuck—*ahhh*."

"Whose turn?" she asked.

"You."

"I think it's you, but I accept your generosity. I'm good—go."

"From where we left off, or start new?"

"Where we left off. I'm halfway there already."

"You have the skirt on?"

"Skirt, heels, no undies, foot propped on windowsill, ready already."

"Curtains are closed, right?"

"*Yes—just go!*"

"Use the middle finger of your right hand. Just the very tip, barely touching, like I do to you."

"Doing that now."

"Bottom to top."

"Ohh, jeezy wow. Why is it so much better when you tell me to do it?"

"Now, let me tell you what that looks like."

~ ~ ~

Henry warned him about store crowds on a Sunday, but his father went anyway. He was intent on buying new clothes, another clear sign of improvement. Henry took the opportunity to carry his mother's final statue to his parents' bedroom. It still had the faint smell of finishing glaze. He hoisted it to the top shelf of the closet and moved it directly above her shirt. Together, they looked dangerously close to the beginning of a shrine.

He pulled the light chain on and off. The shirt swayed on its hanger. The sculpture appeared to move each time the light turned on, like they'd already learned to work together.

On his way out of the bedroom, something caught his eye. He went to his father's side of the bed. A black, velvet-covered jewelry box sat on the nightstand.

He opened it and pulled a ring out; yellow stones set in silver. It was clearly meant for a woman, and it was new. He put it back, taking care to place it in the exact same spot.

~ ~ ~

"Today's the day," Justine said. "I know my timing's been a bit off lately."

"Way off. You say you're there, then it's like another minute."

"Today it's going to happen—together—just like in the movies. Or so I've heard. Literally."

"Then I'm stuck in cleanup mode."

"You've had a lot more practice. You're like a virtuoso with that thing. You could be playing Carnegie Hall if you practiced piano as much as you—"

"We have to talk first."

"About what? Can't it wait?"

"No."

"Seriously? A girl has needs."

"He bought her a ring."

There was a long silence.

"Henry, can you say that again?"

"He bought her a ring. I found it in his room."

"Jesus. They went from talking to... Henry, what the hell?"

"I know, it's weird. She hasn't said anything to you?"

"No, nothing."

"Same here. They talked again last night."

"I know."

"They haven't missed a night in, like, more than a week."

"Do you think this means what I think it means?"

"No, it couldn't be, they'd tell us, right? They haven't even seen each other, have they?"

"I don't know, I don't think so. Why wouldn't she talk to me about this?"

"I don't know. Do you think she would? We haven't exactly been, you know—"

"Phone fucking isn't sex, we've established that." Henry waited, not wanting to interrupt her thinking. "We have to find out for sure, we have to know."

"Agreed. So, you're going to talk to her?"

"Yeah, I have to. Well, I'm not sure. I'll call you when I think of something."

~ ~ ~

Justine wouldn't have thought to do it if her mom hadn't spied on her all that time. At least, that was her justification, though it wasn't an easy one. The whole next day, she thought of little else, except Henry, but that was normal.

It was simple enough to do. That night, when Margaret was in the bathroom, Justine placed her phone under her mom's office desk, under the drawer area, with the voice recorder running. With a full charge, it would record for about three hours.

"Goodnight, Mom," Justine said through the bathroom door.

"You okay, sweetheart?" Margaret asked her. She already sounded distracted, Justine thought.

"Yeah, just tired."

"Okay, 'night."

Later, Justine listened with her door open, waiting to hear the soft murmur of her mom's voice coming from her office downstairs. She messaged Henry from her computer.

The deed is done.

Did it go okay?

Yeah, just waiting. What's your dad doing?

Watching his old surgery tapes.

?

They tape surgeries, for training. He used to watch them all the time, to improve his skills.

Weird.

Kinda freaky cause they're kids, you know?

Damn.

He started watching, prepping to start again I guess.

That's good, right?

I think so.

I hear her I think.

Can't tell unless I go downstairs so update me.

Rodger dodger.

Justine spent the next couple hours on her computer. She tried to distract herself by checking gateways on her old hacks. She reopened some that had closed. She was out of practice; most of her workarounds no longer worked. Hacking was like gardening—you had to keep on top of it.

Shortly before midnight, she heard her mother come upstairs. She sent a quick message to Henry and went to bed.

~ ~ ~

The next morning, Margaret left for work before Justine was up for school, same as usual. Justine got her phone from her mom's office. She charged it while she showered.

She waited until she was on the bus before putting her earpiece in. As the bus lurched, she fast-forwarded through the blank part at the beginning. There was about twenty minutes of nothing before her mother's voice came through.

—it all coming back to you?

The personal, voyeuristic nature of what she was doing came into focus. Her stomach clenched. Her mother's question was followed by a blank section, which must have been Tom responding.

Her mother's voice returned.

I'm sure when you get back in there you'll know which way's up. It's a big step.

Justine stopped the playback. The feeling in her stomach had turned sour.

No more, she decided. The bus came to a sudden stop, throwing her and the other passengers forward before pitching them back again. She could identify the bus driver by the way they drove, and this one was the worst, taking his dislike for the job out on the bus and all its passengers.

Justine decided she couldn't go through with it. This wasn't the way. Maybe she could just talk to her mom, tell her everything she was feeling, and ask her what was going on with Henry's dad. Put it all out in the open. What was there, really, to be so afraid of?

She was trying to delete the recording when the bus came to another abrupt stop. Her phone slipped from her hand and went skidding across the floor. A number of people got out of their seats to retrieve it. Justine sat with a grateful smile, ready to acknowledge the kindness of whoever was about to help the blind girl.

Justine's history teacher, Mr. Latner, liked to dress up as historical figures—Lincoln, Rosa Parks, Napoleon—whoever they happened to be studying. He'd started it when teaching grade school and continued the practice when he moved to high school, despite the smirks and rolled eyes.

Justine's friend, Kara, sat next to her, and always explained to Justine what Mr. Latner was wearing. The previous semester, after Mr. Latner dressed as a pre–Civil War cotton picker, he was called before the school board and told to stop with the dress-up. He argued that as an African American, he had an ancestor who'd picked cotton in the South, and he intended to show farming records from that era that listed his family name as part of the plantation's property, something his grandfather spent years tracking down. The school board was not moved.

Now Mr. Latner taught history like everyone else. He was talking about ancient Egypt, explaining that there were actually seven or eight queens named Cleopatra. "Like *Maries* at an Italian wedding," he said—though Justine could tell from his nervous laugh that he wished he hadn't, and not just because nobody else laughed.

Justine kept hearing her mother's voice in her head.

Phones were not allowed in class—seen or heard—but she took hers out and put in her earpiece. She could get away with a lot because everyone assumed that whatever she was doing, she had to do because she was blind. She could probably eat her lunch in class and nobody would stop her.

The text-to-speech app worked well for some functions, but not for others. She scrolled though the menus but couldn't find the delete command to clear the recording. She heard something that made her stop; a whining, machine-like sound from a random spot in the recording. She realized it was her mother's voice.

I just know if—then silence again. She rewound.

—wasn't something I even understood at the time. There are times I know, I mean I just know if I didn't have Justine, I would never believe it happened.

There was the whining sound again. It was her mother, but Justine had never heard this sound. Was she crying?

She rewound further.

Mr. Latner was talking about Julius Caesar. Kara touched Justine's arm and leaned over. "He said he's going to dim the lights. I think he's going to show some slides." Justine nodded. The room shifted darker.

The recording picked up.

—saying rape, the word. She helped me with that. I was raped. I had to say that to myself in the mirror, because my mind wanted to get rid of it. I was raped. She was the only one who knew. And she knew I got pregnant from it, but she's never met Justine.

There was a pause on the recording. Or maybe the world had stopped. Justine went cold. The pause went on and on, like time had run out and it was the end of everything.

The whine—her mother's anguish—came out of pure, empty space until it filled her ear.

I had to make up a story about her father.

Silence. The ground opened up and she was about to fall into it when a hand touched her. "What?" she said instinctively.

Kara whispered to her. "You're making a noise."

Justine tried to stop the recording. She was shaking. The volume went higher. Her mother's crying pierced though her head.

Something to tell her when she asked.

The hand came back. "Are you okay?"

Justine nodded and pointed her phone toward Kara's voice. "Turn it off, please."

"Your phone?" Kara asked.

"Yes."

Kara took it and turned it off. "You alright?" she whispered as she put the phone back in Justine's hand.

"Ladies?" Mr. Latner said. Justine could hear people shifting in their seats. She felt eyes on her. She pulled her earpiece out and put it in her lap, along with the phone. "You're done? Oh, thank you." More shifting and the lecture continued. Light and dark moved in winks to the rhythm of Mr. Latner's voice.

The weight of Justine's body disappeared. Everything seemed to evaporate. She'd learned about the atomic bombs the United States had dropped on Hiroshima and Nagasaki. Some people were instantly vaporized. She'd tried to imagine what that was like; to exist, and then to not exist.

Maintain control, a stern voice in her head said.

Justine was always jealous of people who could just *be*, and know they were safe. She couldn't do that. No matter how bad things were, she still had to maintain a small amount of control, or she could fall into a manhole or get hit by a bus or get kicked out of school and be made to live with other blind people. There were very few times in her life—not since she was a child, and even then only at home—when she lost total control and everything fell away.

She wouldn't remember a lot of what happened next. She remembered Kara saying, "Are you sure you're okay? Here's your backpack. You left it." She'd left her jacket somewhere as well. She remembered walking and getting lost. It was raining and she dug in her bag for her umbrella. It was the kind that folded up small. She always had it with her, along with her other essentials, but her backpack had come unzipped and some of her stuff was missing. Both her umbrella and her cane were gone.

She smelled flowers and heard doors swoosh; she was outside the Whole Foods, she realized. Soaked by the rain, she looked more like a little girl than a teenager. People tried to help her but she pushed them away. One woman kept trying to pull her into her car, saying she could drive her anywhere she needed to go just please let me help you—Justine had to threaten to bite her grabbing hand.

She found her bus. She shivered as the words ran slipshod through her head. There was no way to turn them off.

I was raped. I got pregnant from it.

The bus lurched forward and back, stuck in traffic. Justine lost track of the stops. She thought they'd gone around the last corner before her house, but now they'd slowed to a crawl.

She heard the pounding of heavy machinery and the shout of voices. The construction crews were back. It took ten minutes to go the next two blocks.

The bus finally came to a halt and kneeled with a hiss as the doors jerked open. Justine felt her way off and into the rain. She turned a circle, disoriented by the thunderous pounding of the digging equipment. She walked a few paces and felt the incline of the sidewalk, telling her she was going in the right direction. She inched along. The pounding got louder.

Slow and steady. She was a block from home when she heard talking and laughing close by. A man said something to her in a gruff voice. A hand touched her arm. Another voice said, "You're not supposed to do that, blind people don't like it."

The first voice spoke again. "Let me help you, sweetheart."

"Thank you. I'm that house up there, with the yellow trim. The rain confuses me." Sometimes it was more effort to resist help than accept it. She just wanted to get inside, take her wet clothes off and crawl into bed.

The man tightened his grip on her upper arm and led her. "Here you go—I got you. I got a daughter about your age."

She could smell it on his breath: peanut butter. They must have been eating lunch when they saw her. It'd be okay if he didn't breathe too close. The rain would help. Maybe not though—she was having trouble thinking straight. Just a little further.

"House with the yellow trim, here you go." He helped her up the steps to the porch as if she hadn't been there before.

"Thank you," she said, and dug for her keys.

"No problem, sweetheart," he said with pride. "You need help with that?" He moved closer.

"No, I got it, thank you so much." She made it inside, shut the door behind her, and locked it.

She was already short of breath.

It'll go away in a little bit.

She didn't want to go upstairs dripping wet so she dropped her backpack and went toward the laundry room as she pulled her shirt over her head.

Something didn't feel right. Her breath was getting tighter. Her head throbbed.

She stood still and tried to think.

It should go away. It was just on his breath.

It wasn't getting better. Something didn't equate.

Best be safe and get the EpiPen.

She went back to the entryway to get her backpack. She felt a vertigo shift and went down on one knee.

Her pack was open. She riffled though it but the pen wasn't where it was supposed to be. It must have fallen out with the other stuff that was missing.

She could feel it in her throat—the tightening. Now on both knees, she put her hands to her temples and forced herself to think.

There was something slippery on her fingers; and something on her face. She knew immediately. Peanut butter. It was on the man's hand when he took her arm. It had gotten on her shirtsleeve and must have smeared her face when she pulled her shirt off.

Don't panic. Maintain control. Take a breath. See, you can still breathe. You've got time. Wipe it off your face as best you can.

She felt in her pack for something to wipe with. Nothing. She leaned down and rubbed her face on the pack.

There. Now, the pen's not in your pack. You have others. You have them everywhere. No problem. One upstairs, next to your bed. At least two downstairs. Where? Where downstairs? Think. Where's the one downstairs? Where the fuck?

She could hear her own breathing now, a ragged, dragging sound.

Where downstairs? Okay, go upstairs. Quickly, now. Justine, go upstairs right now and get the pen in your bedroom and use it. You can do this. This is easy. You've prepared for this.

She stood too quickly and felt herself fall sideways. She landed on her shoulder.

No, not like this. Phone. Use your phone. It's right here.

She grabbed it. It was dead.

Fuck—you forgot to turn it back on. It would take too long. Where was I going?

Confused, she felt for her backpack again.

No, you did that, now you got more on you. Phone. The other phone, in mom's office. Go, Justine. Get up and go.

She stood. She could breathe. A prayer, answered. She'd read about this; it was an adrenaline surge—the body using the last of its resources. She had a window.

Get to mom's office. Use the phone. Dial 911.

She made it. The phone was exactly where it was supposed to be. Easy. She dialed.

"What is your emergency?" the voice asked.

She tried to speak. Her breath was gone. She gulped air.

"Can you speak louder? I can't hear you."

The construction equipment outside pounded a steady rhythm. A smothering darkness came over her as she realized an ambulance would never make it through the construction in time.

"Are you able to speak?" the voice said in her ear. "We have the address associated with this number and our records indicate you have a condition—"

She hung up. She felt something inside her shift.

I'm sorry, mom. I know you'll be disappointed in me.

No. Call her. Call Mom.

She called her mom's cellphone. It rang, then went to voicemail. *Beep.*

"Mom," she managed, but that was all.

Hang up and call Henry. Why? I just want to.

She called him. Her head was spiraling in on itself. Each ring slipped further away.

"Hey." It was him. He'd answered. His voice.

His voice —yes, the last thing before sleep.

She could only listen to the fading sound. "Isn't this your house number? I almost didn't answer, but I'm between classes and—Justine, it's you, isn't it? What? Or is this Ms. Shepard? I mean Margaret? Are you there? Can you... *Oh fuck!* Justine—Justine, are you in trouble? Is something wrong? Are you having a thing, a-a-an episode, like you told me about? Fuck. Justine—just—okay, Justine, if you can't speak and you're in trouble, bang the phone on something."

She did. She hit the phone on the desk as hard as she could, just before she fell.

~ ~ ~

Henry ran so fast that a campus security guard started chasing him, just based on assumption.

His thoughts were clear, almost serene. Thinking a step ahead as he sprinted to his motorcycle, he put his Bluetooth in his ear. When he got to his bike, he left his helmet strapped to the back and dialed his dad's number as he started up. He put his phone in his shirt pocket and sped out of the lot.

His bike slid as he turned onto the wet street. His knee hit the pavement before he managed to right himself. He straightened out and hit top speed, his front wheel edging off the ground.

He slowed as he approached an intersection. Seeing a gap, he ran the red light. His father's phone went to voicemail.

He was doing eighty-five coming down Temescal Canyon when he called his dad's office. The light at Pacific Coast Highway was green. He crouched and hit full throttle. Joyce, his dad's assistant, answered. "Good afternoon, UCLA Medical Center, office of Doctor—"

"This is Thomas Ackerman's son and I have to talk to my dad *RIGHT NOW!*"

"Well—"

"It's a fucking emergency, a fucking emergency, a huge fucking emergency, I have—"

"Calm down, I can page him."

"NOW NOW NOW. Please. Tell him to call me—his son Henry—it's an absolute matter of life and death."

"Henry—"

He was halfway up the hill on San Vicente when he hit the construction. He maneuvered around some orange cones and rode on the shoulder past a long line of cars, then came to a sliding stop just short of a barricade.

A construction worker, holding an umbrella in one hand and a *SLOW* sign in the other, glowered at him. A huge trench was open in the middle of the road, like an open chest cavity.

Henry pivoted and rode up the sidewalk. The construction worker's sign fell to his side as he turned and watched.

Most of the sidewalk was blocked by equipment. Henry stood on the pegs, throttled the bike, and rode up the grass embankment. He slipped on the muddy surface, righted himself, and made it to the top.

There was her house, just a couple blocks up. He began to slide sideways as the grass dipped back toward the sidewalk.

He made it off the embankment and back into the construction zone. He rode along the open trench, swerving around equipment. Men with open mouths dodged out of his way. They looked like fake people.

His phone rang in his ear. He touched the earpiece to answer as he swerved around the last cone and back onto the open street.

"Henry, what—"

"Dad—Dad, help me. Justine—"

"Where are you? What's that noise?"

"I think Justine's had an attack."

"A what?"

"An attack. Her allergic reaction. I'm almost at her house."

"Call 911. Do it now."

"Dad, no, it's already been too long."

"Where are you? You're there?"

"I'm just getting to her house. She called me from there. Dad, please, you have to do something, you have to help me." He rode across her front yard. He dropped the bike and ran up the porch steps.

"She's in the house?" Tom asked.

"She couldn't talk. I don't think she could breathe." He tried the door.

"Get in the house."

"Fuck, the door's locked." He pounded. *"Justine!"*

"You have to get in there. Henry, get in that house, any way you can, just get in there."

Henry took a step back and kicked the door, like he'd seen in movies. It was like kicking a cement wall. "I can't get in. Wait." He leapt off the porch and went to his motorcycle.

"What are you doing?"

He grabbed his helmet off the back and went to the other side of the porch, to the big picture window. He took a step back and swung his helmet as hard as he could. The window shattered but remained intact. He braced and swung again. The shattered glass bowed and the window frame splintered, but it still didn't give.

"Henry—Henry, what's going on? What is that?"

He put the helmet on and took a step back.

"Henry!"

He charged the window and dove through it. He landed in a splash of shards on the soft white rug, next to the piano. He picked himself up and pulled his helmet off. A large slice opened up on his arm. The fresh flesh turned from white to running red.

"I'm okay, I'm in. *Justine!"* He ran to the kitchen. *"Justine!"* He looked down the hall. He ran to the base of the stairs and was about to run up when he saw her tennis shoe through the open office door.

"Henry," his dad said. "What's happening?"

"I found her. Fuck, Dad, she's on the ground. I'm turning her over. She's—Dad, I don't think she's breathing."

"Is she alive?"

"Yes. Yes, she grabbed my arm. Dad, she's blue, her face is blue."

"Henry, listen very carefully. You have seconds. You do exactly as I say, okay?"

"Yes, yes."

"Quick as you can, go into the kitchen and get a knife." Henry pulled Justine's hand off his arm and ran to the kitchen. "A sharp knife, like a steak knife. Not a wide knife. Thin, no more than half an inch wide."

Henry threw drawers open. His own blood arched through the air. He saw the block of knives on the counter and grabbed one of the smaller ones from the bottom.

"Got it. Dad, I got one."

"And you need a straw, is there a straw, like from a fast food drink?"

"What? No."

"Then a pen. A disposable pen."

"I don't know were there's a—"

"Find one!"

"There's no—wait, I think there's pens on her desk."

"You need one of the cheap plastic ones, the disposable kind. Check the cap."

"I'm at her desk now, but I can't find one. Fuck, Dad, what am I doing?"

"Henry, focus."

"Wait—I got one."

"Pull the cap off and blow through it, does air go through?"

"Yes, the end has holes in it."

"Use that. Get her flat on her back."

"She is, she's on her back already."

"Listen carefully. Take a finger and feel the Adam's apple on your neck. Now slide your finger down an inch. That spot right there. Use the knife and push it into her neck in that exact spot. Part way in, you'll feel resistance— push slightly past it. Have the pen cap ready. Do you hear? Do it now, right now."

"Dad, I can't just—"

"Do it now, Henry. Tip her head back, push the knife in, find the resistance, and push just past it. I'm right here."

Justine's eyes went wide, as if seeing. "Justine, I'm going to—"

"*Do it right now!*"

"Alright." Henry slid a hand under her head. He pushed the tip of the knife to her soft white skin. It resisted. "It's not going in."

"Harder, but not too deep."

"Okay." He jerked the knife in. Blood spurted as her body jerked. "*Fuuck.* I think I went past the—"

"Take the knife out and put the top of the pen cap in the hole, so the pointy end is sticking out toward you."

"Shit, I can't get it in. Dad, there's so much blood."

"That's good, it means she still alive, get it in there."

"I think it's in."

"Breathe in it. Seal the area around it with your fingers and push air in it, like a balloon. Can you do that?" Henry made a sound. "You're doing it. I can hear it. Yes, son, you're doing it. You're doing it. Breathe a lot of air in there. A lot of air. Make that same noise if it's working but don't stop breathing into her. Good. Good, I can hear you. That's great, Henry. Now listen, she doesn't have a way to breathe out, and the cap won't let enough air out, so move the cap to the side, but don't take it out. Just pull it to the side to let air out."

Henry pulled the cap to the side but he couldn't tell if air was coming out until he saw bubbles of blood. He put his ear close; air was escaping. "Dad, I can hear it, the air's coming out."

"Gently push her chest, to help expel the air, then move the cap back in place and seal it with your fingers again and breathe in a lot more air. More than you think you should, and as fast as you can. You should see her chest rise. Henry—son, you're doing great."

Margaret had heard mothers refer to a sixth sense. Something only mothers can feel. Stories of waking in the middle of the night and knowing something wasn't right and finding out later their child had died in an accident at that exact moment. She'd lived for years like a bloodhound, nose to the ground, in fear of that moment, secretly afraid she lacked the proper instincts to perceive such a nebulous thing. She'd tried not to expect it, not wanting to bring it on by anticipation, but if it ever did happen and she did sense it, she assumed it would be subtle, maybe touched with a bit of mysticism you could only explain later with the familiar, *I just knew.*

When it happened, it wasn't subtle at all. It was like a sound that only she heard because it came from inside her, followed by all the air being yanked out of her. She stood and nearly doubled over. She had to put her palms flat on the conference room table to steady herself. Everyone looked at her.

She was in a meeting with three attorneys who had flown in from London to meet with her to discuss partnering on a case. She'd turned her phone's ringer off to avoid interruptions.

"I'm sorry," she said. The message light on her phone blinked. She grabbed it. "Excuse me," she said as she left the conference room. She went to her office to grab her purse. She was at the elevators when she heard the message. Justine's faint voice: "Mom." She checked the number—it came from her home line.

Margaret hit the construction backup seven minutes later. She saw the line of stopped cars ahead and kicked her heels off. When she reached the backup, she put her car in park and left it. She hit the sidewalk at a full sprint while the drivers behind her leaned on their horns.

An ambulance shrilled ahead. It was driving half on the sidewalk and half in the gutter as it tried to thread past the backup. Margaret ran past it.

She had her keys out as she ran up the porch steps. Her calculations changed when she saw the broken window and the spread of glass. Scenarios ran through her head in flashes: construction workers, maybe one of the ones from before, had broken in and attacked her daughter, or Justine was home when someone was robbing the house and she had to call without them hearing her, or—

"Justine!"

In the kitchen, blood was sprayed everywhere, as if an ax-wielding maniac had just ran out the back. She heard a scream and turned, expecting to see her mother swinging a gun toward her. But it was her own voice, and her own scream.

"Here!" called a man's voice from another room.

She went to the doorway of her office. Something was bent over her daughter, bloodied, feeding at her neck. She was unable to process the scene. The fiend dipped and came up again. It looked at her. "Ms. Shepard—I mean Margaret—it's me, Henry. Do you have a straw?" It was like being in a game where you're forced to follow the rules. She was being penalized and didn't have the right card, or word, or trinket that would let her move again. She watched Henry until he looked up at her again, blood dripping off his chin, and said in a calm voice, "Margaret, I really need your help."

An image came to her of Justine drinking juice out of a straw. It was something she did when she was sick.

So in the cupboard, there would be straws.

The thought was the key that allowed her to move. She went to the kitchen. The straws were there, on the top shelf, in a box that had a picture of a clown that was watching her. She grabbed one and ran back to the office.

Tom's voice came from a phone sitting on her desk. His voice told her what to do. She snipped the straw in half, following his directions.

So much blood.

Gray started to cloud her vision.

Justine began moving her head side to side. "I need you to steady her," Henry said.

Margaret went behind her and sat on the floor. She held her little girl's head and stroked her temples. "I've got you, my love. Mom's here. You're alright now."

Chapter 20

It was because of that woman. The woman Justine met in the bathroom. The one that taught her to see.

She could see with her own eyes. In the mirror. They were blue, and she knew exactly what blue was, but it confused her. How could she be using her eyes to look at her own eyes? It was as if she'd become greedy, had overcompensated, and was now using some kind of vision that only she knew about, which made it even more like a dream, because dreams are where you can know something that nobody else knows.

It was the woman in the mirror who told her she had such beautiful blue eyes, like she knew what Justine was thinking. She'd always been told her eyes were brown like a tree, not blue like the sky. She couldn't remember if we dream in color. She'd been asked that. "Do you?" she'd ask, really wanting to know.

Then she thought it was death, but that seemed too obvious, like the stupid movies she was glad she didn't have to watch. But who knows how it comes? Maybe it comes through a mirror, when you can finally see, and witness yourself.

Justine always felt she had a unique, secret relationship with death. She knew it like the ugly beast that everyone else was afraid of. The monster only felt safe around her.

They were close enough that she'd forget about it, then it would show up, stalking back rooms and giving her a knowing look that only the blind can see. She knew its kind side, and when it was sad.

It wasn't scary, she realized; dying. When it's happening, you forget about yourself, and it turns out that's all fear is—remembering yourself too much. Yourself, or your idea of yourself, seems distant, because that's what's leaving. Something must kick in, she concluded; a drug or something. God had planned for it and had taken care of that part. It's funny that we think He wouldn't. We're born, we know how to breathe, we die, and it's something else, but Justine never made it to that part. She was going out the back door, having lost her breath instead of finding it.

She didn't remember grabbing Henry's arm. She didn't remember much after calling him, when he'd said he was between classes. She also didn't remember her mom being there. She found that out later.

There was a blank, then the woman in the bathroom. But the thing is, there really was a woman in the bathroom. It was Henry's mom, but Justine found that out later too. It happened when she went to the charity auction with her mom. The event was supposed to benefit kids with medical problems. Henry's dad spoke and they all had a nice dinner and people wrote big checks. She got to dress up. Her mom had bid on a sculpture and Justine kept asking her to describe it, but she couldn't, even with the shorthand words only they used. Her mom just said it reminded her of a statue of a saint that was outside her office.

Doctor Ackerman brought the statue to their table after the auction, and that was the first time they met. Tom said something that made her mom laugh. He was vibrant, the kind of person that makes everyone feel special. It was strange that a man was talking to her mom and making her laugh. Then the artist sat and talked with her mom, because she'd bought the most expensive thing at the auction. Justine couldn't hear what they were talking about because she was so fascinated by the statue that she couldn't take her hands off it.

She remembered going to the bathroom. She always went by herself. If there was one place she couldn't stand people trying to help her, it was the bathroom. Her mom knew not to go with her, even if she needed to go too. Some people see a blind girl and think the poor thing has never had to use the bathroom until now, when they just happened to show up.

Someone was coughing in the next stall.

Justine was washing her hands when the stall door opened and a woman came out. She could smell her perfume. Maybe others expressed themselves by how they dressed, but for Justine, it was their smell. She could identify just about anyone based on their smell, and could usually tell who was walking by in the hallway at school.

The woman's perfume was one she hadn't smelled before, which was rare. Justine was something of an expert in that area. That's when she felt death. It was right there in the bathroom.

Most of the common beliefs people had about blind people were false, misinformed by movies, where drama trumps truth, but there may have been something to the one about developing other senses to compensate. Justine had come to realize that she was aware of things that other people were not—not because they're less capable, but because seeing is just easier.

The water at the woman's sink was going. She coughed a few more times.

"What does it feel like?" the woman asked after she'd turned off the water. Justine thought there must have been someone else in the bathroom she was talking to. "The sculpture," the woman added. "You were touching it."

"Oh," Justine said. "Yes, my mother bought it."

"Do you like it?"

"I don't know, I can't see it."

"But you touched it."

"Yeah."

"That's the best way to tell."

"Then, yes, I like it. I think it's beautiful."

Justine heard the woman leave.

That was it. At least, that's how she initially remembered it. The woman was just a new perfume—a rare treat—and an odd conversation. She had no idea who the woman was.

A few months later, after she'd spent many more hours with her hands on the sculpture, Justine looked up the artist and found out she'd died. There was a video about her work. She listened. In the video there was an interview with her. It was the same woman; she could tell from her voice—it was the woman in the bathroom.

Then death came, this time for Justine, and when it did, she remembered it all differently.

Herself, dying. Her brain, starved and going dark.

Henry's voice on the phone. And when it was happening, or when she thought it was happening, she was back in that bathroom, except now she could see, and the woman was talking to her, saying she had such beautiful blue eyes. Justine saw the woman's face, and her own, in the mirror.

When Justine turned to face her, the woman stepped closer and lifted off her glasses. She touched Justine's face, in the same way Justine had felt the sculpture, like the woman was now blind instead of Justine.

"Your family is so beautiful," the woman said.

"My family?"

"Your parents and you, I saw you all together. You're the handsomest family I've ever seen."

Justine took her glasses back and turned to the mirror. She watched the woman watching her. "Those aren't my parents."

"I'm sorry, I just assumed. You all look so perfect together. What is the name of the sculpture?"

"*The Finite Woman.* It's in the brochure."

"What does it mean?"

"You wouldn't understand, because you're not blind."

"Neither are you."

"Not now, but I was."

"What did it mean when you were blind?"

"That you have to be witnessed. That you're not complete—she's not complete and doesn't really exist, nobody does, unless they've been witnessed. So she's waiting to be witnessed."

~ ~ ~

Justine became conscious of her mom talking to her. "Don't try to speak," she was saying. "You're going into surgery." Her throat felt dry, like she'd been burned up. She wanted to ask for water, but couldn't move her mouth.

~ ~ ~

Tom found Margaret in the waiting room with her hands in her lap. She was looking at nothing. Her blouse was stained with dried blood, a floral pattern of dark red on white. There was still blood smeared on the side of her face and some in her hair. He sat down next to her.

"You should go home. I'm coming back in the morning."

"How's Henry?"

"Fine, just a lot of stitches, but I've arranged for him to stay the night. He wants to be near Justine. Are you staying?"

"Yes." She turned to him. "How did you know?"

"Know what?"

"To use a pen cap?"

"Babies die every year from choking on pen caps. They started putting holes in the end. You see it all in pediatrics."

She nodded. "What a horrible way for a child to die. Unable to breathe." She turned away again.

"Do you want anything?"

"No."

He started to get up but she put her hand on his. "Tom, will you sit with me for a bit?"

"Sure." He sat back down.

Ten minutes went by before she spoke again. "Thank you."

"You're welcome." He wasn't sure if she meant for staying with her or for helping her daughter.

She turned to him again. "They said they think she'll be okay. They wouldn't just say that, right?"

"I checked her MRI myself. Everything looks good so far." He recognized the fatigue in her eyes. "Listen, Margaret, I really think you should go home and sleep." Not waiting for a response, he stood and reached for her arm to help her up. "Did you come in the ambulance?"

"Yes."

"Let me drive you. Come on. We'll come back first thing."

She let him guide her out. They rode the elevator to the parking garage.

"Where are your shoes?" he asked.

"In my car, I think. I'm not sure."

He put her in the passenger seat like she was an invalid. When he got in, she said, "Tom, can we sit for a minute? I'm sorry, I'm just not ready to go yet."

"That's fine. Are you cold?" She shook her head.

It was raining again, hard, like it does a few times a year in Los Angeles, always taking visitors by surprise, as if the final lie had been told. Tom looked out over the ramp that led to the exit; a bright, rectangular space opened to the outside. Streetlights lit the rain. If he blurred his vision, it was like a living picture on the wall of the parking garage.

"I killed a boy," Margaret said. The words stayed in the air so long Tom began to think he heard her wrong. "Not a boy, I guess. I was twenty, I think he was twenty-one."

Things shifted into place. "The guy who raped you," he said.

"Yes. I shot him. Then I smothered him."

"Margaret."

"I killed him."

"He—he raped you."

"I killed him. Smothered him, as he was dying. He died not being able to breathe, he—" She leaned forward with her head between her knees and took quick breaths. Tom looked at the line of her spine marching up her back. "I have nightmares about it," she said to the floor. "I have so many nightmares, Tom. So many nightmares. I don't sleep. It's me, coming to do the killing. It's me doing the killing, over and over, it's me coming out of the woods. And the blood."

He put his hand on her back. Her silk blouse was slippery under his fingers. He slid his hand up to rest below her neck. He kept it there until she finally sat back up.

Tom watched the picture of rain again until it merged with the image of Margaret reflected in the windshield. She was still. Her glossy eyes reflected back at him like those of a sighted animal, weighing to stay or run.

"When I wanted to marry her," he said, "I decided I was going to call her father and ask for his permission. Get his blessing. Very old fashioned. He was this big Indian guy. Huge, like six foot five. Her mother was Irish, so Francis had this exotic mix of dark hair and pale skin, and the Indian features of her father. And her big-ass Indian dad was one of those silent types. The guy was a rock—no emotion, like he was made of granite. He never talked to me, if he could help it, except the occasional word or two. It was always like I'd done something wrong. But I was respectful. Francis would tell me about long conversations she'd have with him and I couldn't picture it because he hardly ever spoke as far as I could see, even to his wife. But I knew he adored Francis—just loved her madly, and she was an only child. She was a miracle baby, because her mother was told she couldn't conceive, that it was medically impossible. Anyway, I figured I'd call him and ask his permission. I wanted to do everything right in those days. According to Francis, he'd always talked about her getting married. And honestly, I thought maybe it would make him like me more—maybe then he'd actually talk to me. I felt confident, the way you do when you're young. I was going to be a surgeon, and thought I was pretty much what a father would want for his daughter. I knew he'd been worried about her, being in Los Angeles, where he'd said—according to her—that long ago the gods had tipped the country and it's where all the fruits and nuts ended up. And here I was, a good person; at least I thought so. So I had it all planned in my head, what I'm going to say, but I'm nervous of course. I call and he answers. I say, *Sir, you know I love your daughter. I'd like to ask for her hand in marriage, and I'm calling to respectfully ask for your blessing. I'd like your permission to marry Francis.* And... nothing. He doesn't say anything, like always. I start to sweat. So I kind of extend it a bit. I say, *And I want to make her happy, and I know I can, and she loves me and— blah blah blah—I'd like your blessing.* And there's this long pause again. I say, *Sir, I'm asking for your permission to marry your daughter.* Finally, he says, *Yup.* Seriously, *Yup.* And I'm like, motherfucker, here I am, laying it all out there, and all I get is *Yup?* Then I got angry. I was hurt. So I say, *Well, great talking to you, thanks for the stimulating conversation. I'm going to go chat with a wall now.* And I hang up. I go in the kitchen and tell Francis what happened. I say I should call him back and tell him what an asshole he is. Francis calms me down, tells me to go in the other room while she calls her mother. So I do. I'm stewing on the couch. Can't let it go. I can hear Francis in the kitchen, talking to her mom. They talk for a long time. Finally, she calls me into the kitchen. I go in there and she's sitting at our plastic table, and she says, *Tom, sit down.* So I do. And she reaches across the table and takes my hands. She's got this weird look on her face, and she says, *Tom, he couldn't say anything because he was crying.*"

Margaret took Tom's hand and held it tight.

"The big fuck. So now I'm crying, and I want to call him back and cry with him. And I feel like such a jerk. All that self-righteous anger." Tom wiped his face with the back of his hand. "Next time I saw him, he gave me a big bear hug that nearly broke my spine. He opened a bottle of this special bourbon and we got shitfaced and it was fantastic. We were close until he died, before Francis got sick. Big man, weak heart. Kind of good I guess, because it would have killed him."

He turned to her. She rubbed a tear from his face with her thumb. Their foreheads met and they held each other, like two old prizefighters using each other to rest.

~~~

Justine came back in layers—the familiar smell of her mother, the sound of a TV from another room, the vague snaking and threading sadness unique to the living—until she realized she wasn't dead.

"Don't talk," her mother said. "You're still in the hospital. There's a chalkboard on your lap if you need to write something. How do you feel? Are you hungry? You can just nod."

Justine felt for the chalkboard. "What do you need, sweetie?"

Justine found the caulk and wrote: *I'm sorry.*

"Please—I just want you to get better." Justine tapped the chalkboard. "Okay, but not now. Right now you should just drink something and rest some more." Justine rubbed the chalkboard with the side of her hand and wrote: *phone.* She could hear her mother's sigh.

"Listen Justine, you're still medicated. You don't need your phone, there will be plenty—"

"Phone," Justine said in a breathy whisper. She felt her mother lean over her.

"Please—no—I said don't try to speak. Don't do that again. Here. Here's your phone. But after you do whatever it is that's so important, you're to rest." Justine put her earpiece in and searched for the recording. "Is it Henry? Because he's okay. The doctor said the most important thing is sleep and nourishment. They have a special drink they said you can have until you can eat." Justine put her phone on speaker. "I'm going to call for the nurse and ask—" Margaret stopped at the sound of her recorded voice coming from Justine's phone.

"Honey—what... what is that? Is that me?"

Justine turned up the volume.

—helped me with that. I was raped. I had to say that to myself in the mirror, because my mind wanted to get rid of

it. I was raped. She was the only one who knew. And she knew I got pregnant from it, but she's never—

Justine felt her mother's fingers touch her hand. She stopped the recording.

Margaret didn't say anything. The silence stretched out until Justine heard a sound and realized her mother had left the room. She pushed the call button for the nurse. When she arrived, Justine mimed writing on her palm.

"You want pen and paper?" the nurse asked, like it was a game show. Justine nodded. "Well, honey that's what the chalkboard is for." Justine shook her head and mimed again. "Alright, relax, don't get worked up. I'll get you a pad of paper. Yes—and a pen. Got it. Goodness."

~ ~ ~

When Margaret came back, she sat and took Justine's hand. Justine tipped the pad of paper in her direction. Margaret read: *I'm sorry I recorded you. I changed my mind and was trying to delete it.*

"It's okay," Margaret said. Her voice sounded used up, like she had fallen apart and was speaking from the pile of broken pieces.

Justine wrote again: *Will you tell me what happened?*

"Yes."

Everything?

"Yes."

You can't leave anything out.

"I won't."

Margaret climbed in bed and slid behind Justine. She reached around and pulled her gently to her chest, like when she was young and Margaret would tell her about the future. Now she was going to tell her about the past.

She talked for the rest of the day. At one point, the nurse came in and told her she wasn't allowed in bed with a patient. She got out, but after the nurse's shift change, she crawled back in. They both slept a couple times, napping like cuddled children.

They developed a coded system. Justine would trace a question mark on her mother's leg if she didn't understand something. An exclamation point meant she thought something was really great, like when her mom told her about her friend, Song, who married a guy that started a tech company and got crazy rich and now lived in Seoul, South Korea. She was the one that paid for her mom to go to law school.

She also told her about Ms. Barden. Justine had a vague memory of her from when she was very little. She used to play in the dirt while Ms. Barden gardened. She remembered her red roses because that's what she still thought of when she thought of the color red.

The next day, Margaret began again, but instead of getting in bed, she paced the small room. She started by telling Justine that she'd lied about some things—about Justine's father, and about what really happened to him.

Margaret left the room a couple times. Justine could tell she'd gotten sick because she could smell it when she got back, under the scent of breath mints. When the doctor came to check on her, he seemed more concerned about Margaret than Justine.

That evening, Margaret told her daughter all the truths, until there were no more secrets.

Justine had her own secret: sometimes she was glad she was blind because she couldn't picture things the way other people could. And sometimes that was good, like now, when her mother told her the most horrible things she'd ever heard.

Henry visited on the third day. Justine found out that he'd been in the hospital the first day as well, getting his arm stitched up. Henry told her everything that happened during the parts she couldn't remember.

On the fourth day, Justine began to get her voice back, but it didn't matter now because she didn't want to talk. She felt like she'd lost her mom; the past had swallowed her up and spit out this stranger.

She was conceived of hatred and violence. She was made of everything ugly. Maybe she was blind for a reason—to protect her from this horrible truth. If you can't witness yourself, then maybe it's not as bad.

She understood now what her mother was trying to protect her from. She knew it was selfish, but she wished she'd have done a better job of it.

The nurse came in to tell them they could go home. Justine tipped the pad of paper in her mother's direction:

What are you going to do?

~~~

Heidi got Margaret's car out of police impound. She also arranged to have the window fixed at her house. When she went to check on the work, she called Margaret and left a shaky message, asking if someone had been murdered there.

Margaret had dozens of messages and emails from work—pressing, urgent matters, things that needed her immediate attention. Gavin, her senior lawyer, after numerous attempts to contact her, resorted to slipping a note under her front door, asking her to please call. After eating the rest of her anxiety pills, Margaret called her doctor for a refill and took more.

Being at the hospital those four days with Justine had made it easy for her to hide, but at home, everything still had dimension and presence. Not just the bloodstains splattered in the kitchen and pooled dark on the carpet, but everything.

Orlando had once remarked that he'd never heard of someone having their own law firm with two dozen employees by the age of thirty-four. How did she do it? Sitting at her desk, dangerously high on meds, Margaret imagined herself on a stage, before an overeducated, self-righteous audience, the kind that still went to art openings, swapped urban gardening tips, and claimed to never watch TV. She was delivering a presentation, with slides projected on a large screen. It was her job to impart wisdom on the wise and extinguish their terminal smugness. Her talk was about how to build your future by running from your past.

"The thing to remember is this," she was telling them, timing it just right and stepping downstage for subtle emphasis, just as her coach had taught her, "there is no fuel like fear. No resource is more powerful." Here she'd pause, at home in the hot spotlight, and make hard eye contact with a member of the audience. They'd be enamored by her intelligence and beauty. "Learn to use that fuel, and it will power—*willpower!*—you, and it will power anything you want to build. Those who have nothing to fear have no chance of accomplishing anything great." They'd be shocked here, this pliable audience, shifting and murmuring. "I know," she'd nod and strut the stage, playing it like she had a secret, another thing her coach had taught her—*That's how you keep their attention, and they won't even know why!* "I know, it's hard to take. Because you're all so soft, you've inured yourself to conflict. You don't want to hear it from me, but I know how to spot fear, I'm a trained professional, and I'm looking at you and I don't see a single fear among you, which means you're all nothing, you don't even *exist*, because without fear—"

"Mom."

Margaret came back to the real world. She turned to the doorway where Justine stood, looking hazy. "What?"

"I was asking you about school."

"You shouldn't speak. Let your voice heal."

"They said it was fine if I speak softly. Can I go back to school tomorrow?"

"Let's wait until Monday. I'll call them and let them know."

"You said you already did."

"Yes, that's right, I did."

"You were talking to yourself. I thought you were on the phone."

"No."

"Are you okay?"

"No. I don't know."

"What are you going to do?"

"I don't know. Maybe nothing."

"Aren't you going to go to work? I mean, at some point? Or do something about—"

"Stop asking me questions." Justine looked close to tears, but Margaret couldn't bridge whatever it was that was sliding wider between them.

"I think I'm in love with Henry," Justine said.

"I know you are."

"You do? I mean, I didn't realize you knew that."

"You love each other, I understand that. Why are you crying?"

"I just—I don't know where you're at. Where have you gone, Mom?"

"I don't know."

After sleeping until noon the next day, Margaret called Orlando. He was still on administrative leave and happy to have someone listen to his troubles at the DA's office. Margaret found it easy to listen. It was a pleasant distraction. Other people's problems seemed so small. It was like escaping to the movies.

"Listen," Margaret said. "How would you feel about being my partner? Full partner. Before you answer, there's a catch. You'd need to start as soon as possible."

Her next call was to Vicky. She left a number of messages before getting a call back.

"Remember that day, a long time ago, in your room," Margaret said. "When you knew something had happened to me but I wouldn't tell you what?"

"You froze me out."

"Yeah."

"Well?"

"You said that someday I'd tell you."

"And?"

"Vicky... I have a huge ask." There was a long pause. Margaret could hear the army of people that worked for Vicky in the background.

"Ask Katrina," Vicky shouted to someone who was trying to get her attention. "Mags, back then, when you needed help, you went to Ms. Barden. That just about killed me."

"I'm sorry. I was already staying with you."

"Fuck. Off. Sorry, not you Mags, I was talking to this idiot. *Fuck off right now or I'll throw you out that window. Edward, open that window.* Sorry again. Anyway, the answer is yes. Whatever it is."

Margaret took a deep breath. "I need you to come here."

Chapter 21

Except for the day after the funeral, Margaret had avoided visiting Nancy Barden's grave. She didn't like gravesites in general because they forced you to think of the person as dead. That was one thing the movies got right—that scene where someone visits the grave of their enemy. That's the way it should be.

Nancy's grave was marked with a simple plate in the ground with her name and dates. That was all she'd wanted. "Don't turn me into a bumper sticker," she'd told Margaret. "I can't stand that. I don't understand people that want to sum up their life with a trite phrase, as if anyone would give a damn."

Margaret sat on a nearby wrought iron bench, where she could see the grave without standing over it. Two cars crept along the curved road a ways up and parked. She watched the group disembark. They were dressed formally, except the oldest, a man that looked about seventy; he wore loose shorts, sandals, and a floral print shirt, like he'd arrived at the wrong location. The eccentric uncle, no doubt, there to damn both death and the weather.

Margaret turned back to Nancy's grave. She'd decided she needed a place to start, and it needed to be a physical place. This was the spot she chose. She took a slip of paper from her trench coat pocket and unfolded it. Under the hospital logo and the—*it's our business to care*—tag line, was Justine's measured writing:

What are you going to do?

This was the easiest place to begin, because she'd only told Nancy one lie—at least that she could remember. She'd make good on it now.

She was going to go see her mother.

~ ~ ~

Ridgecrest Mental Health Institute was the last place Margaret's mother had been placed. At the front desk, Margaret learned they had eliminated their long-term care facility due to budget constraints.

"We're just outpatient services now," explained a girl with tattoos on her neck. "Do you have someone to place?" She reached for a clipboard.

"No, I wanted to visit someone who lived here. Can you tell me what facility she would have been transferred to?"

"No, we can't give out patient information, it's confidential."

"But you just said she's not a patient here anymore."

"Still."

"Let me try again. It's my mother, I'm trying to find her, her name is—"

The phone rang and the girl snapped it up. "Ridgecrest. No *way* shut up right now. I'm not off 'til five but I can get there by then, yeah."

After a few minutes of listening to the girl make her evening plans, Margaret gave up. She drove her rental car back to the Best Western hotel. It was April. The sky was gray and spitting. The Wisconsin winter was over, but there were few signs of spring.

She waited until after five to call Ridgecrest back. She told the manager she was an attorney with the State's District Attorney's Office—that always opened a door. She was told that her mother was sent to another facility, in Green Bay. Margaret called the number she was given and spoke to another manager, who told her that after numerous unsuccessful attempts to place her mother in part-time employment, she'd been sent to a charity home run by a community church. A call there led her to another facility in La Crosse, run by a Mormon group. It seemed the various religious groups networked easily over charitable deeds, helping each other out where they could, even as they differed over who held the keys to the kingdom. The next day, Margaret drove the two and a half hours to La Crosse.

The Mormon Charitable Society was housed, ironically or tragically, in an old Masonic temple. It offered an eclectic mix of services to the underserved. After half an hour in the administration area, Margaret discovered the facility was split into two areas. They were only licensed by the state to provide specific services—those were on the second floor. The first floor was devoted to everything else.

They had a record of her mother, but nothing that listed Margaret as a relative.

"But she's here?"

"She might be," the volunteer said with a cheerful smile, "but I couldn't say for sure. People come and go. You're welcome to take a look."

"You mean, I can just go in?"

"Well, yeah, we're not a prison."

Margaret combed through all the areas on the first and second floors. She even walked through the kitchen behind the cafeteria. "Gotta wear a hairnet in here," a frazzled man said as he walked by while flipping though a stack of papers.

"Excuse me," Margaret said. The man paused and peered at her over his glasses. "I'm looking for my mother. I was told she was here but I can't seem to find her."

"You look on three?"

"The third floor? No, what's up there?"

He snorted. "Career skills."

On the third floor, Margaret found a large room with plastic folding tables and mismatched chairs and benches. There were a few computer stations set up, with giant box monitors that looked thirty years old. A few people sat on a bench, sleeping, draped halfway over the tabletop. A maintenance worker was bent over a mop, pushing it in slow motion along the far wall. Two young kids were at one of the computers; an elderly woman was at another. Margaret walked by the woman and looked closer. It wasn't her.

There were two couches and a stuffed chair near the windows. Margaret sunk down in the chair. A mildewy smell rose up around her. The room had old wood floors and a high ceiling, with narrow windows running halfway up, creating stripes of sunlight. Its drab, colorless aesthetic gave the place a peaceful feel. The only sound came from the wheels on the mop bucket, which squeaked every couple minutes as it was pushed along. The mopper worked around the couch and chairs where Margaret sat, running the mop a few inches from her feet. Margaret noticed a clean line on the floor that went along the walls, around the couch and chairs, then back along the walls, circling the entire room.

She was out of options. If her mother wasn't there, maybe she couldn't be found. The two kids were looking at her and laughing at a private joke. When Margaret looked at them, they turned away and tried to stifle their giggles. The elderly woman slapped her hand on the table. One of the sleepers jerked up, then went back down, like a balloon losing air. Margaret didn't mind being the butt of the kids' joke, whatever it was. She admired their resourcefulness in finding something to laugh about in this gray place.

The squeaking bucket approached. The mopper was back, another lap completed. Margaret watched the mop slide in front of her feet. She looked up and noticed the woman pushing it. A deep scar ran behind her ear and down her neck. A chill scurried up Margaret's spine and burrowed into the back of her head.

"Mom?" The woman didn't pause. "Mom," Margaret said again and stood. "*Elizabeth.*" The woman stopped and turned in slow motion. Her milky eyes found Margaret.

"Are you Elizabeth?" the woman asked her.

"No, you're Elizabeth. It's me, Margaret."

"I'm Beth."

"I know, I—"

"They took my union benefits away."

"What? Mom, it's me, it's Margaret. It's me."

"I voted for 'em. They took my union benefits away."

"Mom, what are you—what are you doing?"

"Took them all away, all away."

"They did?"

"Yes, yes, they did, they took 'em."

"I'm sorry."

"Took 'em."

"I'm sorry they did that."

"I voted for 'em." She turned and went back to mopping.

"Can I help you with that?" Margaret asked. Her mother stopped and eyed her again. Margaret crouched and pushed the bucket forward. "I'd like to help you." Her mother turned back and bent over the mop.

The two of them circled the room, round and round. In the late afternoon, a large woman with skin so dark her eyes looked yellow, came in and gave Margaret's mother a large pill and a cup of water. She stared at Margaret without curiosity as she waited for the cup back.

Margaret continued circling the room with her mother for another hour.

"Mom, do you remember church?"

"I voted for 'em, but they rigged the vote, couldn't have been that way."

"I'm sorry."

"Because I voted."

"I wanted you to know—"

"Yep, took my benefits away."

"—that I'm sorry that I couldn't help you, and I'm sorry if I helped make you this way."

~ ~ ~

"You called earlier?" the police officer asked.

"Yes, that was me," Margaret said.

"I need your driver's license and another form of picture ID." She had them ready. "I need to check the contents of your purse." She put it on the counter. "Wait over there." He indicated a bench against the wall.

Margaret sat as another officer took each item out of her purse and examined it. He opened her sunglasses case and felt around the lining. After putting everything back, the officer came around the counter and handed Margaret her purse. "No liquids inside. They'll keep your phone up front. You can pick it up on your way out. This way."

He led her down a hall and through a room full of desks that looked like the newsroom of a small town newspaper. They went out another door and down another hall. He opened an unmarked door. "The detective will be with you shortly," he said, holding the door open.

Margaret went in. He closed the door behind her. It was a small interview room, like you'd see on TV, with a table and a few folding chairs. Margaret wondered if they copied the TV shows, or the TV shows copied them. She didn't see a one-way mirror, like they always had in those shows, but maybe you wouldn't.

The room had no features; nothing to engage the senses. It made each passing minute seem longer.

Her throat was dry. She tried to remember if they'd passed a drinking fountain. The walls were so monotone she couldn't distinguish the seam at the top; they just blended into the ceiling. Maybe this was what a prison cell was like, flat and shadowless.

She felt her heart rate increase. Using the table, she estimated the ratio of height to width, and used it to begin a Fibonacci sequence. It spiraled from there. Working backward, she pulled numbers and used them to create a periodic function. Her heart pounded in her ears. She couldn't swallow.

The door opened.

"Hello," a woman said and closed the door behind her. She was dressed in black slacks and a yellow summer blouse, which projected off the gray walls like it was floating on its own. She didn't have anything with her, which somehow made her seem more important. "I'm Detective Perillo." She put her hand out. Margaret stood and shook it. "We spoke on the phone."

"Margaret Shepard."

"Sit."

"Do you have any water?"

"Water, sure." The detective went back to the door and shouted down the hall. "Ohmar, bring a bottle of water." She waited, half in the hall, holding the door open with her foot. Margaret felt a surge—an urge to run.

It's not too late to walk away from this. Just make something up. Sorry to waste your time, I guess I was mistaken.

The detective came back in, followed by Ohmar, a gangly man with a struggling mustache who didn't look much over twenty. He put a bottle of water in front of Margaret.

"Don't drink too much, you don't want to have to use the bathrooms here," the detective said. She settled into the opposite chair.

"Thank you."

Ohmar leaned against the wall with his arms folded, a posture that also seemed borrowed from television.

The detective watched Margaret drink. She waited until the silence became uncomfortable. Margaret wasn't sure if she was supposed to start. "I called because I wanted to discuss—"

"Wait," the detective said and put her palm out. Ohmar handed her something. A recorder. She put it on the table between them. "I need to record our conversation. Everything's informal at this point, but it's a department policy. People love to sue. Police misconduct and the like, as I'm sure you know."

"I understand."

"If I determine you have information that's useful to us, we'll write it up and have you sign it. If not, this will be the only record of our conversation. You're from around here, aren't you?"

"Yes, Camden."

"You still have a trace of the accent. Recognized it on the phone, though it sounds like you've tried to purge it. I'm not a local girl. From Philadelphia. You never think you have an accent until you travel the world a bit."

"That's true."

The detective pushed a button on the recorder. "Prelim, Margaret Shepard. Ms. Shepard, I am recording you now, do you understand?"

"Yes, I understand."

"You mentioned on the phone you have information regarding a homicide from 1997."

"No, 1998. A young man named Dwayne Locum."

"What is the information you have?"

"I—I went to high school with him."

"Oh. What high school did you go to?"

"Saint Michael's."

"A shithole, I'm led to believe. Or it was then. Probably still is. No wait, I think it's condos now. That right, Ohmar? What'd they do with that old school?"

Ohmar cleared his throat. "Community center for a while. I think it's closed now."

"It wasn't great," Margaret said. "Back then."

"You seem to have done alright."

"Are you familiar with the case?"

"I wasn't a detective back then, long before my time."

"Of course."

"I've heard of it though. We don't get that many homicides. We're not Los Angeles, after all. But after we spoke, I reviewed the file. It's not currently active."

"What did they conclude?"

"You said you're a lawyer?"

"Yes."

"I don't know what kind of lawyer you are, but even a patent attorney would know that I can't tell you that."

"I'm not licensed in Wisconsin, so I wasn't sure."

"It's federal law. Do you have anything to add?"

"I killed him."

"Dwayne Locum?"

"That's correct."

"How?"

"With a gun. I shot him."

"What did you do with the gun?"

"I took it apart."

"I see."

"And threw the pieces out while driving back."

The detective nodded. "Like they do in the movies."

"What—what do you mean?"

Ohmar shifted. The detective looked at Margaret for a long time before leaning forward and turning off the recorder.

"Why did you do that?" Margaret asked.

"It's not an active file. It's no longer an open case."

"He raped me. In high school. I killed him about three years later. I have a daughter. He's the father."

The detective gave her a synthetic look of sympathy. "I'm erasing what we recorded. It will be like you were never here."

"Why? I don't understand."

"Listen." The detective gazed past Margaret like her mind was already on something else. "All the details of Mr. Locum's past are in his file, but his major accomplishment in life was the distribution of meth amphetamines, back when they were just starting to take off around here. He was a small cog in a very big machine. He likely messed up and was shot by someone who was his best bud the day before. Whoever it was, they're likely already in jail, but I'm not opposed to keeping them there a little longer, if there's an easy way to do it."

"You're not supposed to tell me this. That's what you said."

"That was true before—now, it doesn't matter. But you came all this way."

"But—"

"How old is your daughter now? I'm trying to do the math."

"She's nearly eighteen."

"And you're hear, turning yourself in?"

"I've made arrangements."

"Um. I don't think so."

"I don't understand. I'm confessing. I did it."

"No, you didn't. We've determined it was drug-related. Are you a drug addict?"

"No."

"Were you then?"

"No."

"Do you traffic in narcotics?"

"No, of course not. I think you should turn the recorder back on."

"I think I know what's best."

"Why don't you believe me?"

"Opening a case from fifteen years ago, dragging family though it, interviews, the hours involved—we're a small department." She leaned closer. "Why? So you can get some attention? You were raped, many years ago, I believe you. Is that what you needed to hear?"

"Why would I make a false confession?"

The detective leaned back again and gave Ohmar a look. "It's not unique. As an attorney, I expect you already know that. You see, Wisconsin was the first state in the union to abolish the death penalty. Somehow that distinction has resulted in us leading the nation in false confessions. Can't shake a first impression. We also have some pretty nice prisons, I must say. Some our better than our schools. I don't know your motives. You probably don't either. Some people are just trying to escape, and it's their last option. They remember something from a better time in their life, before it all turned to shit. They attach themselves to something from back then. I'm not a psychologist, but I've seen it a few times."

"I'm not doing any of that. I'm trying to correct something."

The detective stood. "Maybe this isn't the way to do it." She passed the recorder to Ohmar and turned to leave.

Ohmar spoke. "Ms. Shepard, if you're experiencing difficulties in dealing with the trauma of a sexual assault—"

"Oh, right," the detective said, like she'd forgotten her keys. "Good, Ohmar."

"—there are social services we can refer you to that will assist you in getting the help you need."

~ ~ ~

Margaret found the hotel she'd stayed in the night before she killed Dwayne, but only after several attempts. The name had changed, but that was the only thing that appeared different.

It was after eleven at night when she got there. She had to bang the bell at the reception desk until an old, obese woman came limping out of a back room where a TV blared. "Didn't hear ya," she said as she hulked her girth over a cane.

"That's because you have that TV on so loud," Margaret said.

"What's that?"

"Just a room for the night."

"One night, ya say?"

"Please."

Margaret had walked the perimeter of the hotel earlier, in the hope of remembering which room she'd stayed in before. A man wearing only stained boxer shorts came out and glowered at her.

The room she got had a bathroom with a missing door. The bed felt familiar; springy, with mysterious lumps, assuring a tortured night's sleep. She lay on her back and stared at the ceiling, layered with years of ash-colored water stains. The missing bathroom door left an opening next to the bed where yellow, buzzing florescent light spilled in.

She didn't expect to sleep.

The gap. That gap that had stayed with her for so long. The blank space she couldn't fill. She thought she'd closed it. Maybe she had for a while, but now she felt like she was standing on the rim of it; a vast, expanded pit.

Fall in a hole. A forever fall.

She was going to lose herself in that pit. She could feel it. Not just parts of herself, but the whole. All that she was, sucked into that patient, blind black hole.

The calculations were still in her head. She got a pen from her bag, found an old menu in the nightstand drawer, and wrote out the equations she'd used. Distance, velocity, wind compensation. It was all still there, in real time, as if she was now only imagining herself older.

She did sleep a little, fully clothed, and woke a few times without opening her eyes, as if already hunting. When she could tell from the glow on the window curtains that the sun was beginning to rise, she got cleaned up and left.

~ ~ ~

Margaret wasn't sure if she'd know how to get there, having never come from the front. Off the main street was a semi-paved road, the kind locals make themselves.

It wasn't fully light yet. She drove slow, lights out, until she came around the last bend and could see the gray edges of the house. She nosed around the corner enough to see the driveway and front door.

She settled in. Drizzle accumulated on the windshield. The house looked the same as she remembered, only smaller. There was an old truck off the driveway with weeds growing around it; morning was slowly turning it from gray to pale blue. She couldn't be sure if it was the same one.

When it was light enough, she got out and walked up the driveway. She stopped and crouched. There was still a stain on the edge of the asphalt; another cloud imprint.

The front porch creaked, like it might not hold her weight. She knocked. No sign of life. The house might be abandoned, she thought; not uncommon in the area.

She knocked again, louder this time. Still no sound or movement. She went to the edge of the porch and looked up the hill to the line of trees. Her eyes followed the path she remembered taking back then.

The drizzle progressed to a light rain. She walked around to the back of the house. The garage was tilting to the side, as if years of wind had pushed it sideways. She leaned against the wall that faced the trees. The rain had washed everything to slate; the sky, the trees, and the hillside bled together like a monochrome watercolor.

She walked back to her car. Halfway down the driveway, she heard a sound and turned; the front door was open a few inches. She couldn't distinguish anything in the stripe of black.

"You from the city?" a voice said.

"What's that?"

"You comin' from the city?"

"No." She approached the porch.

"What you want?"

"Mr. Locum?"

"You from the city?"

"No, I am not from the city."

"I paid them taxes," the voice said.

"I'm not here for that."

"What you want then?"

"I knew your son, Dwayne."

"What's that you say? Come closer."

She was at the bottom step, looking into the gap, but she still couldn't see the man. "I went to school with your son, Dwayne. I knew him."

"My son? Who? You mean Dwayne?"

"Yes, that's correct."

"You playin' tricks on me? I paid them city taxes, so you don't gotta play no tricks on me."

"I'm not." She went up the first step and saw movement in the shadow.

"I'm an American," the voice said.

"Can I talk to you?"

"What you want?"

"I want to talk to you."

"I don't need nothin'."

"But can I talk to you?" She was on the porch now and close enough to see the edge of a figure.

"You're talkin' to me."

"Can you open the door so I can see you?"

"Who the fuck 're you?"

"I just needed to tell you something."

"What the fuck you want if you're not from the city?"

"Your son raped me. Dwayne."

"What you say?"

"He raped me. Your son, Dwayne. I killed him."

"Raped, you say?"

"Yes, in high school. I killed him."

She could see a grizzled face. A gust of wind blew rain against her back. A gnarled hand ran over the face and chin. "He didn' die in high school, pop tart. You got no brains."

"It was later, a couple years later."

"What in hell you want?"

"I just wanted to tell you. I thought I should. I can tell you more. Can I come in?"

"No."

433

"I didn't mean to—"

"You want something?"

"Just wanted to talk to you."

"They take it out of my Social Security, you know. Because they say I didn't pay my city taxes. I paid 'em."

"Alright, sorry to bother you." She turned to go.

"Now it runs out and I go dry. You got something?"

She stopped at the bottom step and turned. The door was half open. He was the man she remembered, the one Vicky had pointed out—Freak Show Senior, she'd said—but hunched over now, and scraggly, like something that would live under a rock. She smelled something thick and sour.

"Do I have something?" She asked. "What do you mean?"

"You got something for me to drink?"

"No."

"You got something to drink, you can talk to me."

~ ~ ~

She had to wait outside the store until they opened at nine o'clock. When she drove back to the house and knocked on the door, she was holding a fifth of Jim Beam.

She was prepared for anything when he let her in, but it wasn't as bad as she feared. The worst of the smell came from him. There was a wood table with attached bench seats in the main room. It looked like something stolen from a park. She could see an open doorway to the kitchen, where rows of canned beans were stacked on the Formica counter.

He took the bottle and went to the kitchen while she stood by the table. There was no TV. There wasn't much of anything. A bare bulb hung at a sideways angle from a wire, near a gun cabinet mounted to the wall. It was too sparse to be messy.

He came back with a glass and sat at the table. She sat opposite. The bottle was already open and missing an inch off the top. He ignored her as he poured. His hair, though mostly a wiry gray, had faint traces of the same red that ran through Justine's hair.

With a shaking hand, he drank half the glass in deep gulps. He put the glass down and went still. Margaret resisted the tug of her brain as it tried to catalogue the room in a hunt for something to pull apart. His gaze went past her, at something beyond the walls. The rain pulsed as it pushed against the window in gusts. She heard another sound. It was his shoe sliding on the wood floor, under the table. As the liquor coursed his veins, he slid his foot back and forth, like a windshield wiper.

He looked back at her. His eyes narrowed. He seemed to have forgotten she was there.

"Fuckin' government," he said and finished the glass. "I'm seventy years old, know that? Work all my life for that money." She knew from experience the drinking would improve his speech before making it worse.

"Can I tell you now?" she asked.

"Deal's a deal, pop tart." He poured again

She described the events in a simple, matter of fact manner. She wasn't sure if he didn't believe her or didn't want to believe her. As a lawyer, she knew that given enough time, people decided their own truths.

"You done?" he asked.

"Yes. Would you like me to go?"

"Nah. It ain't true, what you said. See, he was a lil' faggot, that's what he was. Scrawny little faggot. Couldn't a done that. I try to beat it outta him. Where you hear this?"

"I didn't hear it, it happened to me."

"He didn't do it."

"He did." The smell was making her nauseous—him, the whisky, his rancid breath. "Can I have some water?"

He shook his head as he waded through his memories. "Nah, he was a faggot. Found him jerkin' it to a magazine once. Should'a seen what was in that magazine. Rather he fuck a goat 'en see that. I try'n beat it outta him. I'm sayin' to you, he didn't want no pussy. I tried. Got him two hookers once."

"I needed to tell you. I don't need you to believe me."

"Believe you? You got no brains."

A clammy, queasy feeling crept through her. "I'm going to go now." She got up. He poured another glass, nearing the bottom of the bottle. "Thank you for talking to me."

"He was killed. It was them drugs he do with them. That kid, I think it was the colored. But police don't care. And now they take my money. Who pays their salary? Workin' folk. He die right here you know, right out front there. I found him, bled out."

"You found him?"

"I found him, bled out."

"I'm sorry."

"Thought he was a—I thought he was an animal, come down outta the woods, an animal that died there. Them drugs got my girl too, stickin' needles in her neck."

"Dorie?"

"Ya." His ruddy eyes locked on her. "My little girl. That was my little girl."

~ ~ ~

Margaret stayed at a different hotel that night. A nice one, in Madison, with fresh flowers on the bureau and a small restaurant attached where she ate a slow, bland dinner in an effort to calm her churning stomach. She checked out the next morning.

She stopped at the store before going back to the house. He answered the door while she was still knocking.

"Knew it must be you—heard your car—not many visitors here you see." He was shaking so bad he was having trouble speaking. She held up the bottle. He rubbed his hand over his face. "What you want now?"

"I want you to tell me everything about him."

"Come in then."

He smelled like he'd begun to decay. He had the bottle at his lips before she even sat down. She watched him tip and hold, and knew he was one to drink himself to death, given the chance, like it was the only thing worth waiting for.

Once settled in, he answered her questions until his speech was so slurred she couldn't understand him. As he spoke, things seemed to poke out of him, like dark spirits surfacing and diving back down.

He passed out for an hour with his head resting on his arms. When he woke, he retched and drank more. She checked his kitchen for food. Brown bananas and cans of beans were all she found. He wouldn't eat.

He had her get a box from one of the other rooms. He dug through it, saying he had a picture of his wife, who'd left when Dwayne and Dorie were ten and eleven. He had two other kids, older, but he didn't know where they were or if they were alive. He couldn't remember their mother's name, which was just as well, he said, because she was an evil witch that would burn down hell. She'd left as well, and took the kids with her. He kept pounding the table as he tried to remember her name. "Damnedest thing," he said over and over.

He passed out again before he could find the picture. Margaret slid the box out from under his arms and went through it.

She found an old, blurry photograph of an infant. The edges were yellow with age. Something had caught the child's attention—he was turning to look. She could tell, maybe from the ears, that it was Dwayne; just a few months old, fresh and unharmed.

She was looking at the picture when he woke. He stood quickly, as if fleeing a bad dream. Expecting him to retch, she turned away. She heard a different sound and turned back.

His back was to her but his hands appeared to be in the open gun cabinet. He pulled out a shotgun and swung it toward her—an old, heavy Remington. He was so drunk that he turned too far. The weight of the gun caused him to nearly swing a full circle. He turned forward again and righted himself for a moment before staggering once.

He spoke unintelligibly as he tried to lift the gun. He looked right at Margaret without seeing her, as if she were a ghost. She didn't move; an animal in the woods, safe in stillness.

"Sheeeelia," she heard through his gibberish. He lifted the gun. "That's yer name." The gun dropped again. The barrel smacked the table top with a thud. "Ha! Shelia." His eyes cleared and landed on her.

A puzzled look crossed his face. He tried to slide the barrel of the shotgun in her direction but it slid off the edge of the table. He jerked and it went off. The sound tore the room in half. He was knocked backwards, like he had no bones. The power of the blast turned her numb, as if she and everything else had been shut off.

A tone was the first thing to come through; an unnatural note that continued and increased as if trying to escape her head. A hot powder smell covered everything.

The sound settled on a ringing pitch. She felt a hard throbbing from inside, then heard the pounding of her heart, whooshing in her ears, then her breath, then the tiny sounds of the man's desperate gibberish again, like a child having a bad dream.

She realized he'd shot the floor. Buckshot splayed out, exposing fresh blond wood from the blackened boards.

From where Margaret sat, she couldn't see where he fell. She waited until he was quiet again. The room was darker, but she didn't know if had been seconds or minutes. She looked up to see the light bulb had gone out with the gun blast.

She slid down the bench to where she could see him.

He was on the floor, laid out against the wall with the gun across his lap. His mouth was open. He looked dead. She looked closer and saw the shallow rise and fall of his chest.

The box he'd had her fetch was still on the table. She moved it closer and went through it. There was more than photographs in it: military pins, animal teeth, a tin of buttons. She dug to the back and found a sealed mason jar. It was filled with a swirling, semi-opaque fluid.

The air was still hazy with smoke from the gunshot. Margaret angled the jar toward the window light. The smoke in the room and the fluid in the jar cleared together. There was something in the fluid. She had to wait as it settled. She turned the jar and held it closer to the window.

She began to see the object, but couldn't tell what it was at first. She stared at it until the shape finally revealed itself: a human tongue, preserved in formaldehyde.

~ ~ ~

She felt like an actor in an old play, making her final, dramatic cross, the climax of three carefully plotted hours. This was a tragedy meant to cleanse souls in mass; who, in the end, is dead, and who is alive? What bodies are left on stage, and who crouches over them? It's assumed, as it was, that life—having it—was the point, not the living of it. Send them home weeping and grateful for the smallness of their own lives.

439

She crouched down and looked into his face for what was left. He smelled like an infection. She lifted the hand covering the gun. He lolled his head back and forth as she slid the gun from his lap. She stood and took a step back.

The shotgun was an old side by side. She cracked it to check the second barrel and found it loaded.

She pulled the cartridge and put it in her pocket. She wiped down the gun with her shirt and put it on the table.

~ ~ ~

She had to go to two stores to get what she wanted: cheap whisky in liter bottles. She bought three of them, figuring that should be enough. When she came back, he was in the same place, but tipped all the way over. She checked him. He was still breathing, just passed out.

Some people, the sicker they get, the longer they live.

She set the bottles on the table, then put the shotgun shell she'd pulled next to the third bottle.

A final look at him, then she left this tragedy to its coda.

Chapter 22

Margaret's street was freshly paved. They'd even painted in the white lines, an indication they might finally be done. She slowed and drifted by her house, not quite ready to end her trip. After circling the block a few more times, she pulled over and called Tom to ask if she could stop by.

When she parked in front of his house, she saw the tire mark on the curb. Her tire, she remembered, from when her wheel had hopped the curb and ended up in the flowerbed.

She knocked, and was about to leave when he opened the door with a book in his hand. "Margaret."

"Hi."

"That was fast." He stepped aside. "Come in."

"No, I don't want to."

"That again. My house does have an inside, you know." He looked past her. "New car?"

"No, a rental. I drove across the country."

"Just now?" She nodded. "You're what they call unpredictable."

"I just got back. Haven't actually been home yet."

"Everything okay?"

"I've had some time to think."

"Okay… Well, that's good."

"I got something for you." She handed him a small package.

"You got something—"

"It's a—it's a candle. I got it in a small town, in a quaint little shop, and the whole place seemed like something out of one of those romantic movies, so I got it. I'm realizing now you probably don't get a guy a candle. As a gift. I could get you something nicer."

"Margaret, are you sure everything's okay?"

"It is, I'm just—I'm starting from scratch here."

"Starting what? And thank you for this, it's more appropriate than you know."

"I don't even like small towns."

"Me either. Starting what?" She bit her nails. He leaned against the doorframe and waited in the silence.

"Tom… I think I should go." She turned away.

"Okay."

She stopped and turned back. "I like you. That's all. It's just—"

"I like you too."

"You don't have to say that."

"I know. I'm not trying to make whatever it is you're doing easier, believe me. I gave up on that kind of thing."

"Our conversations. Our time talking on the phone, and when—"

"Are you worried about that? Is that what this is?"

"No."

"Margaret, listen, I'd never tell anyone or—"

"I know. I've known that. Otherwise I couldn't have."

"How? How did you know that?"

"Because I trust you. More than that. It took me a while to understand it. Until Nevada, actually. More than trust, I have—"

"Margaret—"

"Just—don't say anything for a minute. I have to do this. I... I have to do this." He nodded. "I should have stopped at home first, to at least..." She looked down at the thin crack in the cement between them, where green sprouts sought the sun. "Tom, I've never been on a date. I've never even kissed a man. I'm like a unicorn. I know there are better ways of doing this, I just don't know what they are." She looked up at him. "You can talk now." He didn't respond. "I just don't know how, Tom. I don't know any of that stuff."

"You're doing fine."

"But what do I do now?"

"Maybe I take over for a bit. Then you again. It's like a dance. If I recall."

She nodded. "I can't dance."

"Everybody says that, and it's never true. It's born into us. It's probably the reason we first stood upright. You know, our kids are going to the prom together."

"I know. I'm glad."

"Sure about that?"

She took a moment. "I am."

"I'm glad too. Did you go to your high school prom?"

"I was visibly pregnant, so no."

"That's a shame. They get a bad rap, but mine was great. I went with Donna Halverson. She had enormous boobs. It was hard because all my friends were trying to get in their prom date's dress, and I was trying to avoid mine, because it was just so obvious. I didn't want her to think I only asked her because of her boobs, but the only way to prove that was to completely avoid them. And that was difficult, because she wore this dress that was like—well, she really went all out, so to speak."

"So what happened?"

"She started getting angry that I wasn't even trying, so eventually I felt obligated."

"Very considerate."

"She'd gone to a lot of trouble with the dress and all."

"You didn't want to let her down."

"That's right."

They hit a lull. "I really am going now," she said.

"Sure." He watched her walk to her car.

She stopped at the end of the walkway and turned back again. "You can't ever drink. I mean if we ever—"

"Done."

"I just can't—"

"I understand."

"It's my only weird thing. No, that's not true. My only obviously weird thing."

"I'll find out the rest another time."

"Okay."

~ ~ ~

Conroy was sitting at the dining room table, drinking a glass of Chablis. "I'm impressed, quite frankly."

"Thanks for that," Tom said from the kitchen. He was wearing one of Stephen's floral aprons and stirring a large pot on the stove.

Conroy craned his head around. "Smells good. That stew?"

"Yeah."

"Stephen's recipe? He made some once. Incredible."

"No, something I found and tweaked a little."

"Maybe it'll be ready before I leave and I can bring some home to the missus."

"Already put some aside for you."

"Nice. You alright then?"

"Right enough."

"Good. I'm hoping we're done with hospitals for a while. Seems like everyone's had a turn."

"I think we are."

"Frankly, I hate hospitals. No offense."

"Everybody hates hospitals. It's not just the food."

"What's the occasion? I see lights strung up in the living room. Looks kinda disco in there."

Tom waved a limp hand. "Something I'm working on for tomorrow night."

"You've gone all tragically mysterious, I like it."

"The new me."

"Works."

"I think I'm ready to come back."

"Tykes Initiative?"

"Yeah."

"There's no hurry."

"How about I just show up, see how it goes."

"Perfect." Conroy reached for the candle that sat on the table. He smelled it. "This has me concerned—potpourri?"

"I don't think so. I wanted to ask you something."

"Yeah, what's up?"

"Where did you find Stephen?"

Conroy continued to examine the candle. "I told you that, didn't I?"

"No."

He turned the candle back and fourth in circles. "Francis found him. I thought I told you that."

"No, you didn't."

"Yeah, well, I guess when she knew—when she realized it was for sure, I mean—she made some arrangements. I don't know exactly, but she gave me the number to call. Just in case, she said. If you guys needed it."

"She left that assessment up to you, I assume."

Conroy shrugged. "Wasn't a hard call." He held the candle closer. "Is that the state of Arizona printed on the side?"

"I believe it is."

"I'm not going to ask."

"Listen, Conroy, I wanted to say—"

"You don't need to."

"I just wanted you to know."

"And I do. You'd have done the same for me."

"You overestimate me. That's okay, I used to do it too."

~ ~ ~

Tom pulled the boxes out from under the bathroom sink. He wrapped the rest of Francis's things in tissue paper and packed them away until only her bottle of perfume remained. He carried the bottle to the bed and sat. The wall before him was blank. Nothing looked back at him. He sprayed the air, closed his eyes, and breathed in.

It was all there, eager to show that these were not just memories—those slippery, opportunistic things—but imprints: light shimmering through windows in pastel hues, cool sheets, a few gray hairs off her temples—the invaders, she called them.

He sprayed again and she was holding Henry for the first time, heroic and sweaty. The parking lots and the restaurants and the voracious needs they shared; the songs on the piano and the hours and hours in the studio, under the bellow of arias.

~ ~ ~

Margaret had arrived early and parked up the street so he wouldn't see her. Her calculating made her feel self-conscious; the last thing she needed. She'd been sitting for twenty minutes, and now she was late. He'd said he used to hate it when people were late, but he'd gotten over it. "That's what I get for six months of therapy."

She tilted the rearview mirror toward herself again, something she'd seen women do at stoplights, always with mild contempt. Yes, you're still there, you still exist, do you really need to keep checking? You're not such a mystery after all.

She'd had her nails done. That wasn't so new, but the color was. Instead of a neutral, professional color, she'd chosen one to match her dress. Instead of her usual two minutes in front of the mirror, she'd watched a makeup tutorial and followed along. She even borrowed some of Justine's lipstick.

She'd never dressed for a man and found herself turning in the mirror as she tried to see herself through his eyes. At first, it felt like she'd borrowed a body. Thinking of it in temporary terms made it easier to accept that she enjoyed it. In this play, she got to be the glamorous girl. It could all be washed off.

She felt a grabbing tightness in her stomach. Sitting in her car wasn't going to make it go away.

~ ~ ~

The way he looked at her when he opened the door made it easier. He was dressed in a suit and a dark blue tie. It was the first time she noticed that his eyes were blue.

He stepped aside and she entered. He smelled nice; clean, like the ocean air on one of her early morning runs. "I love your dress," he said as he closed the door behind her.

"Thank you, I made it."

"Really? You have all kinds of skills I wasn't aware of."

"No, that's about it, and it was a long time ago." She looked up at the large paintings lining the entryway. "Your home is very nice."

"That's where the magic happened." He indicated the piano. "Or where it began, anyway."

"Justine tells me you play."

"Only when no one's around to hear it. This way." He took her hand and led her to the living room. He'd cleared out all the furniture and left the middle open. Ball lights hung from the ceiling. Tables were lined against the wall with punch bowls and cups. A butcher paper sign on the wall read CLASS OF 1996, in multicolored paint strokes. "Did I get the year right?"

Margaret's hand went to her mouth. "Oh, my God. Yes. Yes, you did."

"You okay?" She nodded. "I didn't intend to make you sad."

"No. I'm okay."

"I made some dinner. We'll eat, then dance the night away."

"That sounds nice. Except I can't—never mind."

"I picked all slow stuff. All we have to do is not step on each other. Come on." He led her to the dining room.

~ ~ ~

They danced in their bare feet and went though both playlists he'd created. His body developed a familiar feel, warm and rhythmic with his breathing. When he spoke, she could feel the deep resonance against her chest.

Just after midnight, he went to the stereo. "I did a little research," he said as he pushed buttons. "Can't say for sure, but there's a good chance this was your last song." He looked back at her. "You had that, right? A last song?"

"I don't know."

"Oh, it's the most important of all songs." He came back to her as the song began. She settled comfortably into his arms. "See, if you'd been too scared to make your move before then, you had to do it during the last song. Those were the only people left on the dance floor. Everyone else was making out in dark corners. It could be an awkward sight."

"Was that you?"

"I'm afraid it was."

"But that was because you were such a gentleman."

"I was an exception, that's correct."

"And you got there in the end."

"I did." His arms slid up her back.

Then, he kissed her.

~~~

The library never got completely dark. There was always some light from the outside streetlights that leaked through the curtained window. It was almost three in the morning when Margaret heard them come in. She nudged Tom.

"Hum?" he mumbled as he woke.

"I think I hear them."

"They came back here?" He propped up on an elbow and listened.

After dancing, they'd sat on the library couch and talked. Tom eventually made a nest of couch cushions and blankets on the floor. They'd laid down still clothed, but when she woke the first time, he had taken his suit off. She took off her dress in the semi-darkness as he slept, or pretended to. It was when she woke the second time that she heard the front door open.

"I didn't think they'd come back here," Tom whispered.

"Me either."

They listened as their kids went up the stairs. Justine was laughing about something. Henry kept shushing her. There was a clunk as one of them slipped. Justine was talking through stifled giggles. "It's your house, I'm the blind one in a dress and heels, and it's you that can't make it up the stairs."

"Zip it, blinky," Henry said from near the top. "You're used to the dark." Justine snorted, which made them both convulse with laughter. They were in uncontrollable fits by the time they made it to his room.

449

Tom looked at Margaret when he heard Henry's door close. She was smiling, something he hadn't seen before tonight. She put a hand flat on his chest. He saw a shift in her eyes. She slid her hand over his shoulders. He rolled over on top of her as she wrapped him up and pulled him in.

~ ~ ~

Margaret had fallen into a brief, hard sleep. She woke, silent and still, resting on his chest. She felt his heart thump against her cheek. She lifted her head and was surprised to see him awake. He smiled down at her. "Morning," he whispered.

"What time is it?"

"You have somewhere to be?"

"No. Habit, I guess."

"It's about five. Not light out yet. You barely slept."

She moved over him and pushed her hair away from his face. "What have you been doing?"

"Watching you, and listening."

"To what?"

"Your breathing, until recently."

"And what happened recently?"

"Hunger, I think." She looked at him. "Our kids, I mean. I think they're in the kitchen. Though they're being awfully quiet."

"Now?"

"Henry gets up to eat sometimes, then goes back to bed."

"One of the differences between boys and girls." Tom felt her tense. "Would they come in here?"

"They might. We could get in trouble."

"Do you have a shirt I can wear, just in case?"

"Sure, I'll run up and get one."

"No, you stay. I think it would be worse if they came in here and found just me." She started to get up but stopped. "Wait, I'm sorry, of course I shouldn't—"

"No, it's alright." He held her look. "The door at the end of the hall. There's a dresser with shirts and sweatpants."

Margaret wrapped herself in an afghan and slipped out. A light was on in the kitchen. She snuck past the dining room and went up the stairs like a cat burglar.

From above, she looked down at the entryway. Reflected light glowed off the polished lid of the piano. She went past Henry's room, to the door at the end of the hall. She hesitated before going in.

Inside, she closed the door behind her. It was completely dark. She rested her back against the door and let the afghan fall.

When her eyes adjusted, she could make out the door to the bathroom. She went in and found the light switch. She expected a harsh response, but a soft light above the mirror went on. When she turned to go back out, something on the counter caught her eye: a bottle of perfume. The glass bottle looked cut from a hundred different angles, like a diamond that holds light in a prism. She picked it up. It had no markings. She sprayed the air and took a step back. There was something familiar to the scent. She turned the bottle. It threw off colors like an old parlor trick.

Margaret turned to the mirror and looked at her naked form; the mirror Francis must have seen herself in thousands of times.

When she went back to the bedroom, she kept the bathroom door open so she could see her way around. She found the dresser and got a pair of sweatpants from the bottom drawer and pulled them on.

She checked the top drawer for a shirt. There was a framed photograph on top of the neatly folded clothes. She took it out and angled it toward the bathroom light.

It was her. She looked younger than the one time Margaret had met her. Her beauty was astonishing, the kind that actually takes your breath away for a moment. She was between Tom and Henry, with an arm around each, as if protecting them. Henry looked about twelve. She wore a man's blue flannel shirt and had a big, open smile.

Margaret looked up from the photograph. An angle of light cut through the closet, where she saw the same blue shirt hanging. She put the picture back and got a t-shirt from the next drawer.

She told herself to leave, but instead went to the closet. The shirt hung on a bare wooden rod. It moved as she approached; a subtle, coquettish turn. There was something on the shelf above. A sculpture.

She reached up and pulled it down. It was heavy. She slid to the floor in a dark corner and cradled it in her lap. Its density betrayed its delicate appearance. She closed her eyes and slid her hands over its textures, contours and angles until she understood its form. Three dancers. A perfect triangle.

~ ~ ~

Usually it was the smell of her perfume. If not that, then some other scent preceded her. Now it was the smell coming from the kitchen—a dish she used to cook, or a spice she'd used.

Tom rolled back and covered his eyes with his arm.

Not now, Francis. Please, not now.

~ ~ ~

Unlike Henry, Justine was wide-awake. She was hearing noises. Something downstairs. And someone had walked by the door. But which way were they going? Was it Tom, going to his room? But she would have heard the front door, and she'd been listening.

She knew she wouldn't be able to go back to sleep. She'd kept Henry awake by pestering him about what he thought had happened with their parents until he'd finally fallen asleep while she was still talking.

Earlier, when Henry came over to pick her up for the prom, he looked at Margaret and did a double take. Justine felt it in the air.

"What was that?" she asked him in the car. "You made a weird noise or something when you saw my mom."

"Nothing," he said. "I didn't make any noise. She just looked different; good, I mean. I'd never seen her like that. Maybe for once you were right." Justine kept asking him to tell her more. "Like, how good? What do you mean by that? Like she was trying to be sexy?"

Justine sat up, which caused Henry to murmur. She'd heard more noises downstairs. Her mind raced through scenarios. It must be Tom. Who else could it be? Had they left and come back? If it was him, she could go down there and ask him how it went. No, that would be extremely awkward. And what if her mom was still there? Henry had said he didn't see her car. And what excuse would she have for going down there? She could say she just came down to get some water—something like that.

Henry stirred. If he woke, he'd tell her not to do it, and of course he'd be right.

She slid out of bed and found a pair of Henry's shorts and a t-shirt from his closet. After making sure his breathing was steady, she opened the door as quietly as she could and started toward the stairs. A smell stopped her. A perfume. She stood still as she tried to place it.

Another sound came from below. She slid her hand along the railing toward the stairs. She paused and listened, then padded down the stairs. When she made it to the ground floor, she reached and felt the cool, familiar edge of the piano. There was another smell now—something cooking. She could see a blurry shimmer of light toward the kitchen. She continued to the archway leading to the dining room.

When she made it there, she felt death and stopped.

"Hello, Justine."

"Stephen?"

"Yes. You like eggs, right? I've never made you breakfast."

She approached him. "Stephen, did somebody die?" He didn't answer. She moved closer. She heard the sizzle of eggs being poured into a pan. She got close enough to reach out. Her hand touched his back. She wrapped her arms around him. He went still as she rested her face against the back of his neck.

~ ~ ~

Margaret came down the hall. She stopped when she saw that Henry's bedroom door was now open. The bed was messy and empty. The digital clock read 5:31 am.

She continued to the top of the stairs and stopped again when she looked down. Through the archway, she could see the dining room light was on. Sounds drifted up. Voices. She came down the stairs toward the light with no idea what to expect.

~ ~ ~

Margaret got to the dining room and stopped. Justine was sitting at the table. Henry sat next to her in a robe. He was reaching for a casserole dish piled high with scrambled eggs. Tom stood opposite, wearing boxer shorts and a dress shirt, passing out plates. The table was cluttered with assorted breakfast foods: fruit salad, a plate of sausage and bacon, a vegetable quiche and a basket of warm pastries and croissants.

Before Margaret could speak, Stephen came in from the kitchen, carrying mugs and napkins. He stopped. "Hello, Margaret," he said.

She took a deep breath. "Hello, Stephen." She looked at Tom. He nodded to the empty chair between himself and Justine. She sat. Justine turned to her but Margaret didn't say anything. Tom poured her coffee. She noticed the candle she'd gotten him was lit and sitting at the center of the table. Justine nudged her, but she still didn't respond. She watched Stephen sit in the last chair. He looked across at her. They locked eyes for a moment. He smiled and took the bowl of fruit and served himself. Henry was bent over his plate, alternating between fork-fulls of eggs and the croissant he clutched. Stephen passed the bowl across to Margaret. She scooped some on her plate and passed it to Tom.

Justine nudged her mother again, harder this time, causing the table to jolt. "Sorry," she said.

Margaret reached under the table and drew a slow exclamation point on Justine's thigh. Justine let out a sound somewhere between a squeak and a contained sneeze.

Luca Brasi trotted in.

"Dog," Henry said around a mouthful.

"Thank you," Justine said.